T HE EVENING OF SUNDAY May 10 in the year 1863, Hettie Childs called her son, Robey, to the house from the old fields where he walked the high meadow along the fence lines where the cattle grazed, licking shoots of new spring grass that grew in the mowing on the edge of the pasture.

He walked a shambling gait, his knees to and fro and his shoulders rocking. His hands were already a man's hands, cut square, with tapering fingers, and his hair hung loose to his shoulders. He was a boy whose mature body would be taller yet and of late he'd been experiencing frightening spurts of growth. On one night alone he grew an entire inch and when morning came he felt stretched and his body ached and he cried out when he sat up.

The dogs scrambled to their feet and his mother asked what ailed him that morning. Of late she'd become impatient with the inexplicit needs of boys and men and their acting so rashly on what they could not fathom and surely could not articulate. In her mind, men were no different than droughty weather or a sudden burst of rainless storm. They came and they went; they ached and pained. They laughed privately and cried to themselves as if heeding a way-off silent call. They

were forever childish, sweet and convulsive. They heard sound the way dogs heard sound. They were like the moon — they changed every eight days.

He scratched at his head, knotting his long hair with his fingers. He felt to have been seized by phantoms in the night and twisted and turned, and his body spasmed and contorted.

He told her that he did not know exactly what it was possessed him, and did not even understand what happened enough to be dumb about it, but thought it was a condition, like all others, that was not significant and with patience it soon would pass.

"That seems about right," she said.

As he walked the fence lines that cold, silky spring evening, he let a hickory stick rattle along the silvered split rails. He was thinking about his father gone to war. Always his father, always just a thought, a word, a gesture away. He spoke aloud to him in his absence. He asked him questions and made observations. He said good night to him before he fell asleep and good morning when he woke up. He thought it would not be strange to see him around a corner, sitting on a stool, anytime, soon, now. He had been born on the mountain in the room where his mother and father conceived him, but it was his father who insisted he was not really a born-baby but a discovered-baby and was found swimming in the cistern, sleeping in the strawy manger, squatting on an orange pumpkin, behind the cowshed.

Swarming the air about his head that evening, there was a cloud of newly hatched mayflies, ephemeral and chaffy, their pale membrous wings pleating the darkening sky. Not an hour ago he'd watched them ascend in their moment, like a host of angels from the stream that bubbled from a split

rock and pooled, before scribing a silver arc in the boulder-strewn pasture, before falling over a cliff, and then he heard his mother's plaintive voice.

When he came down from the high meadow, the dogs were standing sentry at her sides, their solemn stalky bodies leaning into her.

She said softly and then she said again with the conclusion of all time in her voice when he did not seem to understand, "Thomas Jackson has died."

"It is now over," she said, not looking at him, not favoring his eyes, but looking past him and some place beyond. There was no emotion in her words. There was no sign for him to read that would reveal the particulars of her inner thoughts. Her face was the composure of one who had experienced the ir-revocable. It was a fact unalterable and it was as simple as that.

He held his bony wrist in his opposite hand. He shuffled his feet as if that gesture were a means to understanding. He patiently waited because he knew when she was ready, she would tell him what this meant.

"Thomas Jackson has been killed," she finally said. "There's no sense in this continuing." She paused and sought words to fashion her thoughts. "This was a mistake a long time before we knew it, but a mistake nonetheless. Go and find your father and bring him back to his home."

Her words were as if come through time and she was an old mother and the ancient woman.

"Where will I find him?" he asked, unfolding his shoulders and setting his feet that he might stand erect.

"Travel south," she said. "Then east into the valley and then north down the valley."

She had sewed for him an up-buttoned, close-fitting linen shell jacket with the braids of a corporal and buttons made of sawed and bleached chicken bones. She told him it was imperative that he leave the home place this very night and not to dally along the way but to find his father as soon as he could and to surely find him by July.

"You must find him before July," she said.

He was not to give up his horse under any circumstance whatsoever and if confronted by any man, he was to say he was a courier and he was to say it fast and to be in a hurry and otherwise to stay hush and learn what he needed to know by listening, like he was doing right now. She then told him there is a terror that men bring to the earth, to its water and air and its soil, and he would meet these men on his journey and that his father was one of these men, and then she paused and studied a minute and then she told him, without judgment, that someday he too might become one of these men.

"Be aware of who you take help from," she told him, "and who you don't take help from." Then she eyed him coldly and told him, to be safe, he must not take help from anyone.

"Don't trust anyone," she said. "Not man, nor woman nor child."

The jacket on the one side was dun gray in color, dyed of copperas and walnut shells. When she turned it inside out, it showed blue with similar braids of rank. She told him he was to be on whatever side it was necessary to be on and not to trust either side.

"Secure pistols," she said, "and do this as soon as you can. Gain several and keep them loaded at all times. If you must shoot someone, shoot for the wide of their body, and when

one pistol is empty throw it away and gain the pistol of the man you have shot. If you think someone is going to shoot you, then trust they are going to shoot you and you are to shoot them first."

Her voice did not rise. It betrayed no panic. She instructed him with calmness and determination, as if the moment she'd anticipated had finally arrived and she was saying words to him she had decided upon a long time ago.

"Yes ma'am," he said quietly, and repeated her words back to her. "Shoot them first."

The dogs shivered and mewled and clacked their jaws.

"Remember," she said, reaching her hands to his shoulders, "danger passes by those who face up to it."

He remembered too how she had told him at twelve years of age he was old enough to work the land, but he wasn't old enough to die for it. To die for the land, he had to be at least fourteen years old and now he was.

When she finished her instructions, he drew a bucket of icy water from the well and splashed himself down to the waist. He toweled himself dry and unfolded a clean linen shirt. He dressed in black bombazine trousers and a pair of his father's flat-heeled leather brogans and then he donned the shell jacket. His square hands and bony wrists extended beyond the jacket's cuffs while the trouser legs gathered at his shoe tops. He plucked at his cuffs and tugged at the bones to make room for his chest.

His mother observed to him that he had growed some on top, as if it were a mystery to her and his face colored in patches for in her voice was carried a mother's tenderness, but for the most she remained distant and did not change

her mind and did not suggest he eat and sleep and wait until morning light before he departed.

After a time, long and purposeful, she cast her eyes on him, but she did not gift him with her smile. She reached up and he bent down and she hesitantly touched him at the side of his face. Her fingertips lingered on his cheek and neck as if she were not one with eyesight but was a blinded woman seeing with her fingers, and then she held a button and tugged and he felt as if she was pulling the inside of his chest.

It was then he realized just how sad and how futile his journey was to be. She was sending him in the direction of his own death and she could see it in no other way and she could do nothing else than send him off. Even if he was to return alive, she'd never forgive herself for risking her son's life for the sake of his father's life.

"You take off the coat," she said, changing her mind, and she helped him free the buttons and shuck the coat sleeves from his shoulders and arms. "Be a boy as long as you can. It won't be that much longer. Then use the dyed coat. You will know when."

"Yes ma'am."

"You are not to die," she said, though in her face loomed darkness.

"No ma'am."

"You will be back," she said, her eyes suddenly alive, as if they were eyes seeing the life past this life.

"Yes ma'am. I will be back," he said, glancing toward the darkness of the open door.

"You will promise," she said, commanding his attention.

"I promise."

"Then I will wait here for you," she said, and reached her

other hand to his face and drew him to her as she raised her body to his and kissed his lips.

In that kiss was the single moment she reconsidered her imperative. It passed through her as if a hand of benediction. He waited for her to say more words to him, but she did not. He felt her blue eyes wetting his face. She kissed him again, more urgently this time, and they both knew she had to let him go and then she let him go. He stepped away, gave a final wave of his hand and then he left out the door.

Outside, in the cooling, anodyne air of the mountain reach, evening was fading into night. His mother's touch still warmed his neck, his lips still heated from her kiss. He bridled a cobby gray horse with pearly eyes, saddled up, and rode from the home place and down into the darkness that possessed the Copperhead Road. If he had looked back, he would not have seen his mother but the dogs sitting in the still open doorway, their cadent breathing slow and imperceptible.

It took half that night to leave the sanctuary of the home place, to leave the high meadow, the old fields, and descend the mountain switchbacks into the cold damp hollows and to leave the circuits of the hollows and ride through the river mists of the big bottom. The trees and ledges sheltered the starlight as he passed beneath them. The mountain night was uncommonly still and the moonlight eerily shuttered by drifting scud, but in unshrouded moments the moonlight broke through and found the hollows and in long moments he was bathed in its white light as if the hollows were not made of stone but were channels of mirrored glass. So bright was the light he could read the lines in his hands and the gritted swirls in his fingertips.

He was still a boy and held the boy's fascination for how

light penetrates darkness, how water freezes and ice melts, how life could be not at all and all at once. How some things last for years without ever existing. He thought if the world was truly round he always stood in the center. He thought, Spring is turning into summer and I am riding south to meet it. He thought how his father was a traveling man and ever since he was a child he too dreamt of traveling most of all and now he was and he felt a sense of the impending.

He let float in the dark air his free hand and then raised it up and reached to the sky where his fingers enfolded a flickering red star. The star was warm in his hand and beat with the pulse of a frog or a songbird held in your palm. He caressed the star and let it ride in his palm and then he carried the star to his mouth where it tasted like sugar before he swallowed it.

2

———

T HAT MORNING OF HIS leaving there was no sunrise. There was no reddening in the eastern sky but rather a lessening of darkness from black to gray by degree. The dark hours played with the trilling calls and countercalls of wood frogs on the edges of ponds. A flock of blackbirds bound north traced the night sky with their arrowed wings. The ledges leaked thin runnels of trickling icy water. From somewhere deep in the sanctuary of the laurels a vigilant stag was belling the herd.

Those close-walled hollows were deep and cold and sepulchral. Their towering bore in and seemed poised to close. The switchbacks were wet and their path of stones was smooth and slippery, and more than once the cobby horse slid and each time she did he tightened his legs on her stout barrel affording her what small surety he could. But frightened, she would halt and leg-stiff refuse to take another step. He sat her patiently and spoke softly into her flicking ears and after a while she would snort and begin to move.

The path continued its falling for mile upon mile into the green of the rising springtime. He let his feet slip from the stirrups and he lay back until his head was over her croup. He could not imagine coming down this road in darkness and spring runoff, but tonight that's what he was doing.

To reach the bridge that morning was as if to return from a long journey that began beyond the rim of the world. Memory of his mother and the home place traveled with him in only the vaguest sense and his sudden concern was that if he crossed the bridge he would cease to remember them altogether. He turned in his saddle and looked back to the place where he'd come from. He angered over the distance, the fastness and the resistance of the home place. How could a night be so long? How could a few miles suddenly be so far? How could a place be so singular and so selfish as to deny itself to your mind once you have left it?

His eyes were wet and for reasons he could not name his chest throbbed. He wiped at his stinging eyes and cursed out in the darkness, but he did not know what he was cursing. Just a boy's last curse when he's told he has to do something. Even if the boy secretly wants to do that something, by nature he will curse the redirection of his will. Where before he had possessed time, now time was no longer his. He was being sent into the world and him now fourteen years old and so ignorant of its ways.

When he crossed the bridge the land opened and spread and lay flat as if a length of ribbon unfurled on a cobbled lane. On the densing air was the smell of leaf mold and opening buds. The sound of running water filled his ears and then receded and then increased again as he approached the junction of waters where the Twelve Mile doglegged and plunged into the turbulence of the Canaan. He continued southeasterly to the roar of the spring runoff and the boulders knocking in their chambered course.

He'd not slept or eaten the whole of that night and his body

was weak and qualmish. The land continued its widening and already the cobby horse was becoming too tired for the journey ahead. She blew heavy and shivered. The stones in her path were drenched with dew and her bare feet struck with increased concussion. Then she stumbled and stopped altogether and would not go forward. She snorted and tossed her head, slinging froth from her bit chain into the air. He kicked his heels into her flanks and slapped her rump, but she was unyielding. She cocked her head and flicked her ears forward and then back where they stayed.

Then he heard what she was listening to—the pinging sound a hammer makes on an anvil. Ahead was the little timbering village where old Morphew's mercantile stood on the way to the Greenbrier. He let her stand and shake out a repetition of long shivers that rippled her hide and once she settled he dismounted. He stroked her soft cheek and blew air into her wide waffling nostrils until she tossed her boxy head.

Her mouth was worn raw and bleeding where she'd worried the bit through the night. He told her she was surely in a state and he understood why because he was in one too, but it was going to be all right. He leaned into her left shoulder and when she gave him her weight, he folded her leg up. Her foot was heated and tender and the frog bleeding where it was penetrated by a sliver of shale in the shape of an arrowhead. With his folding knife he removed the stone sliver and she was relieved, but the damage was done. He set her foot down and with a coaxing of words, he was able to lead her forward.

Now he heard the squealing eeek of the wooden frame that held the suspended bellows, the rattle of chain as the leathers

expanded and collapsed, wheezing spurts of pumping air. The ground of the forge was strewn with plowshares and coulters. Beneath the worktable was a comb of grass and on top was a clutter of hammers, chisels, and punches.

The smith hovered over the fire, intent on the blue-straw color crawling up the metal from the depths of the forge. Then he turned at the shoulders and quenched it in a banging hiss of steam. The smith, a bent and hunchbacked German, had forged the iron hook that hung in their chimney. He pointed their turning plow. He made his mother's knitting needles.

One end of Old Morphew's porch was clasped in the branches of a lilac bush and backset; on the other end was a long lean-to stable and gray smoke purled from a smokehouse chimney. A boy, not much younger than himself, was walking across the porch floor on his hands, the unhitched galluses of his denim overalls clicking across the boards. An upside-down pocket was sewn into his pant's leg and stems of black licorice sprang from it.

The hiss of quenching heat blunted the air as the smith again plunged the working end of his pliers into the slack tub. The boy walking on his hands stepped aside for Robey as he mounted the porch and then followed him inside. In the air was the rank sweetness of molasses and coffee, cured bacons and ham.

Old Morphew looked up from his ledger book as the door slapped shut but made no gesture of greeting. He was so much older than Robey remembered since last he had seen him, his chest now gaunt and his body cadaverous. His stertorous breathing came husky and tubercular. They held each other's gaze.

"Mister Morphew," he said, and in the spoken name of the man was his question to the man: Do you remember me? Do you know who I am?

Morphew let go his grasp of the plank table and made up his pipe with tobacco. For the pain of bursitis in his shoulder he lifted his arm over his head and stretched it out and then let it back down. Inside the mercantile the smith's pinging hammer was only a pitched ticktack sound.

"Get'cha some crackers and set down in that cane-bottom, soft-back chair," Morphew said. He pointed to the cracker barrel with his pipe stem and then took a tin can and drew molasses from a black spigot bunged into a cask. Beneath the cask the wooden floor was puddled with a wide black stain where the spigot leaked.

He took the offered can and dipped a cracker. He was hungry and his stomach had begun to gnaw. He ate another, but the gnaw would not be satisfied. While he ate, Morphew studied him from behind his ledger, and when he caught his eye Robey told him what he knew and what he was sent to do and asked where he might go to find the best fighting.

"I know that's where my father will be," he said.

"I ain't heard about Thomas Jackson dead," old Morphew said, pulling on his chin. "Thomas Jackson being dead is hard to imagine. I don't know if I can feature that."

"Ma says he's dead."

"Your mother would know such a thing. She has the gift," Morphew said. "Though I will say one thing to that."

"What's that?"

"Prophesying the death of a man at war seems a safe-enough adventure."

Morphew nodded toward the cracker barrel that he should fill his fist again, then told him what he had heard of the fighting but warned the news was a week old and even if it wasn't it was unreliable at best. He hooked his finger into the spigot and licked them clean.

"Where would I go to find the army?"

"Which army?"

"How many are there?" he asked. He felt his growing tiredness in the warm sweet room. He'd not slept the entire night and understood the ache in his belly to be as much of weariness as hunger. He settled more deeply into the soft-back chair, feeling as if heavy weights had been hung from his limbs.

"There's a lot of them," Morphew was saying. "Last I heard they were in the valley and then they were on the Rappahannock. There's a pile of newspapers there by your feet. You could read up on it, but I wouldn't trust 'em. It's news what's all thirdhand and second best, if you ask me."

"My mother told me to travel south and east to the valley and then down the valley."

"Far be it for me to contradict your mother, but that won't put you on the Rappahannock."

"Where's the Rappahannock at?" He could hear himself speaking the words. The river made sense to him. His father told him to always defend a river on the far bank rather than the near bank and if the near bank was to be defended then do it behind it rather than at the water's edge.

"You go east," Morphew said, and pointed in the direction of east with his pipe stem with such precision that Robey thought east must be a place just outside the wall of the mercantile. That's not so far, he thought.

"Ma told him she'd whip him and hate him forever if he went to war, but he went anyways."

"You can't pound out of the bone what's in the blood," Morphew said.

"He said it was in in my blood too."

"Yessir, he's the travelinist man I ever knew."

"You know you orta whittle a new bung for that molasses cask," Robey said after a lull in the conversation, but already his brain felt thick with tiredness and collapse.

He did not know how long he slept in the soft-back chair. It was a short dreamless sleep that concluded as quickly as it had begun. He could hear the ticktack of the hammer and smell the sweetness. The boy was staring at him upside down, his legs bent at the knees and thrown behind him.

Old Morphew was still at his ledger book holding himself erect on his stiff arms. Again he said Morphew's name as if he had just arrived.

"You ain't running away to fight, are you?" Morphew said sternly.

"No sir," he said, and he was beset with an urgency to get on his way. It was clear to him he never should have stopped. So early in his journey and already he'd conspired to delay himself at the mercantile. It was not his prerogative to doubt his mother's advice, was not his to question or confirm the recondite principles of her clairvoyance.

"You wouldn't lie to me?" Morphew demanded.

"I don't lie."

"No, I don't suppose you do." He pushed a pouch of smoking tobacco across his ledger. "Take this here for your father. He'll want it sure enough, and this too," he said, and pushed

forward another pouch full of coffee beans. "He can settle up when he gets back."

"I will be leaving now," Robey said, and stood. "I have a long ways to go and I am anxious to get back soon."

"Good luck," Morphew told him and, stump-legged, followed him onto the porch, with the upside down boy tagging along. The sun had lifted from the horizon and held at a quarter in the sky—he'd slept that long. The cobby horse was lathered and woebegone, her head hanging on her neck. Parked beside the road was a work-sprained ox cart and the teamster carrying a bucket of water to the team. Roped inside the bed of the cart was a nailed coffin made of undressed white-bleached poplar.

"Who you got there?" Morphew yelled out from under the porch roof.

"Mister Skagg's boy," the teamster said, after he located the voice calling him.

"He used to live around here," Robey said.

"Wal', he don't no more," Morphew said.

They watched the teamster deliver another bucket to the thirsty oxen. He wore a black felt hat, a bright red shirt, and trousers ragged at his ankles. His unlined skin was the color of coffee.

"Where you bound from?" Morphew yelled.

"We come up from Lynchburg. Mister Skagg's boy died in hospital there and I am to bring him home."

"How'd he die?"

The teamster dragged his felt hat from his head and held it to his breast. He rubbed at his head trying to figure an answer.

"I just don't know, sir. He was asleep when it happened and didn't tell."

"Damned old fool," Morphew muttered, and then turned his attention to Robey. "It looks to me like you got to the bottom of that horse. How you gonna get where you're going on that ride?"

"I'll just have to walk when the time comes," he said, experiencing an awful sinking of the heart. One look at the cobby horse and he knew that time had come indeed.

"It's a long ways from here and it looks to me like the time is closer than you think. Maybe I can fix you up."

He looked to the teamster and then to the smith down the road at his forge and gestured that Robey should follow him. Behind the mercantile in the lean-to stable, a horse could be heard thrumming through its nose and stamping the wall. Morphew entered the shadowed light of the lean-to and when he returned he was leading the horse forward. It was coal black, stood sixteen hands, and it was clear to see the animal suffered no lack of self-possession.

"That is an oncommon horse," Robey said, unable to help himself in his admiration.

"He's a warm blood," Morphew said, "and I will tell you one thing. When he goes, he goes some bold."

"Who does he belong to?"

"The man who rode him in here died in that cane-bottom soft-back chair not a week ago and I buried him in the cemetery. That's to say the horse's ownership is in limbo but in my possession, so you can say he's mine right now."

"I have never seen a horse like that."

"The German says he's a Hanovarian. He's a fine horse,

with an equable disposition, but I'll warn you, he don't much like other horses."

"Which side were he on?"

"The man or the horse?"

"It don't much matter, does it?"

"Not if you're dead now, does it?"

From the darkness of the stable's interior, Morphew fetched a bridle, blanket, and saddle with holsters draping the pommel. He then fished into the black space where the rafters crossed the beam.

"You know what these are?"

"Yes sir."

"What are they?"

"Army Colts."

"Of course you do. They are .44 Army Colts. Do you know how to use them?"

"Yes sir."

"Show me how."

Robey cradled one of the the revolvers in his hands, hefting its weight and sighting along the length of its barrel. He deftly knocked out the pin and removed the cylinder and then looked to Morphew who produced a box of cartridges, percussion caps, and grease. Robey tore the covering from one of the cartridges and poured the powder into the chamber and then seated the bullet. After he loaded the cylinders he greased the head of each bullet. He then set a brass cap at the rear of each chamber. Then he repeated the process with the second revolver.

"Take them," Morphew said. "The horse and the pistols."

"I can't do that," he said. "Ma said I warn't to ask for no help."

Morphew thrust out his lower lip and scrutinized him before he spoke and when he finally did he began in anger and with impatience.

"Talking like that tells me you ain't got half sense to be out here doing what you're doing."

Morphew's breathing caught in his throat and he had to draw down into his lungs to find it again. His face reddened and his words became dull mutterings as water slid from his right eye. A pain passed through him taking the color from his cheeks. When he spoke again his throat was constricted and his words were as if winnowed in his throat channel.

"I respect your mother. She is an uncommon woman among women, but you just can't go boggling around the countryside. Things out there ain't like they used to be."

"How's that?"

"You used to be able to trust people."

In old Morphew's urgent composition were unspoken words: But I still trust you.

"You saddle and bridle this horse and you meet me out front. I will write you a paper saying this horse is mine, which by rights it is, and that currently it is in your custody."

Morphew turned his back and stumped over the worn ground, making the short distance between the stable and the mercantile.

He was alone with the horse and as he studied it, he understood the horse to be making decisions about him as well. He'd not known such a horse as this had ever been made and could not help but feel inferior to the animal. He was a young stallion and through his body he was deep and big set. His head was light in build and his eyes were large. His neck was

long and fine and his tail set high, but his shoulders were built massive. His muscles were dense and ran strong and wide in the loin. His legs were short in the cannon bones but his joints supple, strong, and substantial. His hoofs were high in front, behind and below, and the frog carried well off the ground.

He stepped forward and touched his hands to its long face. The coal black horse let his stroke to its cheek, neck, and muzzle. He then stroked its back and shoulders and worked his way down each leg, increasing the strength of his touch on the wide forearms and gaskins. He caught the horse's eyes with his own and the horse seemed inclined to tolerate him, if not be actually fond of him. After working his hands firmly over the animal's body, he bridled the coal black horse and set the blanket. He cinched the rig, and after telling the horse what he was going to do he caught the stirrup, swung up, and settled in the saddle. He then told the horse he was ready and the horse was willing.

When he rode around front, old Morphew was sitting in a rocker he'd dragged onto the porch. The upside-down boy was playing his hands as close to the rockers as he could without pinching his fingers. Morphew had a gunnysack for him with cans of deviled ham, pork and beans, and condensed milk. He pulled himself erect and labored his body from the porch.

"Don't get cocky riding that horse," he said as he adjusted the stirrup leathers. "A man rides a horse like that he begins to think he's above every other man."

Old Morphew then stepped back from the horse's side. Youthfulness twinkled inside him. He enjoyed the businessman's satisfaction of a completed transaction well done. It

was in seeing his pleasure that Robey determined the old man must have experienced a recent great terror inside his heart cage or the depths of his mind and only now, frightened and wounded, was returning to himself.

"Rupert," Morphew yelled over to the German, "how is it you're not drunk today?"

Without pausing in his work, the bent man thrust the middle finger of his right hand over his head. Morphew laughed at this—a mischievous little game they played.

"Hunchbacks are often smarter than we are," he said, as if it were a truth underappreciated.

"Don't that boy ever stand up?" Robey said.

"No," Morphew said, casting a glance at the boy walking on his hands. "As a matter of fact he don't. He is an upside-down boy. Bet you've never heard or seen one of them."

"No sir. I don't believe I have."

"Well, you are in for an education and I just hope you live long enough to tell about it."

"I will."

"That's right. You find your father," he said, waving him away, "and you bring him home and we'll settle up."

With that, he rode off on the coal black horse with the heavy revolvers in the holsters at his thighs. As he disappeared from sight, Morphew noticed the German had wandered to his porch and was suddenly standing at his side. The German marveled on the beauty of the horse's flowing movement, its grace in stride, and he commented with small wonder on the horse's affinity for the boy.

"It's a horse that leaves quite an impression," Morphew said.

"It is the kind of horse that can get you killed."

"I thought about that."

"And what did you think when you thought about that?"

"I thought a lot of things. I thought about his mother. I thought about how he's his father's son and he is a-goin' either way he can. I thought how gettin' in trouble ain't hard, but gettin' out of it is."

"I thought you'd think how where he's going the horse might be smarter than him."

"I thought that too."

3

I t was beautiful to ride the back of the coal black horse and in those first days of journey they traveled constantly. The valley when he discovered it was luxuriant with grass and clover. The red-clay roads were wide and hard packed and the road cuts were dry and banked.

As the days drew by they passed silently through fields, swamps, pastures and orchards. They rode through marsh where the water table was only a few spades deep, but the corduroyed lanes of passage were high set and well staked. They crossed acres of fresh turned earth, plowed straight and harrowed and sown with wheat, rye, and oats shooting the surface and knitting it green. They encountered walls of pine so thick it took days to skirt to find a throughway and when they did it was through a land of wind-thrown trees, or dead on the stump, the crooked and angled limbs bleached white with sun.

In his urgency, sleep was Robey's bane and he tried with all his might to stay awake days at a time, but finally he relented and learned to fall asleep on the back of the coal black horse as it seemed to share the same mind with him in the direction it maintained. From then on, when he grew tired, he merely

pulled a blanket over his head and dropped his chin upon his rocking breast and slept and the horse would sleep too, walking on in its repose, covering a length of four miles every hour, its hooves invisible for the dust and gauze of heat, or veiled by lightning on the black path as the flashes directed their way in the electric, combusting, and starless night.

Whole days and whole nights went by; how many he lost track of and could not tell. He'd not known there was so much country beyond the hollows and so flat and undulating and the deep-running streambeds, the dense thickets of wild rose, the sudden, vertical-walled mountains. Although with his own eyes he had seen the vast distances to be witnessed skimming across the mountaintops, he'd not seen so far inside the land, not seen such verdant meadows and lush pasturage and the great built houses he saw, ever in his life before.

In moments he thought he'd have seen the ocean by now, or the majestic cities his father talked about. He thought he would have crossed shiny iron rails or entered the funnels of tree-lined boulevards terminating in the grand squares where government and business did their work. His father had told him of how broad and limitless the world, how close the woods, how endless the tidy green forest, how steep the climbs and sharp were the switchbacks' rocky descents. Out west, his father had told him, nature's work was as yet undone. The rivers still sought their beds and in their seeking they swelled to measureless proportions and were as if vast inland seas appearing and disappearing. The mountains were high and tumbled and rose to invisibility. There was desert land and canyon land. There were trees so wide at the stump they were impossible to chop down and in some places there

were no trees at all as far as the eye could see. The weather was big beyond the Mississippi and angry and lasted for weeks. The cold was too cold, the hot was too hot, the water was too much or none at all. Nature was laid bare naked: sparkling sand, wind-scored stone, leeching mineral, hanging and split rock dividing the buffeting wind. Wetness sought dryness and the wind the tallest trees to strike down and the light-ning the flattest land. Out west was the mine, the quarry, the nursery, the smithy of a maker.

At first he collected what he could of food and weapons and there was plenty to be found and picked over. But then he stopped his hoarding and rode on with only a blanket, oilcloth, loaded pistols, a knife, and a canteen and managed to find a handful of parched corn, or buttermilk, ginger snaps, a sack of navy beans whenever he needed to satisfy his hunger and often there was to be found in the ruins of the army's plumbeous-colored wagons such odd fare as sardines, pickled lobster, canned peaches, and coffee. He thought he'd starve before he'd steal, but that was before he was faced with starving.

As the days went by, he began to attend the smells of fry-ing bacon and stalk the cow paths spattered with fresh dung. When necessary, he filched field corn from the cribs or caught stray chickens, a cooling pie, a ham hung in a smokehouse, and when there was none of this to be found he ate berries, ramps, and wild garlic. He ate watercress and drank tea he boiled from acorns.

He left the valley in an easterly direction and he crossed again where mountaintops were wreathed by terrible winds, where mountains were heaped on mountains whose cloud-capped summits seemed to call him and he thought someday

he'd like to return to them and search through their aerie mists to stand on their peaks.

There were also beautiful and isolate moments in his searching days. He followed deer paths into their notched parks where thirty or fifty head grazed like cattle. He saw pools of water where there were so many fish they climbed on each others' backs, sparkling in the sunlight, to tongue the hatch. Down lanes he traveled there were estates, brightly lit against the night's darkness and untouched by war or the news of war. He saw tiny villages set in mountain glens, pretty farms and houses whose existence was pristine and without evidence of what was overcome to be so pure.

One night in the twilight world of an early evening, he heard organ music playing in the trees and could smell the heavy scents of burst pine pollen. Somewhere there were people gathered and they were worshipping and their choral voices hymned in the darkness. His mother had beliefs, but his father was a freethinker and was fond of saying that with soap, baptism could be a good thing. He suspected that his beliefs fell somewhere in the middle between his mother and father. Curious as to the music's source, he suggested the horse in its direction and anticipated arriving at its source, but it ebbed and then disappeared as mysteriously as it had occurred and he wondered, What could it have been?

He continued on until he found wedged in a declivity of stone a standing horse that'd hung itself up a long time ago. It was made of white bones whose ribs grew moss and legs sustained runner vines and the bone of its skull was a garland of white-flowered creepers. The horse must have plunged through and broke itself and become trapped and could not

escape, and now when the wind was right it sounded music in those bones.

HIS FACE ALTERNATELY wind galled and sunburned and his limbs numb with cold and listless with heat, he had descended into the vast green northeasterly valley, crossed the upheaved blue mountains, and descended once again onto the piney plain, where the air quaked and trembled as it endured its own heated weight. His mother had told him to continue up the valley, but by all other accounts it was to the east where the army was to be found.

By now he was joined as one with the horse. His thighs and legs were soaked with its lather, his clothes stained through with its sweat. So too his hands and where he rubbed his face and finger-combed his hair, and he could not imagine ever parting with the jewel of it. The horse held possession of both his waking and sleeping mind. He dreamt of the horse and in each sleep the horse multiplied until they became so many horses he could not keep count of them. The coal black horses were the first horses and the only horses ever to have been. They were not horses, but like something of the other—the man-eaters: the lion or wolf or bear, or man himself. Only they were more true, more noble of birth, more singular of purpose and intent. When they ran, they ran in a glorious periphery of whiteness that disappeared the earth beneath them and the air above the earth to the spring of their ribs. There were no legs on boy or horse. He was blank from the knees and the effect was that of riding light, as if light were spindrift and he was borne in its froth and was swept along on the horse he rode: the winged horse, the born horse, the

horse out of the blood, the horse pulling the light of day across the sky.

He thought to tell the horse of these events visiting his mind in dream, but could not bring himself to do so for how weak and lovesick they left him. Every time he tried he felt as if he would collapse to the ground. He thought if he were to tell he would lose what little there was left of him. To tell what he believed the horse already knew would be to lose himself forever in the horse.

It was during this time that he resolved he would keep the horse and by whatever means possible he would pay Morphew the price of its purchase and he would find the heirs to the dead cavalryman who owned the horse before Morphew and he would pay again.

HE RODE ON THROUGH the snarled forests of the flat land, rough and bluntly savage, and over sweeps of inexplicably burned and gouged terrain, and it was here one day when he came upon death.

It was long before he arrived at the shattered and blown house, long before he even knew it existed that he was drawn in its direction. Perhaps it was the eerie silence in the place he sensed beyond the tree line. Perhaps it was the emptiness he felt in the atmosphere. He felt a falling-off inside himself and a telling in his mind that he was entering a place of grave dedication. Then there was a flush of vultures and on the shadowed ground movement into light, and a pack of dogs slunk by and with the dogs was carried the unmistakable smell. It was in their jaws and chests and soaked into their shamed faces.

For no apparent reason, men had been killed here, their

souls set astray and their bodies left piled like rotting cord wood in ditches and behind files of sharpened stakes. The men's bones wore tatters of flesh and cloth and where they were piled it was difficult to tell how many men there were. He had no one to guide him through these ghostly regions of horrible event and him with so little understanding of how many people on the earth, in this moment it seemed as if half of them were dead and left unburied. Their smell was like a fresh poison possessing the wind to become the wind. Though he had never smelled the death of men before, he knew the smell as if it were a knowledge born into him.

He dismounted for vague reasons of respect and together with the horse he walked across the battlefield to its border and into the dark woods. When he turned to mount the horse his foot sank into the ground and his ankle became trapped in the rib cage of a single man buried alone in a shallow washed-out grave. The man's bones were chalky and withered and broken and one arm was raised to his gray skull as if in salute and his finger bones were clenched in the fist of a painful death. The man's death must have occurred so long before the others. Had this clearing seen war before? Was this a place where war resided like a natural animal in wait?

He did not know the answers to his questions and did not even care to think about them for very long. He simply knew with all these men dead he must be getting close. He thought with all these men dead fighting war, it must be that war was winning.

AT NIGHT MOST PEOPLE went to bed, but not all. To be en-countered on the roads was the sound of pounding hooves

and to be avoided were bands of armed men on the backs of their hard-ridden horses. This was easily done, but not so easy to avoid were the lone riders slipping along silently in the dark. He met such riders on the road, men whose violence always seemed to be within them, violence that was convulsive and dangerous. They rode with their reins loose in one hand and with the other they held a carbine or a double-barreled shotgun, upright, with the butt resting on their thigh.

When he could not avoid these encounters he slowed and half-raised an arm in the common gesture of lone riders meeting on back roads. Most often they were as wary as he was and wanted as little to do with him as he wanted with them. They had their own secret fears and reasons to avoid being seen on the roads. They were on their own private missions. But then seeing the coal black horse materialize from the shadows and grow upon approach, they'd swivel in the saddle for the better look and he could feel their eyes on his back.

Then came one late evening when he was riding down a deep-cut bowered lane with a snake-rail fence running along both its sides. The air carried heavy and was too dense to carry much reach of surrounding sound. From ahead there came the profile of a dark rider in relief from a dogleg bending the road. The dark rider paused to consider them and then came on. He grew as he made his approach and when they passed on the lane the dark rider pulled rein and hailed him by a name that was not his own. Fooled by this trick of mistaken identity, he stopped in the road and turned, but the coal black horse did not want to stop and he quickly wised up to its misgiving when he heard the muffled sound made by the rider's thumb drawing back the hammer on the shotgun

he carried. His heels raked hard, but it was not necessary. The
coal black horse was already driving into a sudden run. The
horse broke fast and drove all out for the dogleg ahead and
he held as tight as he could because the horse was making for
it with a power he did not know it possessed.

Bent to the horse's neck, he clung hard so as not to be unhorsed and still had little hope for when they made the sharp
corner. He feared for how fast the ground would rise because
he knew he'd not be able to hold on when the horse set left
and threw right to make its turn. But rather than drop its
shoulder to make the turn, the horse continued to climb in
stride and at the last instant made a great winging leap out
of the cut and over the high snake-rail fence and into a wall
of briars that grew on the other side. His body whipped in
the saddle but he clenched up and held with the last he had.
In that same moment the shotgun fired, and simultaneously
a covey of quail went up in their wake. There was a raucous
thrashing as the briars tore at them for some distance until
they burst free onto brushy ground and then across a cutting,
where they disappeared into a wood on the other side.

But it was not this dangerous encounter that lingered in his
mind. Rather, it was the poise and equanimity of the horse
that he wondered on, its sense and knowledge of men. Afterward, there would be other episodes, but he did not need to
wait to hear the hammer drawn back or to feel the spray of
buckshot falling on his shoulders before they were dodging
into the next bend in the road. It would happen again and
again, but by then he was digging his heels into the horse's
sides and it was rising into the bit on big floating steps and
they were disappeared.

ANOTHER DAY PASSED and then another and he could feel
the urgency of his mother's imperative weighing on his mind
and body. He could feel the responsibility of the promise he'd
made her. He was to find his father and bring him back to his
home where he lived. And he remembered she said he was
not to dally along the way but to find his father as soon as he
could and to find him by July. But why July? What did she
know about July before it even happened? Or had it already
happened? He wondered what month it was. Surely it was not
yet July.

"Tomorrow," he repeated. Maybe tomorrow would be the
day when he would find his father. But then tomorrow came
and went and he felt no closer to the river where the army was
said to be than he did the day before. He had no idea the land
was so big and the many crosses its roads made.

He was now in a hot and wet country ridden with flies and
he often wished for flight and to enter the realm where the
birds darted and sliced the air. He wished the coal black horse
to grow the wings he dreamed and fly him through the air.
The wind on the plain east of the valley was long and tangled
and he was homesick, fatigued, and disillusioned. His strength
was about gone and his limbs felt as if borrowed from a man
a hundred years old.

In darkness, he left the road and followed a stitch of path
into the trees and then left the path and urged the horse to
find a route in the pathless forest. He continued on, desiring
distance from the traffic of humans. He wanted a place remote
and undisturbed where he could collect himself, where he
could lie down and sleep, lest he slide from the horse's back
and tumble to the ground. He needed to lie on the earth and
rest his thin sore body and renew his thowless spirit.

He unsaddled the coal black horse to let its back cool in the moon-dappled shade. He ran his hands over its legs and lifted each foot to check for cracks in the hoof walls. He sorted the cockleburs from its high-set tail. He wondered at how indifferent the horse was to pain, how immune to weakness. He had long since come to understand and accept how superior the animal was to him, and he did not mind this fact but appreciated it.

"You are tough as a old ox," he said, briefly catching an eye's lateral vision with his own.

He shook out the sweat-stained saddle blanket and lay down in front of the horse on a bed of green ferns and where arched fiddleheads unfolded and a lead tied loosely to his wrist.

He looked up into the horse's face and told the animal to be patient with him, that he was still a boy and that he should sleep awhile before they moved on. He did not want to slip off and break his neck in the dirt.

"I am tired," he said as if tiredness were a thing of longing. The horse responded by nosing his chest and blowing gently against his face.

"I am dirty as a pig," he said in agreement. The horse lifted a foot and set it down heavy. It grunted and then found bunches of grass at his side to enfold with its lips and tear free. Its head shot up as it chewed and it glanced to the rear.

You eat a little bit, he thought. Just a bit of sleep for me and we'll be on our way.

But it was a troubled sleep waiting for him. That day on the road he'd seen something his mind would not let go of. It was not that they were men alive or dead. It was not that they were men torn or ravaged or made horrible. Then his mind did let go and his eyes closed and his breathing steadied and

he listened to the horse cropping again and chewing what it'd found, its eyes, its ears, its nose always ready for reasons to fly.

WHEN HE AWOKE, he was refreshed. He sat up and swept the May bugs from his face and hair. He stood in light and when he did he learned that beyond the small clearing and its edge of woods where he'd slept was a bow made by a flat river where swallows danced lightly on streams of air. The sunlight was clear and strong and he could see the river's glaring sparkle without seeing the water's surface. He led the horse in its direction where he found another green and there he tied the horse to a lead where it could browse the fresh grass.

He proceeded on to the riverbank, wading through deep ferns and a flowering thicket, a hand held in front of his eyes for how bright the sun glare reflecting off the riffles. He stepped forward and then he sat down and let himself slide the bank on his backside to dangle his feet from the edge of the bluff overlooking where the broad flat river looped. His father told him rivers were difficult to defend. They created meanders and meanders needed to be closed and in doing so they tended to suck up troops.

The bluff was littered with softened pine needles and the water under the sun was the color of caramel. He thought to dangle his legs in the water, but it ran too far beneath the rim of the bluff. His father said rivers break lines of sight and impede lateral movements. It was rivers where possibilities began and ended.

He sat for a long time, resting on a bed of pine needles in the cool shade. He knew he needed to be on his way and soon

enough he would mount the coal black horse and follow east into the sun. Behind him he could hear the horse snuffing and tearing grass. He realized he'd not eaten in several days and needed food as well as he needed travel. Lately the by-ways had been clogged with the traffic of refugees, mule drivers cursing, men teaming haggard draft horses, high-piled wagons teetering with trunks, home goods, and furniture. There were women with green hides sewn to their feet who drove cows and pigs before them and there were barefoot boys and girls cutting the air with switches behind flocks of imperious geese and waddling ducks who griped like spoiled children. He saw a lone man shabbily dressed with a kid goat slung over his shoulders, a little boy carrying a rabbit by its ears. They pushed wheelbarrows and pulled handcarts that were laden with carpet sacks, churns, hand tools. For the most they were poor and motely. Their bodies were thin and drawn in stark contrast to the fattening food stock—the beeves, hogs, and milch cows that were leading them south and west.

And there were the lone teamsters with their cargo of the maimed and dead. He wondered if they were the same drivers he'd seen in the far distance from the high place above the Twelve Mile, old men with their rude wagons and broken horses hauling the casualties of war back to their homes, only to return again for another load of the torn and shattered. Sometimes there was a box and other times there was tightly bound swaddling in the shape of a man. Some men waved to him and others just stared as if he were the strange one who'd crossed by accident into the land of limbless men. Maybe these teamsters were but a few in number, the designated, and this was their mission, their destiny—freighting

the damaged from the sundered world. Two days ago it was a black phaeton with glass sides pulled by a matched pair of carriage horses. It didn't matter, the old man at the footboard holding the reins and whip, the box inside the glass walls, it was still the same.

There were other travelers also to be seen on the roads and byways and on first occurrence he did not completely understand who these strange bands of men and women were, and these his mind could not let go of. It seemed common enough to him that he should see black men wearing checkered homespun and walking behind the horses the white men rode and not so unusual that the black men themselves would sometimes be riding. But he'd not seen before in his life a black man with a leather strap collaring his neck and being led down the road by a chain. His quickest thought was that the man was a criminal, but in the next instant he knew better.

These encounters, they increased in number and frequency until yesterday. He did not know what told the horse there was a strangeness approaching from the north, but it stopped and raised its head and directed its ears forward. He pressed with his left thigh and clucked in his throat and they stepped off the road and into the tree shade and waited. He was not so intent on hiding as he was avoiding being seen by the silent, alien caravan that was approaching, for advancing on him was no jingle of harness, no rattle of a bridle, no cough, no muffled tramp of feet or plodding hooves. There was no gabble of voices or creaking wheel axles, not even the silent approach of the lone rider he'd learned to detect in the extension of his mind. There was not a sound or feeling he could

name, but an eeriness. It was as strange as the birth of an unnatural—the oncoming surround of utter silence they carried with them as they moved down the road, as if a troupe escaped from hell, seemingly without motion and heated and on the edge of burning.

When the vanguard hove into view they were the roughest men he'd ever seen. They rode all manner of horse and rig. They rode gaunt horses with pinch-nosed hackamoors that wrung their tails alongside warm-bloods wearing blinker hoods and four-reined bridles. There were wild and bony horses snubbed short that didn't so much walk as they skittered and pawed across the ground sideways the way an insect does. Some of these men were shirtless and rode without blankets or saddles. Their faces were painted and their long hair knotted with leather. He wondered on the vanity in these men as some wore feather plumes in the bands of their slouch hats and red and paisley kerchiefs at their necks. Others wore ropes of shells around their necks and their heads were made up with blue and vermillion. There was also a black man, face tattooed and wearing a beaver hat, who rode among them, the silvered butt of a short-barreled muskatoon bouncing on his thigh.

Following behind were runaway slaves that'd been rounded up and formed into coffles and marched back south. When the chains had run out they'd been yoked with forked branches cut from trees and lashed at their necks. They were a silent dusty procession and fantastic in appearance. Their clothes were often a flannel patchwork, or torn calicoes or canvas cloth, or cut-up blankets sewn into smocks and trousers suspended at the waist. They wore coverlets gashed in the center,

dropped over their heads, and closed round them with a belt. The children were dressed in overshirts with no underclothes beneath them. While most wore rags and castoffs, a few were better dressed than the riders. One chained man wore a smart black suit and a low-topped bowler hat.

Bringing up the rear was another knot of the manhunters and a two-wheeled dog car with penned and slobbering hounds riding beneath the driver's high seat. The dogs looked his way with their drawn red eyes but didn't make a sound. They were dogs trained to hunt what they hunted without a care for anything else, and their chained and yoked quarry walked the road before them.

After that, he wanted distance from human beings and the roads they traveled. He wanted the ancient overgrown animal paths found in deep and trackless country. He wanted the parallel roads traveled by the drovers and the livestock, the poor, the runaways themselves.

4

THERE WAS A RARE SETTLING accomplished by a silent concert of light, air, and water. His still-tired mind lulled into repose where it stayed for a time until disrupted by a thrashing in the leaf mold beneath the brush. He smiled at how a foraging squirrel could make more of a racket than a mast-rooting hog. He knew he had to be on his way and, this morning, ached with the guilt of recalcitrance. He wanted his days back. Wanted time to be his again. He idly tossed a stick in the direction of the racket. There was a long silence and then a scraping sound and then from a branch high over his head the squirrel began to chatter, scolding him for throwing the stick in its direction, scolding him for his presence on the cutbank.

The sun soon shifted in the sky and found the patch of ground where he sat and he was blotted with light. He thought what sport it would be to fish this river. From the hard-twigged bushes came the chit notes of songbirds. Swallows were diving for the riverbank below his feet, building their nests. In the tops was a breeze combing the spiring trees and then it was quiet again as if a hand suddenly raised had been let down. Behind him he could hear the horse tearing away tussocks of grass.

He tried to recall having slept the night through but could not.

On the far bank emerged the figure of a human, a bent little woman. A cob pipe protruded from the shaded confines of her bonnet. A length of braided hair extended down her back. She carried a wooden bucket and a cane fish pole rocked on her shoulder, no more than a harmless curiosity. She stepped down from the grassy mull bank to the stony shore, the toes of her shoes poking from beneath her gingham skirts.

He thought to slide away into the woods, but following her was a gaggle of squat white geese and this was walking food. A duck was selling for twenty-five cents and a goose was fifty cents or about that.

He watched as she studied the water downstream and then wandered back upstream along the stone-cobbled shore. The geese followed her in both directions, bumping into each other as they toddled to turn and catch up. He didn't have any coins. Maybe she'd take trade, but what to trade? He could steal just one, but in his thieving to date he'd never stole from anyone he'd seen to be an owner.

The little old woman did not seem intent on fishing and after a while she dropped the fishing pole, sat down on her bucket, and concentrated on smoking her pipe. The geese wandered about in idleness and mild confusion until the little woman spat. They gathered on the spot, bumping into each other, inspecting her phlegm for some time. Then a goose found a grub and drew the attention of the others and they gathered there next. The woman continued to enjoy her pipe, sending a steady succession of gray puffs into the air. Over the pines, crows in flight made their raucous calls. Their sound

came on suddenly like a snapping bough. A mobbed owl hove into view and crossed his vision over the river's surface. The owl slid low, found the dark understory on the near bank, and disappeared. The crows, having never shown themselves, broke off their pursuit.

It was then he noticed the lazy water browning in color and beginning to rise. At first it was slow and he did not know if it was happening at all, so slow was its beginning, but then it rose more rapidly. The current quickened and there came wreaths of feather-white foam swirled about the edges of vortexes that made ripping sounds as they sucked shut. Stems and leafy branches followed and then a broad limb of dried wood.

Upstream, there must have been a powerful rain as the river continued to swell until it had become a black muddy wash. The little woman stood, took her bucket in hand, and walked backward as the water followed her, nagging at her feet with every step she made. The geese assembled on her steps, flustered and squanking in confusion. She stepped cautiously and he wanted to yell that she should run. Then she did. She turned into a trot that took her to higher ground where the sand and gravel was closed over by hummocks of grass sewn into the red earth. She jumped the grassy step, the flustered geese climbing behind her, and watched as the river gently heaved and cuffed its high-water mark.

It occurred to him, as it continued its rising, that it just might not stop, so fast and powerful was it coming on. He left off his concern for the little woman and began to scamper backward on his palms and heels. But this was not quick enough, so he stood to run, and it was in that moment of standing that a great chunk of earth the river had slowly been

carving began to subside. The bank gave way beneath his feet and he was being let down into the caramel water on a slab of red dirt collapsing into the river.

His descent was slow and inexorable, and however hard he strained to scuttle the falling bank he could not keep himself from being shrugged away. He went under the dirty surface and even as he pushed the bottom to rise for air the deluge was already receding, and when he stood he found himself standing waist deep in muddy water. His wetted body cooled and yet was heated as if hornet-stung in the sluggish frothy water. His clothes skimmed with a slick of red clay and sluiced from his fingertips as if milk or blood.

"Yo, boy," a voice called out. It was the little woman with the cane fish pole coming down to the water's edge from the dry bank. Other than her nose and the bowl of her pipe, her face was shrouded in bonnet. "You drownded yourself?" she inquired.

He cleared his burning nostrils and spit. He dragged himself into the shallows and pawed his way through the flooded briars, his shoes slogging through the scum until he reached a hard bed of silt and stone. He pawed at his face and eyes again. He shook out his arms, shucking their wetness into the air.

The little woman was laughing at his calamity. She was a strange and ugly woman with narrow shoulders and a long beakish nose that ran constantly. Just as she'd wipe at it, another drip would form. About her being was the rank smell of old sweat that surpassed even the stagnant earth of the riverbank. With her geese jostling to flank her at the water's edge that they might stare at him too, he thought she also made quite the comical.

"Don't you look a picture," she cackled. "You have got to be careful. Accidents happen out here."

"Is this the Rappahannock?" he asked as he climbed the bank to stand at her feet. Hers was not a very kind face. Her face actually made him dizzy to look at as her skin seemed to run in the sunlight with a swarming fluidlike vibration. His body iced as he realized that she was crawling with lice. They were running her skin in streaming volutions that swirled her cheeks and forehead and across her lips and yet she did not seem to notice.

"This little trickle?" she said. "Don't be a ignoramus." And then she said, "What do you want with the Rappahannock?"

"You ain't a woman," he said, before he could stop his voice in his throat. "You're a man."

"Every beggar's got his stick for beating off the dogs," the little woman said.

She then swiped the bonnet and braided hair from her head in a single motion and she was indeed a man. The little man then unbuttoned the dress and shed it from his shoulders. Without the dress he was a queer, spindly little man, built like a boy with a boy's frame and a boy's muscles, but in the light his face skin revealed to run evermore with the motion of vibrating water. His bare neck and the wisps of hairs at his collar were beset. His naked arms and the backs of his hands were likewise a struggling infestation, but beyond belief he seemed to pay it no mind. Still, there appeared nothing to fear from him except his infestation.

"You really never know a man's true nature." The little man laughed.

His face held an expression behind which little could be seen for the crawling mask he wore. The little man rooted in

his ear with his finger, as if there could possibly be something that would irritate him, and then looked at it.

His voice turned to sharp rule and still looking at his finger he said, "You intend to jine up, or what?"

Robey shook his head. His stomach had become a turning of knots. He could not look at the man's crawling skin and he could not look away from it for how mesmerizing. He was not afraid, but he felt better when he knew where the little man's face was, the same way he wanted to know where a disappeared snake crawled to when he came across one in the forest.

"No," he said.

"I were in the army for a time," the little man said wistfully. "I spent my days in the mud marching through wet cornfields. I was trod on and ridden over by every big-mouthed son of a bitch who had a horse. I'll be hanged if I know anything more about the matter than that." Then he paused and said, "I couldn't wait to get back home."

The little man was funny to him and he began to take pity on him for how lost in the world a man so little as him must be when all other men were so big.

"Food?" the little man said.

"Lately I been kind of off it," Robey said.

"Hungry then, ain't ya'."

"I been feelin' like a walking belly," he said.

"You afoot?"

He told him he wasn't and asked that he should wait while he forded the river to retrieve his horse and kit. The little man agreed to this and Robey slogged through the water to make the far bank. The horse was waiting where he'd left it but was

contrary this morning and had little intention of crossing. He patiently saddled the animal and slung his haversack over the pommel. He jammed a pistol in his belt and then coaxed the horse to the riverbank, but again it shied when at the water's edge and kicked that it should not get wet. He stopped to stroke the animal's eyes and soft muzzle.

"Can you handle it?" the little man yelled across through his cupped hands.

He spoke to the horse how they'd feed and water and get on their way, and only with the utmost of patience was he able to convince the horse across the river.

"Boy, I like the looks of that horse," the little man said when they came up from the river.

"He's a good horse," Robey said.

"I had me a good saddle horse I was riding," the little man said. But by then he was back in the branches and was striking a path in the woods with the white geese waddling along behind him.

Robey followed the little man and the geese to his house where the window glass was broken and from inside there were more geese stretching their long necks and staring out from the jagged openings. Or they tottled on the wide veranda, curious and birdy about events they found significant, yet were invisible to the human eye. The little man told him to stay put and not to move while he fetched them food to eat, and he was to refrain from using the well as the well house was charred over from fire and still stank of wet smoke and its water was rancid.

The little man disappeared inside the house and it wasn't long before he came out carrying an immense platter heaped with half-warmed sauerkraut, fried onions, salt pork, and cold

beef. In his other hand he held a coffeepot. He squatted in the yard as he set the platter on the ground between them and after taking up a handful of kraut and a slab of beef, he urged Robey that he should also take some food and eat. He was so hungry he did not pause to reach into the plate after the little man.

They ate in silence, gorging their food and grunting the way dogs do. For Robey it was because he was so hungry, but for the little man it seemed to be the way he knew how to eat. Between mouthfuls the little man began telling Robey the long story of how he'd just come home from the war on furlough, the hounds of hell on his ass all the way, only to find that raiders and renegades had been at his house. When he told of their destructiveness his swarming eyelids quivered and his hooded eyes blanked with hatred.

"There is no sign of my family and I can only hope they are safe," he said. But there was no hope in his voice, his affect flat and melancholy.

"You're going to look for them," Robey said, sympathetic to the little man's plight.

"Why yes I am," he said. "Thank you."

The little man patted his full belly and belched and insisted Robey do the same and when he did the little man thought that hilarious. He slapped his thighs and insisted they do it again. Then they reclined in the grass and while rolling a cigarette, the little man told Robey that war had its other sides too.

"In war," he said, "the best bad things are often obtainable," and then he offered him the coffeepot, but when Robey thumbed the hinged lid it smelled of whiskey inside and he declined.

"Oh, go ahead," the little man said. "Have you a little shot

in the neck. It won't hurt you none. They's a twenty-gallon demijohn settin' right inside the door."

The little man took a long gulping drink as if to prove how abundant the amount of whiskey.

Robey thought how the little man must have had a rough go of it, being little and all and then to come home and find what he'd worked for wrecked and vandalized and his family missing and maybe dead. But now he was wary for the changes in the little man. Within short time of his whiskey-drinking, something had come over him, or had risen up from inside him. Either way he was being overtaken and it was coming on fast.

He told the little man whiskey was nothing he'd ever drunk before and at the moment it just didn't interest him, but he was grateful for the food and thought he should consider being on his way.

The little man laughed, as if satisfied with the logic of his answer, but it was an ill-tempered laugh. He continued to drink and then he tried again to interest Robey in joining him, but he declined.

"But it ain't no fun drinking alone," the little man said, as if an appeal remembered, one made to him by another somewhere in his past.

"No," Robey said again. "I don't want any whiskey, thank you."

"But it's good whiskey. It slows time," the little man said, his voice sweet and wheedling. He told him it made all your cares a will-o'-the-wisp. He drank off another full draft and then another until he was swirling his finger inside the empty pot to catch the dregs.

"It's time I was going," Robey said again and he felt a flush of anger for how foolish he'd been and a sudden unreasoned fear came over him. He was now ensnared by the little man and he'd allowed it to happen.

"Before you go, sell me that horse," the little man suggested, licking his fingers. "So's I can ride it to search for my family."

"It ain't mine to sell," Robey said, fighting to quell the apprehension in his voice. He knew he could no longer be timid, no longer hesitant and compliant. He didn't know who this man was, but he knew this man's mind was set and he would never give up the idea of possessing the horse.

"You stole it," the man said, and when he suddenly stood Robey pulled himself from the ground to also stand.

"It was lent me," he said.

"You love that horse, don't ya'?"

Robey did not reply. His hand went to his waist where the butt of his pistol hung in his belt.

"What every horse lover don't understand is that every horse is someday gonna die," the little man said. Inside his swirling complexion his eyes had reddened. His voice was shrill as a child's.

"There is other horses in the world, I'll grant you that," Robey said.

"Sell it to me and tell your man it were killed."

"I can't do that."

"I say nobody lets out a horse like that."

"Mister Morphew let me that horse. I have a paper to prove it." His face burned at the charge, that his honesty should be questioned and that he should stoop to defend himself.

He also knew it made no difference to the little man that he should have such a paper to prove his word.

"I could kill that horse," the little man said, and drew the revolver he wore in his belt and aimed at the coal black horse. Robey knew it was true and he knew the only witness would be the wind and the trees. "Give to me that horse or I will blow the top of its head off."

Later, he remembered feeling a numbing shock to his skull and remembered singling out the shot that fired from the gun and then seeing in the rail of his vision the little man holding the gun. He knew he shook his head in disbelief when the revolver turned on him and at the same time knew his own hand held a revolver and that he fired his weapon into the dirt at his feet and then his brain convulsed. His mind split open and without there being a sense of light, there was an eclipse of light and then there was only a throbbing blackness and then there was only blackness.

When he finally came to consciousness it was in night's darkness and the sky was lit with stars. He did not fully understand what had happened to him but understood there was nothing he could do. Days may have passed, but he could not tell because he had no idea of time. Neither did he have an idea of place—the sky above, the earth below. His head felt broken and seemed lifted from his shoulders and detached from his neck and yet it was the source of a great pain that held his entire body in an iron grasp.

The bullet had cut a groove in his scalp and his head still bled profusely. His blood was everywhere, soaking his head and neck and shoulders and still leaking from his body, leeching into the ground.

My blood is on the other side of my skin, he dumbly thought.

He was dizzy and had no control over his stomach. In frightening moments his gut heaved and threatened to overtake his life with its launching. Then it did. The heaving motion would not relent and his body shook with paroxysms involuntary. The bouts came without regularity but were still chained with one inciting the next. When his stomach had emptied, the violent attacks continued until finally his stomach was played out and his muscles too exhausted. In the meantime he'd torn away his linen shirt and knotted it around his wounded head as best he could.

"It's the best I can do," he gasped, appealing to no one but desperately pleading none the less.

A sickness passed through him and then dizziness. Jittery, he lay back in case he should fall. He wanted to curl up in innocence, but knew he never would again. He settled into the cool ground and the world stopped turning and he waited to slip from consciousness once again.

It was in daylight when he finally stood and climbed the porch and crossed the threshold through the broken door. Geese followed him, scrutinizing his every movement, as if he were the oddity entering their house and for reasons they neither trusted nor understood.

Inside, the house was in a shambles, the work of the little man. Fragments of utensils, boots, torn paper, and candle molds were strewn about as if disgorged from the open doors of the cabinets and hanging drawers by a furious wind that had been bottled up inside them until they exploded. A stove stood in the middle of the two rooms so to heat both the

big kitchen and the front parlor. On the wall was a tear-off calendar.

In the parlor there was a fireplace with a heavy oak mantel. Inside the redbrick fire chamber were the burned remains of a spitted goose. The carpet fluttered with down and was stained with geese droppings, and scattered about were shards of broken dishes and blue crockery. Each step he took raised a white floating in the air, enough down to make a bed mattress. The geese looked at what he looked at and poked their heads in the direction of his face and looked him in the eye as if an explanation would be forthcoming.

As he climbed the stairs he let his fingers drift over the embossed wallpaper. At the upstairs landing his vision blurred and a wave of pain sawed through his head and sat him down to rest. He looked below to see the geese gathering at the foot of the stairs. He closed his eyes and opened them and they cleared for the time. He pulled himself erect and continued on to the hallway.

In the bedroom, at the head of the stairs, was a corded bedstead with turned bulbous posts and a deep featherbed resting atop a thick straw tick. An overstuffed wardrobe stood in one corner. Its doors hung on broken hinges and its dresses, similar in pattern to the little man's disguise, bloomed in the door's opening. The bureau drawers had been dragged from their slots and their contents strewn on the floor. There were so many things in the room. There were more shoes and clothes than he imagined a whole family could own all by itself.

A woman's straw hat was lying on the bed, and a lace handkerchief and a scattered collection of briar and cob pipes and a wild-turkey-wing fan. On the other side of the bed he

found the woman who owned the dresses. She sat on the floor propped with her back against the wall. She'd been stabbed in the neck, the bone-handled knife left in the wound, and her swollen intestines filled her lap and spilled over her splayed legs. Her scalp had been cut and ripped away from her head. He felt no shock at what he saw. He felt no horror for what had happened. He was reminded of his own wound and tore a supply of clean garment material to wrap his head in the days to come.

In another room he found a variety of mechanical toys. There were painted cast-metal rabbits that beat tin drums, birds with keys beneath their wings, and when the key was turned and let go their wings beat and they sang tinny songs. There was a monkey who clacked brass cymbals, toy soldiers in flared red coats and blue pantaloons who played cornets, tiny clocks that chimed, and music boxes that'd fit in the palm of your hand. There were two tiny unmade beds against the wall that still held the shape of the small bodies that used to sleep in them.

Outside the air was pure when he staggered into it and he could not breathe enough of it into his lungs. In the barn he found a little mud-tailed pony that was fat and unworked. He found a pail of axle grease and slathered a handful into the wrapping that held his wound. He studied the charred remains of the well house and thought to pull an armful of flowers and drop them inside its column. He knew to do this without ever having done it before. He thought to go back into the house and maybe let toys to fall into its stony black maw. He wondered why he would be moved in this way af-ter all that he'd seen. What was it inside him that would ask

him to pause and consider these gestures on behalf of this dead family? He did not know this woman or her children. He did not know whose people they were or if they had been good people or bad people. Surely the children had been good people and the woman had been a good woman, but what were they to him? If the lead ball had been better aimed, he'd be like them. He'd be dead too.

He took time to eat that morning. He killed a goose and pawed open its chest skin. Then he cut away a breast and this he spit-roasted in the fireplace while the other geese watched. He found mustard pickles and a crock of salt pork. He found caps and bullets of the necessary caliber, but he had no gun.

As he ate, he did not wonder on all that had happened thus far, but rather, he wondered how he should think about it. He knew what was in the well and he knew how close he'd come to being there himself. He'd been very stupid and it was a condition he now pledged to avoid. He remembered old Morphew telling him he was in for an education and how he hoped he'd live long enough to tell about it.

He decided he would live without actually deciding it. He just knew he would. Something inside him told him so. He could feel a distance inside his head. He was in pain and his mother always said that pain was weakness leaving the body. He would eat his meal and then he would continue to search for the army and if he should find the little man and the coal black horse he knew what he would do, but once he had, he'd not apologize to the horse. This he swore. He'd not apologize to the horse no matter how right the horse had been in mistrusting the little man.

When he was done eating, he caught onto the mane of

the mud-tailed pony, the children's horse, threw a leg over its back and swung upright. The pony shied and almost sat down for how spoiled it was, but his hands and legs and the words he spoke told the pony it did not belong to itself anymore. It belonged to him. He sat the pony, letting it build its strength beneath his weight. He wanted with all his heart to be past this moment and into the next when he would be healed and would be wiser than he was before. He was learning his lessons and he was still alive and he thought that was worth something.

"Walk," he said to the pony. "Walk on."

However unworked and lazy the pony was, the instant he dug his heels, the pony understood it was to obey and stepped off and then broke into a jarring trot.

In a sack he carried a jar of molasses, dried peaches, a haunch of venison, and handfuls of black walnuts. He had coffee beans and cornmeal. Behind each of his legs hung a goose by its neck. He started north, following the hoof prints of the coal black horse.

5

OT AND DRY, the locusts were sawing the air and the roads were powdery and thick to breathe. He traveled all that day and then slept and woke at sunrise and traveled on again through a thinly settled country. So miserable was the sight of him, his head wrapped in a blood-crusted rag, he determined there was no need he should avoid people.

There were towns he passed through where people came out to watch his passing as if he were an army unto himself and there were other towns where his passing went wholly unnoticed for sakes of commerce or play or worship or conversation. Children older than he stood at the roadside and stared at his passing, and gaunt and pellicle dogs silently trailed him in the dust, lunging the sweltering air. The mud-tailed pony proved to be a sly and insolent animal by nature and sulked and like a spoiled brat exhibited displays of bad temper. It kicked at him when he gave it a chance and attempted to savage his knee with its teeth as he rode, but he remained patient and determined to persuade from it with his heels whatever miles he possibly could.

His head throbbed with pain in the dry heat. The pain wavered through him, consuming his head and neck and shoulders,

but he knew he was slowly healing. It was only common sense to him the way the pain made flash upon flash in his body and then peaked and lingered and in some days' time it began to dull and diminish. He discovered hidden beneath his experience of pain an unconfused state where his mind fixed on his mother's counsel and his father's existence and he found new clarity. He admonished himself for breaking every word of advice she'd given him. Except to have followed her imperatives to the letter would have left him afoot not a mile from old Morphew's mercantile. He determined that he would learn from the lessons taught him thus far and by gift of chance he was still alive and from now on he would be a fast and dedicated learner.

The land was beginning to crop with limestone and a darkening green and increasingly there were wells of cold water and burbling springs where he could drink and rinse his body. In the next days he stopped often to wash the wound, fix a new compress, and tie a clean bandage. His chest and back ached as they carried his head pain and each time he removed the wrappings he winced at how strange the sensation as he tore away scab and dried blood from his mending scalp.

The easterly roads turned swampy for some miles while to the northwest lay a range of blue mountains and these he kept to his left and fading behind him as he traveled in the direction of the the rising sun, the direction of the ocean. He rode on, and after the mud-tailed pony played out he left it tied in darkness, entered a banked barn, and stole his first horse, a copper-bottomed mare he quietly led away. After that it became easy enough to do and he felt the need to change mounts at every opportunity, and so by necessity

he became an accomplished horse thief, exchanging the copper-bottomed mare for a big cream horse and then for a broad-shouldered, parrot-mouthed chestnut, and then for a sturdy bay with failing eyesight when the chestnut spavined.

Each day his wound dried and knit shut and knotted with building scar that tugged at his scalp, and overly sensitive to light his eyelid would slowly close on him if he let it.

Wounded and face-hideous riding the backs of common horses, he was afforded an easy passage through the places where people lived, a world of boys, old men, and women. They offered him food and water and so miserable he must have looked that if they recognized the horse he rode, they said nothing, so he took their food and asked after the armies and while news was inconsistent, the coal black horse was re-membered more than once for its beauty and for the unlikely little woman with the cob pipe that rode its back.

It was in these wounded days the beginning of the man he would grow to be. He bore his pain and endured his wound as if a sign he too had been blooded by the madness that'd taken ahold of the land. He no longer shied from people, from the lone riders, from the reenslaved herded South. He no longer feared their presence on the roads and his conversion was be-lievable to him. He had lived and did not die. He was breath-ing. Still, it was only the beginning and he was not old enough to know these changes, did not even know enough to think this way yet.

The land had taken on a haunted feel since meeting the goose lady. What had been new and beautiful was now old and strange, wrong and unfamiliar. In one town he sat on a low stone wall and watched boys his own age wearing fresh

white linen shirts with hard, starched collars take copperhead snakes from a picnic basket and nail them by their tails to a barn wall. The barn wall had been painted with a black skull over a set of crossed bones. When the boy with the hammer and nails, a boy a head taller than the rest, gave the command each boy let go the copperhead he held by the neck, and yelling and hooting they all ran away.

The snakes swarmed across the face of the door, twining and dangling themselves about each other, dropping their bodies and lifting again. They opened their mouths and bared their fangs. They bit each other thinking to find the source of their pain. The boys laughed and slapped their thighs. Then they began to stone the snakes from safe distance.

An old man with tufts of gray hair springing from his skull, investigating the thumping noise, came to the corner of the barn. In one hand he carried a galvanized bucket and in the other a gutta-percha walking stick. He shook at the boys with his walking stick, castigating them for their grotesque play. They laughed at him and turned their stones on his person. The old man ducked his old head and stumbled in his escape, slopping his trouser leg with spilt whitewash that lipped from the rim of the bucket.

He righted himself and hobbled away, coming in Robey's direction where he sat beside him on the rumbled stone wall. Without introduction and as some people are wont to do, especially the old and foolish, he took up with a left-off and ongoing conversation. He told Robey his old wife had recently died and he was now sad in his heart and considered a lunatic by many in town and had nerve storms because he was alone and because he and his wife, he said, wanted to die together.

"Her eyes were always the brightest," he said.

The old man still possessed his teeth, remarkable for one so elderly, but they seemed to protrude straight from his gums and closed in a beak that his thin lips rode. He paused to sneeze and when he opened the palm of his hand mucus webbed his fingers.

"Those boys are quite exceptional in their stupidity," he remarked, but Robey continued to make no response: no word, no nod, no shrug of his shoulders. Where they sat the stone was warm with captured sun and not uncomfortable. He did not mind the old man, and after a time in his presence the old man seemed calm and less agitated.

"Their time is coming soon enough," the old man added, his words swashing in his beaked mouth, but still Robey made no response. He thought, Let the old man talk himself out.

But the old man persevered in his one-sided conversation, prattling on and occasionally pausing to ask Robey if he was listening. He took Robey for a young soldier and so talked about having fought in Spain with Napoleon when he was in his youth. He claimed to have eaten dead horses to stay alive and one time to have actually eaten the forearm of a dead man. He told how he found it very sweet and for that reason had to swear it off because he feared he would get a taste for human flesh.

"More was not enough," he said, and then he speculated on the hell he would surely go to after his death for eating human beings, as well as for other unnamed transgressions, and at this thought he laughed.

From the barn door continued the hollow resounding of the thrown stones. From the inside came squeals of pigs

and the fierce rustling of their bodies. One by one the snakes dropped their heads and their broken angular bodies hung limp. The boys carried on with pitching their stones, breaking the snakes' bodies, until the cut bloodless pieces fell away and gathered on a bed of chaffy earth.

"Are you listening to me?" the old man demanded.

Robey took a deep breath to say he was.

"You have also done bad things," the old man said. "Bad men can talk to each other. Bad men can understand the other. For thousands of years we have understood this, but that doesn't change anything."

"No," Robey said, regretful at having spoken even as he spoke. "I haven't," he continued, and he knew the sound of his voice betrayed his words.

"Maybe not yet," the old man said. "But you will. You are experiencing one of life's great lessons. Specifically which one, you do not know, but in time you will know."

IN ANOTHER TOWN was a baseball game and he had never seen such before so he stopped to watch. When he became noticed he moved on again, content with only the witless beeves and skulking dogs and mild cows watching his slow passage.

He continued to think about what else the old man had said to him. The old man told how he was now worthless and no good to anyone anymore because he was filled with despair, and despair was useless in times such as these. He told him to remain angry, because anger was more useful than despair and would deliver him. But to despair would surely lead to failure and tragedy.

They were the words of an insane, but he could not escape

them. They were committed to his mind and once learned he could not unlearn them. It was fate, he thought. Then he thought how people loved to talk so very much and even had a weakness to talk. He himself had done so and it made him laugh at how foolish his gliding mind. The bay shortened and tossed its head at his sudden outburst. He quieted the animal and let his hand to the long-barreled pistol he wore in his belt. It was an odd piece of indeterminate make and had been a gift from the maundering old man.

He traveled on, following the rumors of great armies encamped to the east on opposite banks of a river, but in the days that came his long slow ride through the landscape of war became so like chasing the wind that when one night a cold wind swept the open land, he took refuge in the scorched shell of a burned house.

The bay tethered, he entered cautiously, as if testing the floorboards. Outside its stone walls was a constant moaning of the soft wind streaming through the trees. He had at first mistaken the pump in the yard to be the black silhouette of a figure, and even after he knew his mistake he kept looking to the yard to assure himself it was not, kept looking to the trees where the bay was tethered.

He lit a tallow candle inside a box lantern of punched tin and cautiously passed from one room to another and upon determining that he was alone in the house, he built a tiny fire in the hearth and it soon lit the room with a warm glow. He reclined on the hardwood floor and with the fire's coax the aches of the day began to melt from his limbs. There was a burned stairway to the second floor and from the fire-gutted ceiling hung a beautiful chandelier, its pendants like carved diamonds.

At first he had thought it a spangle of stars in the night sky and then he understood it was the stars through the room's charred ceiling and the shaped and fitted glass that gave to him such a sparkling sight. He could only think that someone had hung the glass after the burning for how its icicles were clear and untouched and cast prisms of light from the fire.

The wind outside died away and ceased its quiet moaning in the trees. The sound had existed beneath sound and he'd forgotten it until now it was disappeared. In the new silence came a ticktock sound, ticktock. He searched the room to find its source and then was a clean and unlikely striking sound and a tiny door unlatched and he found the source just as the cuckoo shot forth.

Someone had wound the clock and hung the chandelier, and however pitiful the gestures, they were trying to return to a time that he was afraid they would never see again. It was a time on earth he realized that he himself had never witnessed because of his seclusion on the mountain, but was seeing it now in its havoc and devastation. What was life like before all this? What did people do and what did they think about before they warred and thought about war? He tried to remember what he did before he left the mountain and what he thought about in his seclusion. He recalled chores and quiet and solitude. He knew there was more than that, but he could not remember and he knew it had not been so far back in time. He tried hard to recall who he had been and what he was back then then, but however much he longed to he could find nothing to remember.

He banked his small fire with the kindling he'd gathered, the wood spurting blue and red flame, and the room took on

more light and he found other moments of longing and desire. There was a wooden inlaid box filled with shiny stones. There were other boxes, tin and copper and lacquered, and woods he did not recognize and could not name. Inside their shells were coins and buttons, ribbons, marbles, pins, tiny bones, a doll's leg.

There was a mildewed bench with a hinged seat and while the inside was empty, its interior smelled of wool and lavender and contained a porcelain-faced doll wearing a blue felt hat and long hair made of straw-colored yarn. A leg had been torn away from the torso, but when he polished the dirty face with his sleeve it shown in the firelight as if newly made. In the silence, the burning wood made hissing and cracking noises and there was a sudden flicker of shadow in the air as vesper bats took flight and filled the chamber with their silent wing beats, black on black, spearing the air and fleeing the lighted room through the empty doors and windows.

He set a pot of coffee to boil and fried the last of his bacon in a tin pan. He made a thin dough of water and salted cornmeal and set that to bake in the open fire on the blade of a broken hoe. He thought how he'd boil his coffee and scumble his biscuit into it. That would taste fine and feel good in his mouth and warm his throat down into his belly. His hunger grew and as the food heated he fixed his gaze on the porcelain-faced doll he'd propped at the fireside. Absentmindedly, he rubbed his scalp where the healing skin felt as if pulled by tiny paws. He fit the doll's leg to her hip and it matched.

He wanted to feel the hatred that possessed him when he dragged himself off the ground that was drenched with his blood. He wanted the anger the old man told him he must

have to survive. He wanted it lodged inside him like an iron spike, but tonight it wasn't there. Tonight he was too tired to hate and hoped in the morning when he was rested he would hate again.

"What do you have to say?" he asked the porcelain-faced doll, and when there was no reply he whispered the word "nothing."

When the coffee was boiled he poured half a cup into the drippings and could not wait, but was so hungry he burned his fingers and mouth. He slid the cake off the hoe into the gravy and ate the slurry with his fingers. He scraped the sides and the rapidly cooling bottom of the pan with the backs of his fingers and licked them clean and wiped at his mouth and then licked the back of his hand and then it was over. He knew enough to know he'd eaten like a ravenous dog and how disapproving his mother would be if she had witnessed such and how nice it would be to someday again not eat like that.

"Soon," he sighed, and sat close by the fire, exhausted for how voracious his hunger had made him and still amazed at how quickly the food had disappeared. He knew he should climb the stairs to sleep, or crawl under the floor, or go outside and sleep with the horse. He could not help but mistrust the dead calm stillness of this night's windless turn.

But his belly was full and he was tired and wanted to sleep and for so long now he had been vigilant. He closed his eyes and bars of fire darted across his eyelids. Sleep came and overwhelmed him as if a slowly crushing weight, though he fought it the best he could. Its strong hand brought ache and defeat and then relief, and when he knew he could not hold it off any longer he finally collapsed beneath it.

When he lurched forward he saw the fire in the hearth had died and gone to the an orange glow of mere embers. The porcelain-faced doll was slumped beside the fire as if she too had been asleep. He righted her and as he stood to stretch his aching body, he concentrated on the faint sound that had awakened him. A muscle in his stomach began to flutter. Then he heard the sound coming from outside the stone walls. It was a man goading an ox, and then came the scrape of a travois on the hard ground and then a woman's voice, thin and plaintive, complaining how difficult her situation. He kicked at the fire and stamped out the sparks. He gathered his kit as quickly as he could and as they were almost in the yard, he could do no other than climb the charred stringers and escape to the second floor.

6

A T THE TOP of the stairwell, the roof was open to the sky and the weakened and ravaged second floor was cast in the shadows of the stone-built gable walls. Up there the night was not so dark under the sky, and from where he stood in the gable shadows he could see an ambling gaunted ox approaching the house. There was a man and a girl attendant. They were walking beside the ox, and riding on the jouncing travois was a woman. She was large and rode as if in repose, but when the ox stopped she slowly climbed erect and clasping her hands under her belly she lifted its weight as if she were lifting herself. The girl hastened to help the woman stand and the woman thanked her. The man told them this was the place from where he smelled the fire and the bacon and the coffee cooking. He made a show of sniffing the air and then a scraping cough from depths of his chest expanse doubled him over. The man was otherwise robust and wore a born thickness in his wrists and neck and shoulders. He was built wide and drumlike and conducted himself with raptorlike self-regard.

"You get a fire started," he said to the girl, pushing her in the direction of the doorway. The girl stumbled and cursed him over her shoulder as she went inside and then the man led

the woman inside, and through the fire-ravaged second floor he could watch the progress of their spectral shapes passing underneath him, moving from place to place as if they were blown by a steady wind.

The girl found embers in the fire he'd left and momentarily looked about but made no mention of them to the man and woman. She stirred the embers to red life with an iron rod. She fed the fire with one of the small wooden boxes and in the first light that held her he could not see her face because it was flanked by her hair, but when she drew her hair together and draped it to one side he could see how thin and hollow her young face.

"I fear we've reached bedrock," the woman moaned. She held her arms stretched out before her as if discovering her next place in the air while she moved in the direction of the fire's warmth. Her hands found her way and she eased herself onto her knees on the bare wooden floor, touched the floor with her hands, and settled on her hip.

"Get the parfleches," the man said to the girl.

He spoke to her harshly and she responded in kind, as if an old enmity festered between them. The man fished in a gunnysack until he found a green bottle, which he held between himself and the firelight to measure its content. He then uncorked the bottle and took a drink. In the light of the fire he could be seen for his sparse white hair, his powerful neck, his white muttonchops and all black livery. Some minor affliction was tormenting his leg as he kept scratching and cuffing at it. After a second drink he gave a final cough and seemed content.

"Get them yourself," the girl said, not moving from the fire she was kindling to life.

"If I have to get them you're going to get it good," he told her.

"They empty," the girl said, and the woman groaned, clutching at her swollen sides.

"Don't sass me," the man said, crossing the room to strike the girl a fierce blow that knocked her down when she stood to meet him. Robey flinched, watching.

"It's her time," the girl said, as she cowered on the floor.

"It ain't her time," the man said, taking another drink. "It ain't her time until I say it's her time."

Robey's body pressed more tightly to the stone wall of the standing gable as he watched them move underneath him. He let his hand to the grips of the pistol he carried in his belt, its long barrel extending past his hip. The wood of the grips was smooth and the chambers were recently primed. He would not be shot again. That knowledge was as deep in his bones as a knowing could possibly be.

"There'll be a black frost tonight," the man said, and then surveying the empty room, he said, "I wonder where they went off to? They couldn't have gone off for very long."

"They probably scared off when they heard us coming," the girl said, her voice a bitter sulk. "There won't be any frost," she said, as if it was the most recent of crazy ideas.

"Help me with these boots," the man said, sitting on the bench. "Or I'll lick you again."

The girl stood and approached him warily and then she was tugging at his boots and letting each of them drop to the floor. The man then paced the room in his stockinged feet, scratching at his leg again. He told the girl to get busy and gather up what would burn so at least they should not freeze to death on this cold spring night.

"It ain't gonna freeze," she said as she found another of the boxes. This one she studied for a moment without opening it and then set it gently in the fire. She then found the cuckoo clock and this too she placed in the rising flames.

"That there too," the man said, indicating the bench with the hinged seat. "That's wood. That'll burn good."

The girl tipped the bench over and began kicking at it until its wooden pegs broke loose and it came apart at the joints. While she worked, the man stood in the center of the room drinking from the green bottle and to his own amusement began whistling poor imitations of night birds, the more complicated ones requiring him to pocket the bottle so to twine his fingers and cock his clasped hands. He waited, but he received no countercalls.

Then, bored with that, he picked up a piece of lath and swatted at the chandelier, making a game of breaking its tiniest glass pendants. Then he stopped at the girl who knelt at the hearth feeding the broken bench into the fire. She stiffened as he lifted a lock of hair from her neck and whispered something into her ear.

"You're just a dirty dog," she said, and swung around and hit him on the head with the iron rod she held. Stung so, he screamed and ran out of the house holding his head.

"What happened," the woman cried out, sweeping the air with her arms as if pushing the invisible. "What's going on in here?"

"It were just a dirty scoundrel dog," the girl said with disgust. "Don't be so nerve-raw all the time."

"A dog?" the woman cried. "What dog? How did a dog get in here? I don't like dogs one bit."

From behind the stone of the gable wall, Robey could see the man in the yard where he skulked about in the darkness for a time. He wandered in the direction of the bay but stopped well short of its hiding place. He tried the pump and when the handle broke off in his hand he kicked at it and staggered.

Below where he stood, the girl worked to make the blind woman comfortable near the warmth of the fire. The woman kept asking what of the dog, but the girl hushed her and would say no more about it.

When the man returned, it was as if nothing had happened between him and the girl. He sat on the floor in the same place where Robey had fallen asleep and by primitive gesture appeared to sense there had been another presence resting in that same spot against the wall. But then he settled as the odd moment passed. From his pocket he produced a handful of hardtack and breaking off piece after piece he fed them silently into his mouth. The dry crumbs that flecked his black coat he plucked from the material and fastidiously licked from his fingertips.

"If I had my choice," he pronounced, "I would have goose and oysters and scrambled eggs and pecan pie."

"If," the girl scoffed. "If frogs had wings they wouldn't bump their asses every time they jumped."

The man cackled and slapped at his leg. Then he skimmed a piece of hardtack across the floor in the direction of the fire where the girl scrambled for it and held it to her chest.

"What's that?" the woman said, near hysterical, fanning the air close to the floor with her hands.

"Nothing," the girl said, sucking on the piece of hardtack so not to make noise.

"Don't you tell me nothing," the woman said. "I am not stupid. I know there's rats in here."

"We can spit-cook that chicken you got hid up," the girl said to the man.

"What chicken?"

"The chicken what you got hid up."

"But it is my chicken," the man said, philosophically.

"I was the one that stol'd it," the girl said.

"I am so hungry," the woman groaned. "Please cook the chicken."

"At least feed your woman," the girl said.

"Please," the woman said again, and the man scratched his head as if it were a proposition that required deep thought. Eventually he must have decided because he opened his coat and took from inside the carcass of a chicken he wore strung on a rope around his neck.

"Take the god damn chicken," he said, throwing it to the girl.

Robey watched as the girl plucked and gutted the chicken, setting its innards aside on the hearthstone. She then skewered the carcass with the iron rod and held it over the flames. As its skin heated and blistered, fats dropped into the flames where they hissed and flared. The man drew near to her and together they watched it cook.

When the woman asked, the man took it upon himself to explain to her what was happening. She informed him that although she was blind, she could still hear and she could still smell. The man looked at her as if it was news to him while the girl snickered behind her hand.

"What I'm asking is it done yet?"

"Soon," the man said.

After they ate the chicken, the room became a pleasant scene as their need for anger and violence toward each other appeared to have been satisfied with food. The woman said something to the girl he could not hear but watched as the girl assisted the woman to her feet and guided her through the rubble into the yard where the woman gathered her skirts in her hands and squatted down to make water. Then the girl gathered her own skirts to her waist and did the same.

When they returned, the man helped the girl make beds on the edge of the warmed hearth stones, close to the flames. The girl eased the woman to her side and covered her with a woolen blanket and then she let herself down not far away from the woman and pulled her own blanket to her chin. It was then she discovered the porcelain-faced doll and in an instant pulled it to her chest and had it hidden beneath her blanket cover.

Once settled the man insisted they pray before sleep. His words were those of the sincere and well-practiced divine. Robey listened to the man's holy and dramatic pronouncements. A strange man of the cloth. If only, when he ceased his praying, they would fall asleep, because Robey was tired and his legs ached for standing so still for so long. If they slept he could slip down the stringer and be gone in the darkness.

But the man upon finishing his prayer took up his green bottle again and continued with his drinking. Still agitated by his leg, he shook it beneath his blanket, banging the floor with his heel. Then he stood and set to a fretful pacing again until finally some thought occurred to him and he took down his trousers to inspect the spot he'd been itching.

"God damn tick," he slurred.

He shuffled to the fireside where he took the iron rod from the fire and held its red-hot point to his naked leg. The smell of burning hair and flesh rose to where Robey stood against the gable wall and in the closed light he could see the man, a grimace stretched tightly across his mouth and his eyes no more than black holes in his face as he held the red iron to his thigh, causing the tick to back out of his hide.

Through the floor he watched the man who remained naked from the waist down. The man lolled his head back and forth like an angry bull slicing the air with his horns. He then tipped the bottle back and emptied it. He pulled up his trousers and resumed his pacing, from time to time raising his burned leg and shaking it. His leg now relieved, he seemed conflicted with some new thinking that was growing inside him. He lay down on his bedding, but he was too restless for sleep.

Robey waited patiently, hoping the man would settle as had the girl and the woman, and soon he would be able to slip down the stringer and away in the darkness. He looked to the rickety sawtooth he would have to descend and then looked off the gable wall in the direction of his anticipated departure and then back down through the floor. The man was up again. He was moving about the room. This time, he was on all fours and slowly scuttling toward the sleeping girl, tucking his legs underneath him, reaching forward and pulling his body to his reach. Turning in her sleep, the girl awoke as he made his approach. She watched him coming to her, a hand to her mouth.

"Are you a-sleepin'?" he was saying as he crawled toward her. "Are you already a-sleepin'?"

But she did not answer and when he was near enough she pulled back the blanket and kicked out at him. He caught her small foot as it struck into his head. He held that foot and when she kicked with the other one he caught that foot too and dragged her from her bedding and into him so quickly she seemed to have disappeared inside him.

At first she did not know to resist, but then she fought him, her body coiling and twisting on the wooden floor. She struck out with her fists and tore at his white face-hair and he fended her off, trying to quiet her, but she would not relent so he wrapped an arm around her neck and punched her in the face.

Still, she kept struggling and so he punched her again until she groaned and folded in his arms. He punched her one more time and then let her onto her back where she did not move. He waited and then he lifted her skirts and tore away at her underclothes until she too was naked from the waist. But when he moved between her legs she roused herself and fought him again. She kicked her heels into his haunches, arched her back, and clawed at his face. He took her thin arms in his hands and twisted them until she cried out and then he stretched them over her head and held her arms as she continued to kick, but he was now between her legs and so wide was his body she could not find the angle to strike with her heels.

"You help me here. Now," he yelled out to the blind woman. "She has gone crazy in the head."

At first the woman cried and fretted and when he threatened her she dug more deeply into her bedding.

"Take her damn legs," he said, but the woman would not move.

"You're hurting me," the girl moaned.

"I don't give a god damn if I am," he said, and struck her a blow to the side of her head.

Her cries of pain and her pleading with the man to leave off her rose up from the cold floor and filled the stone-walled chamber. The man pushed himself up on one hand and with the other he struck the girl a savage blow to the head and she went quiet again. He gripped her by the hair and pulled back her head revealing her white throat.

Then the moon went behind the clouds and all was lost in shadow, and the wind came up and there were the faintest sounds of the man working and the girl whimpering beneath him like a small held animal. Robey let his head back against the stone of the gable, his hand on the butt of his pistol. The sounds from below broke inside him and then hardened and the hard pieces — they broke too. He banged his head again and this second time cracked open his wound. He began to bleed into his collar. He knew he should do something and he knew he would not.

When the man was done he slumped and lay quietly across the girl's trembling body and then he fell back from between her legs as if tearing himself from her. Panting for air, he crawled across the floor to lay on his pallet where he went into a fit of sneezing and cursing and then was silent. He reached down between his legs to cradle himself in his hand and soon harsh sounds of sleep came from his throat.

The girl lay crumpled in the moonlight, her bare legs white as bone. Then she curled her legs inside her skirts and folded her knees to her chest and held them in her arms.

Robey waited until he thought they were all deep in the sounds of their sleep and then catlike he went down the stringer where he paused over the sleeping bodies, scrutinizing

one and then the next, the pistol in his hand, its barrel pointing the way.

When he stood by the girl, he found her still awake and she raised to him a thin, worn and childish face. At first she seemed to have lost all touch with the earth. She just lay there staring up at him, staring at nothing, not blinking, or breathing, or speaking, or whispering. She had been so harmed, maybe she had died.

As their eyes fixed on each other, the moon came out again and thinned the darkness near the floor and shone on her face. Her lips were broken and she was bleeding from her nose. She caught her lower lip between her teeth and he thought she did die and was just now returning herself to the living. In her eyes there was condensed hatred that had split off inside her and she could not return from, could not return to, sadness or pain or joy or any other emotion. It was there inside her where it would stay.

She paled and her mouth opened as she stared at him, but her heart so full, her voice failed her, and in that stony world was only heard a moan of the soughing wind.

Ashamed, he draped the blanket over her closed body. He then hastened from her side and passed silently among their bodies and left out of that place to find the bay horse tethered in the coppice of trees. All that night he followed the bends of the black road jeweled by starlight until the wan light of the dawn touched the east with red and the pastures turned green. The roads became white and then was the coming gold of the sun and that day's worth of heat, and he was miles away before he stopped to sleep.

7

HEN, IN A RAILWAY CUT, the bed of cinders gave way and the bay horse, near to blind, went down, tumbling him to the ground and with its fall was the cracking sound of snapping bone. At the last instant he had pulled the animal's head back and it had tried to check its fall on its stiff forelegs, but it was too late to stop what was already happening.

The horse's hind leg was trapped under the rail where the ballast had eroded, but still it thrashed and pawed to right itself. Its shod hooves struck sparks on the parallel rail and thudded on the ties. The bay's right front leg was as if jointed between the knee and fetlock, and it swung wildly as it heaved its body, trying to stand until finally the splintered cannon bone stabbed through the leg hide, white and ragged and sharp as a pickax.

He stood a ways off and spoke to the horse, telling it to settle, and when it did not he moved in to take the horse's tossing head in his arms and cover its terrified eyes. He held on as the strength in its neck dragged his feet and lifted him off the ground. Then it did settle and there was a panting silence between them and he let go his hold. The horse stretched its neck and sniffed him. He stroked the horse's cheek and forehead and did not let go his touch.

"You have gone and broke your leg," he whispered into its ear, his face that close.

The horse lay on its side staring at him. Its skin quivered and it snorted and he took this as a sign of understanding. He knelt down in the cinders and put his face to the horse's soft neck, his hand to the velvety muzzle and he told the horse how not to be afraid and it was only then he felt his own ankle begin to throb inside his shoe and he silently cursed.

The horse raised its head and then let it down again in the cinders where its wet breathing made gusts of dirt and grit. He told the horse it had been a good horse and a loyal horse and a noble horse and when he found the coal black horse he would tell it so, and when he returned home he would tell the other animals and then he felt foolish and tears welled in his eyes. A shank of anger entered his chest and the tears began to sting his eyes.

He stood and formally apologized to the bay horse, asking that it might disremember his boyish thoughts and actions. He asked that it might forgive his momentary weakness, for they'd been on good terms since he'd stole it and then regretfully he collected himself and drew his pistol from his belt. He set the muzzle behind the horse's ear and held not a moment before pulling the trigger.

He wanted to rest after that because he was painfully tired and sore, but spiritless he shouldered his kit and took the bridle and trudged on for the duration of that hot day through a sparsely settled country, his sprained ankle paining him not a little. He was soon road-dirty and his soles blistered.

He followed the train tracks until evening shed a bluish twilight over the land and far off could be seen the white spire of a

church steeple and then the dim lights of a town. He climbed a grassy bank in the town's direction and stepped out onto a plank road running parallel with the rails below. The town, now within reach, glowed dully in the glove of the night. He took up the plank road and after not long his shoe broke open and began to flop as he walked. After so long his journey and however bleak his prospects, he knew he was arriving at a place significant. He felt it in the air, in his skin, inside his composing mind. He knew he needed to find another horse.

In the distance was the drift of small hills and green islands of pasture running into abrupt mountains and there was the cool dank smell of a flat river on the air, and even further, a purple line of forest between the mountains and the green islands of pasture. The country here was cultivated with prosperous farms and the low-walled buildings were of red brick or gray stone. The roadside was crossed by veins of limestone forming knotty points and there were thin cracks where artesian springs seeped water to the earth's surface. He thought how easy it would be to farm this deep fertile land. A warm rain had begun to fall on the dry land and then from out of the dark he heard the cadence of hoof beats pounding hard on the planks.

He stepped off the road and onto the soft ground where he stumbled across deep ruts and passed into a thicket of brambles in the twilight shadows of a little paintless house. Two dark riders swept through the gloaming, and then cavalry by twos passed the brake and then was the heavy sound of iron-shod wheels grating on the planks, and a wagon came jolting out of the darkness, winding through the trees, the lathered team flat-out for speed.

It was an open four-horse coach with seats across from door to door and nine men dressed in blue were riding the benches, and behind that wagon was another one and then came ten more after that. Without hesitating he stripped off his jacket and worked to turn it inside out blue. More wagons followed the coaches and cavalry and a battery of horse artillery. He climbed higher from the road, a steep ascent made craggy with broken rock and dark with pine trees.

From there he could smell wisps of smoke and cresting the low rise he could see the town sprawled out beneath him where a river made a great oxbow turn, and at the extreme arc of its curvature, crossing the river twice, were the railroad tracks nicking past beneath the night's first veil. There were engine houses, water towers, and fueling stations. There was the meander of inbound dirt roads feeding plank pikes cut straight as dies. Wagons and soldiers were converging on the town from all directions, their dashing black shapes spectral in the last bands of red light that seamed the western horizon. A cold fog was drifting in and had begun to numb and wet the empty fields.

The pain in his ankle dulled with the night's cooling and it no longer concerned him. He knew he was now near to something big, an army, a battle, a horse. He felt himself on the very edge of the fields of war, the ever-moving place of grinding violence whose turbulent wake he'd been following for days. The winding river, the rails, the hard-riding cavalry told him so, and he had little idea how deep he was or how far they sprawled before him. No matter the distance, no matter the depth, he'd come so far, and no matter what he'd been through he concluded he was at the beginning once again.

He did not know what to do right away, so he sat down and held his arms clasped round his folded legs, his chin on his knees. Where before he'd been desperate to travel and driven foolish in his decisions, he now felt a calming patience hard learned. The rain was falling more heavily and was cold and the air turned unseasonably bitter, and he had the passing notion he was going to freeze to death, but he knew it was fatigue and hunger and the lingering effects of his head wound. He felt the darkness pressing his eyelids and there unconsciousness momentarily caught him.

His short dream was the brief and repeated experience of falling without end. Each time he fell, he could not stop himself no matter how hard he tried. He was shot and falling to the ground. He was tumbling past the windlass and falling into the tomb of the well. He was falling from the coal black horse. He knew he was dreaming even as he dreamt. He murmured and called out to himself but could not break through to consciousness. When he did wake he did not know that he had even slept, but he awoke in darkness and a heavy shoe was kicking at his swollen ankle.

"What are you," came a hollow voice from over his head.

The voice was coming at him from a great distance and he could not see its source. It was as if he'd awakened at the bottom of a pitch-black well. As he found wakefulness he felt himself arriving for a long time until he understood it was a soldier's voice asking the question and the soldier was now prodding him at the leg with the point of his bayonet. When he did not answer the soldier's question, the soldier set the point of a bayonet against his thigh and pressed. He could not feel the pain for how frightened he was at the shock of

discovery. The soldier leaned harder and his leg spasmed and kicked when the blade went into his skin.

"I know'd you weren't dead," the soldier said with delight. "What's your purpose and I don't want to hear any lies come out of your mouth."

He looked up and saw standing over him a man dressed in a blue uniform and his heart went cold. The soldier wore a thin black beard and gold-rimmed eye glasses and off his shoulder was the rising moon. The soldier stepped back so he might stand, and when he did the soldier flicked open the shell jacket with the point of the bayonet revealing its dyed interior. The soldier relieved him of the pistol he wore in his belt and his knife and then they waited not long before another soldier walked in on them.

Immediately the two soldiers disagreed over the appropriate password and this issue they debated between themselves for an inordinate amount of time. Each claimed his was the new password and the other was still using the old password. Without arriving at any satisfactory conclusion as to what course of events they should pursue, they finally lost interest and let it drop and turned their attention to Robey.

"You got any money hid?" the second soldier asked. "Got any 'backy? You rebs always got 'backy."

Robey shook his head no, in reply.

"He don't talk?" the second soldier asked of the first.

"He ain't talked yet, 'cept in his sleep."

"What'd he say?"

"I don't talk sleep so's I don't know."

"Cat got your tongue?" the second soldier said to Robey.

Again he shook his head and the second soldier snickered.

"Maybe he's got a head full of cotton," the second soldier said. "By God, he'll talk when they stick a rope around his neck."

"He's just a boy," the first soldier said.

"A boy'll kill you as dead as anyone else," the second soldier said. He then unfolded his pocketknife and slipped the blade into each of Robey's pockets and sliced them open.

"He ain't got nothing," the first soldier said, impatient to be relieved of sentry duty and already tired of the responsibility of the prisoner he'd taken on.

They determined that maybe he was not the curiosity they'd thought he was, but still, the coat was suspicious enough and he was armed and so should be delivered to the major. The second soldier told him to cross his hands behind his back and then tied his arms at the wrist with a piece of twine and twisted the bindings tight with a stub of wood he carried. Then the first soldier indicated with his bayonet that he was to move in the direction of the town below where torches had been lit and the streets were bright and lined with wagons.

The walk down the hill was a torment to his swollen ankle now that it'd been put back to work. He stumbled in the tufted grass and tripped and the soldier accompanying him prodded him at times and at other times assisted him as if he could not decide which way to treat him.

Eventually they reached the town and as they passed through the narrow streets, curtains were folded back and squares of pale yellow light showed from small-paned windows. Soldiers were everywhere in the streets and wagons were positioned to barricade side lanes and alleys. Soldiers stood posted at the junction of intersections. They milled about in conversation

and squatted on the ground wrapped in oilcloths, hunkered against the rain.

Stable hands and draymen sat in the clutter of hand trucks and upturned carts, their shafts thrust into the air. They were eating crackers and cheese, scraping out cans of sardines with the backs of their crooked fingers, licking them clean and lighting cigarettes. A large poland hog, its throat already slit and blood gushing to the cobbles, was being clubbed to its side with an axe and slaughtered in the street under a dozen knives. Soldiers roamed in kitchen gardens, stabbing the earth with bayonets looking for silver plate, gold coins, and jewels. Many of the them conversed in languages he had never heard before and all seemed used to the chaos that swirled around them. Tonight this town and a few days ago it was another town and in a few days it'd be a third and they'd do it all over again.

In one garden there were soldiers eerily lit by an oil lamp and tied to a tree branch by their wrists and gagged with bayonets.

"They're drunkards," the soldier told him without being asked.

From an alley came a shriek that stopped them and when they looked into its darkness they could see a cabal of soldiers lifting the skirts of a servant woman to see if her master had hidden any money or jewels close to her body. When they found none they still did not let her skirt down, but began to cut away its folds with their clasp knives.

"You're too young to see that," the soldier said, and prodded him in the back that he should continue along.

More cavalry were arriving by the minute, unsaddling their

lathered mounts and tethering them to bayonets stabbed in the ground. The soldier stopped him, handed him his rifle, and held to his shoulder as he bent to pick some gravel out of his shoe. Where they paused, a shutter flapped open and a woman's head filled the opening, her hair let down and draping her shoulders. Soldiers milled at the wooden steps to the side entrance of her house. A sentry, sitting by its closed door, occupied himself by tossing his hat in the air and catching it. One soldier laughed and observed to another that he didn't think the town would have any old maids left after tonight.

Peddlers moved amongst the soldiers and queued at the women's doorways, hawking their common wares of writing paper, sewing kits, candy, and tobacco. Knots of teamsters paced about, smoking and restless with their prolonged wait while the draft horses stood shifting in harness. Ahead of them lanterns hissed as their reflectors threw coves of light that cut into the cold and drizzle and showed stockpiles of lumber, kegs of nails, horseshoes. Sacks of oats, potatoes, and flour were already loaded in the wagons. There were ducks, chickens, and turkeys in slatted crates. Beef calves blatted for their feed of milk.

The light they passed through showed a gang of black men dressed in rags and cast-offs standing quietly on a long expanse of railroad platform. The men of the perimeter were made to hold up a rope that encircled the lot of them and outside the rope there were soldiers with sharp-edged bayonets fixed to form a hedge of steel blades pointed at their chests.

A soldier with a megaphone was warning them that if a single nigger hand should ever let go the rope and it should fall below their waists, they'd all be shot where they stood.

They continued to wind through the back streets, seemingly lost in their maze, when finally they came to a large square, the majority of which was taken up by a dry stone fountain and at the head of the square, behind a tall wrought-iron fence, was their destination. An immense house glared with white lights that emanated from three tall windows across each story. Rising to the house's deep-set front door was a half-story granite stoop manned by guards and under which was an entrance below ground for tradesmen and servants.

They climbed the stairs and entered into a foyer where the light softened and filtered through an interior door's glass panel. A guard opened the interior door and told them to wait where they were and shut the door on them. Then the guard came back, opened the door, and led them into a hallway, where an old woman greeted them. She wore a white veil and white gloves. Around her neck was a string of pearls and each pearl was the size of a marble. Behind her stood a maid and coming up behind the maid was a young officer. He carried before him a wide leather book stuffed with papers.

The old woman told them they'd have to wait as the major had yet to arrive but was anticipated shortly. She told them there were others seeking an audience with the major and she was looking forward to meeting him herself, as if the occasion was not military occupation but one of a social nature. His guard and the young officer with the book of papers exchanged irritated looks and exasperated, the young officer swirled a finger next to his head.

"Go ahead," the young officer said, resigned to the old woman's hospitality. "It's her house. We are here as her guests."

Her intentions affirmed, the old woman glowed. Gracefully she showed them down the hall and through a doorway where

inside the parlor, the blended fumes of tobacco and whiskey and the heat of the room's wood fire overwhelmed him. There were other people in the room, standing and sitting, and these he avoided with his eyes. He asked his guard that he might sit and the guard agreed to let him.

Here they waited in the company of more guards, bored and hardened men standing at ease and, oddly enough, talking about shooting quail. Inside, the house was as if outfitted from the China trade. There were silver clocks and rosewood tables, enameled screens and porcelain vases blooming with peacock feathers. He imagined each room like this one: crystal chandeliers, dark paintings hung in ornate frames, the embossed spines of books, silver snuff boxes, upholstered furniture, and heavy curtains misty with condensation.

His brain began to unreel. The heated room was slipping from his mind. Could this be what people were fighting over, the many possessions that surrounded him? These objects with so much value and so little use? He thought how the sweep of a hand or the lick of a flame and they would be broken and burned. Maybe it was the weak and the fragile and the beautiful that made you the craziest and made you fight the hardest.

From the hallway came the commotion of opening doors and crossing the parlor's threshold, the words of an angry exchange. Robey was tired and hungry, but he was not concerned. He knew he would be delivered. He did not know why he knew it, but he knew this was not the end of his journey.

"What kind of dodge is this?" a voice came from the hallway. It was the young officer with the leather book of papers.

"He says he wants to hold a prayer meeting," the old woman was saying, "and is here to seek the major for his permission."

"He's the worst in love with God of any man I ever known," said a woman's urgent voice. "He prays on his knees and sometimes his eyeballs roll around backward inside his head."

"I'd like to see that," the old woman said solemnly.

"But, ma'am," the young officer said with all possible forbearance, "we don't want a prayer meeting."

"Well, why not?" the old woman declared. "I can think of nothing more appropriate."

"He has a mighty voice," the woman said. "Sometimes when he prays it's so awful powerful he has to put his face in a cracker box."

"Put them in the parlor," the young officer said in exasperation, and then commanded that the guard in the parlor be increased.

When Robey saw the girl, she was following behind the man in all-black livery with white hair and white muttonchops bushing his cheeks, and behind them was the blind woman, haggard and tired. The man was pink-faced and wore shoulders that rounded above his chest. He limped in one leg, but it did not seem the limp of a real injury. Robey could feel himself in the direction of the man's wicked little eyes as they scanned the room. The girl had lightened her skin with the slightest stroke of chalk powder and reddened her hard shallow cheeks but could do little about her broken lips.

The soldier guarding him leaned down and whispered how her appearance surely did not go against her. Another of the guards caught the eye of the girl, hooked a finger inside his cheek, and made a popping noise. He then smiled and kissed his fingertips. Her panicked eyes flew to Robey's where they stayed, and then they dulled and grayed.

8

HEN THE MAJOR ARRIVED he was carrying his watch in hand and Robey was made to stand as the major, shedding his oilcloth, entered the parlor. The major's head was large and his face was shaped flat and pale. His eyebrows were great white wings that flared dramatically from his brow as if threatening flight from the surface of his forehead. He was by appearance a horseman, for he was bow-legged and walked with his legs turned outward and his toes turned in. He handed his sword to one of the guards, took off his cap, and said to the old woman shadowing him that, yes, a broiled chicken would delight him to no end if one could be found at such an ungodly hour.

"Is that altogether necessary?" he said, pointing to the bindings at Robey's wrist.

"He's a prisoner-spy," the soldier said and tugged open the blue jacket to show gray.

"Please," the major said. "Untie the young man. We'll just have to take our chances." Then, to the young officer with the leather book, he expressed the sentiment that someday this war would be over and when it was they would all have to live with each other once again.

The woman directed her maid to immediately kill a chicken and broil it for the good major. She then told the major a fire had been built in the library and he should sit by the fire and warm himself as the night outside was turning cool and wet.

"It's spring nights like this that the cold can deceive you the most," she said, to which he agreed. She then told him he should rest himself as the train was running late but should be along shortly, and when it finally arrived he would surely be busy with the off loading.

The major looked at his watch in the palm of his hand and asked her how she knew his train was late.

"I have ears to hear with," she tried in her most alluring manner.

"Yes. Yes you do," he said. He found the young officer's eyes with his own and communicated reprimand. He told the woman not to concern herself with the train. It was his business to know when the train would arrive as it was his train and then he disappeared through a doorway deeper into the house's interior.

It wasn't long before the young officer with the leather book came to the parlor and indicated they were to follow him. As he stood, Robey cut his eyes to the girl, but she sat quietly, her hands folded in her lap, her vision cast in the direction of a tall window.

The young officer led them down a long lamplit hallway, smoky and orange and hung with family portraits set in ornate gilded frames to a room that fronted the square. Inside the room, a gallery walled with books, was a fireplace and the major straddling a wooden chair close to the crackling wood. He'd removed his damp jacket. His collar was unbuttoned and he sat as one who wanted proximity to the fire. His arms

were hung off the chair back and in one hand he held a glass of amber-colored whiskey. He was teetering back and forth, letting himself onto the front legs of his chair and then the hind legs and closer to the flames where he was sweating and seemed to feel the strange need to do so.

In the doorway stood the old woman whispering to a much younger version of herself. She too wore pearls and a tightly bodiced peach dress with ample skirts. The woman's daughter, Robey concluded. Though they were whispering about the major, she seemed intent on another individual in the room, a black-haired cavalry officer.

"Too old," the woman was saying, and Robey could see how right she was in her observation. However alert and vital the major at first had seemed, in repose he showed himself to be too old to be in a uniform, his smiling head perched on its stiff collar, his purple-spotted hands hanging from his shirt cuffs, tufts of white hair similar to his eyebrows rimming his red shell-like ears. His face, though elderly and care-worn, was the man's face returning, as some men's faces do, to its original boyish likeness.

"He's a very important man," the daughter was saying, impressed with the major, his staff and attendant military trappings.

"Not down here he ain't," the old woman said, her voice betraying the truth and depth of her bitterness.

The major turned on the blabbing women and then smiled broadly to let them know he could hear their imprudent hallway whisperings. They fluttered at how unsettled they were made by the gaze of his clear blue eyes and the knowledge they'd been found out.

"It's a young heart that beats in this old body," he told their

fleeing backs, and then he saw Robey and his guard and gestured with the wave of his hand that they should enter.

When they made their way into the room, there were two
tall guards standing inside the entry and another officer
lounging crossways in a reclined chair, his legs slung over
an arm. This officer wore the gold braids of the cavalry and
of all the men in the room seemed most secure in himself.
His hair was black and glistened with oil, as did his tall shiny
boots. He held a gold-framed hand mirror and scissors and
was trimming his elaborate waxed moustache. On the floor
beside him was a half-eaten bowl of buttered popcorn.

"I am tired to death," the major said to no one in particular, and turned back to the fire that was reddening his face.

The guards took this as a sign, for they smiled and shifted
to stand at their ease again. Then propping his arms on the
chair back, the major turned his eyes on Robey and said to
his guard, "Who is this young man you have for me and why
so urgent?"

"He's a peculiar one," the soldier said, prodding him forward with the stock of his rifle. "I sketch him a spy."

The cavalry officer could not contain his laughter. "A spy,"
he scoffed, and caught his image laughing again in the mirror glass.

"Don't be shy," the major said to Robey. "Can I offer you a
drink on this wet night?"

"It might help warm me up some," Robey said, and gave
off a shiver at the suggestion of how chilled and thirsty he
might be.

"He talks," the guard said, as if it were a suspicion confirmed.

"He talks," the cavalry officer mimicked, and then made a sound of disgust in his throat.

"Has he not talked before?" the major asked.

"Nope, not a word come from him."

"Then how do we know he is a spy?" the reclining cavalry officer said, without breaking concentration with his mirror.

"Are you a spy, son?" the major asked, looking again at the watch he held cupped in his hands.

"No sir," Robey said.

The major continued to ask questions as if his aim was to ask a certain number in the shortest amount of time and the substance of the answers did not much matter to him.

Robey didn't know how to reply after the first question and so he clasped one hand in the other and said little more.

The major looked up from his watch and, seemingly taken by Robey's face, caught his eye and smiled and would not let go the stare. The major held the stare, looking him straight in the eyes and Robey met his gaze and would not turn away and before long it was as if neither one of them was located in the room. It was no longer night or day and neither of them was in the environment of war. The major was somewhere else—another place and another time and that's where he was seeing Robey.

"Have you had any formal schooling?" the major softly asked, and when Robey did not answer he explained how before the war he'd been a schoolmaster in Connecticut and he had taught boys much his own age and how much it saddened him to now see them in uniforms and carrying swords and rifles and slaughtered in battle.

Robey thought for a moment as to what he might say to

this man who was experiencing an occasion remote and ruminative. He folded his shoulders and out of respect he looked down at the worn carpet beneath his feet. The cuffs were worn from his trousers and the fabric ragged and thready. He'd not realized how tattered he'd become and had the odd thought it was time to find another pair of trousers. He was learning that fear was like danger and passed by those who faced up to it. The straying thought lingered: new trousers. He thought this day would not be his end. He decided he feared nothing from these men and looked up. He looked straight at the major, unmoved by the old man's rheumy solicitation.

"Well," the major said, draining his whiskey glass and clumsily setting it to clatter on the stone floor of the hearth. "So be it. What do you have to say for yourself? Nothing at all?"

"I am searching for my pap," he said.

"He is a liar," the soldier bawled, and to this the major shrugged, still holding his gaze as he let the watch dangle on its short fob.

"Son?" the major said.

"I am to find my pap and bring him back to his home." His voice became no more than a whisper on his lips when he said, "I were shot right here in the head and my horse were stole from me."

"The bastards," said the cavalry officer trimming his moustache. "They'll take the eyeballs right out of your face."

Again the soldier guarding him called him a liar and the major informed the soldier that he was no longer needed. Disgusted and long since tired of the duty he'd assumed, he shouldered his rifle and stamped out of the room.

"Sit down," the major said, pocketing his watch. "Let's have a chat."

"It is the truth," Robey whispered without moving.

"You wouldn't be pulling my leg?"

"No sir."

"Tell me what happened."

"A tiny little fellow back down the road. He was swum with skin fleas and dressed in women's clothes he stole'd off a woman he killed. He shot me here in the head," he gestured, "and stol'd my horse. It was a very fine horse black as coal."

"By gawd, that's the boy's horse," the major shouted, and punched his fist into the palm of his open hand. "We found the fellow who stole your horse. He's in the hoosegow as we speak. He's one of ours and I assure you in no uncertain terms, he will be taken care of."

"How do we know it's his horse?" demanded the cavalry officer. The mention of the horse had caused him to set aside his mirror and scissors and lunge to his feet. As he spoke he cut the air with his hand.

"No," the major said, wagging a finger at the cavalry officer. "The boy speaks the truth and you, sir, are working on my last nerve. I think you like that ill-tempered horse better than you like people. The story is impossible to contrive. You will give the boy his horse."

"I will not."

"You will give back to the boy his god damn horse and you will do it now and that will be the end of the matter."

What was between the major and the cavalry office was personal and what had been smoldering now burned hotly. The major was clearly pleased with his display of anger in

command. In a sulk the cavalry officer shook down his trouser legs and, hands clasped behind him, looked to the ceiling as if in supplication. After enough delay to communicate that the final decision was his and his alone he left through the door, the guards snickering at his back with full intention that he should hear them.

"I will write you a letter," the major said, "explaining your purpose and signed by me."

"I had a letter before this happened," Robey explained, "and it didn't do much good."

"It is the best I can do," the major told him, and when he gestured the young officer with the leather book of papers stepped forward, opened its cover, and laid out a clean sheet of paper, a pen, and bottle of ink on a stand. He then held the book as a surface to write while the major dipped the pen and in flourishing script stated Robey's business and his stewardship of the coal black horse. He periodically cursed as ink spurted from the scratching pen and from time to time raised his hands that it should be blotted.

"Just sit quiet, son," the major said to the book of papers as he wrote. "It won't be long and you'll be on your way."

While they were still sitting by the fire the woman of the house ushered in a man and his wife. She said outside it had begun a plague of rain and the parlor was full and asked if the major would agree to sharing the fire with these itinerants, and to this he consented.

"Will my broiled chicken be much longer?" the major asked as he continued to write.

"There is a terrible downdraft," the woman said, and then told him the fire was being fickle, but it was apparent that she had completely forgotten about the major's chicken.

She sat the man and his wife by the door where they maintained themselves in mute sadness. The man was bare-legged and carried a large bundle on his back. The woman carried an infant less than a year old, wrapped in a blanket, and the presence of the baby seemed to soften the major. Clearly, he himself was a fond father and Robey could only conclude it'd been a long time since he'd seen his children.

The child was placid in the woman's arms, making not a sound, and still she spoke to it, saying its name. They were both wet and chilled and about them was the mystery and awe of hunger. The major ordered for them a mug of hot cider, then entered into conversation with them while he continued to improve his letter on Robey's behalf.

The man stood when the major addressed him and listened like he was used to it. The man told how he was by trade a weaver and his wife was the great-granddaughter of the Reverend Mr. Lamb, formerly minister of Baskenridge Church. They had been burned out and were traveling west to escape the hostilities.

"You travel a long way from home," the major said.

"Yes sir."

"Is Emily your daughter's name?" the major asked, glancing down at the watch he again palmed in his hand as the young officer folded and enveloped Robey's letter of safe passage.

"It is," the weaver said.

"It's a beautiful name," the major said. "I also have an Emily."

"God bless you," the woman said.

"Satan especially hates women," the major said with an exaggerated wink of his eye.

He then took out a purse and gave the woman a silver dollar,

telling her it was for the infant child, which overcame them both with gratitude. He called to the maid and ordered for them coffee, bread, butter, and honey, if there was any to be had. He then crossed the room and pulled back the curtains to let his knee rest on the sill and peer out at the street.

"Why haven't you joined up to fight for your country?" he asked the weaver, still staring out the window.

"They won't take me," the weaver said.

"Why not?"

"I have a black heart."

"Oh, Christ," a sentry mumbled, letting the butt of his rifle knock on the floorboards.

"What is it that constitutes a black heart?" the major asked, without the least interest and as if in reply came the haunting banshee wail of an oncoming train whistle.

"He has a mind disorder," his wife said with some panic in her voice.

Then came another long blast from the quills and the sound of exploding exhaust. The men in the room came to life as if from a long rest. Then was the sound of the engine's volcanic eruptions bouncing off the hillsides and splitting the wet night with their echoes, with great back blasts of soot, as the engine hammered up the last grade and began its run into town.

At that moment the front door flung open and a soldier yelled down the long hallway, "The train is coming," and the sound through the smoky and orange lamplight, past the portraits set in gilded frames was raw sound in its coming from some far-off place, booming through the streets and entering the house. The major turned on his heels and made for the

open door, his guards following close behind with his coat and sword.

Robey waited expectantly, but they seemed to have no more concern with him. The woman carried her baby to the window to look out, but she could not see so she unlatched the window and let it swing open. She called out the arrival of the train and when she left the window's opening the drapes followed her on a wind that would not let them down. The sound increased and the room was washed in a sweep of white light, and he thought it would be a good time to slip away to reunite with the coal black horse. But something was wrong. He felt it before he knew it and then he knew it.

"Don't you go out there," the bare-legged weaver hissed at him, hunching at the window to see into the night.

"You stay here, boy," the woman said, shifting the baby from one arm to the next and sliding a revolver from the blanket's folds.

Still, he went down the hall to the open door where the old woman was fingering her pearls as she and her maid stood looking off in the direction of the train yard and the major and his guards mounting into their saddles and departing on horseback.

"Don't you go down there," the woman warned, and she reached for his collar to hold him back as he passed her by. He could feel her crabbed fingers at his neck and dragging across his shoulder as he slipped her grasp.

Already he was leaving through the open doorway and into the chaos of horses and teamsters, officers yelling out orders and cavalry dashing over the cobblestoned street. As he passed through the streets he detected the townspeople watching

from behind their fallen drapes and from between the slats of their shuttered windows. Men broke from doorways still stepping into their boots and dragging their suspenders over their shoulders, their shirttails flagging behind them.

He didn't know why, but he crossed the square and walked the street in the clear direction of the glistening engine, its rods slowly rising and falling. Shotgun blasts of steam filled the black vault of the night. Frightened horses were rearing in harness and had to be quieted. A shaft of white light still bayed from the tinplate reflector, splitting the wet darkness as white carmine-tinted plumes swept past the reflected light.

A cavalryman yelled at him and he jumped back as the horse and rider surged over the spot where he had just stood. Inside the light was visible the red star of the headlamp while the iron clapper continued its tolling on the bronze walls of the bell, as if calling to him again and then again: come see what you have never seen before in your young life.

Robey gazed at the shining steel and copper of the engine that pulsed before him. A red line bordered in gold made a long stripe down its wet glistening barrel. The black-faced men were slowly being herded forward, treading warily, as if they feared they would be fed into the very noise of the engine.

The doors of the boxcars banged open and lanterns were lit inside the cars and they became incandescent and shown from within as the men collected forward and began handling the boxes and crates from the cars' interiors and into the wagons. The black skin of their raised arms was wet and silvery in the light and their faces streaked as if they were crying silent endless tears. A red mouth would open or the light would catch

the white of an eye, and this would cause a soldier to shift and raise his rifle and yell and then another soldier would yell and the yelling would erupt down the line.

He turned away and it was then, through a white blast of steam issuing from the cylinder cock, that he saw webbed in the sweeping steel slats of the low pilot the torn and masticated head of the bay horse, its eyes huge and pearly and fixed on the distance forever. He turned over inside himself and felt his jaw fixing and reminded himself of hatred and how anger was more useful than despair. But still that a horse should receive such an outcome, even in death. Then the strangest feeling came into him as he marveled at how powerful the machine and the way it'd cleaned the bay horse's head from the rest of its body. He found his breath again and thought to find the coal black horse, a revolver, the infested little man who shot him so cold-bloodedly.

Then a soldier screamed, God almighty, and fell and he could hear a sound coming from the walls and cobbles like hot spattering grease. Then, beside his ear, he heard the crying sound the air makes when it splits. Then another soldier was toppled and then a rider hove up and the word went out that a large force had struck the pickets and they'd been drove in. Then came the first of the pickets pouring over the river, the rail cut and in from the countryside, and in the same moment was begun the screaming sound of artillery in the night and in stark detail. It was as if the whole world about him was suddenly flying apart.

9

From out of the darkness continued a coruscating gunfire. Spent bullets were flattening on stone walls and dropping to the cobbles below where they hissed in the puddled water, or whining through the leaves of dogwood and cutting the green needled trees and falling to the street like elements of heavy rain. He saw a young soldier boy struck in the hand from a great distance and the force of the bullet seemed to fling the hand from his body and spin him in place until he fell down in the street to dumbly stare at his hand, as if an appendage newly attached and sourced with a baffling pain.

The horses standing in harness held their heads high as their lathered flanks heaved with every breath. They danced and trod heavily and then they too began to fall onto their haunches and sides but not before eight or ten bullets found their wet-sleeked hides, their withers, their long necks, their ribs, their croup, their powerful beating hearts. It was never the intention to kill the horses, but that was how thick and crossed the fire was in those first minutes of chaos.

He could see a cannonball striking sparks as it bounded over the rounded cobbles and then slowing and gently rolling his way. He jumped aside, but another soldier, his gaping

mouth still gobbed white with a paste of crackers and cheese, held up his rifle as if stepping into water and put his foot out to stop the cannonball and in an instant his foot was gone and blood was gushing out the stumped end of his leg onto the street where his blood showed like red glass in wet sunlight. A second cannonball blew a soldier's head clean off and continued on to smash another man to death. The headless soldier walked three more paces before falling to the street where his dead body shook fishlike before extinguishing.

Robey lifted on his toes to damp the tremors circuiting the ground and a shock of fear went through him and it was like candied syrup running the lengths of his extremities. His belly swooped low and dashed at his pelvis where it fluttered. This night was war. The falling rain was war. The clipped moon was war. The earth where they stood and the sky they stood under was war. He had to fasten his mind to stave off the urge to piss himself and when the urge passed he armed himself with a dead man's revolver and then a second one he jammed in his belt. He determined, as if it were his prerogative to do so, that he would not be shot again by any man on either side of that small earth if he could shoot the bastard first. War would not kill him.

Horses reared and shrieked as the din of noise rose again and then surpassed itself. They kicked over the traces and kicking out with their hooves became entangled. A jack, braying and honking, plunged across the square, its ears swept back and its tail straight up in the air, a muleteer running behind, slipping and falling with broken leads still in his hands. Streamers of blood flowed from its nostrils, breaking and flattening and spattering its hide. It ran headlong through an

iron fence and into a stone wall where it broke its neck and crumpled in a flower bed. Another soldier, his ribs blown out by an exploding shell, was revealed to him in lantern light, his throbbing heart, and he spoke on in delirium of a particular woman before he too expired.

Sparks flew from minié balls and grapeshot that hit stones in the hard gravel yards. The major, now mounted and crying out a babel of orders, rode up in a flurry of lather and sweat and stopped where he stood, and he could feel the fling of heat from the horse, panting and about to drop as it skittered to keep its tangled feet under it.

"Get down," the major yelled at him, and when someone pushed him from behind he scurried for cover in the wet grass behind a spiked wrought-iron fence.

Sharpshooters were now picking off the teamsters, the soldiers in the train yard and the soldiers in the tight confines of the streets, their flesh blurred by bullets. The major screamed out in anguish as a bullet passed through his black boot and entered his horse. A surgeon approached, dragged the boot from his leg and insisted upon immediate amputation, but the major kept him at bay with his drawn revolver, and the surgeon bound the wound while the major stayed in the saddle and continued his steady contribution of incoherent orders. Another bullet struck his wrist and his gauntlet filled with blood before he let it slip from his hand and slap to the ground where it lay red and bloated.

Then, from back a lane unlit beyond the great fountained square, came the long dense sensation that comes in advance of a great force marshaling. Then there was the force itself and that alone was fearsome and powerful to witness and then he

heard the officer's command and the sound of slotted steel swords clearing their scabbards.

"Form fours! Draw sabers! Charge!"

Then came a sudden hurtling through space and behind it were the raiders materialized on horseback, kiting through the hedges and emerging from the alleys and gathering into the parallel streets where they charged like the bore from a burst dam, and then they were in their midst and abrupt explosions were erupting from the ends of their arms. Horses screamed and fell with groaning exhalations. A gush of blood spewed from another's mouth as it whirled on its hind feet and bolted. A blade flashed and a hand was cut off at the wrist. Another flashed and a man's head was nearly severed from his body and ropes of arterial blood tapped into the night's darkness.

There were now a hundred horses in the street, rearing on their hind legs, churning through the smoke and fire, the drizzle and blood. One soldier dropped his rifle and raised his hands and he was shot dead. Men were sitting up trying to staunch their own bleeding chests. A horse sat on its tail, both hind legs broken beneath it. With their swords the raiders slashed the gray canvas that covered the wagons and killed all who were revealed inside.

From broken windows in the upper stories, soldiers continued to fire and when hit they collapsed where they stood, falling to the floor or tumbling out the window to the ground below.

The major fought on, receiving saber cuts to the head and arms. His horse's feet pounded the air at Robey's face. The major grabbed a double-barreled shotgun from one who would

shoot him and shot the man with his own load and then shot another and in short order he cut a third by the throat.

"Close up," he cried ferociously. "By God, close up."

But battles are determined by the soldiers fighting them and not orders from the top. The major was sitting bolt upright in the saddle when a minié ball came singing through the air and passed into his head and then he was dead and falling. The palings of the fence spit into his side and he was held there, stopped in his abrupt descent, his body pierced with black iron and dangling aloft like a great speared fish. His white face went blood red and gently came to rest in Robey's lap where he sat on the ground. His head still smoked where he'd been shot and his eyes were mere glass as they'd had their last flickering before his body fell.

Then it was over. And the air was possessed of an unnatural silence, but it was a silence that did not last long before it was replaced with hissing and roaring, with moans and screams. The enduring sound beneath sound. The silence had lasted for as long as it took the listening mind to return from where it had sought refuge from the gun's detonations to the timeless human sounds of pain and expiration.

On the ground around him came the moans and the sibilant cries of the wounded and dying men, the men stranded at the simple ends of lives. Horses had broken loose, and riderless they galloped about like the charge of a strange maneuvering ghost cavalry. He wondered what you did when a man shot in the stomach cried for water and you didn't have any water to give him. He stumbled across the face of the young officer who carried the leather book. He sat crumpled, half upright, and stared mutely at the red bubbles frothing from a hole in

his breast as if he were aware of watching his life floating from him, his comprehending mind understanding how soon it would be and his active mind helpless to do anything.

They dragged into the light of the lit fires the cavalry officer with the elaborate moustache whose hair was black and glistened with oil. He no longer wore the gold braids of the cavalry but was wearing civilian clothes instead. He had been wounded slipping out the back door of a house on his way to escape.

"Put him through," one of them said, his voice half lit with whiskey, unable to stop what had been started.

"He ain't hurtin' nobody."

"It's a ugly bull that never hurts anybody," the first one said, and drew his pistol and shot the officer in the forehead.

"He's dead," the second observed, bending down and dumbly peering at the body before stripping it of boots and spurs.

"He is indeed dead," the one said, and freely conceded the hell he was already destined for. He then congratulated himself on how consistently true his shot and rode away.

"He loves to kill them," the second one said to another.

What soldiers had not been killed or wounded were gathered into the train station and made to huddle on the floor where the mutilated and dying lay packed together. Those who had fled were taken after by raiders on horseback and for some minutes after the battle came the sound of single shots from deep in the night's gloom as the hunters found their prey.

The blood was already turning black as the peddlers reappeared and began hawking their wares to the customers newly arrived. The raiders hardly paused in their killing before they attacked the slat-sided army wagons, where they discovered bologna sausages, hardtack, and sponge cakes. They

turned the muzzles of a cannon on the train engine and blasted holes in the boiler. The water jacket ruptured and steam geysered into the air. Another round went through the cylinder and still another destroyed the crank pin and the driving wheel as curtains of water rained down on the cross ties.

After the battle, it was not long before he could hear the clack of dice inside a cracker box and after the battle there was food: milk, butter, eggs, and chickens brought from their hiding places and into the kitchens and onto porches. Stoves were fed with wood and pots set to boil. Afterward, doors and windows were flung open and invitations to eat were extended, and from a chapel the mounting voice of a choir followed the building strains of a pipe organ.

He walked the streets in search of the coal black horse. He thought too he might see the girl. He ate while he wandered, crossing street after street, discarding chicken bones in the gutters as he walked, but he could find neither the horse nor the girl.

These men he now walked among carried a sudden fatal danger with them. They seemed without cares and seemed as capable of turning on each other and even their own selves as they were of killing their enemies. They wore low crowned, broad-brimmed hats. They were long-haired and unshaven and their overshirts were dirty with camp grease and fire smoke. Their gray trousers were black stained with saddle sweat and horse lather. They wore three and four Navy Colts in their belts and carried shotguns slung on their backs. Their faces were darkened with sun and gunpowder. They did not walk but loped the canted walk of traveling wolves.

"Murderers," the veiled old woman in pearls said to a pass-

ing raider wearing a gold cord wrapped around his black slouch hat.

"Just murderers, ma'am, every one of them," the raider said, without hesitating and without looking her way.

THAT NIGHT HE SPENT what passed for sleep in a shed while a dog nearby sent up an intermittent barking and howling. During his wanderings he had learned that a regular army, one he concluded to be his father's, had crossed back into the valley at Front Royal and when he inquired he learned he was just days behind. A voice in the night told the dog to shut up its yap, but it continued its noise until there was the sound of a single muffled shot and then there was silence. Morning was only hours away when he could no longer hold off the crush of sleep and later it was still dark when he awoke, and in that short time the raiders had departed. They had disappeared as silently as they had appeared.

The morning air was damp when he came to and a dense grimy river fog rolled in across the grain fields. While the rest of the town slept, he hurried through the compact streets under the colorless sky, the faint light of morning still on the river. The gutters were now dry of runoff, but the damp was running from the walls and fences as if it were spring's last thaw. A keen northeast wind was sweeping the stony streets and at each corner a hot wet draft struck his body and cut into him. He was well armed and past the want of hunger and thirst. His clothes were mildewed and rotting on his body, but that could wait. His ankle was swollen and ached to his leg and into his hip and he felt his thin body was down to nothing but muscle and bone, but he did not care.

In the train yard were the dead buildings and there were the boxcars and there was the engine and the twisted trucks and all were shrouded in the wet acrid smoke of their burning. The streets were strewn with debris and mottled with swatches and runs of cracking blackness and he knew they were the bloody stains of the fallen soldiers. He needed a horse and he found one, a big cream workhorse with knotted shoulders cropping a trampled kitchen garden. It still wore a collar and the last vestments of a broken harness draped from its neck and dragged on the ground. It was a wounded and sorry mount, one jaded and abandoned by the hostlers, but it was stout, clear-eyed, and of even breath.

He mounted the horse and beat its hind end and jabbed his heels into its sides. The cream horse remained obstinate and heavy as a log as it slowly understood its charge. He jerked the makeshift bridle he'd fashioned and swore and slowly the horse understood and began ahead. It crossed over the tracks, its wide hooves grating on the ballast of broken stone and gravel between the ties. On the other side was a deep ditch and instinctively the animal sat as they plunged into it, stood, and bounded up the other side. Then they were on the brambled and nettled waste ground beyond the station and cindered rail bed and the cream horse, encouraged and not finicky in the least, breasted through them.

Here the land settled to the river bottom and was bathed in runners of fog and mist, and the wind was now slicing over his head in hot gusts. The horse slowed and stepped gingerly as the ground disappeared in the gauze of whiteness below its chest. He kicked the horse, but still it stepped no more quickly for his efforts, picking its way over the rough and uneven ground. From the east came broad trails of pale silver

presaging the advent of another day's light. Then rising to his
nostrils in a sweep of dank air from the earth below came the
sweet cloying smell of newly wrought death.

His craw surged and he tried to bend away as he retched a
clear fluid, but it drenched his knee and pant leg and when
he opened his eyes he could see revealed in the passing
windows of tattered fog, the soldier with the thin beard and
gold-rimmed eye glasses who'd taken him prisoner and then
the kind old major surrounded by his guard. His face was
gray and his large head seemingly misshapen in the bone
plates. All about him were the men in blue where they'd been
carted and strewn for burial and the sight of them was as
eerie as drowned fish. They were dead and face up and their
eyes were open, as if watching his departure, as if they'd momentarily paused in this low wet place to witness his leaving
before resuming their own eternal travels. He understood if
he had to be dead to keep his eyes open and not forget to do
that because that was the habit of dead men.

As he left that dead ground he entered a forest on a path
that the cream horse found and it wasn't long before he heard
a whickering in the trees distant, and pulled up. The fog was
so dense he could not see what was before him and he leaned
forward and stretched his neck and waved his hand before his
eyes as if fog could be sorted away.

The whickering came again and it was close and then he
found its shape and he could see it was the coal black horse.
It had been watching him as he rode in and now snorted and
pawed the ground. It tossed its head and made a sound as if
impatient and even castigating. In disbelief he called out to
it and it tossed its head again and then beside it he saw two
legs dangling from the round bottom of a white dress. On

the ground beneath the feet was a straw hat and a parasol. It was the little goose man and he was hung by his broken neck. He'd been unhorsed in the fork of a low branch. His tongue was purple and swelled from his mouth and spread across his chin. His eyes bulged from his face like hen's eggs and he smelled from where he'd pissed and shat himself.

At first he thought to apologize to the horse and would have except for fear the horse would not accept his supplications. He slid from the back of the cream horse and his face stinging with tears of restraint, he spoke gently to the coal black horse as he led it away from the little man's hanging. They walked slowly at first and then he stopped and pulled himself into the saddle. Then he urged the horse on and it hesitated before re-sponding as if to acknowledge that its rider had learned some valuable lesson and should now be rewarded for such.

They bore off from the river and struck the forest. They came to rails and crossed them and descended the other side. It was a gradual descent but a continual bed of rocks or large stones. In some places, the horse was at a loss how to proceed through the wild and dreary land but figured its path on the move and pursued it with abandon. Throughout the hilly land was a profusion of springs where the water came from beneath the limestone ground, clear and fresh. The timber grew large and the woods became crowded with underbrush and fallen trees and rocks, and more than once the coal black horse found passage that would have scraped him from its back had he not lifted his legs or bent low on its neck. But it did not matter. Nothing mattered as they traveled deeper into the North to intercept the army.

10

AYS LATER AS HE neared the wide flat river of his destination, where the army of his father was said to be, there were fresh rumors of a movement in a northeasterly direction and it was as if the eddies of seventy-five thousand men up and tramping the dusty roads could be felt in the very earth itself. He was only days behind the march when he turned in its direction, following its tremors.

Long afterward, he would remember how fifty miles away he heard the thunder of cannons echoing through the blue mountains, the reverberations of the bombardment that preceded, as he was to learn, the final charge of the fateful battle. The next afternoon, he rode through a drenching rainstorm that leeched the July landscape of all color and after dark he met the saturated vanguard of the gray retreating south.

Another storm cut loose in the morning, one that was more vicious, and in moments the tide of men and horses, the drovers and their herds of braying beeves he was traveling against, were forced by the deluge to wade through the deep cloying mud like hogs, the turning wheels clogging from spoke to felloe and locked in its hold skidded over the ground. Insensate, he was drawn against the tide of sutlers and ambulances, the carriages and caissons, the long parade of the hip-shot, the

mud-spattered, the blood-dirty, and the slaughter-gutted, the wheeling army of the dead and the dying. For twenty miles they came against him and the coal black horse in a relentless tide and he rode on without hesitation through their broken and driven ranks. Their calls of foreboding and their hollowed silences were a testament to the great killing and dying that had taken place where they had departed. They had died on the battlefield and now they died by the road and they died in the road and those that did were ground to pulp from the rolling iron-shod wheels, the treading of horses' hooves, the tramp of so many barefoot men.

At the end of that road, it was as if evil had descended and taken up inside man and caused man to flail and step before the bullet and receive the bullet and receive the blade and man could not help but put up flesh as shield against metal. For man to enter those fields had been to give up all will but the will to kill, or be killed, and to survive those fields was somehow to be cheated of death. At the end of that road, he knew was his destination.

He did not call out his father's name as he moved against the retreat, did not ask of those sunken and glassy-eyed men where he could find his father. He did not want to intrude on their suffering, but more so he did not want to be heard or to be seen by them. He wanted to pass through their gabbled ranks as if he were not there and as if he were something of an essence and was capable of splitting time and walking the seams of place unknown and unseen. He had done such before, walking quietly through the place of deer or bear, walking up to a rabbit and taking it by the neck as it watched him come on. He simply knew he would find his father because he knew his father would be where he went to find him.

As he approached the town, everywhere the eye looked was the litter of war. There was paper torn from the cartridges rain-pasted to every surface, shreds of ripped clothing, blanket, and sack trodden into the ground. There were sprung watches, broken plates and shards of crockery. He saw a boot, and then he saw a boot with a foot inside, a sleeve and then an arm inside a sleeve, a glove and then a hand inside a glove. There were dead horses, splintered caissons, the litter of corn cob and the brass tubes of cannons seated in the earth with their white oak carriages staved and broken and the tubes of the cannons blackened and bulging and cracked. A white horse, its forelegs shot off, lay on its side calmly cropping the tufted and trampled rye.

The trees were made white and glistening as bone where they'd been peeled of their gnarled bark and whole men lay in rigid contorted shapes and some others lay as quiet and as peaceful in death as if they truly were asleep on the picnic ground.

In the deadened woods where the bullets had stormed and the air still crackled with the smell of heat, sharpshooters were hanging in the trees by their cinched leather belts. Their bodies were turned out and they occupied the air like great frozen birds intent on kill and in a flash their flights arrested. They hung dead and could not raise their bodies, but it was as if at any moment they would come to swift and fierce motion, and for anyone to pass under their bowers would mean certain death.

Those were but the small images where his mind could isolate what it found and save it into memory, for about the fields of milo maize were fifty thousand casualties, fifty thousand men who were killed, and wounded and missing from the roles. They were in parts and pieces. They were whole and

seemingly unscathed and wandering about as the future dead while others were vapor or grease or but rags of flesh and pulverized bone. Strewn over the few hundred acres was everything a man carried inside and out. There were enough limbs and organs, heads and hands, ribs and feet to stitch together body after body and were only in need of thread and needle and a celestial seamstress.

Their blood, gummed and clotted, was beginning to draw flies in the wet air. They lay with their broken legs twisted and contorted so, to even unfold a man in the attempt to configure him as a man would be near impossible. It was a horrible scene to witness, replete with sorrowful pleadings for water and assistance, while the silent dead resided in strange repose, their stiffened arms reaching to embrace a heaven. He decided from that day forever after that there must live a heartless God to let such despair be visited on the earth, or as his father said, a God too tired and no longer capable of doing the work required of him.

In places there were swarms of movement, bodies still wriggling as if with souls attempting flight, but in these environs he knew even the souls had been killed and he knew this down inside himself, though he'd been told by his mother when the body dies the soul is immortal. Then a head lifted and a death drawn face caught his eye. It smiled and called a name his way, its eyes large with recognition. He approached, and when he leaned closer hands took hold of him and tried to claw out his eyes and he could do no other than boot the man's head to save himself, and he thought, In war even the dead will kill you.

He continued on afoot, walking from face to face, the coal

black horse following behind, stepping gently over the dead and not addled by the rank iron smell of cooling blood. In one field, he found a lineup of dead dressed in butternut uniforms. It was below the brow of a western ridge and their hands were tied behind their backs and a single bullet had passed through their brains. He didn't know what it was and could only figure they had tried to run from battle. One had a handkerchief tied over his mouth, perhaps to shut up his whimperings. He too was wounded mortally through the brain and they must have done it to keep him from hollering on the occasion of his imminent execution. Or maybe he'd gone mad. Or maybe he'd been wise. It didn't matter: he was dead.

His blood went hot and pulsed in his veins as he determined this was not to be feared for its horrible import but to be embraced for the knowledge it imparted. It was something to learn and to depend upon, another rule of the chaos. It disabused him even further of what he'd brought with him from the mountains. He saw that even they will kill you and if that is so, then anyone will kill you and he was relieved to know such and could plainly see how simple an equation war was becoming to him.

In one wood was collected a field of the dying, a long, sad row of men who lay on the bare ground, moaning and twitching fitfully, blubbering in wave and cadence. They were left wholly to themselves. These were men who'd been severely wounded through the head, some with both eyes shot out. They were all mortally wounded and had been put aside to die without hope as quickly and peacefully as they might.

Not far away from them was a long table where the surgeons worked from first sun to twilight and through the night,

lopping off arms and legs with the quick gnawing strokes of their bone saws. Wagons carted away the bloody limbs and came back empty, wet, and glistening in the blaze of surrounding lanterns and again were loaded and hauled away.

It was as many and again and again into infinity as the most people he'd ever seen in one place—in his whole life together—and they were all limbed and dead and dying and their air smelled fetid as if an ocean shore captured for days at low tide, close and unmoving, quaked by no wind. He knew this was no brittle edge of the world he'd entered. This was the world itself.

There, in that wood, in the fleeting light of a declining watery sun was where he found his father. He was lying there, in that field of the dying men under a purple sky. He recognized him and he clasped his hand and his father stared into him with the look of an expectation at long last fulfilled.

A bullet had smashed into his father's cheek where it had left a black hole. It had then made a circuit of his cranium and exited out the back of his head. He could feel the ruptured path of broken bone the bullet had left as it coursed beneath his father's scalp before exiting through the wall of the parietal bone. When his father tried to speak, Robey encouraged him to remain silent. As they held to each other, all around them were the constant murmurations of the dying: giving orders, fighting, praying, calling out the names of women and children, gasping, gurgling, and throat breathing.

"I came as quick as I could," he said, fighting the panic that had seized his voice.

"It's a good thing it weren't any quicker," his father whispered.

"I tried hard," he said, his father's head on his lap.

"I know."

There was a low moan he could not contain cidering from deep inside his chest.

"Hush," he told his father. "Hush now."

The moan began to grow and overwhelm his body and take possession of him. He had no control over it because it was his heart and lungs and backbone and he fought hard to not fly away into the thousand pieces of a boy flung into the sky and through the air and down into the earth.

His face burned with what he had discovered at the end of the road. He could never have imagined what he found, could not confront how terrible his failure. His mind fled from him and his body ached from trying to keep it somewhere inside his body—his arms or legs or hands if not inside his skull. The feeling ran the ridges of his spine like a dragging knife-point. Then it passed and he was not panicked anymore.

WHEN HE FOUND his father in the field of the dying, he tucked his jacket under his bound head and found another jacket, a blue one with torn yellow piping, so as to move freely about the fields. For several hot days and wet nights to come, the departing troops would be parched by the sun and pelted by the heavy rain that washed the soil where the stains of battle did not run too deeply. The days: a relentless baking sun, which sets cloaks of steam and breeding flies to rise in the air.

That first morning he awoke before light and tied the lead of the coal black horse to his father's wrist and pinned the major's letter to his father's blanket. His father roused and under cover of the blanket he let Robey curl his fingers around pistol grips and only then, with the horse standing sentry, did he set out to forage for food and water.

As he wandered the fields, he thought himself to be in his ghost form, the died boy who lived with the dead and ministered to the dead. He was not yet dead, but was still young enough to not attract attention from the slowly gathering marshals who were intended to bring some order to the ravaged fields of the battle's aftermath. He foraged for what nourishment he could find to sustain his father and his fallen com-

rades. Inside the scattered haversacks were crocks of butter, mutton, veal, lard, and jars of sweet preserves. There were bottles of wine and oddly enough to be found were old bonnets, baby shoes, women's gaiters, feather pillows, silverware, and jewelry. He heard in the town there were cart loads of bread, but these were soon gone and in the days that followed no more was delivered.

There was every imaginable form of wound to be seen, horribly mutilated faces and men without arms or legs, and yet they were still alive and floundering in the mud like something left by a great swashing tide. Men drowned in the puddles where they lay for lack of an unbroken bone in their extremities by which they might turn themselves over to face the sky. At night they lay out upon the cold and wet earth, staring into the glowering darkness of the sky as they whispered their final prayers. While the fortunate were bedded on straw and hay, a blanket, an overcoat, most were stripped and being robbed and had nothing, not shoes or boots, not hat or coat or tunic or trousers.

In the first hours he wore a lady's kerchief around his face, wrapped layer upon layer and would let it slide down when he went back to his father's side but after a while he became used to the universal smell of death and gave up the kerchief and forever after was immune and not bothered by it again, the iron odor of blood outside the body, the living stink of the wounded, the peculiar smell of expiration and soul escape.

As he walked, there were to be seen dead men, surrounded by scraps of writing paper, who'd torn up their letters and the images of their betrothed they carried against their bodies, lest they come into the hands of some uncaring individual

and be published in the Northern newspapers. The still living beckoned to him and they thrust their last pages into his
hands and he carried the letters to keep them from the scavengers moving about the fields.

The scavengers came like flights of starving birds. They
were collecting what tokens of affection they could find sewn
inside pockets and talismans worn about the necks, for the
soldiers carried into battle braids of hair, lockets, curios, and
women's scarves. The scavengers moved like crows in the garden, skipping from one dead body to the next, furtively going through each pocket and lining to steal what single item
they could find. They twisted rings off fingers and with their
single prize they shamefully slunk away. These were intended
as the anonymous memento mori of one of earth's great battles and were destined for a drawer, or a closet, some private
museum, or to be sold as reliquies, ransomed to bereaved
families. The more industrious collected blankets, harnesses,
and rifles. They led off horses, cannon limbers, caissons, and
even ambulances they would rebuild as milk trucks and forage wagons.

Sticking among the rocks and against trunks of trees were
hair, brains, entrails, and shreds of human flesh cooking
black in the heated air. There were men and horses swollen to
twice their size, and in the days that followed he witnessed the
shocking distension and protrusion of their eyeballs and he
would eventually see them bursting open with the pressure of
foul internal gases and vapors, their bloomings like horrible
flowers exploding their petals and leaves and spewing them
across the ground.

Grave diggers came to work, men hunched over their shov-

els and the earth they turned in plodding fashion in every place heaving the ground uneven. There were two he watched as they filled one grave with the turned earth of the next. He thought they must have been at it all night for how long the sweeping, lifted mound of rolled soil they'd already left in their wake. He watched them until they paused with fatigue and one of them hoisted a jug to his shoulder only to find it empty. He wasn't close enough to hear their exchange of words, but apparently it was an argument over the empty jug. One of them dropped his shovel and doubled his fists, whereupon the other lifted his shovel in the air and slammed him on his shoulder cuff. They closed in a hold and struggled against each other, while beneath their feet were dead men, their eyes white as milky glass, until finally the grave diggers fell among the dead where they did not move except for their breathing chests.

In a peach orchard, he came across young men gathering up the amputated limbs and filling wooden barrels with them. When he asked them what they were going to do with all that limbage, they said they were medical students and they were going to bury the barrels in the ground until the limbs had decomposed and then ship them to Washington to the medical college to use in their studies. Another team of students was boiling the flesh from the skeletons of the fallen gray soldiers, working diligently with paddles and hooks as the flames licked at the sides of the steaming black iron kettles.

There were two scavengers he followed that first day and studied for especially how they worked. Over the course of time he learned how they were unlike the others in that they were not interested in keepsake or memory or usefulness

but rather had a professional way about them. They arrived with the same tools as those of the surgeon or mechanic. They would wear carbide lamps to move about the field at night and maintained a variety of disguises. They camped a safe ways off and were not greedy for the accoutrements of war, and what they did take of war's implements they were selective about the pieces they stole. The two were searching for jewelry and certain personal items. They wanted anything with an inscription or an address which they might then sell to loved ones back home. They did not go through the pockets or the linings of the dead but slit them with razors they wore in their sleeves to be the quicker about their business. They carried iron shears in their pockets for cutting off fingers to get rings and wielded jawed pliers to remove gold from the mouth.

By that afternoon, the citizenry had begun arriving in flocks and tramping out to tour the battlefield. They were old fathers and mothers, brothers and sisters hunting for their wounded and dead. The fields were strewn with rifles and all manner of outfit, and these likewise were collected up as trophies by the citizens and more than one of the innocent and curious was killed by the accidental discharge of a rifle still loaded and cocked.

Side businesses sprang up. Women were charged twenty dollars to move a husband or a son from the ground into a wooden box and onto a cart, and he took advantage of this opportunity and his arms ached so for helping that day he could not lift them from his sides. When the women tried to pay him, he refused at first, but finally he relented, whatever they wished to give, and accepted the few coins they left for him on the ground for fear of touching his blood-slick and fat-greased hands.

With the money he walked into town to buy water and a clean dressing for his father's head. He saw two women, one older and one younger. They were sitting in the open doorway of a gray stone house. By their doorstep, the syringa bushes were in bloom and white lilies had unfolded on bowed stems. He took their relationship to be that of mother and daughter. They were laughing as if nothing had happened and he could not help but smile at how happy they appeared in spite of their surroundings. He opened their gate and his throat parched, he called out to them for a sip of water.

"Water," the mother said. "You want water after what you did?"

He slowly shook his head. As hard as he tried he could not think what he had done.

"You can't tell?" she asked, and then answered her question for him. "You scared all the birds away and they won't ever come back." Both women laughed at this for how funny it was to them.

"A sip of water is five cents and by the glass is fifty cents," the younger woman called to him.

He held out his hand to show her the coins he possessed and she motioned for him to approach. He went to them along a path of red bricks lined with trampled yellow flowers. She was a blue-eyed strabismal woman with a high color in her vein-traced cheeks. She held her legs clasped in her arms, her chin hovering her knees. The older woman had a boiled look to her face, as if she'd been burned, but she wasn't burned. Sweat ran down the sides of her thin face and collected in the bones of her shoulders and chest. They each clutched a square of cloth to their face from which they inhaled deeply and between them sat a stoppered bottle of rose water. He held out the

silver coins again and the younger woman indicated he should drop them in the berry pail at her feet. When he did, the older woman stood and disappeared inside the house.

"Bread?" he inquired.

"A loaf of bread cost two dollars," the younger woman said, growing impatient with his trade.

This money he also let drop into the hollow of the berry pail and this time when he did he leaned forward and looked down and saw it to be full of coins and greenbacks.

"You stay back there," she said sharply. "Don't get so near. Bring a loaf of bread," she called into the house.

The older woman returned with a glass of water and a loaf of bread less than the size of a muffin. She waved him off and when he stepped back to the gate she set them on the bricks in front of him. She then returned to the step and nodded him forward after she sat.

"Drink the water and go," she said. "And take that with you. You can't eat that here."

"Would you have some linen to bind a head?" he asked, after draining the water glass.

"Two dollars."

He paid her this money as well and taking the rolled material he left out the gate. Behind him, they resumed their private laughing, at what he did not understand.

Making his way back through the gathering crowds, he came upon a cemetery where a woman was digging a grave beside a file of dead men. Inside the wrought-iron gates the grass appeared blue and he was drawn to step inside and stand in that grass, and when he stood inside the fields of war beyond the fence appeared white in the bleaching sun.

Possessed by the orderliness of the place, he walked among

the riven stones of the cemetery. War had even been made upon the cemetery and in places the ground looked as if plowed. The tombstones were broken into fragments and graves had been turned up by plunging shells. The monuments had been toppled to provide cover for a time and so they were pocked and scarred by the scrape of bullets. The bodies slumped behind the stones had absorbed the bullets made of pure, hollow, soft lead, arriving to kill at a thousand yards, fracturing and shattering bones, blasting tissue, and causing large gaping wounds that draped like cut mouths in the sun.

He counted there to be thirty-four of the dead that she was burying and when he asked if he could help he learned she was six months pregnant, but she made no mention of a husband or father to the baby she carried.

"How did this happen," he asked, not quite sure what he meant, even as he was asking the question.

She looked at him oddly, her head cocked to one side as she leaned on her shovel.

"You are not from around here," she said.

"No ma'am."

"Why are you here?"

"My mother sent me to fetch home my pap."

"Did you find him?"

"He is over thar. I was to get water, but I drank it all myself. Then I paid for a bandage and I did not have any more money to buy water for this canteen."

"You can help if you want to," she said. "I will give to you water to take, or I'll just give you water and you can go."

"I have never had money before."

"Then it will give me pleasure to pay you in water."

For a time he helped the pregnant woman plant the dead. Their various causes of death were most apparent as the minié ball was a terrible, crippling, smashing invasion of the body, shattering and splitting bones like green twigs and extravasating blood in a volume of tissue about the path of its ferocious intention. The killing wounds were to the head, neck, chest, and abdomen. When the minié ball struck it flattened and tumbled, fissuring and comminuting bony structures. Shards of bone and broken teeth often flew from its path, wounding one body with the bones and teeth of another.

Most of the killed in the cemetery had received long-distance mortal head wounds in the lee of those signifying stones, as if the stones were waiting and would not be denied their purpose in life. Many had been shot in the left hand reaching up to slide the ramrod into their rifles.

He silently dug into the earth, his hip close to hers. Stray hairs floated about her tired face. She would tuck them away and they would come free again and she would stop to rearrange her hairpins. He thought of his mother and for the time he was a child-boy again and he was home and they were working in the kitchen garden, digging, planting, and hoeing, and soon he would share with the world the advent of an infant brother or sister.

When the hole was deep enough, together they would lift in a man and then beside that grave, they'd dig again, filling in that one with what they excavated from the next one. He worked his shovel hard so she might have that much less to do, but she dug steadily and held her own.

As darkness came on that first long day, he stood up from the new grave to grasp the next man and he saw that it was

a boy his own age. His teeth were broken in his mouth and the bone cup for his hip must have been shattered because his leg was extended at an odd angle from his hip. Simultaneously, he felt horror and dignity for how young the boy was. The woman began silently to cry, the back of her hand at her mouth and he knew it was not so much for the young boy as it was for the little straw he was and the weight he added to her already heavy burden. Her chest caved and her shoulders shook and she wept quietly into her hands. He helped her to sit and stood by her side while the anguish passed through her like a steady racking wind.

"I am sorry," she said, daubing at her wet face and leaving it smudged with graveyard earth.

"He were a drummer boy," he said, bending to take the broken sticks from the boy's hand.

"Dear God," she said. "He was so young."

"Yes ma'am. Just a pony."

"You take his boots," she said, tears filling her eyes again.

"Ma'am?"

"I think you will need his boots."

They buried the drummer boy with the earth of a new grave and when they had completed the mound, he took up the broken drumsticks and slid them into the black dirt.

"That's enough for now," she said.

Then she led him to a stone house that stood nearby, its walls pocked with bullets. From a cistern she took a jar of milk and made him drink from it until his belly ached and then she filled his canteen with fresh water and made him also take a loaf of bread. She continued to apologize to him for reasons he did not understand. There was nothing he could

determine that was her fault, nothing she could possibly have done wrong. She told him with conviction that people should be born twice: once as they are and once as they are not. He did not understand this either, but the way she said it convinced him it was true.

"Someone believes something that's wrong," she said, "and that person gets others to believe it too. And then everybody believes in the same mistake."

He asked her which mistake she was talking about and his question made her voice go cold to him. She told him he could just about take his pick if he wanted and then she warmed again and her voice pitied.

"You be careful," she said, her hand on his shoulder.

"Yes ma'am," he said, relieved that she had recovered herself.

"You will take your father home?"

"I promised my mother."

"A broken promise is worse than a broken bone."

"Yes ma'am."

It threatened to rain again as he made his departure, the dry lightning illuminating the faces of the unburied dead at the cemetery gates. He hastened back to his father to cover him with gum blankets he'd secured. His father was sleeping as a soft, insignificant rain began to fall, and was at peace and only woke when he tucked the blankets to his sides. The coal black horse shook out a muscle in its shoulder and blew. For the horse he'd found a feed bag full of oats and its contents he spilled out on the ground.

"Son," his father said, pleased to see him. "I should say I am feeling a little puny tonight."

His father smiled up at him as he lifted his head so that he might have a sip from the canteen. He tipped the canteen and let the water leak into his father's mouth. He then let his father's head back down to rest on the jacket his mother had sewn.

"The church pews is full of wounded men," he told his father, "and outside the window is a wagon where they toss the arms and legs. They say they've run out of chloroform and sharp saws there's so many. Near twenty thousand."

"Oh, it was a big thing," his father said of the late fought battle. "Biggest thing you ever saw in your life. Some of the boys had to get drunk three times just to get through it."

"There's rows and rows of 'em laying dead," he said, trying to understand what he'd seen.

"When they advance, they are afraid and they want to be close to each other," his father told him. "They want to feel the cloth of the next man, but they need to spread out."

"They need to spread out," he said, repeating the words to himself.

"It was a terrible event," his father said. "It was as if whole brigades disappeared in a cloud of smoke."

"I have a clean bandage."

"Yes. The bandage should be changed. We will rest tonight and in the morning we will go home with a fresh bandage."

He touched at the crust of the bandage wrapped about his father's head. It was black and hard.

"Where was the sun today," his father asked. "Did it not come out from all the clouds?"

"It was sunny all day," he said, and it had been, hot and rainless.

"Not here," his father said, and he could only think it was the coal black horse who had walked the sun from east to west and made a shadow that shaded his father from its rays.

He cradled his father's shoulders in his lap and with a pocketknife he began cutting at the old bandage as gently as he could. The horse stopped its feeding as the bandage came away in chips as if it were tree bark and he could not tell what was skull bone or rotted bandage as it came away in his hands. He looked up to see the horse watching them with what seemed like mild curiosity while it ate.

"There is a law of nature," his father said, "that produces rain or snow after a great battle. It is the same in France and Germany. I knew your mother would endeavor to find me."

"She sent me when General Jackson died."

"I was there," his father said.

"When he were killed?"

"I was there," his father said.

As the bandage came away, so too came more patches of scalp and shards of bone and necrotic tissue. Revealed to him was the black hole bored into his father's cheek.

"That does itch not a little," his father said, fumbling a hand in the direction of his head but then giving up and letting it drop back to the ground. "Maybe another day for us and you will take me home to your mother."

"Yes," he said, and his throat constricted as he held the back of his father's macerated head and felt the maggots falling through his fingers and away into his lap.

His father gave off a convulsing shiver and then sighed and settled again, and it was as if another piece of him had died and departed and there was little hope of recovering it. He worked

quickly, scraping lightly at the wound rot with the knife blade. He then bound the wound with the clean linen he'd bought from the two women earlier that day and lay down beside his father and held his broken and ravaged head.

"Mayhaps, when it gets a little later, you could find a cart and a pony. I would not suggest you steal for they are something we could return."

"I can do that," he said, and he thought, This is my father and I am his son and it brought him a degree of peace.

"Or maybe tomorrow night," his father said. "Another day's recuperation would make me stronger."

"Tomorrow," he said, and thought he might cry for the storm he felt in his face, but he didn't. "Now would be a good time to get you some sleep," he encouraged.

"Soon," his father said.

"Soon," he said.

That night he awoke to the sound of a shot and a man crying out. The night had brought no relief to the day's heat and now a gunshot. He sat up to see the shallow graves in the moonlight giving off a phosphorescent glow. It radiated from the fresh turned earth above the burial pits, and passing through the light of the glow he could see low-running, slab-sided hogs come to root out the dead bodies already inhumed. At the far end of the field of the dying came a scream and a scuffle and a cursing that awakened and traveled the length of the head wounded in a long mimic of moaning sound.

He took up a length of broken sword and went down the row until he came to a soldier propped up on one arm. He was gibbering and pointing in the distance with a revolver. His eyes, his nose, his lips, his face were shredded by shell fragments.

"It is my own leg," the soldier kept saying, again and again.

The soldier waved the barrel in the direction of a nearby feeding hog and he did not understand the full import of that until, plaintively, the soldier explained, it was his very own leg the hog was feeding on and in his mind he knew the leg was no longer attached to his body, but however he tried not to, he could feel the teeth of the gnawing hog.

"I can feel the pain as that hog gnaws at my shin," he cried, pointing the revolver into the darkness.

Beside the soldier was another, lying face upward taking breath in rattling snorts and blowing it out in sputters of froth which slid down his cheeks in a white cream, piling itself along one side of his neck and ear. A bullet had clipped a groove in his skull above his temple. From this opening his brain protruded in bosses dropping off to the ground in flakes and strings. Then he stopped breathing and then and there he was dead.

"Stay here," the soldier said. "Don't leave me. I cannot see."

"They are over there," Robey said, pointing at the hogs' flat shadows crossing in the darkness.

"I am blind," he said.

"My father," he said.

"Stay until I die so as I will not to be eaten alive by that hog. It won't be long now."

He did not want to leave his father's side, but still he took up the sword and for the next hour he guarded the field of the dying. Of all that he might wonder on, he wondered on why the blind soldier was blind.

"Why blind?" he whispered as he walked. "Why blind and still not dead."

He walked the fields length, turned smartly, and then returned to the soldier who'd endured the phantom pain, and after several such circuits he was tired and impatient, so he went into the field where the hogs were rooting and lay down on the surface of the flat wet grass with the sword at his side.

He waited and finally one of the curious beasts came close and nosed at him with its great tusked snout and when it did, he brought the sword up swiftly and skewered it through the neck. The animal screeched, and open-mouthed it lunged at him as he twisted the blade sharply and hot blood flushed from its neck and down his arm and it made no other sound again. He slaughtered it where he killed it, taking what fresh pork he could carry and leaving the rest for its own kind. In the morning he would fry its bacon and fat which had been nourished with the flesh and faces of dead soldiers and he could not but think that when he fed them, he would be returning them unto themselves.

When he returned to the soldier who had endured the phantom pain, he was going to tell him that maybe he was blind because God thought he'd seen enough for one life, but when he arrived at his side he found him to be dead. On his chest was the revolver, a six-shot Remington. It was loaded and he understood that the soldier had left it for him. He also came to understand that he was finally finished with his believing in God.

12

THROUGHOUT THE NIGHT HE was restless and in the early-morning darkness he awoke to the silent movement of women. He sat up and without passage into wakefulness he was alert and saw them wandering from body to body in the field of the dead. They cried into handkerchiefs they'd scented with pennyroyal or peppermint oil. They were stark, tormented creatures with unpinned hair and bent shoulders, wandering in the dawn, kneeling beside bodies, and collapsing to the ground. He wanted to call out to them, to touch them, to be assured that he saw them and was not dreaming them.

He looked to the horse silently standing watch and sketched its face with his own sadness and drew strength from its passive and mannered distance. Surely the horse felt what he felt. Surely the horse knew what he knew. The women were sisters, or mothers, or lovers, he did not know. They wept and stumbled on and he wondered if they truly wanted to find the men they were looking for. He himself had found what he was looking for and wished he hadn't for how slender and proscribed hope was now.

When he awoke again it was in the morning and it was because someone was throwing pebbles at him. When he opened

his eyes it was to see the girl. He knew it was her before he saw her, but still he closed his eyes and opened them again and she was still standing there.

She stood looking at him without moving, her body in black silhouette against the sun, and he shielded his eyes to see her the better. He rolled to his side and could see that she was looking at him queerly. She was wearing a plain black dress with the sleeves cuffed in white lace and he made out she was carrying a drum on her hip. She stood beside the coal black horse and in her black dress was as if she was of the horse, born of the horse, and the thin sliver of yellow light expanding between them was their separation completing itself.

She cocked her head and squinted at him, studying him in her mind. Some part of her knew him, but she was not sure and he felt compelled to tell her in what ways they were acquainted. How their paths had crossed. He was tempted to say, Yes, you know me, but he did not. He returned her look and the guilt of their history must have been written in his face.

"You thought I wouldn't recognize you," she finally said, her lip caught between her teeth. Her words held no accusation, but still he felt accused.

He stood and gathered himself and not knowing what else to do, he began walking away from her, but she followed him to the tree and then her voice was asking to his back, "Who are you?" And then her voice was rising and she was cursing him and saying, "You could have stopped him."

"I could not help," he said, turning to her sad and stricken face. "I had to find my father."

She stood very still, disbelieving him.

He fought for control of the sound in his voice that it not be weak or pleading. He'd done nothing to stop the man and however much he tried to tell himself that he'd not known what to do, the after-knowing, the knowing that follows experience, was burned into him and what he'd thought before was slight and weak and not worth remembering. He could not deny that he'd become bound to this girl that night in the fire-gutted house. He could not deny that it'd been in his power to stop the man.

"And did you?" she said.

"Did I what?"

"Find your father."

She had begun to cry and her tears were strangely wet and glistening as they streaked her dirty face. But she did not raise her hands to wipe them away. She stood in the black dress with the drum on her hip as if she were the one struck with accusation.

"Don't cry," he said, wanting to console her, but his attempt only made her the more angry and he felt as if anything he might say she would think was lame and stupid.

"It ain't me crying," she said. "It's my eyes."

"My pap is under this dying tree," he whispered, and pointed where the coal black horse stood watching them, making its long shadow in the light of the morning sun.

"What's your name," she said.

"Robey."

"Is that so?"

"Yes," he nodded.

"How old are you?"

"Fourteen."

"You have not been broken yet, but you will be and when it happens you will know what it was like for me. What he did to me a animal wouldn't do to another animal."

He wanted to tell her he'd been shot in the head and so had his father. He wanted to tell her he'd already been broken and he lived, but he knew his father would not be so fortunate. It was a thought he'd not yet allowed himself to have and felt something structured that he had depended upon fall apart inside him and it made his eyes burn.

"What's your name?" he said.

"Rachel," she said. "Like in the Genesis."

"How old are you," he said.

"Fifteen."

"People should be born twice," he said.

"I'd rather not be born a'tall," she said bitterly.

"How could he do that," he asked foolishly, and a look crossed her face as if he were the incredible questioner and he prepared himself for another tongue-lashing, but her anger was too great for her to sustain. Her body wavered and he wanted to suggest she sit in the shade and rest, but his mind was made too awkward by her presence and he could not cobble his thoughts into words that made half sense to him.

"He thinks he's above ever'one else," she said. They were words she'd had a long time to think about and decide upon in her struggle to understand. "He talks about turning over a new leaf, but he'll never change, not one bit. He carries snakes in his pocket and throws them at people. He claims he can't be killed."

Speaking the words had the effect of sending her back

inside herself. He wasn't there anymore. It was just her and these words she was fashioning to express the thoughts of her mind that could not explain or escape the memory of what had happened to her.

"Ever'one can be kilt," he said, and he waited for her to say more, but the girl named Rachel was now lost and confused, and however immediate and profound her surroundings she did not seem to know where she was. She lifted a hand and let the palm of it open, and that was the best she could do. He waited as she slowly made her return, looked at him, and sighed.

"We are lodged in that cow barn," she said, and then, "You can see the roof over yonder." She pointed across the hull of the battlefield and he could see the cornice of a roof, its dull surface flaring with muted sunlight.

She told him she wanted him to know.

She then stared in his direction, not focusing on anything, but weighing a thought in her mind. There was a long silence between them that neither felt the urge to break.

Then she told him she was tired and she needed to rest and turned and walked away.

THIS DAY BROUGHT MORE of the scavengers and more of the relatives and citizens and now there were the tourists arriving by train to be added to their numbers. The air was bone dry and the heat of that July day was relentless beneath a high blinding sun, and soon after their arrival they became a vomiting lot, fainting and puking on the ground beside the dead.

He walked among them with a shovel over one shoulder and canteen straps slung over the other, the hollow sound of

the knocking canteens reminding him of his day's obligations. He wore the revolver tucked in the back of his trousers hidden behind his coattail and a knife in his new boots. He watched them as they went down on all fours like dogs and heaved their guts until their insides were empty and there was nothing more to heave. Then he'd move on, finding it increasingly difficult to extend sympathy or pity.

One old gentleman he encountered, wearing a sombrero hat and a short sleeveless cloak, was sitting on a large tricycle inside a circle of the dead and unburied and for no reason he stopped.

"Are you looking for anyone in particular, sir?" he asked.

"Thank God no," the old man said, "but please give to me a shovel and I will help you with this terrible work for it is awful and shameful. There is no one here to cover these poor boys with even leaves."

"They's grave diggers working," he assured the old man. "They'll be along shortly."

"The very birds would do that much for them if I did nothing and left them lying here so."

He felt no patience for the distress this old man was experiencing, so he gave him the shovel and walked on, securing another not far away. He too had been innocent. He too had believed.

Today as he walked, there was a second landmark that kept him oriented. The first had been the comb of trees where his father lay dying at the feet of the horse and now there was the cow barn where the girl named Rachel was lodged, the cornice of its roof, its dull surface. He thought of her there, still with the man and the woman. He trusted they would meet

again, trusted their lives had crossed for reasons he did not yet understand. The thought seemed natural to him. He would see her again because he'd seen her before.

As the heat persisted, finding water to drink for the coal black horse and the men in the field of the dying had become a chore. When it rained the first night he had been able to collect rain water in gum blankets, but it had not rained in a while. He knew of a well where the owner had removed the crank handle to those who would use it except for those willing to pay a high fee and that morning he had worked up his resolve to shoot the man if he would not give up the handle to his well. So hot was the weather. So thirsty were the dying men.

By the time he arrived to do the deed, a provost marshal was there and had taken the handle from the well's owner. He was spinning it in his hand as he threatened him with arrest. However, if he should choose, he could file a claim and the federal government would pay him for use of his water. The provost then returned the handle to the well and posted an armed guard while the owner went to file the necessary papers for reimbursement. Robey was first to fill his canteens at the well and returned to his father who had not spoken since the night before.

"ALL ABOUT US," he said to his father with wonder, "there are niggers burying the officers."

"They followed them into battle," his father said.

"They cry a good bit. Some are old and some are young, but they all seem to cry a good bit."

Robey tipped the canteen and water ran into his father's

open mouth until he choked and it blew from his eyes and nose. His body was stiffened with an arrested fit of coughing and then he composed himself. He daubed at the beads of wetness on his father's face and neck and emerging from the corner of his eye and then let him drink again.

"Which ones cry the most," his father asked.

"I would say it were about even."

"When someone dies that you love it is a very hard thing. They were like brothers to those men who died to keep them in bondage. Who can figure out such a kinship?"

"I asked of one fellow, 'Where are you going, walking in that direction?' I reckoned the direction he was going to be south when he could have just as easily have walked north."

"What did he say?"

"He told me he had to go back home to where he lived. I asked him why and he said, 'I have to tell them what has happened here. I have to tell his momma.' So I gave him some bread I had and he told me his name were Moses. He seemed like a good enough fellow."

"He was a slave."

"He said he were slave of a captain, mortally wounded and not yet twenty-two year old. He buried him under an apple tree over there. He told me after the war he would come back and get him. 'Why would you do that?' I asked him."

"What did he say?"

"He said to me his momma will want me to."

"You have never seen such gruesome sights and you so young," his father said, and made a rattling cough.

He took his father's hand in his own and held it tightly to steady him and could still feel the strength in his father's

returning grasp. He didn't tell his father what he'd seen on the road, the sight of the shackled slaves rounded up and herded south like cattle, the slave hunters in their garish dress, their plumes and cold-blooded horses, their hooves scuttling like crabs in the dust, the coiled whips lashed to their saddles.

"I helped some fellows today and they gave me a handful of coins."

"What for?"

"Over in the place with the big rocks. They were taking picture-photos of the dead and asked if I would help them and so I did."

"What'd you do?"

"I helped carry them where they wanted them to be for their picture-photos to be taken."

"It was good of you to help," his father said, but was so tired he knew their conversation was ending for now.

"I caught sight of those scavengers again. They'll surely come to no good if they keep going."

"You stay clear of them," his father warned, and the strength of his grasp made him know how strong he felt his imperative and he returned the grasp, strength for strength. They held like that until his father's grasp weakened and released.

Then his father said his name and then said to him, "Do you think you can make that kind of decision?"

His words were as if a veil had been lifted on the moment. Their lives were in balance and asking and considering this question they were stepping back from fear and hopelessness and emerging into prospect. They were a teaching father and a learning son, timeless in their existence, the father born into the son as is the grandfather and the father before him and

all the way back to the first. The father's life is foreclosed and the son's life is continuing and as always, only the unknown privileging one state of being over the other.

"I don't know what to do," he said. "I feel like I have to do something."

"You've got to ration it out in your mind," his father said. "I will not be there to help you."

"Yes sir," he said. He then gently rolled his father onto his side and he added more letters from the dead at Gettysburg to thicken his father's mattress.

13

HILE HIS FATHER SLEPT, he could not help but be drawn to where he anticipated the scavengers' next foray among the dead and dying soldiers. It was a place he knew well with a curious array of round boulders wedged beneath a ridge with a stream falling from a saddle and passing through to course the orchard fields. It was the place where he helped the photographer position the bodies and set their rifles to their shoulders as if just shot.

He slipped away and it was this deep rocky place he went to, far distant from the town where the hospitals had been sited. The ground there was gullied and barren, and the fitted boulders seemed tumbled into place and seated in the earth at improbable angles. Some were strewn and others were cropping from the earth and others of the boulders could not be understood for how they came to be there. For days the stream had run red through that place and still it was not clean, but brown and murky.

The ground there was too difficult for burial, too distant from the hospital tents, and besides, the dead in that place were from the South and so they still lay out on the field of battle where they'd fallen. The few yet living were gathered on a scattering of straw under a canopy and were tended by

kind women and their children who came out from the town during the light of day and went back home in the evening before dark.

With all stealth he moved on to this place and stood high over it in the shadow of a boulder. He could not sort the scavengers from the boulders and the black trees. White vapors that rose from the earth drifted the land in slow tatters.

He moved slowly, ten paces at a time, and then waited and listened. He moved forward again and listened and then heard a high faint wailing cry he at first mistook for a night bird, but it was not. He glimpsed a light and went down flat in that dense place on the duff of the forest floor. As he did, another light that came from behind him swept the ground where he'd stood and pointed into a ravine before descending. He watched the light dodging in accordance with the gait of a running man who carried it and remembered the lay of terrain as it was momentarily sketched in light before it went to dark again in the trees.

The moving light went down into the deep ravine and converged with a second light.

"What the hell," an angry voice panted.

"What's the matter?"

"The bullet-hit son of a bitch bit me in the hand."

"Well, whack him. One good rap to the back of his head and he'll be dead as a doornail."

There was a pause and then he could hear the dull thud and crack of a flat object striking what he took to be head bone. He slowly crawled into the place where they were and suddenly he was on the periphery of the intersecting lights that came from the scavengers' heads and pooled on a fallen officer crumpled at their feet.

"Did you kill him?" the one said.

"How the hell do I know?" the other one said, holding a hatchet in one hand and nursing the side of his other hand.

"What's the matter with you?"

"I tol' you the son of a bitch bit me."

"Get it done, god damn it," the one side. "We have got to get out of here."

"I will do as I damn well please."

The one leaned over and poked at the officer laying at his feet. He hooked his fingers in the officer's nostrils and drew back his head until his mouth gaped open and filled with the yellow light that came from the head lamp. He then let go and the officer closed and groaned.

"Well," the one said, "I shall be very happy if you'd please get that gold plate out of his mouth."

The other one took the hatchet to the mouth of the officer for the sake of the gold plate it contained and to which a set of false teeth was attached. He raised it over his head and then it flashed down through the yellow light. With a single chop, he sliced through the side walls of the officer's mouth, separating the mandible from the maxilla and leaving the officer's mouth a gaping and bloody maw.

"He's a rascal, that one."

"I'd like to see him bite someone now," the one said.

"He will not bite again," the other said. He then reached down and drew a straight razor under the officer's mangled jaw and cut his throat. His razor hand dallied in the sully of gurgling blood and when it came to light it held the dripping gold plate.

He followed the two scavengers that night as they contin-

ued their bloody work and continued to follow them as they took what they'd stolen back to a redbrick house a half mile from the battlefield. It was no bigger than a one-room cottage, built of stone and roofed with tin. The doors and windows were missing. and the north side collapsed into rubble.

From outside the small house, they entered into a small shallow cellar, no more than four feet high, and from under the floor came a light and he could soon hear the wheeze of a bellows. He did not think to leave off. He did not ponder his father's question, could he make that kind of decision? He had no choice, but thoughts such as these never entered his mind. It was as if what he was doing had already been decided for him and to not question them was part of that decision.

The dim yellow light built beneath the floor and began to glow from the cracks in the foundation. He found an opening where the sill had rotted and closed in on it, crawling to the light on hands and knees. When he lay flat on his belly he could see into the cellar and he could see them and when he did, a nameless emotion passed through him. It was the mere wisp of a feeling and he was galvanized by it.

They sat cross-legged on a dirt floor, a light between them, as men have for thousands of years, but this light was a small forge and it heated a crucible and into the crucible they were feeding, one by one, the gold teeth and the wedding bands and the gold plate just taken from the mouth of the murdered officer. One after another they emptied their pockets of the gold tokens, sentiments, declarations, intentions, and cures they'd scavenged.

"I don't like killing," the one said, working the hand bellows. "But what else can you do?"

"It is done," the other said. "In the morning we will follow the army when it moves south. I've had my fill of this place. The smell of it could bend nails."

Robey studied them for a long time through the foundation wall and he was not appalled but intrigued by their methods. Behind him a horse snorted, and startled, he rolled away and reached for his revolver. Back in the trees was hobbled a long-legged roan and a second horse stood beside it, a white-faced chestnut tearing at leaves.

Down below, the men were not concerned as they'd not heard the anxious horse. They unstoppered a liquor bottle and passed it back and forth and smoked cigars, and when the metal was molten the one took up iron tongs and lifted the tiny crucible while the other pushed a sandbox forward, its insides just big enough to hold a deck of playing cards. The one with the tongs poured off the liquid metal and it formed a rectangular light more lustrous than the sun, more lustrous than any light he'd ever seen before.

The two continued their drinking and smoking their cigars while the yellow light cooled, but his mind never seemed to lose the memory of how brilliantly it glowed. With their bloody hands, they flicked at the dirt on their trousers, inspected their buttons, and straightened their lapels. He concluded their work was done for this evening.

"I say we go to Harrisburg tonight and take the train back to Philadelphia," the one said. "I say we got enough and we can't be hogs about it."

"Why not?" the other said. "Hogs get fat."

"Pigs get fat; hogs get slaughtered."

"I stand corrected."

In the light of the cooling forge and the hardening metal,

he could see the one to be a lynx-eyed man, the skin of his face scarred and pitted as if by fire or explosion. His ears were truncated and actually appeared to have been cropped. The other took up a hot glowing ember with the tongs, leaned into it, and lit another cigar.

"They are backed up on the Potomac as we speak," the other said.

"Why are they there?" the one asked. "That ain't very smart."

"The river is too high for them to cross," the other said. He savored his cigar, rolling it in his fingertips, dipping the mouth end into the liquor bottle and sucking on it.

"That could be the end?"

"That is why we are not going to Philadelphia."

"I believe we should saddle the horses," the one said, "and get out of here this very night."

"I believe," the other said, "I will saddle the horses and I will be pointing them south. We aren't done yet by a long shot. There will be another battle at the river and we are going to be there when it is over."

The other one then stood and brushed his hands over the seat of his pants. He made his way up the incline in a scramble of rubble and disappeared into the thicket where the horses were hobbled.

Robey watched the one still sitting in the cellar, paring his nails with a penknife. He drew the revolver and cocked it, folding his body over the hammer to muffle the mechanical sound. He held it with the barrel straight up and could not recall how it was so very heavy to hold.

He then worked his way along the side of the stone foundation to where he could see the other one saddling the horses and feeding bits into their mouths. One of the animals

suddenly tossed its head in the air. The man stepped back and cursed it and when it had quieted he punched it in the side, causing it to squat and then tremble and tread on the ground where it stood.

His work finished, the other man came back to the red-brick house. He spat in the dirt and took a step down into the cellar, ducking his head low. When his body filled the opening, closing off the light within, Robey stepped up beside him. He steadied the revolver on the bridge of his forearm, placed the tapered octagonal barrel at the man's ear, and pulled the trigger. The lead bullet traveled in an instant through his brain behind his eyes and left the vault of his head out his opposite ear. He collapsed and tumbled forward with the gun's explosion to sprawl across the legs of the one still sitting on the dirt floor.

The light below ground went out with a flare as he stepped back from the opening and cocked the revolver again. Then there was a long silence and he could hear the hissing embers, could hear his own breathing. He and the one still alive both knew there was no way out of that cellar except through the opening he now covered.

He waited, holding himself close to the stone of the foundation. If someone had heard the shot and came to investigate, he'd have time to slip away into the darkness, but it wasn't likely. Shots in the night in those fields were not uncommon occurrences. Nightly, there would be the lone banshee wails of a crazed echoing across the fields, then a shot, whether accidental or intentional, self-inflicted or inflicted on another, and then there would be silence again. Then another shot without preface or consequence, the fields armed and that dangerous. War still not satisfied. War still lurking.

"Who are you?" came the voice of the one from the black cellar. Acrid smoke from the smothered fire was beginning to wind in the air aboveground and mingle with the burned powder charge.

"Nobody you know," he said.

There was another long silence. The smell of burned hair came to his nostrils. Soon enough he'd know if someone was riding out to investigate the shot, but he doubted it.

"What do you want?" the one asked.

"I don't know yet. I just killed a man."

"You killed him all right."

"I was hoping to kill him," he said. He felt no knocking in his body nor in his chest or head or legs. His arms had not weakened but felt stronger and his resolve fastened.

"Well, that you did," the one said.

"He's dead, isn't he?"

"He couldn't get deader."

"It weren't hard to do."

"No. I'd say you have a regular talent."

He scanned the black line of the horizon for moving lights. He listened for the sound of horsemen. He could detect neither. Down below the ground there was only quiet.

"What's your name?"

"None of your business."

"Tell me your name, friend. Everyone's got a name."

"I don't want your mouth on my name."

"You've got mustard, I'll say that."

Again was the overwhelming silence. It held in the air as if the draping darkness was knit with yarns of glass.

"Parley?"

"What have you got?"

"I got a sack of gold down here hid up in the wall. Silver too. Do you want it? It's yours if you want it, friend."

"I hadn't really thought in that direction."

"Anyone hear that shot, the provost will come."

"If he does, I don't believe I will be the one they ketch."

"I have an idea."

"What?"

"I will throw you up these sacks."

"Suit yourself."

The sacks came up out of the darkness and fell to the ground where he could see their black shapes in the moonlight. He moved to retrieve them and when he did the scavenger in the cellar shot. The bullet missed him wide and he returned to the wall with the heavy sacks.

"Did I hit you?"

"No."

"I had to try."

"I 'spect that."

"I am sorry to've tried, but he was my brother."

"I didn't mean to kill no one's brother."

"Ah, he didn't know enough to come in out of the rain."

"He was a very bad fellow."

"Oh, he was all right, but you know what?"

"What?"

"You just can't polish a turd." The scavenger had a laugh at his own joke and then he said, "What are we to do now?"

"I think I am going to take your horses now and slip away from here."

"I appreciate that."

"I don't need your 'preciation."

"Then I will wait to come out if you do not mind."

"Suit yourself."

"Hey, boy. What if, say, that you just lay back there in the dark and shoot me when I come out?"

"I did not think of that."

"Boy?"

14

HEN HE RETURNED to his father's dying side, the coal black horse was restless and scolding. He muzzled it with his hands and it tossed its head and streamed slobber in the air when it smelled the scavengers' horses on him. He'd sold the roan and the chestnut to the man who owned the well. He woke him from his bed and told him it was best to send them upcountry for their health and the man understood and bought them without asking any questions.

He gentled the coal black horse and then he lay down on the warm ground with his head on his father's shoulder. He felt his father's arm lift and and his fingers fumbling until he hooked them to his belt. He lay quietly with his arm across his father's chest and his father's arm holding him. He felt the rise and fall of his father's breathing and he wished that sleep would overtake him and painlessly carry him from that place. He now knew that when he left, his father would remain.

He wondered would he remember all that he was experiencing. Would he remember these offenses he was committing, these days on the road, his search for his father. Memories as terrible and horrible as these would make it all the more

important to forget them if he could, forget the names and faces, the land and the objects upon the land, forget everything he had learned of what there was to know about war.

"Where have you been," his father asked, without turning his head. He thought his father had found sleep, but he hadn't.

"To fetch a pony and cart," he lied.

His father gave off a cough that rattled from deep in his throat. There was an unmistakable smell to him and when he opened his eyes they were filled with vision and urgency and his breathing was elevated. Robey unwrapped himself from his holding arm and took his father into his arms.

"You have to know, son. What happened here was not enmity or brutality."

"Yes sir," he said. "I know. Rest now."

"This was not the raving mad. This was not for love or greed or ignorance. These are the well bred and the highly educated. This is humanity. This is mankind, son."

"Yes sir," he said, but he wondered, what about himself. Would he be able to face up to what he had done? Had his own actions not arisen from pride and righteousness?

"This is the nature of man and this is the world and if you are to live in it, you need to know what you have to do."

"Yes sir," he said, and he thought, Let the past go. Let it go. He thought, Be the judge inside your own mind and not let anyone else do that work. Determine for yourself because either side will kill you and those without a side will kill you and the women and children will kill you—all the instruments of war—and he had killed and he knew he would kill again without pause or hesitation or even thinking he had to

before he did. In his bones he felt his lessons and once learned they would never be forgotten. They were lessons that could never be talked away or thought away. They were lessons as old as the history of the sun.

"You have to do what I think you did tonight," his father said.

"I know, sir."

"You know that I will not be leaving here when you go."

"I know."

"When you go, you are to travel south. Find Moxley and Yandell and Tom Allen and Little Sandy. They are with the battery on the Potomac, for the water will be too high to ford. They'll take you in. They will teach you. They'll take care of you. Tell them you are me. Say you are me."

"I am you," he said.

"It is so cold," his father said, and these were the first words he'd spoken that conveyed his pain and despair. "I don't believe I have ever been this cold before and I have been cold before."

He gathered his father into his arms and held him. His father's head was a great putrid mess against his chest. He held on to him, and as he did he cared little for all that had happened and cared not at all for what might come in the hours and days yet to be. They were here and alive together no matter how short the time, no matter how fast the moment that was approaching, and when it arrived it would be less than an instant.

He held his father through the night and his father, already weak and frail, lost ground as the night bore on, but he did not let go his hold on him, as if it were possible that his hold-

ing could stave off the certainty of death. His father shivered and his body was cool to the touch and dry about the face and eyes. His father whispered something and he asked him please say it again and leaned in to hear better his voice.

"Where did you go tonight?" his father asked, his voice clear and strong again, as if recovery were a possibility.

"To find a pony and a cart to take you home."

"That's a good son, but I say I don't think I'll be leaving this field."

"I know."

"I think this is the last day of my life," he said, and then he made the abrupt sound of laughter halted. "Your mother won't like this one single bit. You'll have to tell her the news because I won't be able to."

He then clutched at his son's sleeve as he was seized by a great paroxysm that ran through his body more than once before leaving him alone. His breathing rasped and stopped and then it started again and he sighed. A heavy dew had fallen and the wetted field that stretched out before them beneath the moon was so like a wide path of white jewels on blue velvet.

"Oh," his father said, as if he were quietly relieved of another piece of his mortality.

He held his father's head in his lap with an arm across his chest. His father clutched that arm and would not let go his grasp. He felt his father's fingers curl and a strength transmitted.

"I am very tired," he said, and then another convulsion swept through his body, lifting him into the air as if a man fighting inside his dreams and then he was quiet again.

"It is time," he finally said.

"No sir. I don't think it is time yet."

"It is."

"No."

"It will be today."

"Not today, sir. Please."

"We will meet again in the old fields," his father said in his shallow fast breathing.

He knew his father's time was at hand, for he was assuredly on the path of the dying. He now knew everything died sooner or later and knew life meant little. He knew everything that was had been before. He knew the lives of men were mere and fragile wisps regardless of action, declaration, and self-opinion. He knew the earth was angry and evil was as alive as any man or woman. He knew life meant little to him, but this was his father's life.

"I am passing myself into you," his father said, "and you are already an old man." And then he said, "I will be coming."

However strange the metamorphosis of the son receiving the father into himself and in turn the son becoming the father, it was substantial and whole and he could feel it inside himself. He could feel it fastening its hold as the words were spoken. Then it was over and he was no longer a boy because his father was dead.

That night, when he cut a lock of his father's hair, he felt strangely calm and the reason was because he'd experienced the horror that left one so. When the experience began, he could not say. Was it a week ago or a month ago? How long he would be haunted by shadowy sadness he did not know. He wondered who could explain a world where human words

and human bonds and human thoughts had so profoundly failed. He had the feeling of an inexorable tide rising up inside him. His eyes had seen so much death so near to him. He had the feeling he'd been just a hollow, hungry, empty boy held on the mountain waiting and waiting until the call came, until it was his turn to become one of these failed humans. But in the cradle of the mountain he'd never felt hollow or hungry or empty. He did not understand it, but he knew he was no longer afraid of death. He knew he no longer felt the half of something but felt whole and finished in his making.

15

E WATCHED AS THE MOON slid into the woods. His father's grave lay beside him. In the last hours he'd wrapped his father in a gum blanket, folded its ends and bound them with twine. He then dug a deep grave, carried his father to its opening, and eased him inside, and around him he placed the sacks of gold and silver, the letters from the dead. He then returned the earth and replaced the sod and broadcast a scattering of twigs and branches that no one should ever find him until someday he might return and take him home.

Done with his work, he saddled and bridled the coal back horse and gathered his kit. He calculated he had but a few hours before sunrise cracked the horizon with its red. There would be heated air and a dense fog that would not burn off until late morning. That was if this day was like the day before it and when it came to weather, he reckoned it usually was.

He walked alone with the coal black horse across the open ground, its size and strength and equanimity becoming his own. He passed the ever-lengthening earthen mounds that had swept over the dead and swallowed them under. He remembered where the bodies lay, the thrown-over, the back-arched, the headless, the drowned, the sundered, the men held

tightly in each other's arms. He did not care that war should be so terrible. He'd had no choice and still he had chosen it. In one hand he held the reins and in the other he carried the capped and loaded six-shot Remington. It was his hand. It was his arm. Should he meet anyone this morning, he knew what he would do.

The cow barn was where she told him she would be. There was no stock, but there was oats and oat hay and straw, and implements were strewn about the ground. The walls had been shot through and at first the bullet holes were not apparent to him as in the darkness they were so like black knots in the rough pine boards. He picked his way through the rubbish and litter, scattered tools, milk cans, stools, buckets, harness, barrels, a dung cart, torn and broken and shattered, the hot sheen of a small dying campfire.

He found the man. He was in one of the stalls sleeping the sleep of the dead. His body was gray and slumped and his mouth sagged open with great exhausts of air and the guttural noise of his breathing. His broad chest moved slowly up and down, lifting the blanket that covered him and the stems of straw he'd tossed over himself in finding his sleepful repose.

He shook out an armful of feed for the horse and then a scoop of oats. The horse had become impatient and ready for flight. It had indulged him long enough. He promised soon and went back to the barn wall where he made his way along its splintered surface.

In the next stall was the blind woman. Her size had increased evermore since last he'd seen her. She lay on her side, her vast belly in front of her and her arms and head and legs

made small by how huge with her belly she had become. Her face was misshapen and bespoke a grave and internal malady. What did the blind see in their sleep, he wondered. He remembered feeling kindly toward the woman before and even after what he'd witnessed in the shell of the burned-out house so many weeks ago, but now she was just another being in the shape of a human. She meant nothing to him and he knew if he allowed himself she would mean less than nothing.

He moved on and when the shadows shifted he could see her. She was in a last keyhole of moonlight that entered through a rent seam in the board wall. She lay under a blanket in a bed of straw in an empty stall. Her loose hair fell ragged across her bare arm. He patiently watched her sleep, waiting for her to awake and look in his direction.

Sensing a presence and still in sleep, she finally did stir and sat up and opened her eyes, the spears of moonlight cutting across her bare neck. She raised a hand that held a knife and slowly it turned with her wrist as if it were the knife turning her wrist and not her arm. She concentrated on the faint sensation that had awakened her. She knew something was outside the wall and close beside it in the darkness, and if it should come inside she would fight it to the death.

He watched her stand, a thin sliver of a girl in a dingy shift. Her hair fell past her shoulders and she held her crossed arms to her chest as if cold, the effect of which was to make the knife seem as if its blade was not attached to a handle but was a blade protruding from her body. She stared at the wall he was looking through but did not seem to understand that someone was actually on the other side. She stood erect and pulled her blanket over her shoulders. She stepped into the

alleyway and after looking at the sleepers in their stalls she went outside where he met her and she was not startled to see him there but rather was as if she expected him. She let the knife slip from her hand, stepped close to him, and when she leaned in to whisper he could feel her warm sleeping breath on his face.

"You were watching me sleep," she said.

"Yes, I was."

"I felt you," she said, her eyes moving over his face, searching out what was wrong, as surely she knew something was.

"Me?"

"Yes. I felt you. I have been waiting for you."

"You knew I would come?"

"Why the long face?" she said, and then touched her fingers to her lips. Over his shoulder she could see the coal black horse and it was then she knew what it was that had brought him to her.

"My face ain't long," he said.

"I know why you came."

"Were you sleeping?" he said.

"I wouldn't call it sleep."

"My pap died," he said.

"I am sorry to hear of your loss," she said, and then she held open the blanket for him to walk into and he did so, without hesitation, and she closed the blanket and her arms around his shoulders. He let his face to her neck, let himself be held inside the blanket, let his body rest against hers. She smelled stale with sleep and sweat and days without bath water. She told him that everything dies and then, in time, it comes back. He felt her breath warm on his neck. Over their

heads was the last slow wheel of the stars. Morning was only a few hours away and he had the sense it was a first morning, the morning of a beginning.

"He's not in this world no more," she said as if it were a relief and a blessing visited upon him.

"No," he said. "He ain't."

"Are you leaving?" she said.

In answer he nodded his head, his cheek to her neck.

"Take me with you," she said. "I have to leave too."

"Yes," he said.

Her arms tightened around his shoulders and he responded by drawing her body more closely to his own. He was here and he was leaving and he would take her with him. She asked that he wait a moment and when she returned she told him the man was asleep drunk. She then found for him a sweet potato buried in the ashes of the campfire. The skin was blackened and crisp, but inside the flesh was orange and still hot and steamed when he broke it open. Overcome with hunger, he could not help himself as he wolfed it down.

"Stay where you are," she said, pointing at him with her finger as if to fix him to the spot where he stood. When she returned this time she carried whatever kit she owned in a carpetbag and a small tight bundle of clothes tucked under her arm. She set these on the ground and then she held out a pair of scissors. He took the scissors from her, and when he did she bent at the waist, collected her hair in her hands, and held it from her scalp, telling him he should cut it away from her head.

The scissors were sharp. He cut through her hair and she threw it away and then prepared another skein for him to cut

and he cut that one too. Then she stood and he worked his way around, cutting her hair until it was short and tight to her head. She ran her fingers through her scalp and told him it was good enough for now.

Then, standing with her back to him, she let the blanket fall and shed the dingy shift from her shoulders. Underneath the shift she was naked and the white skin of her body was blue in the night. Her body was thin and lithe and built with narrow hips. The bones in her long back were well defined, her shoulders, her ribs, the sunken shapes of her hind end, and there was a space between her legs made by how thinned and sticklike they were and he thought how much better he'd fared with his foraging than she had. But she moved with strength and sureness and without a single wasted gesture.

She wanted to leave as quickly as possible, she told him, and she intended to do just that.

She unrolled the bundle at her feet and it was a pair of boy's trousers wrapped around a linen shirt and a moleskin jacket. There was a wide leather belt and socks and shoes and a forage cap. Before she dressed in the clothes she turned to look at him, her hands on her hips. There was a boldness in her stance, her telling him to take his look if he was going to. It was as if she were challenging him with her body, as if she was asking unspoken questions: What will you do with me? How will you be?

He answered her when he did not move and did not look away. He then looked away to the east where the sun would soon rise and then to the horse which pawed the ground and then back at her as if to say, time is wasting and hurry with yourself and we need to get down the road.

When he turned his look a second time in her direction she was pulling the trousers onto her hips and cinching them with the belt. She was telling him she would from now on not be Rachel to him but a boy just like he was and if it came down to it she was his brother. She would be Ray. It's what her mother used to call her. At least it's what she remembered. Then the shirt and the jacket. With the prospect of escape and her decision made, she now could not move fast enough. She could not stop talking. She insisted that he understand how important this was and he told her he did. He told her he understood.

She sat on the ground and dragged the socks and then the shoes onto her feet and it was when she was tying the laces there was a rustling inside the cow barn and a groan and the man came stumbling out. He was so desperate to relieve himself he did not see them until he'd unbuttoned himself and his piss was steaming on the ground.

"Pay no attention to me," he said, as if he found the moment amusing.

He then finished his business and buttoned up after wagging himself dry. He approached the girl and when he reached to touch her clipped head she swatted at his hand and backed away from him.

"What happened to your goldilocks?" he said, pretending a posture of meticulousness and refinement, his hand still raised. "You know you don't sell for what you're worth unless you look good."

Rachel seemed paralyzed by him, her words stolen from her mind, her determination vanished. He felt it himself, the honeyed voice and created gestures. The man's size ran to

proportion that was beyond his physical being. He asserted himself into the world, as if he should possess other human beings and they should willingly submit to him. Somewhere a cock began to crow and the light changed as if a first curtain had been drawn open on the day to come.

"We have to go," Robey said. He'd already drawn the Remington from his belt and the angle at which he held it, though not pointing at the man, declared his intention to use it.

"Who the hell are you?"

"None of your damn business," he said. He wanted to tell the man who he was and what he'd seen and what he'd endured and what he'd lost, but he had no reason to be known by him, to be known by anyone.

"But you are going?" the man said to the girl, his voice demonstrating how incredible he thought the idea.

"We're going," Robey told him.

"I will come for her," he said. "You know that."

"It's a big country."

"It ain't that big."

"No, I 'spect it ain't."

"Then take the horse," the man said to her as if he were that generous.

"I don't want your god damn horse," the girl spat out.

"That isn't Christian," the man said.

"You shut up your god damn mouth, you old blister." She held her hands over her ears. She hated him. She did not want to hear what he had to say. "You sinned against my flesh," she cried.

"Rachel," he said, her name in a voice sweet as the vine.

"He wears a money belt of stol'd money," she said, her eyes

closed and her hands still clapped to the sides of her head. "Get it."

"Where is it?" Robey said.

"Don't be a dunce," she told him. "It's around his waist."

"I will find you," the man said. "You know I will find you."

"Shut your hole," she said, and this turned him mean as he understood his hold on her was breaking.

"You will rue this day as long as you live," he told her. "When I find you, you will regret you ever treated me this way."

"You did this to me," she said, "and what did I do to deserve this. You are the one who'll pay in hell."

The man suddenly went down on his knees in a stylish and practiced gesture. He closed his eyes and clasped his hands to his breast as if in prayer and his pursed lips began to pulse as if his silent prayer was so profound it required release. She paused in her anger for how dramatic an effect this had on her.

"Please forgive me," he said to her, and then he let his prayers be aloud and they came in a torrent, rote and passionately, about the sins of men and the frailties of human flesh.

She told him to stop, to please stop and then to stop his jabbering, but his fervor increased as he struggled to reach dominion over her mind.

"Don't do that," she cried, and kicked at him. "God damn you," she screamed. "I hate you."

Robey stood witness to them in their opposite struggles, the crying girl who sought escape and the cruel praying man who had harmed her. He knew the scene had been played before in tents and sheds and under the bowers of trees. He could see the past, the power and belligerence of the man's

imprecations. He could see them wearing down the girl and turning her against herself and making her forget her own experience at his very hands and hostile to her own wishes.

She stamped the ground and cried that he should shut his praying mouth and should kill himself to death for all he'd done in life. His words continued on, penetrating the air with their ferocity, and were so like falling wood and she screamed at him to stop, but he wouldn't stop. A moan came from deep inside the barn. The woman had awakened in darkness and was calling out for someone to help her.

"Make him stop," she told Robey. "Put him through," she said, and grabbed for the Remington he held, but he would not let her have it. He'd stood by and watched this man harm her and he had done nothing when he could have. It was not so much that he felt guilt for not acting that night in the fire-gutted house. He was different then and now he was changed. Then he was a boy, and he thought like a boy. He angered and hated, but he thought the world still had a chance. He thought they all had a chance. Perhaps somewhere inside him he knew his fate and that night in the fire-gutted house it was not time yet for him to leave his past and enter his future, but only the damned can see their future and know nothing of their present.

No matter. He had already made his decision. What was another man like this man to him? The praying man wanted her forgiveness. It may have been true. But sometimes you have to revenge before you can forgive. Familiar to his ears was how loud and certain the mechanical sound at his thigh when he thumbed the hammer on the Remington. If the praying man heard the same sound, his voice did not betray him.

He raised his hand to sight the barrel with the praying man's

forehead and was to pull the trigger when the girl dashed in between them. With both her hands, she raised a long-handled implement above her right shoulder. At its highest reach she did not stop but drove it down with all her might and as hard as she could, and in that instant the three thin tines of a pitchfork pierced into the praying man's kneeling lap.

They were like fangs the way they entered into him. They were a sharp curving blink that found no bone in their sharp passage. They stopped his praying and opened his eyes with burning pain. His lap was suddenly on fire. She jumped her weight at the handle and drove it again and it was this second effort that overcame the silence of shock and delivered to the heavens the screams of the well stabbed.

He let down the hammer of the Remington, belted it, and pulled her away by her shaking shoulders. She fought him because she wanted to jump the fork a third time and send it deeper, even though deeper was not a possibility.

So much killing and so much violence. So much malice and fraud. He saw them. He saw her. He saw the praying man and he saw himself. How to explain the way violence needs violence? Is that the explanation itself? Violence demands violence. This was not the pagan retribution: an eye for an eye, a tooth for a tooth. This was the law before there was law. This was vengeance and a rebellion to law. How to explain the failure to understand this and the failure to not understand there are things that cannot be understood?

He knew in the end there were no answers. There was no illumination. The world was chance and was not revealed to us, but it revealed us to ourselves, our fragments of idea, our false memory. There was neither vision nor wisdom to be

discovered. We only became more seeing and less ignorant. Sin could not be washed away and minds do not heal except for the guilty and the foolish. Our confessions become our weakness and our wisdom our vanity and both our harmful fantasies. He looked at the praying man and knew one thing: we have chosen ourselves to be the chosen.

He thought his father's words and then he thought about the girl as she struggled in his arms to reach the handle and drive it again. He feared she would not return from where she had just been. He had thought that maybe she had a different way of looking at the world whereas he had none that he knew of anymore and just maybe she was a way back for him, but now he did not know. He only knew he could not let her kill the man any more than she already had. As he held her, he held the moment of life in his hands, his own life.

He looked to the praying man and he appeared to still be doing so. His hands were raised in supplication and his mouth gaped and tears streamed down his straining face. He fought movement for how consuming the pain that had discovered him, but his body could not endure the pain and wanted to reject its source and so the handle of the pitchfork quivered in the air as his body tried to tremble it out.

Robey pulled the girl away from the man to the side of the coal black horse. He took her foot and placed it in the stirrup and then with both hands he heaved her into the saddle. He began to walk and the coal black horse followed him.

THEY TRAVELED SOUTH on the coal black horse, leaving that place of the dead. He could feel her body slumped against his back, her arms clasped around his waist. When they were

chased, she rapped on his head with her knuckles and he turned an ear to her speaking lips. She told him to ride into the fog, but the horse already knew to do so and was already disappearing inside a vast gray cloud come to earth.

On that ride to the river, all time was present time. There was no past and there was no future. They were beginning in their flight and rode the coal black horse hard like a fleeing deer. They might this time leave the earth, he thought. They might ride through the sky. They might ride forever until it was all behind them, until it was over.

What he remembered was the silence of that leaving and it was a very complete silence. He sensed that those men who offered blood and presented blood and threw blood were not ravaged by war, but for all the dirt and black powder and slick of blood they had been prepared by war, prepared for their irrevocable and irreversible deaths. The wounds were horrible enough, but only of a kind. They had their faces or did not by increasing degree until there were men with no faces at all and in the end it was remarkable to him how little there was that can be done to a man once all that can be done has been done to him.

He had experienced the horror that leaves you calm and unafraid, but for her something inside was broken and he did not know if it could be be mended. Her life, her horror, he could not tell.

As they rode out of there and down that road, the pink and green dawn came and the sun when it rose looked to be a globe of red-hot iron. The air was still and heated, and as if that were not enough, women and children could be seen piling wood on dead horses and setting them afire. Their

immense bodies lay on the ground, their elegant necks and finely shaped heads, the round spring of ribs. For miles were the collapsed and bulge-eyed beasts and in places the ground was blackened with their grease where someone had already burned one of them. He remembered also the sight of those two ladies sitting in their open doorway selling water and laughing as if nothing had happened and he thought what a strange world it had become and he could not understand it enough even to tell of it if someone had asked him.

It was days afterward and miles south when the rain-washed air began to clear of its death smell and they were at the banks of the Potomac where they stole their way into the lines. On their heels, as if in pursuit of their own persons, the Federal Army had finally mustered and appeared in the fields and woods beyond the sentries.

By then the field works were up and the engineers were completing a pontoon bridge to make the crossing. They were as if an ancient forlorn people gathered on the grim shore of an old river. He found Moxley and Yandell and Tom Allen. They were with the battery as his father had said they would be. He told them he was Robey Childs and they told how his father was good as gold and if anybody ever needed him he always came a-runnin'. He was the bravest man any of them ever knew.

Thereafter, they would call him captain, as they had called his father, and that night he sent off a letter to his mother but could not bear to tell her all he knew.

As to Rachel, the men of the battery said nothing to him. It was a mystery to them what was between the son of their fallen comrade and this girl who traveled with him posing as

a boy, but they made no judgment and spoke not a word of it among themselves.

After Gettysburg the rain had resumed with a vengeance. Rolling thunder shook the night's darkness. The rains were torrential and the lightning flashes left them momentarily blind. They sat in the rain with the water running from the cuffs of their jackets, waiting for the crossing.

Finally came the nights of July 13 and 14, wet and black, and these were the nights they chose to escape across the pontoon bridge. Supplies were critically short. Men were hungry and picking kernels of corn out of the horse dung. With tarpaulins they sheltered their smoky fires of green and snapping pine logs, so they would continue burning and give the impression that men still fed them. All that day a line of the tallest men, their arms locked together, had stretched from bank to bank so others might make the crossing. Then the word went around that the river was falling steadily and that the thin line of the pontoon bridge had been completed.

On a rainy and foggy night torches were lit and bonfires were built of fence rails to light the way to the other side. Robey and Rachel waited in the gravel at the dissolving edge of the river as the water rose and curled. When it descended, they rode the coal black horse onto the bridge, cut loose its mooring and under a wetting drizzle, the blossoms dropping in the water, they floated to Virginia.

16

PERIOD OF SHADOW drapes from her shoulder to the swell of her small belly as if a length of long black hair. In a flawless china sky the sun is bright and coming through the panes of glass as it makes its crossing east to west.

He is asleep, sitting up in a chair beside her. His hands are palms down on his knee caps. A loaded Springfield rifle lays on the floor at his feet and beside it the six-shot Remington. She thinks she's had a dream and she's frightened. She cannot separate what she dreams from what she thinks.

They travel nights and sleep by day and it will soon be dark again and time to travel the twisting roads one day closer to home. Getting himself home. At night the darkening air brings silence before the walk of the predators, the hunters. For them the night will bring invisible passage for their escape.

"Would you like to live here?" she said, turning her head slowly.

"No," he said, as a sleep-talker without waking. "I wouldn't want to live here."

"Where would you want to live?"

"Where I am from."

"There's too much light out," she said. "Can't we sleep at night?"

He'd already told her so many times before that they couldn't sleep at night. They slept by day and at night they traveled to travel unseen. She pulled the blanket to her shoulders and moved her arms beneath its drape, and when she did she was strangely limbless and birdlike, her arms winged and flightless in the windless, airless room.

"It ain't safe," he said, and stretched out his legs, a boot heel banging on the floor. It was getting late in the day, and now awake he'd not be able to sleep again before it was time to leave.

"I dreamt we were asleep together," she said.

Her voice was matter-of-fact and he thought she meant him, in her dream, together with her. But he did not presume she meant him and so wondered whose dream company she was recounting. She carried her life with her and could not flee from it, even in her sleep. She tossed and turned and cried out in her sleep. She insisted upon sleeping with her knife and that he keep the blade sharp. It was inside her and knocking at her ribs and fluttering her lungs as if they were wings startled and throbbing with urgency.

"You should try to sleep a little," he said. He'd told her this so many times before and was beginning to understand that opposite his intentions, he was counseling her in the direction of her terror.

"Where do you think she disappeared to?"

"I don't know," he said, sitting up and looking about the room as if there were still the presence of a third person.

In the house where they lodged was a raggedy old woman with a sun-stained and stroke-twisted face. One of her eyes was bloodshot and the other was as white and round as an

ivory marble. She had welcomed them into her house and with a hand grinder she had made flour and with the flour she had made balls of dough as big as her gnarled fist. She fried potatoes for them to eat, and there was bacon, and she made up a sack of the same for them to take when they rode away. She had moved about the house as if a phantom impaired and more than once burned herself as she cooked and took an awfully long time to realize it. As her presence in the house seemed odd to herself, they inquired but could not sort from her if it was her house or not.

What they did learn was that her ears did not work too good and so it was hard for her to hear them from both sides of her head at once. They learned she had not seen a soul for months, not even a stray dog, and they learned she had a son named Horace. He was a crackerjack of a young man, but he had been killed by which side she did not know and what did it matter anyhow? She declared her heart and mind were broken by it. She knew this, she said, but she claimed love and prayer were enough to get by on. She declared herself a good saint of God regardless of what he had done to her. When she said these things there was a breath around her that shined as if it was not air or light but was something from within.

"I can't sleep without knowing where she's at," Rachel said. "Do you think she's still wandering about? She gives me the cold shivers."

"Try counting," he said. He rubbed his face hard, as if trying to rearrange his features. He wanted to comfort her, but she contained inside a wall of vigilance and suspicion she had built around herself. Not since she had comforted him upon the death of his father had she acted kindly toward him.

"One, two, three," she said. "It doesn't work."

That was when he told her he loved her.

"Why?" she said.

"I just do."

She raised her draped arms and slowly turned her face to him. The point of her knife prodded the blanket material.

"Don't be such a straw-head," she scoffed.

She lay back down on the divan in the strange room, pulled the blanket to her chin. She turned to face the back of the divan and pretended sleep. She was exhausted for the weight she carried inside her and did not understand why she shouldn't be able to sleep, why he should say he loved her.

"I almost love you," she said, relenting, and was to say more but was stricken by her own words and shook her head violently—no, she did not mean to say what she said. She seemed ashamed of her mistrust, or inability, he did not know which. As time had gone by his mind had increasingly become confused when it came to her. He wondered if the debt he was paying could ever be paid, or if she even thought about it that way, or knew how he thought about it.

"How much longer?" she said.

"A few more days," he said softly. "Rest a while and we will go."

Their stay with the battery on the banks of the Potomac had been brief. He secured a hard-mouthed bay mare for her to ride, the rare horse that the coal black horse would tolerate, as well as provisions, ammunition, a brass telescope, and the Springfield. The army was still precariously encamped when he asked the men of the battery how far it would be home and how long it would take. They told him two days if he didn't sleep and killed the horse in getting there. Otherwise it would

take five days. He was to figure 150 mile as the crow flies and ride by night and each day rub down the horses.

Hole up by day and sleep with the sun, they told him, and when there's nothing left and there's five miles to go, cut deep gashes in the horses' shoulders and pour gun powder into their open wounds. Yessir, by the Jesus, that's what they would do to get home in a hurry. But then again, riding that black horse to death ain't worth gettin' to anybody's home and who the fuck needs a home when you got a horse as fine as that one?

They'd ridden hard the past days and in their imaginations it was as if the whole world was chasing them. They slept under rock ledges and in hollow logs and moved their position when he had the instinct to do so and each dawn they halted again. The highways were beset with a confusion of regular and irregular troops. There were partisans and bushwhackers. There were profits to be taken and old scores to settle. He'd learned in no uncertain way that this was war too, name it the war inside war. No matter, it was as much a part of war as war itself and in war you get killed just for living.

Their shortest route was west by southwest but this took them against the intentions of all flowing water and the corrugated upthrust of every folded mountain. They crossed rivers and streams and waded dense sloughs and after a time he could glimpse the green front of the Alleghenies they would have to ascend. In places the front was ramped foothills and stone-bound windy gaps and in other places flat walls of forested stone and cobbly switchbacks and the whole effect was like that of a great resting beast, its legs tucked beneath its body and its paws extended from beneath its chest.

"Two, three more days," he said.

"Nights, you mean."

"Nights," he agreed.

He worried her mind would give out in that time. It had become that bitter and was that near to its breaking point. It seemed she had not slept as long as he had known her. She held to her fear and her mind would not give it up no matter how hard she tried to persuade it into a different direction. She began to tremble and then she sat up and let the blanket and then the dirty sleep shirt slide off her shoulders.

"Lay on top of me," she said, letting the knife slip to the floor from her hand and laying back and opening her arms to reveal her naked body. But he did not move. He was not sure he could move.

She called to him again and told him what to do and when he still did not move she told him if he wanted to marry her he had better be nice to her.

He was clumsy in his movement. He moved to sit beside her on the divan and then let himself forward to be caught by her and in a tangle of arms and blanket and sleep shirt he was pulled down against her body.

"Don't move," she said, and held him to her shaking body.

He let his face to her skin and breathed in the smell of leather and sweat and horse and wood smoke they both shared. He wanted his face against her skin and to not move it. He could feel something pulled from inside him and extending toward her. He wanted to say words that would tell her this, but his feelings were not clear to him and they would not be for a long time.

"You aren't the worst," she said with sweet resignation, and pulled him even closer to her body than he already was. She stroked his back and kissed his cheek and neck.

When they awoke the old woman was still absent the house and at first they did not talk about her and the longer they waited for the other to mention her absence, the more impossible it became to acknowledge she had even existed. He stepped out into the yard and scanned the circle of the horizon. He cradled the Springfield in the crook of his elbow. It would be dark soon. Sun-fires lit the western horizon as the sun in its setting was burning down the earth.

He wandered the yard and there was still no sign of the old woman. Then the curl of a low branch at the edge of the porch caught his eye through the porch railing. At first he thought it the tiny face of a child peeking at him from the bushes or the tiny face of a shy wood sprite caught in mischief. He stepped onto the porch and cocked his head and saw what it was: a whorl of dried needles that looked nothing like the face of a tiny child or wood sprite. He tilted his head again and his eye could barely catch what he'd seen, but there it was again.

"I see you," he said.

He played this game until his mind could find face and then left off to bridle and saddle the horses. When he went back inside Rachel was at the sugar chest, wetting her finger in her mouth and feeding sweet scrapings onto her tongue. He watched her eat the sugar and when she looked up he encouraged her to continue until she'd had her fill.

"Have your dinner," she said, and led him to the stove for potatoes and bacon. He was hungry and, no utensils at hand, he took up the plate and ate the heated food with his fingers.

They mounted the horses in darkness and rode into the ink black night and when they stopped to rest the horses she told him she was in a better state of mind but still far from feeling the way she wanted to.

"I thought it would get better by now," she said, "but it hasn't."

He made to speak, but the words would not come. He wanted to tell her it was a matter of time, but did he know this to be true? He carried his own sadness and hatred and to these his mind was fastened and enlivened. He did not want to forget, not ever. How could he suggest she move on from her own? He led with his hands, as if words were found by touch until finally he gave up and let his hands drop into his lap.

She waited to see if that was all he had to say and then she laughed at him.

He found for her a can of condensed milk, punched it with the point of her knife and this they shared beneath a grotto of stone where a spring ran out while the watered horses cooled in a stand of trees. His eyes searched the shadowy patterns of the starlit forest. He was calculating another move tonight, weighing the advantage of another mile against what it might cost to her and the animals. He knew the bay would soon give out, but they were close now. He did not know this ground, but he knew the terrain and recognized how it would lead them through.

"The stars have moved closer," he said, squatting beside her. He made up his mind; they would spend the duration of that night where they were and make one more move before daybreak.

"Do you think she was ever there?" she asked of the old woman where they had spent the day.

"I don't know," he said. "I never thought she wasn't."

"It's probably just as well," she said.

As to staying where they were, he suddenly changed his

mind and they climbed into their saddles once again. He needed to get home. He needed to return to his mother to know she was safe.

EARLY IN THE MORNING they saw turkey vultures sailing the uplifts, the air above the air, and their eccentric rises and descents were slow and screwlike. Old wood smoke still filtered through the pines, a stove fire let slowly to die. There was an old woman wearing a shawl and carrying an umbrella. Beside her was an old man leaning on a walking stick. They were watching the sunrise from a hilltop and then they moved on and disappeared behind the hill. He took them to be more of the nice women and good men staggered and shattered by the spiral of events begun and that once begun begat their own private, terrible, and willful force.

When they reached the place, it had the look of abandonment after years of decline. For some reason he had the instant passing memory of a complete story his father told him about an ancient athlete who ran up a mountain with a newborn bull calf on his shoulders. He did this every day in the belief that as the bull calf grew he would likewise build himself and become a stronger man. His father declared it to be an impossibility but an idea capable of dogging the mind. Maybe bull calves didn't grow so fast in ancient times as they did now. No matter. His father said that he could never give up the thought of that man and despite what he knew to be true about growing bulls, he sometimes still wondered why it couldn't work.

Aside from the obvious reasons, why not? his father had opinioned. It's the kind of idea that holds sway on the thinking

mind. Maybe all people were this same way. Maybe they carried on in belief against a bad idea but nevertheless carried on until it collapsed them.

The cabin door bore a huge iron padlock, sized for an armory or a ship, and the cabin seemed to wear it not for its security but as if in punishment for grave transgression. Likewise, the shutters were nailed fast, but contrarily the kitchen garden had been recently tended and what used to be flower beds of considerable proportions still bloomed with garish heads tottering above new weeds. Wild roses chafed at the log walls. There was a cistern filled by a wooden pipe with amber-colored water. There was a neatness that made him think the old people would be returning in a day or so.

He called out, and as he expected he received no reply. The only sound to be heard was that of the horses tearing and champing sweet clover and the trickling of the water's ropey fall from the pipe's end.

The sty they found empty and overgrown with thistle and the sty's earth was dry and settled. There'd been no rooting hog that season and runner vines had curled and woven the barked and gnawed logs. Orange trumpetlike flowers toppled on their green stems. They moved on to the stable searching for inhabitants. Inside its board walls it smelled of mildew and clay, the ferment of manure and hay. In one stall was the rotting smell of seed potatoes gone unplanted.

Out the back door on a grassy sward they discovered the attraction of the gyring vultures. In the trampled grass was a maiden mare and a new foal lying beside each other as if died in parturition. The mare had thrown down the foal bed and her shrunken pear-shaped womb lay to her hocks, blackening

in the switch grass and pea-vine. The feet of the newborn foal were frayed and flaky and still wore a fringe of soft horn so young he speculated it was preborn.

"She were a very fine horse," he said of the mare.

"Do you think they've gone somewheres?" she said, her throat constricted with the grisly spectacle they witnessed but did not want to acknowledge.

"Recent," he said, and told her how he'd seen them through the telescope departing on their approach. He speculated the death of a mare such as her was enough to break a frail spirit.

The sun was most risen when they washed in the cistern and fried bacon and onions they took from the garden. There were also baby carrots and tomatoes. After they ate she undressed and rinsed her clothes in the cistern and then she decided to climb in after them and wash herself. There was no suggestion that he look or not look and in her immersion she found peaceful occupation. She let the trickling water run through her hair and splashed him and told him that he ought to take a bath because he stank to high heaven. He kicked off his boots and still wearing his clothes climbed in too. She thought this funny and laughed and then coaxed them from him and as he gave her each article she scrubbed and beat and wrung the water from them. His hands and neck and face were burned nut brown from the wind and sun. She inspected his head wound and declared it to be nicely scarred.

They draped their clothes over low bushes in the sunlight and wrapped themselves in blankets. She wanted to sleep in the grass under the shade of a tree, but he insisted they sleep in the stable with the horses. So, exhausted, they closed the stable door and bedded down to sleep the day. The darkness

inside was incomplete but crosshatched with thin shafts of infiltrating sunlight.

He told her the light stems traveled in the straightest lines to be found in the natural world.

She held her hand up and slowly moved it until it found one. She then pulled away as if burned or cut and laughed at how funny the game she was playing. She returned her hand and let the light play on her open palm and then touched her palm to her face as if to carry its warmth to her skin.

At her insistence they lay close together to whisper, even to touch. He felt her breath dance on his face as light as an eyelash. He felt the air in the barn cool on his skin. His eyes found her eyes and she looked away.

"He ain't dead," she said.

"No, he probably ain't."

"He'll come, you know. Sure as heaven and earth. She's dying and he'll come for me."

She continued to play in the light as her thoughts let words to her mouth. She let herself look into his eyes and then she pretended to carry the warmth to his face, his cheeks, his eyes, his forehead, the lines in her hand pressed and held against his skin.

"He ain't like anybody I ever met," he said, "and I have met some odd ones."

"You can't listen to him talk or he'll change you," she whispered as if it was a mortal secret. "He is the mesmerizer. He opens his mouth and begins to preach and they're walking the aisles, ya-hooing and boo-hooing." She deepened her voice and mock intoned, "How does a black cow eat green grass and produce white milk, yellow butter, and orange cheese? Don't you tell me there isn't a God. Ya-hoo. Boo-hoo."

He asked her who she was to the man and the woman and how they came to be traveling together.

She told him her father was a preacher in Baltimore and had answered a call to mission in Africa for two years. She told him her father was a true man of God who always said there's a thick black line between okay and the right way. It was when her mother and father left for Africa the man and the woman were assigned to be her guardians until their return. But her mother and father were killed in that far-off country.

"Their riverboat overturned and they swam ashore and were attacked by a lion."

"A lion?" he said, as if their existence were confirmed.

"A lion."

"God, I never knew anyone kilt by a lion."

"It's not an everyday thing," she said.

She continued to talk as if once begun she could not stop. She told him one day he'd scream at her and the next day he'd beg forgiveness. He commanded her life and no decisions were her own.

"I was going to run off," she said, "but I guess I just run off too late for my own good."

"A person can get used to just about anything if it happens slow enough," he said.

"Not that," she spat, and then she turned her back and went silent on him and they did not speak again before sleep.

Late that day when he broke from sleep it was because he could not breathe. He thought to feel hands on his chest and at his throat, so difficult it was for him to receive air. He turned over and on all fours he hacked and coughed. His eyes stung and his face was as if poisoned. The stable was filled

with smoke, the horses stamping and screaming, their hooves knocking on their wooden stalls. At first he could make nothing of this noise and smoke. His mind moved slowly and then all at once. The stable was on fire.

Half suffocated, he crawled naked for the door, but it would not open. The flames were close and had begun to roar for the heat they generated. He kicked at the door with both his feet and it gave with each blow but fell back and he could not hold it enough to squeeze through. It was chained or jammed, he did not know which. He pawed at the earth beneath it and then finding a broken shovel he dug with that and flattening his body he was able to scrape underneath. Outside, he waited to be shot, but the shot never came. He held to the earth and breathed deeply and from where he lay he could see gray smoke pouring from the windows and snaking across the roof. Above the door the track had separated and a wheel was stuck in the gap.

He cut away his hold on the earth and lifted and tore at the door with all of his strength until the door, track and all, fell away from the opening and a wall of black smoke poured from the opening. He crawled back inside, breathing the lean air close to the ground and found her lost and struggling and fought with her and dragged her free as the coal black horse found the opening and bolted through with the bay mare following behind.

From that moment on her panic returned and would not abate. Her hands shook and her thoughts came from her in a frenzy or not all, but mostly not at all. He thought how barn doors, worn with constant use, were always coming off their tracks and it could have been just that, but he did not know

how the flames could have started or why. He searched his memory as to when they ate and where they built their cook fire and whether or not he sufficiently doused it. And if it was someone who'd lit that fire, why did they not shoot him when he crawled to the air? He could not answer these questions, and as night fell on that day he concluded he never would.

In those next hours they experienced the sense of being pushed before consequence while carrying it with them. Their bodies were in the fugue state of turmoil and relentless fatigue that is felt by both the hunter and the hunted. They rode out of there, abreast and in step, the horses' hooves powdering the red-soil dust of the valley floor. He carried the Springfield floating upright, the butt resting on his thigh, as they dodged through the dense forests enameled green in the unfriendly daylight and the horses played and lathering, they continued on, traveling into the night, all the while looking back and waiting for the gunshots that never came.

He insisted they travel the long way by woodland lanes and pathless crosscuts and from time to time they took refuge in cool starlit woods where they hoped they would be safe. When he heard hoof beats, they bushed up and waited in blackness and soon he could hear the ring of so many pounding hooves it was as if an entire calvary was pursuing them. He understood there was no reason for them to be pursued, but he wanted no encounter, no delay, no possibility of all the trouble there was to be found on the roads in those days after Gettysburg. They waited and watched and the sound grew and then it bore off and there were no sounds and the night returned to silence.

He pointed to her the stars that guided him in case she

needed them. In the northwest was Ursa Major, the bear, and in the northeast of that month the first stars of the Great Square of Pegasus were rising above the horizon. There is Polaris, he told her, the North Star.

"If anything ever happens," he said, "don't you worry about me. Just start running."

She assured him he had nothing to worry about on that account.

They waited until they were sure the road was clear and then crossed over and struck through the open countryside and by then it was close to morning. They found a path, a ribbon that went winding between the willow stems and it was there they lost the bay. She came up lame in her right foreleg, so tender she would not let down her leg. A hairline crack in the hoof wall had split open and the frog was likewise split and hot and raw.

He hiked Rachel into the saddle of the coal black horse and led them for a while and then he mounted behind her and they rode double under the waning moon, a half shell in the sky, west through the measureless dark forest.

17

HERE THE MERCANTILE had once stood was
burned over and now a blackened patch of
ground. The fire had spread and consumed
the lean-to stable where first he had seen the
coal black horse. It had climbed to the rock walls that stood
behind the stable and now the rocks were scorched black and
leaked variegated runnels of coppery water. The smith was
likewise burned to the ground and where it had stood was
now a junkyard of iron and charred timbers. In the center
stood the great anvil, untoppled and settled upright, as if it
rode the burning stump upon which it rested down to the
ground to wait patiently for the next hammer that would presume to strike it.

There was no sign of old Morphew or the hunchback German or the upside-down boy. There was no sign that human
life had been recent and one day would resume. The site was
lonesome and haunting and its borders already greening and
closing over with the nature that would repossess it.

They did not linger in that place but rode on into the hollow
in precise reverse of the descent he had made what seemed so
long ago. He was now different. He was older and born over and
had lived out the ends of so many men's lives, his father's life.

In this dry season the leaned-out Canaan was pools and riffles fed by tiny veins of feeder streams. The Twelve Mile was the same, but its water was colder and blacker and its banks more grown and wild with the tough and sunless varieties. Trees had toppled into the moaty water and raised to the air great fans of scrabbled roots that clutched boulders in their twisted fingers. Sweeping trunks of mountain laurel met, intersected, and wove together and all about was as if a ferocious and violent nature had walled the mountain in waiting for his return.

They rode on, higher and higher, and found a sunken place near the bridge that once spanned its surface where stone and gravel had washed in. The coal black horse, without hesitation, stepped off from the bank and forded the slow cooling flow, belly deep and sure-footed.

The air closed and cooled around them as they continued their ascent and late that day they came upon the old fields grown with mullein and yarrow and then was the high meadow in the sling of the mountain wreathed in juniper, and it was a flash of wet grass in a startle of sunlight when they broke from the rock walls and stepped out on what seemed the top of the world.

The cabin, when he finally saw it, was smaller than he remembered and in the time since his departure seemed to have endured a great weather. Its logs were cracked and silvered and its cedar roofing was lifted, twisted, and ramshackled by the torment of a vagrant wind. Slivers quilled the rounds, and moss and vine were abundant in their reclamation. No aspect was square. No surface had yet to begin its return to nature and yet all seemed perched and more precarious than a balanced eye.

But there was a greenness and an abundance he'd not imagined possible. It was as if the garden, the fields, and the mountain had blossomed. There were new lambs gamboling on the hillside and stiff-legged spring calves blatting for their mothers. A litter of mewling pups gadded about. It was as if his mother had bred animals and increased nature to replace men and children. It was as if he had returned to the realm of dreams.

He dismounted and crossed the cabin's threshold. She could see him in her mirror when he stepped through the doorway. She was touching her wild hair as if anticipating an arrival, as if it were an aspect of her being newly recognized.

"Who's there?" she said fondly, because she already knew it was him. "Come out of the shadows where I can see you," she said, and it was only then the dogs flattened their ears and rose up bristling for how fooled they were by his approach. They exploded with deep shocked barks, slobbering and clacking jaws and the scratching of the paws skittering on the rough floor to reach their lumbrous bodies between her and him. They could not hide their embarrassment when they saw who it was.

"They've known you were coming," she said in their defense. "They just didn't know when. They have been antsy for days."

Her hair had whitened and her face had taken on the purity that is found in the sick and the holy and the season-changing sky. She moved about with steps so silent she was as if nature in transit drifting the floorboards. She'd not seen another human being since he left. She'd not heard another human voice and had long since left her own voice inside her head as

the faintest whisper of sound enough for the animals to hear when they were called to milk or feed or from one pasture to the next.

"You've been gone a very long time," she said. "Are you really here?" She touched his face in the manner of the reading sightless.

"Did you receive my letter," he said.

"No," she said. "It hasn't come yet, but it will."

It was then she let go the slender hope that her husband, her son's father, was still alive. She knew then he would not come stamping across the threshold and take her in his arms and lift her off her feet.

But she had long since entered the world of loss and enduring silence and now was the beginning of its infinite and companionable grief. Later she would tell him she'd dreamed his father was dead and admitted she was not shocked when he did not arrive home. She just didn't know until then it was actually true. But she'd never dreamed Robey dead and so looked for him every day and thought he would surely come home to her.

"You must be tired," she said looking past her son to the girl.

"I need to lay down," she said. "I am so tired and my shoulders ache."

His mother directed her to sit by the window in the cushioned chair and then he followed her into the kitchen where, composed and inhabiting herself again, she daubed grease into a skillet.

"Who is she?" she finally said as the grease popped and she let the eggs slide in to fry. "Where does she come from?"

"I don't know much about her," he said.

When she turned and looked at him, she could see that he had changed. She could not imagine what he had seen while he was gone. She could not imagine the black curve he carried inside him. But no, he hadn't changed. He was her son and the change was from a boy to a man and that was to be expected.

"What did she tell you?"

"We talked some."

"What did you talk about?"

"I wonder about that sometimes."

"I'd like your part of the story," his mother coaxed, but this conversation was not her interest. It was simply an effort to fill the silence.

"She said her mother and father was killed in Africa."

"That seems an awful place to die."

"There are better ones?" he asked.

"I think I'd prefer my own bed for one, but then I am not the world traveler you have become."

His face flushed red with shame and he wanted to apologize, but he said nothing. He sat with her while she cooked eggs and bacon and there was bread in the warming oven. She gave account of the farm, its progress, and the necessary work to be done now that he had returned.

THAT NIGHT ON THE MOUNTAIN while the women slept, he sat outside in the cool summer air, the coal black horse staked to a long lead. In the farthest distance he could see the faint glimmer of a light and then another one. They were miles away and lights he'd never seen before. When his mother

came out she was wearing her nightgown and a sweater and carrying for him another plate of food. He apologized to her for being a smart mouth and wished to take it back and she accepted his apology and agreed to let him.

"That's a fine horse you've brought home," she said.

"I owe Mister Morphew for it," he told her, and explained how he'd lent it to him, but he did not yet tell her the mercantile was burned out and so too the smith. Instead he asked after the distant lights and she told him they'd been burning for a month.

"They must be homesteaders," she said. "There were bonfires at first."

"Homesteaders," he said. The thought was incredible to him. Did they not know what was going on in the world?

He then said in answer to the question he knew she was thinking, "It's a hard place to talk about what happened east."

"There's time," she said, and then with a sigh that escaped her, "Time's what we have now."

"He told me to tell you he loved you more than anything on earth."

When he said these words to her they broke her and she tried hard not to, but she began to weep. He thought of all the tearful women, the mothers and daughters and lovers weeping for the men and boys who were lost souls no longer in possession of living bodies. They were prisoners of their dreams to come and powerless over their dominion. He thought of the men and boys who would come home and would never heal, the broken and wounded, the not dead. Those who would never see, never walk, never chew food, never speak a word, never sit up, never dress themselves, never again have a

thought in their minds. What would their women do? Would they still love the men and boys? What would love become? He thought better dead and lost than maimed and crippled.

She cried until her shoulders caved and she could not breathe. She choked, but when he tried to hold her she would not let him. He knew she wanted to be alone but understood that she did not want to do it by herself. He sat quietly with his hands folded and ready.

Then it passed and she gathered herself and wiped at her face with the backs of her hands. There was a long silence until she spoke again.

"Do you know she is going to have a baby?"

"No," he said, shaking his head. "I didn't know that."

"Is it yours?"

"If she wants it to be."

That night they sat under the stars long past tiredness as they did not want to be separate from each other's company after so long apart. They watched the distant lights flickering against the atmosphere that existed between them and the homesteaders.

He wondered aloud if it was wind or mist or maybe someone had crossed in front of a window between them and the light that made it come and go. He wondered to himself how she must have known Rachel was going to have a baby and thought back to those days on the road and when he did his mind failed him. Could she have burned the stable? She was already a mystery to him and so the news of her having a baby made little difference to his mind. If she had tried to burn, what difference did it make now?

Together they listened to the intermittent call of the night

birds and the sawing sound that is made by grazing animals. For neither of them was the reunion complete and joyful, but they would gratefully receive what was left to them as they watched together the moon set beneath their feet, beyond the rim of the earth.

THEY WERE NOW in the cooling weather of the fall and descending in the country was haunting autumnal stillness. The sky was high and smoky-colored and mornings the fodder was frosted with hoary crystals and steamed in the air when broke open. The sun came flat and its light was not warm but white and cold. From miles away plied the wet smoke of burned slash as somewhere in the country more land was being cleared with fire. However pleasant that summer had been, however abundant the crops and productive the stock, it was the harbinger of the darker days to come.

It was not strange to him how his mother had grieved that summer as she experienced, drop by drop, the pain of pain remembered. Early morning, midday, and after supper she would disappear from their table, lost and broken-hearted, and into the fields, into the forest, into darkness, and he would hear her stirring in the night preparing to go and he would follow her into the night always at a distance and always she would be comforted by his watchful presence. He would cut the pain from her if he could. It was as if when she ate she fed grief into her mouth and when she walked she took it into her legs and when she carried, she bore it in her arms and shoulders and slowly and imperceptibly she was altered.

It was during that summer Rachel's belly began to grow and as it did her body diminished as if consumed and contained

within her prodigious belly would be an astonishing yield and when delivered there would be nothing left of her and she would disappear. His mother engaged her with activity, prodded her when she moped, and by dint of will refused her the deep blueness she would surely have sunk into. He did not know what was between them. He knew it was not a peaceful understanding but was an understanding distant and by appearance respectful and at times was as if both women shared sorrow's affliction, one in death and one in gestation.

Each day he went out alone to the fields to work and to see what would come up the Copperhead Road. At first his mother urged the dogs on him in his daily rounds, but he wanted no warning from the dogs, either for himself or for who would come. The coming he looked for was a consequence he'd anticipated from the first time he saw the man. He carried the Springfield rifle with him and had long since determined never again would he wait to be called, to be told, to be steered in one direction or the next by any man.

On rare days he could hear rumbles coming up the mountain from across the Twelve Mile and all the way up the Copperhead Road. The sound, emanating from the dark clouds in the east, would rumble all day, and after it stopped rumbling, it would still rumble, echo over echo. At the time he did not understand the source of these detonations and explosions, but later he would learn it was the phenomenon of acoustic shadow, the traveling sound from a far distant battle skipping on air. But at the time he did not know this and thought a battle raged nearby and below and was drawn to it as if answering a call and was disquieted by these thoughts.

What he had not anticipated coming up that road was the

scavenger brother of the scavenger he'd killed behind the ear with the six-shot Remington. The morning he saw him was so quiet and still it was as if a murder had already taken place.

He was lying in the dish of an ungrained, wind-scalloped stone, high above the mountain's southern flank. He wore a blanket pulled over him and his cheek nested on the pillow of his clasped hands. Sprawls of needle-leaved juniper, knotted and stunted, scented the air. The Springfield lay beside him.

The weather was seasonal that day and it had just broke noon. He had put up dried and dented corn in the crib that morning and in the afternoon he would complete the task. He'd drunk his coffee from a jar and was eating the hard bread and pork sandwich he made for his lunch, licking the grease from his fingers. He was at his leisure, visiting with infinity, wondering what was in the rock that made it dish this way. Or was it not the rock but volition latent in the wind that slowly razored stone in so tailored and peculiar a fashion? Or was it the ancient ice his father told him about?

He was watching the mountain route that rose from the big bottom, the only way to arrive at the home place. He was nestled in a tiny high place that looked out through an ever-widening angle where it reached full degree at a hackly ridge two hundred yards very distant and then dropped off abruptly into a hollow, an inescapably tangled ravine bound with the interlocking trunks of laurel.

He had taken several deer on that ridge when they crossed and it was not so much the challenge of taking the deer but in not shooting the deer so it would carry itself over the ridge and into the jumbled back side of that ridge. His father had always warned him, You carry a deer out of there one

time and you learn it's not something you ever want to do again.

And this day was different in ways other than he could describe. Rachel had not slept and he had sat up with her through the night as she seemed to hold silent conversation with what was inside her. And he felt different that morning when he loaded the Springfield and capped the revolver and filled the jar with coffee and made the meat sandwich to take with him. He did not know why, but it was in his arms and across the width of his back, his shoulder blades in particular.

He raised the brass telescope to glass again. Any other day he would have been back at work by now, but this day he lingered to watch an unfolding natural encounter on the hackly ridge.

When he had looked before, it was to see a young button-horned buck watching a red-tailed hawk perched on the open rib cage of a dead deer. The deer was old and must have broke down in the night because it'd not been there yesterday. It was different that the deer did not find a hidden place to do its dying but died there on the ridge. It is not uncommon for animals to make mistakes. Often they miscalculate in their leaps and bounds and rip their hides or break their legs. As with humans, animals are born and grow old. They are smart and some are stupid. They make mistakes. They have accidents. They live and die.

But for some reason this was different and his skin warmed with the thinking and he lingered long after it was time to return to the cornfield. He didn't know why he knew what he knew. He just knew to keep doing what he was doing.

Through the glass he watched.

The hawk was plucking shreds of intestine and gulleting them as if they were stringy worms. From the angle of his perspective the curious buck looked as if he was standing right next to the hawk rather than standing off. The bird raised its wings and flared them broad as a sail full of wind. It screamed from inside its throat. He smiled as the young buck feinted and fled.

The ridgeline was now empty except the picked carcass. It was the middle of the day and the crest of that ridge was struck with light, as if it were flint and the sunlight were steel. He had wanted to see the red-tailed hawk one more time before it flew off. He had wanted to watch it eat and take flight and pivot through the air on its powerful wings, but it'd already flown away.

Then he saw a man he recognized riding into the glass. He was riding a slowly walking horse, and though it was not the man he expected it was a man he knew, and only when he saw him did it make sense to him. The man paused within his round view to look at the carcass.

"Don't be hasty," he whispered. He spit out the gobbet of sandwich in his mouth, pressed his body to the stone, and with total certainty pulled the butt plate of the Springfield into the cradle of his shoulder. He eased the forestock onto its makeshift rest at a point behind the sling swivel and he found the blade of the front sight with the notched rear sight. He made his calculations instinctively.

When he finally left his perch he went down to find the scavenger draped on the ridgeline. He lay on his back where he'd fallen as if struck by the arm of a gigantic. His head was balding and his nose beakish. He was sunken about the

eyes and his skin was pale and from where he'd fallen he was bruised yellow and purple in the face and yet even in dying he wore the hungry vulpine look.

"How's it look?" the man asked, his teeth gritted against the pain that wreaked his body.

"It ain't pretty," he said. "If that's what you are asking."

"You're a mean bastard," the scavenger muttered. "That's all you are."

"I 'magine there are some who have the exact same thing to say about you."

"I believe I asked one time your name?"

"Robey Childs," he said.

"I'll tell 'em when I get where I'm goin'."

"They'll want to know."

"Jesus, that hurts," he said. He did not motion to indicate, but clearly he spoke of the black hole in his chest.

"You ought to have been more careful," he told the man.

Blood was milking from one of the man's nostrils and in staggered moments the man did not seem to fully understand what all had happened to him. He reached his right hand in front of his face as if to clear his vision but then let it drop and his arm to dangle at his side.

"Where's my horse?" the man asked.

"He run off."

"I guess there's a lesson in this," the man said wearily, and then he said Robey's name, "Robey Childs."

"What would that lesson be?" Robey asked, but the man was now dead and thereby prevented from answering.

He made a sound with his tongue and looked to the sky. What has happened has happened, he thought, and what will

happen will happen, and when that happened he'd count himself fortunate because he could get on to the next.

Overhead the thick leaves were daily turning red, orange, and yellow. The dusty water ran under black shadows and the dried corn shucks scraped and scuttled with the winglike breezes that cuffed the mountain. Those hot lovely days of July through September were now gone forever. Soon would be the driving wind, and the beating rain would become snow and the high mountains would become impassable, and in that fastness only then could he rest. He continued to stand by the scavenger's body. Why, he did not know, but felt he should do so for a while before taking his guns and whatever else of value he possessed, before toppling him over the ridge. Then he would retrieve the runaway horse and go home.

"Was it the one you'd been waiting for," his mother asked him late that night as they sat outside bundled against the chill.

"No. It weren't him."

"It was someone else," she said.

"Yes ma'am."

"How many more is there?"

"Only one," he said. "But then I thought that a'fore this one."

"I should have just had dogs," she speculated. "At least they grow up in a year."

If there was whimsy in her voice he could not detect it.

18

HEN THE END of the waiting time for the next one came it was months later and he was astride the coal black horse. They were riding the bed of the rock-bound Copperhead Road. Ice plated the slow water and eskers of snow fingered the cloud-shadowed ground.

Cold and weary, he'd come down from this day's aerie, an overlook made, he speculated, where rocks had gathered when rocks were sentient and moving, as pretime pilgrims had arrived and were exhausted from their difficult journeys and so slumped together against one another. Below this place was the concealing snow and above this place was the bottom of the wintry universe, and when he stood there he could not resist his desire to reach out with his hands in the hope he might touch them both.

The sun was lost in the sky, eclipsed by the deep cut he rode and had been so for several days, as if it was ruled by darkness this winter and so it was cold and frosted and the rock walls were blackened with frozen water. It was early evening still, and already the lights of the night had been set in motion.

The winter thus far had been the one he wished for: prolonged cold, snow and ice and a penetrating darkness that

came in the late afternoon and the body never so tired as to sleep through it. There was nothing but long dark winter and the endless evergreen forest that fell from sight to the horizon miles away. There were cows to milk and feed in the wet barn and there was waiting while Rachel changed daily before his eyes as her time grew imminent.

These months spent in gestation she had remained for the most part closed to him, dark and angry and forlorn, yet she needed to be near him and always know where he was. She told him of the strange-bodied feeling of her ribs un-sticking and spreading to accommodate her belly. The pains that flashed through her like wildfires. Her small bones stretching. Her faints and haunts, and sins. At times she did not seem to know where she was or how she got there or what day of the week it was and when she did know she did not care. He'd come to know fear again but not for himself. It was for how dear her life had become to him.

Last night, her voice ragged with tears, she told him she was ready to die and wanted to do so. She told him if she could not go back to the beginning she would just as soon get this life over with and be born again. He felt a shiver working into his chest bones.

The coal black horse suddenly snorted and tossed its head and scraped at the ground in stride. Robey had heard noth-ing odd on his own ear but retrieved the Springfield from the saddle scabbard and slipped off the road and dodged behind a dense screen of root-sprouted coppice shoots.

"This could be a bad day for someone," he said to the steady horse. Then he could hear the snow-muffled stride of a rider approaching. He did not know the outcome and that moment

did not care in the least. He knew he had found what he was looking for. What would follow would be a rest of one kind or another.

He made a sound and the coal black horse rose and pitched forward into the road. The horse wheeled as he drew rein and then willfully spun in place one more rotation, jumped straight sideways, and held. He sat the horse barring the road with no perceptible movement to be seen in the hands or bit, the rifle balanced as if a scale across his lap.

The man was coming on, riding a sorrel with a white mane and four white feet. After his long search the rider was bringing conclusion as fast as he could without even knowing it. He did not stop until he brought the sorrel abreast of the crossed coal black horse.

Beyond mild surprise, the man had nothing in his eyes, but the face of him recalled the bone midden of those killing fields he'd ridden away from so many months ago, leaving his father dead and buried beneath the signifying tree. It recalled to him the night in the fire-gutted house and Rachel and the blind woman and his own head wounded by the little goose man and dressed in the torn garments of a murdered woman.

"I know you," the man said, and at first seemed pleased to have suddenly met up with him. "I been looking for you," he said.

But it went without saying. There was only one reason to be on that road and being lost wasn't likely. The man's eyes were now lively and fleeting about their sockets and it was then he determined they were not the eyes of the killer but the eyes of one fleeing sin and consequence and death.

"That's a fine horse," the man said. "Any man who'd seen that horse once would know you again."

"The hell with you," Robey told him.

"But I have caught you," the man said, setting his jaw on the words, cold and fixed. He then smiled in an attempt to take back a degree of his provocation.

"What part have I in your life?" Robey asked.

"That is what I am here to talk about."

Kill him, he thought. Put him through, he told himself, and a prefigured order of ideas deep in the map of his mind illumined as if divine. There would be no discernment, no discretion, no proportion to his justice.

"We are already dead," the man said, "you and I," and he swept a hand to indicate the high stony walls of the narrow sepulchral hollow. "Ours are the souls of the ruined," he observed with delight.

Then the shot rang out in that sunless, starless, timeless place, but by then the man was collapsed upon the neck of the sorrel horse and the unchecked horse was rising up and the man was sliding off the back of it and falling heavily to the beaten ground as if thrown down from the highest place. Midway to the snowy earth the man turned his body and folded and he landed on the point of his shoulder and with a great exhalation of pain he slumped to his back.

And it was only then the shot Robey fired across his lap was heard shattering the air.

Before dismounting he stepped the coal black horse forward and horse and rider stood over the man's fallen body. The bullet had entered his chest but had not come out. It had traveled bone and lodged in his shoulder. Eely blood trickled

down his face where his skull had broke open when his head bit the stony road. An incessant groan was the best the man could do in the furor of his pain. He breathed heavily as his mind was delivered a commotion of messages that did not conflict. In his agony was the escape of his earthly and spiritual power, the tenebrous and the menace and the dark energy that ruled his life.

"I believe you hit the mark," he gasped, and tried to look down at the bubbles that pocked his chest.

"You believe that?" Robey said, dismounting and standing over him.

"Yes, I believe I do." Blood was fogging the red wheels of his glassy eyes. His colorless lips tried to shape more words, but it took several tries. "Should I not?"

"You should."

"Tell her the woman is dead. She'll want to know."

"I ain't telling her nothing," Robey said.

"My head is so heavy," the man said. "Like lead."

Nothing more was said as they waited together. He thought to feel remorse for his actions. Had he now made enough of his own needless contributions to the world's killing? No matter how just and righteous his actions? Had he not ended life the way others had ended his father's life? He thought of guilt and invited it inside himself, but it would not enter his mind or heart and it remained a cold and dormant place inside him. Did he kill himself when he first killed and so was already dead?

When his work was done he mounted the coal black horse, caught the polished reins of the sorrel, and rode toward home. As he traveled that thin stony path, he thought how a kind of

wickedness had died, but what it left behind could not be undone or unremembered. Ahead could be seen the light from the flaring lantern shining through the windows. He thought how the wickedness lived inside his own house but could not be killed when it was born and must be loved without condition. He wished to shudder or tremble. He wished to regret his actions, to lament, to cry. He wanted to long for the past when he was a boy and lived as a boy.

But he could do none of these. His bygone days were mere shapes and scenes played against a shadowy wall. He had no past because he was too young. He had no past, except the past of a child: hunger and satisfaction, heat and cold, wet and dry, squares of yellow light on a wooden floor, companionable animals, the love of a mother and father. There was no bite of conscience, no thought to retrace the life and live it differently from what was done before. He wanted nothing to do with such wandering thoughts or feelings. He was so minded as he rode through the evening vapors, away from the man he'd killed beneath the moon's rising face.

That night she wandered barefoot into the room where he sat. The only light was the nimbus of a tallow candle centered on the table where they ate their meals.

"What is it?" she said.

"Can't sleep?" he said.

"My eyes won't close when I sleep," she said.

She stretched until her body refused to go any farther and then she made a surprised sound and let it back. She came close to him and tapped his knees that he should make them a place for her to sit. She looked like a child with long tangled lashes that wove and unwove each time her eyes closed and

opened. She scrutinized the palms of her small hands and then let them fall helplessly against the round of her belly.

"You ought to put on your stockings," he said. "The night's cold."

"It is surely cold," she said, and as if in agreement came a swoop of wind that scattered snow like buckshot against the cabin walls.

"This is the cold that brings the warm," he said, and she told him it was the same thing his mother said.

He wondered what she might be tonight. Her mind seemed improved. Would he tell her? Could he not?

"What's your idea of heaven?" she said urgently. "Do you think we are saved by hope?"

"I don't know," he said. "I don't have any answers like that tonight, nor no questions."

"Do you pray?"

"No," he said. "I don't think I do."

"Well. If you decide to start, just don't do it where I can hear it."

"I will remember that," he said.

"What is it?" she said again. "Are you going to tell me?"

"I seen him," he said, and she turned her eyes on him with all their clarity.

"You seen him?"

"He told me the woman is dead."

"Was it bad?"

"He didn't tell me and I didn't ask."

"Where'd you see him?"

"On the road. He's dead too."

She then looked off to a place that was inside her mind. He

watched her thoughts as they crossed her eyes. In her head were mysteries he could not decipher.

"Are you sure he's dead?"

"He's dead," he told her, his voice resolute, and yet he realized that even in the state of death, life-blind and quelled, the man would haunt her and he would continue his possession of her forever. He wondered if there would ever be enough peace to stop this turning for the wound that had been cut into her memory.

The room filled with a great pressure and it was as if the air was being squeezed through the cracks and jambs. The stove banged again as the fire's temperature increased and there came the visitation of memory from Gettysburg, the portal through which the past might come into the present. The stove joints ticked with expansion and a beam in the wall pealed out as it chafed on a peg. Outside the wind was running and in the morning would be white sculpted fields, the ground swept bare and strangely grassy and in other places the earth would carry hanging drifts higher than his head.

"His was the blackest soul," she said as if the news of his death was all so long ago.

She held out her hand, a fist unfolded, her mouth open and wordless. For days she'd struggled to find the strength to bear down on the pain. She thought she must get it stopped before it continued. For days she'd felt her tiny bones shifting and moving, finding positions of accommodation. She prayed for the strength, but it just hadn't come. She suddenly groaned and cried out as her leg was seized by a cramp. She stretched the curled leg and held it in the air above the floor where its muscle quivered beneath her skin and finally loosened. The

infant was ready to be born, and known only to her it was rushing its birth.

"The pain when it comes is worse than knives," she said. "I want to die." Then she said, "Lift me up," and when he did she said, "Come to bed," and he followed her to bed where she asked he lay down behind her and press his knuckled hand against her back.

"Don't rub," she said, her voice reed thin. "Just push hard. Push as hard as you can with your fist."

When the pain subsided she wanted him to hold her in his arms and rock her gently. He found the back of her neck with his face and breathed deeply her sleepy smell. She moved her back into his chest and pulled his arm to her chest, his hand to her breast. There was about nothing left of her, not back or shoulders or chest, her belly so huge. She moved his hand to her belly and there her skin was stretched and taut and it was holding her this way they slipped into the lull of exhausted sleep.

He did not remember when he fell asleep but his gesture upon waking was to resume the pushing with his fist. Yet when he lifted his hand he found nothing to touch and when he crawled up through sleep, he could not find her and the bed was cold and soaking wet. He stood from the wet bed and with his first drink of water rinsed the taste of sleep from his mouth and with the second slaked the thirst brought on by the dry heat of the wood fire. He thought to have found her in the darkness by now, but he didn't.

Then he called out to her and tore the quilt from the bed and barefoot he was running for the door.

Outside the night was blue and vivid and continuous with

its blanket of scraping winter light. He could hear his mother come from sleep and calling out his name at his back. In the forest the pines wore their mantles of snow and from the barns and stables was drafted a strange and serene silence. He called out her name in the stillness and the sound of his voice ran out to distance across the brow of the snow-covered summit.

"Rachel," he cried. "Rachel."

He felt the sting of cold in his lungs. His heart was pounding in his chest, but there was no answer returned. In the sky Pegasus was due west and the Big Dipper stood upright on its handle. The flight silhouette of an owl, its shallow wing beats passed over his head and he looked off in its telling direction.

Then he could see her in faint illumination lighted by the moon. She lay at the misted and unfrozen stream bank, where she'd carried herself to the place where the hot waters bubbled up from the earth. She was trembling and moaning and he began to run to her, but when she saw him coming she stood. She held up a hand and yelled at him, "Let me die," but she did not speak whole words before they were torn with her cries of pain. He kept on, dragging the blanket he'd pulled from the bed. She waved her hands, no, telling him to stay away, and when he did not stop she turned and threw herself full body into the warm water.

He saw the flash of her white legs as she fell down into the pool. He was running across the frozen ground, so near the clouded and steamy shoals of the spring. She then stood upright, her wet shift a sheen in the moonlight and stepped into the eddy where the current circled a boulder before taking a sharp cooling swing, before quickening and roping with

heavy turbulence and troughy rapids, before falling off the mountain.

Here she let go from her grasp and there was a white bobbing that floated from the shallows and made for the current's catch. There was first one and then there was another one and both of them dunking and rising like tiny pumpkins, the second one floating after the first one.

He splashed into the shallows of the birth-stained water as the current carried them toward the falls. He threw himself forward, rasing a great flounce of water that swiftly closed to submerge him. He stood and ran and dove again, his thighs breaking the surface, and he was catching them in his hands, first one and then the other, their tiny faces red and soundless and contorted with the unimaginable terror of being born.

Afterward, he wished to console her, but she seemed to want nothing from him. She turned her back on him and in her stance was written the question why: Why did you do that? Why did you save them? Who gave you the right to do that?

She told him, "I want to hate you for what you have done, hate you as much as I hate him who did this to me," but he made no reply.

For several days there was nothing of motherhood that kindled inside her, but Hettie would not relent and finally she gave in and let them nurse at her breasts. They were two little boys with fine downy birth-hair on their shoulders, backs, and their odd-shaped heads. Their faces were like those of tiny old men and they beat the air with their fists and their cries were hearty and healthy exercises. She refused to name them and they were not concerned because for this there would be time.

Then there was more cold and a chilling rain that turned to snow and lasted for days, and winter on the mountain that year seemed longer and colder than any winter before. The snow and cold, as if an edgeless sea, enveloped the dormant earth, the arrowed pines shrugged to the skirling wind. Hung in the sky was the white sun, the desolate glistering of far bright stars, the cooling remnants of old stars. Outside the candle-bright cabin was a tide of white-locked fields in deep suspended silence.

During these days of snow-pent darkness he was seized by a sleep with an iron grip, senseless, nameless, and peaceful sleep, and only afterward did he sense the flow of time gone by and feel what was inside him begin to ease. He had died a first death and a second and a third. He knew in this life he was not done with death and killing.

It was a sleeper's world frosted, silent, dark and starkly beautiful, and he remembered tranquillity. He remembered the days in the valley riding the coal black horse. The horse rising to the bit, its hot breath blowing back at him, the shedding sweat from its sleek black neck, flecks of foam from its quivering nostrils. He remembered his father. He remembered the dead. He remembered nothing moving in the darkness of those nights, but one night he awoke to a chorus of baby cries and Rachel cradling a baby in her arms and feeding the baby and then feeding the other baby, and when she lay down she lay down beside him, her belly tucked against his back and her face at his neck. He remembered her arm reaching across his chest and gently taking her wrist in his hand. Sleep, he remembered thinking, sleep a little while longer.

COAL

BLACK

HORSE

A Conversation with the Author

A Reading and Discussion Guide

READERS ROUND TABLE
ALGONQUIN

Although the novel is largely about a boy's journey, it is also about a very particular moment in history. Much of its power comes from the Civil War battle scenes, which feel so real and visceral. What kind of research did you do to re-create those scenes?

It began with a visit to Gettysburg. As a boy growing up in New Hampshire, my war of fascination was the American Revolution, but when living in southern Pennsylvania I began to wonder about the Civil War. So I went to Gettysburg to see the battlefield and slowly but surely began to feel myself drawn into that experience. I was trying, as a curious person, to learn about it and understand it. I began to read and one thing led to another. I visited other battlefields and somewhere along the way I decided I wanted to try to write this novel. Again, as a way to experience it. I was as ignorant of this world as Robey Childs and in a sense I invented him so that we could discover it together. I remember I was at Shiloh for a major reenactment and was standing inside a battery of cannons. I could feel the concussive force of the explosions against my body and coming up through the earth. My face felt wet and when I wiped at my nose it was bleeding. I thought how that

must have happened to the artillerists and for a moment I had the tiniest glimpse of their experience.

You're not from the South, yet you capture your characters' voices and diction so well. Did you read Civil War accounts or did it come by way of instinct?

It's true, I'm not Southern born but was raised in the country in the northern reach of the Appalachian chain. A lot of similarities up north and down south along that spine of those mountains. And the mountains of West Virginia, the fictional setting of Robey's home, exists in a kind of not-south not-north ether. Even in ancient times it was a place where the northern tribes and southern tribes brushed up against each other and was a kind of no-man's-land, contested territory and a place where you could get killed. As to the voices, I think of them as rural and arcadian, naturally sardonic, and trenchant. My family had an amazing talent for the aphoristic and the epigrammatic. This went a long way in establishing authority in a character. When Hettie Childs first spoke she came onto the page as if she'd been waiting 150 years and finally this was her moment. She is real to me in every way.

It seems as though the coal black horse is equally real to you. Did you grow up with horses?

Horses, cows, pigs, sheep. Yes. The farm is still there and I get home every chance I can. The coal black horse began as a simple means of conveyance. The boy needed a good horse if he was to carry out his mother's imperative. He needed a horse with experience he lacked. So I came up with the coal

black horse and then the strangest thing happened. With each draft the horse became more and more prominent. The horse grew in my mind and grew on the page and in time the horse was the same to me as it was to Robey Childs. I mean that literally. Such a horse as I imagined was lustrously iridescent. Like coal when turned to the light. I was amazed when I first saw the hardcover jacket my publisher did for the hardcover. It is so arresting. It really took my breath away. And of course there is something ancient and timeless about the horse and the rider. The horse is consort and for thousands of years we have lived together by agreement. I think they are very beautiful. Sometimes I think, like Hettie, the coal black horse was out there the whole time and just waiting for Robey and me to come along.

In the process of writing the book, did you think about how warfare has changed since the Civil War?

Combat actually changed during that war. Take for instance the minie ball, invented by Captain Claude-Étienne Minié of France. This was a high-caliber grooved conical lead bullet. It could be loaded quickly, and because it was grooved, when fired from a rifle it was very accurate over a long distance, and yet the generals still believed in massed lines of men in close formation charging over open ground. New weapons, old tactics. Wounds were especially horrible and so many wounded required amputation because the minie ball did not just break bone but actually shattered whole sections of bone, and the bone could not be mended.

But however terrible and chaotic war is, I think instances of courage and dignity and sacrifice in warfare are timeless

and universal. I am not sure if it's true, but I read that the men who retreated after Pickett's famous charge walked backwards because it would have been ignoble to have been shot in the back.

Even now I think the reasons why boys and men go to war haven't changed. We must recognize what a great adventure war is. If not for the Civil War thousands and thousands of young men were destined to live their entire lives in the same place, the same town. They saw the war as an escape from daily lives that were relentlessly boring and tedious. War is extremely liberating and purifying and for so many men, they were never so alive as when they were at war. It is not acceptable to talk about this love of war, but I think it's real. I do not think this has changed. William Faulkner wrote, "The past is never dead. It's not even past."

What was the biggest challenge for you in writing the novel?

I think all writers are more interested in what they don't know than what they do know. Naturally, helplessly, hopelessly curious about everything. Research is so fascinating. I just loved all that reading and those experiences, but ultimately I am a dramatist, not a historian. So, two things: First I had to acknowledge how inexhaustible the information is and literally begin to turn away from it. Second, I had to find a way to animate the story I wanted to tell. But, where to start? And how to start? And where to go from there? In a sense, all stories are about what we mean to ourselves and what we mean to each other. It's really that simple, but every one of them has to be different. I thought about the boy leaving home and entering

that landscape. He was really quite the innocent. He was born in remoteness. It was his story I wanted to tell—a boy sent out to bring his father home, a boy looking for his father. I think for all time mothers have been sending their sons to bring home their fathers. I think about how hard it was for her to send him. I assumed a vein of iron in these people. I think there are people who have such faith in each other.

Your characters do seem to retain faith under very difficult circumstances. Did any of them surprise you?

Yes, late in the novel, at Gettysburg when Robey takes justice into his own hands. I remember the days when writing that scene. I do not approve of what he did, but I could not stop him. It was as if his will was discovered and he became a powerful influence in every rewrite thereafter, and there were quite a few. Hettie seemed to come onto the page all at once and it was only afterward that I realized how powerful her presence is throughout the book. She is present in the opening and the ending, but for me she was never very far away. She possessed a kind of strength and wisdom and equanimity that the world so lacked. And of course the coal black horse becoming more prominent by increments until finally it became the title. I still have dreams about them.

Are there any other characters who are entering your dreams? Is there another novel unfolding in your mind?

I have never thought of writing as something I do but as a place where I go. There I find a community and a language and an experience of totality. So, yes. The event at the end of

Coal Black Horse, the birth. When I first realized that Rachel was pregnant, I felt an overwhelming responsibility and only later, when she eventually gives birth, did I know she was having twins. As I have mentioned, there are days you remember when you are working and these were two of them: her being pregnant and then having twins. I just couldn't let that go, so in the book I'm working on now, I am telling their story, only it is years and years later and they are grown men.

1. Why do you think Robey's mother sends him on a dangerous journey to find his father? How do you feel about her
decision?

2. Robey is reminded of his mother as he travels. For example, when he is shot: "He was in pain and his mother always said that pain was weakness leaving the body" (page
53). Where else in the story do you find her presence? How
would you characterize their relationship?

3. In what ways does the landscape at the farm, on the road,
on the battlefield, and in Gettysburg inform the story and
affect Robey and the people around him?

4. In his travels Robey sees a lot of strange, beautiful, and
gruesome things. For example, the horse skeleton covered
with vines and flowers (page 26) and then the description
of the man's skeleton a few pages later (page 29). What
other examples of this juxtaposition can you find? How do
they affect how you understand Robey's journey?

5. Robey meets so many characters on the road—Morphew,
the German, the upside-down boy, the goose man, the major, the pregnant woman in the graveyard, the scavenger

brothers. How do these secondary characters help (or impair) Robey's quest to find his father?

6. What role do fate and second sight play in the novel? For example, Robey's mother knows that Thomas Jackson has died without being told and that Robey must find his father before July. What other examples can you find, and how do fate and premonition guide your own life?

7. Morphew tells Robey that he is "in for an education" (page 21). After a battle later in the story, Robey has this encounter with the coal black horse (page 112): "Then he urged the horse on and it hesitated before responding as if to acknowledge that its rider had learned some valuable lesson and should be rewarded for such." What is Robey learning? How does he acknowledge his education?

8. Throughout the course of the novel Robey has to make hard decisions such as stealing food and horses. How does he feel about these decisions? In what ways do they seem to change him?

9. Robey doesn't kill the man who rapes Rachel even though he has the opportunity and cause to do so. Why doesn't he?

10. Religion plays a significant role over the course of the story, perhaps most dramatically in this revelation on page 116: "He decided from that day forever after that there must live a heartless God to let such despair be visited on the earth, or as his father said, a God too tired and no longer capable of doing the work required of him." How do religion and spirituality shape the novel?

11. Pages 124–26 describe the scavengers and minor businesses that spring up in the wake of battle. How does Robey seem to feel about this? How does this affect your perception of the Civil War?

12. The pregnant woman in the graveyard tells Robey that "people should be born twice: once as they are and once as they are not" (page 130). What does she mean by this? How does this tie into the themes of the novel?

13. How would you describe Robey's relationship with his mother, the coal black horse, his father, and Rachel? How is each relationship different and alike? And how do these relationships define Robey as a boy and Robey as a man?

14. War has affected the land and the people—for example, the "raggedy old woman with a sun-stained and stroke-twisted face" (page 178). To what extent have the characters, the land, and even the animals been affected by the ravages of of war?

15. How does the birth of the twins change Robey? How does it change Rachel? Do you have the sense that things will be better or worse for the family? Why?

16. How has Robey's story altered the way you think about war and violence? Has it made you think about love and faith differently? Are there particular passages that reflect your opinions and feelings?

MOLLY ULINE-OLMSTEAD

ROBERT OLMSTEAD is the author of five previous books (*River Dogs, Soft Water, A Trail of Heart's Blood Wherever We Go, America by Land,* and *Stay Here with Me*). The recipient of a Guggenheim fellowship, an NEA grant, and the 2007 Heartland Award for Fiction, he is a professor at Ohio Wesleyan University.

Hast thou given the horse strength?

Hast thou clothed his neck with thunder?

He swalloweth the ground with fierceness and rage . . .

—BOOK OF JOB

Published by
ALGONQUIN BOOKS OF CHAPEL HILL
Post Office Box 2225
Chapel Hill, North Carolina 27515-2225

a division of
Workman Publishing
225 Varick Street
New York, New York 10014

First paperback edition, Algonquin Books of Chapel Hill, May 2008.
Originally published by Algonquin Books of Chapel Hill in 2007.
Printed in the United States of America.
Published simultaneously in Canada by Thomas Allen & Son Limited.
Design by April Leidig-Higgins.

This is a work of fiction. While, as in all fiction, the literary
perceptions and insights are based on experience, all names, characters,
places, and incidents either are products of the author's imagination or
are used fictitiously.

Library of Congress Cataloging-in-Publication Data
Olmstead, Robert.
Coal black horse / Robert Olmstead.—1st ed.
p. cm.
ISBN-13: 978-1-56512-521-6 (HC)
1. Fathers and sons—Fiction.   2. United States—History—Civil War,
1861–1865—Fiction.   I. Title.
PS3565.L67C63 2007
813'.54—dc22   2006042914
ISBN-13: 978-1-56512-601-5 (PB)

10 9 8 7 6 5 4 3

Robert Olmstead

ALGONQUIN BOOKS OF CHAPEL HILL | 2008

secrets, he may need that protection. Certainly, however, he knows something about the first big scandal in Mayor Lindsay's official family.

In the case of Marcus, who resigned after his indictment, pleaded guilty to a charge of bribery conspiracy, and is serving a fifteen-month jail term, Lindsay commented: "I've been through some rough ones but I guess this is the roughest yet." He didn't elaborate on the other "rough ones" he's been through, but, given the history of New York, Lindsay's two years as mayor—up to the Marcus-Itkin-Corallo imbroglio—might be just a warm-up. The ghosts do not chuckle; neither do they envy him.

The shadow hanging over New York is no darker than the shadows that have gone before. The hoods who cried for their mothers as they roasted over the hot coals in the Mafia furnace and the sophisticated, high-riding gangsters of today are separated by many long years of violence, but the play seems always to be the same. Only the actors have changed.

THREE

BUFFALO:

Niagara Powerhouse

In the files of the Buffalo police department there lies the murder story of narcotics smuggler Al Agueci, of how the Mafia took his clothes, his skin, the very flesh from his bones. Agueci was a man practically no one, except the Mafia, knew. His widow found out, though, what it means to cross the barons of the brotherhood, however right you may be. Crossing the top Mafiosi does not necessarily involve going against their wishes; it is enough to go against the grain of their egos, for they believe they can do no wrong—and there is little chance for appeal. Indeed, it is the insecurity that they themselves feel when they wrong one of their own that apparently leads, at times, to violence.

"*Sangu lava sangu,*" The Mafiosi say. "Blood washes blood." And a lot of blood, other than Agueci's, has been spilled in trying to wash the slate clean. Because of Al's murder, his brother Vito set his sights on the throat of one of the top gangsters in this country, Stefano Magaddino, Buffalo-based Mafia powerhouse servicing the western New York, Ohio valley, and Toronto, Canada, areas.

The Agueci brothers were born and raised in Sicily, eventually working their way to Canada, where they became heavy traffickers in narcotics for Stefano Magaddino's Mafia family. The brothers then obtained Magaddino's permission to branch out and soon began to engage in the narcotics business in the greater Buffalo area. On July 20, 1961, however, they were arrested in New York City for violation of the federal narcotics law, thereby setting in motion a chain of events that eventually led to Joe Valachi and his remarkable testimony concerning the Mafia.

Magaddino's agreement with the Aguecis called for a percentage of their profits to be paid to Don Stefano. The don, in turn, was bound to provide protection for his boys: freedom from the interference of other gangsters, bail money in the event of arrest, and many other things.

The evidence indicates, however, that Magaddino, perhaps on a whim, reneged on his end of the deal when the arrest was made and did nothing to aid the Mafiosi brothers, who were depending on him for assistance. Al's wife finally managed to provide bail for her husband, and the angry man set out to avenge himself on Magaddino. He was not seen again until November 23rd, when his burned and mutilated body was found in a field near Rochester, New York. The Buffalo police department records the murder thus:

> On November 23, 1961, the body of Albert G. Agueci of 21 Armitage Drive, Scarsborough, Canada, was found in a field near Rochester, N.Y. His hands were bound behind his back, and his ankles were tied with long cord and he was strangled. His jaw was broken, half his teeth had been kicked or knocked out. Substantial portions of meaty tissue were removed from the calves of his legs. His body was doused with gasoline and ignited. His body was mutilated beyond recognition. This was not only to cause his death, of course, but this was to send a message to anyone else who had the temerity or the gall to try to resort to vengeance against one of the dons of the empire.

Al Agueci had learned the horror of a Mafia death-lesson, and in his tortured and ebbing consciousness at the end he must have begun to realize the wisdom behind the old Mafia proverb: *"Tra la legge e la Mafia, la piu temibile non e la legge."* "Between the law and the Mafia, the law is not the most to be feared." The message was clear, but to one the message appeared to have little meaning: brother Vito.

Vito Agueci was convicted on the narcotics charge and sent to Atlanta federal prison. There he met up with Joe Valachi, who, as a member of Vito Genovese's New York family, had been invited to share the Genovese prison cell with five other inmates.

Agueci told Valachi he would like a meeting with Genovese, and since he didn't know the don personally, he asked Valachi to arrange it. Valachi relayed the message, but Genovese refused to meet Agueci. Vito had already made known his declaration that he would do anything to avenge his brother's murder, and Genovese knew what "anything" meant. Consequently, he looked on Agueci as a personal threat to himself as well as his close Mafia *compare*, Magaddino.

From that moment on Genovese began playing Agueci against Valachi, and vice versa, hoping thereby to do away with Agueci. Genovese told Valachi to walk Agueci around the prison yard so he could identify him. This Valachi did, and within a short time Valachi found himself under surveillance by other ominous members of the Mafia also doing time in Atlanta—Johnny Dioguardi, a convicted extortionist, Trigger Mike Coppolo, and Joe Beck, alias "Joe Palermo," all of them high-ranking Mafiosi from New York.

To add to Valachi's suspicions of a plot, Agueci, at the instigation of Genovese's pals, began calling him "a rat"— an informer—while Genovese in his cell at night began telling him to "get" Agueci for calling him names. Valachi testified later that he became convinced Genovese wanted to "kill two birds with one stone," for Valachi knew that his killing of Agueci in prison would also seal his own destiny, as far as the law was concerned. He realized he was being used as a tool and that, as a button man, he was expendable to the Mafia.

According to Valachi, his reluctance to do the job assigned to him caused Genovese to give him the Mafia kiss of death, which greatly increased his continuing fear for his life. Valachi became almost paranoid in suspecting everyone in the prison of being determined to kill him and even had himself thrown into solitary confinement, which, he said, was the same as walking into the safety of a police station.

Upon his release from the "hole," Valachi's fears rose until he was almost irrational. For days he sat in his cell and wouldn't leave it even to eat. Then, during an outdoor rest period one day, Valachi went for a walk in the yard. Near a construction project he suddenly looked up and saw a man he thought was hoodlum Joe Beck; he was sure that Beck had been sent to murder him for not following Genovese's instructions to eliminate Vito Agueci. Valachi felt that this was it. Grabbing a piece of pipe, he began slamming it down on Beck's head until his adversary lay motionless.

Unfortunately, for Valachi, the man he killed was not Joe Beck, though he looked very much like him. Fortunately, for the American public, Valachi was tried and convicted of murder and sentenced to life imprisonment—fortunately, that is, because Valachi's sentence decided him to ask for the protection of the law and to "blow the whistle" on the entire structure of the Mafia, for he knew that if he ever returned to prison, no matter which one or where it was, the violent black hand of the Mafia would search him out. In prison it would be kill or be killed. So he talked, and the nation listened.

But while Valachi filled in one side of the picture, the repercussions of Al Agueci's murder were providing some details of the other side. For example, Assistant Chief of Detectives Michael Amico, who was in charge of the criminal intelligence division of the Buffalo police department, reported to the McClellan committee about the "Niagara Powerhouse" himself.

Stefano Magaddino, alias "The Boss," "The Old Man," and "Don Stefano," lives at 5118 Dana Drive, in an exclusive area of Lewiston, N.Y., with his wife. His luxurious home is located on a plot of land adjacent to a similarly luxurious home occupied by his daughter and son-in-law, James LaDuca, who was in attendance at the Apalachin convention.

Don Stefano (who is 77) is the irrefutable lord paramount and titular head of syndicated organized crime in the Buffalo-Niagara Falls and Toronto areas.

Stefano is known to be the "don" and in absolute control of all illegal operations in the area as pertains to organized criminal activities. No crime by members of the organization is permitted without his permission and guidance.

Don Stefano was arrested on August 16, 1921, as a fugitive from justice relative to a homicide at Avon, N.J., and turned over to the Avon, N.J., Police Department.

Informed police authorities believe Stefano Magaddino was among visitors to the notorious Apalachin meeting, November 14, 1957. His clothes were found on the premises where the meeting was held.

It has been reasonably theorized that a meeting with such magnitude of important notorious Apalachin guests would not proceed without the presence of Don Stefano Magaddino, who has extensive criminal interests and influence in syndicate decisions.

Don Stefano, before the Apalachin disclosures, was known to wield a great deal of influence in Niagara Falls politics. In the late 1930's Magaddino was reported to be associated with John C. Montana in the Empire State Brewery in Olean, N.Y.

It was during this time that Montana was regarded as a trusted lieutenant of Magaddino, and second in command. This close association with the Stefano Magaddino dynasty of criminal activity in the western New York area has been more closely cemented by intermarriage of the two families.

Also closely associated with Magaddino is Herman Weinstein, who is alleged to have profited handsomely from his illegitimate transactions with the mob in the way of bootlegging, black market gasoline operations during World War II, and many other illegitimate transactions. Weinstein is now regarded as a successful motel operator, owning the plush Peace Bridge Motel, which is considered a meeting place for prominent syndicate members.

I mention this association because our surveillance, I might add, takes us many, many times into this plush motel, where many of these syndicated individuals from in and outside of the Buffalo area tend to congregate.

Since Apalachin, Stefano Magaddino has relinquished immediate control over legitimate businesses such as Magaddino Memorial Chapel, the Power City Distributing Co. of Niagara Falls and Camellia Linen Supply Co. of Buffalo, N.Y.

Stefano Magaddino is ostensibly considered to be in retirement from legitimate business holdings, passing on his interests directly or indirectly to members of his immediate family.

Magaddino's present chief lieutenant in charge of Buffalo syndicate operations is Fred "Lupo" Randaccio. Randaccio indisputably controls all gambling, labor racketeering, and other illegitimate activities for the old man.

Associates of Stefano Magaddino include John C. Montana, Samuel Freedman, Herman Weinstein, Roy Carlisi, Fred Randaccio, Fred Magavero, James Zerilli (Detroit), Joseph Falcone (Utica), Anthony Perna, James LaDuca, Dominic D'Agostino, Samuel Rangatore, Dominic Mantele, and Benjamin Nicoletti, the last five from Niaraga Falls and Samuel Pieri, of Buffalo.

I have given names there of those associates.

He truly did. The men Lieutenant Amico named cannot forget Agueci, the lonely field, and the pitiful remnants of a man seared beyond recognition because he stood up for his rights—or for what passes for them within the peculiar government of the underworld. Suffice it to say that Magaddino's funeral parlor did not handle the funeral, though Amico pointed out to the Senate committee that "we see no illegitimacy at this time [in Magaddino's undertaking business] other than, of course, he enjoys a virtual monopoly of servicing those individuals that are deceased from the families of individuals from the criminal underworld."

Not content merely to name names, however, Lieutenant Amico also sketched the full extent of Mafia operations in the Buffalo area—a sketch substantiated by details collected from many sources. For instance, Lieutenant Amico explained to the senators the business perhaps best loved by the dons—supplying snowy linens to restaurants, barber shops, motels, and other places—using the Buffalo area as an example.

The boys attend to the smallest details of the linen business with consummate courtesy, and it is this occupation that enables the soldiers in the Mafia army to work their way up from bedsheets to the more serious business of winding-sheets—where the money really is.

Camellia Linens typifies the Magaddino operational ploy. According to Lieutenant Amico:

> This is a type of business that catered to restaurants and barber shops, and what came to my attention, not in the form of an official complaint but undertones of perhaps extortion in this respect. Many times they would contact these barbers, perhaps some of the members of the gang would get a haircut and perhaps tip them a substantial amount, and then go in a few weeks later and indicate to them that they would like to leave their business there, their linen supply business.

> These individuals would indicate to them a tendency not to change because they certainly were happy with their linen supply at that particular time. Well, the mere presence of these individuals many times, dressed in the way they were, the demeanor that they showed, would tend to sort of discourage some of these individuals to resist them and to, in effect, acquiesce, and it is said it is better to get their linens than to fight them.

> Now, you might wonder what is so important, perhaps, with some linen supply. They might, at the outset, even come in and say, "We will supply your linens for maybe a penny or two per linen cheaper," but after the individual has once changed his services or supply, he is then stuck, and this

outfit might, and it has been in cases in the past, perhaps not only increase the prices to where they were, but even add to it. This wouldn't be all.

In many instances, if there were, for example, 50 pieces of linen that were counted by the barber-shop proprietor, and this individual would come in and say you had 100 pieces of linen this time, and he would say I only counted 50, and he would say we counted 100, and because of his presence and because of what he represented, perhaps, the fellow would acquiesce and say, "Well, I guess I had a hundred." This was the means, at that time, whereby I feel they gained monies in an illegal way.

Amico, a staunch individual, held the senators spellbound as he traced, in a simple, sometimes ungrammatical but always sincere way, syndicate workings at the operational, money-making level:

The same will go for cigarette vending machines and jukeboxes. I had an experience in one instance where they had made a movement; [Fred "Lupo"] Randaccio and a fellow named Fred McGove really had gone into business in a cigarette-vending-machine operation. They had attempted to monopolize the entire predominantly [Italian] west side of Buffalo. In many instances they did this in a legitimate manner.

However there were instances where some were recalcitrant individuals who felt that certainly after some other supplier had been loyal to them they didn't want to change individuals in the middle of the stream. They again came in there in their typical fashion and dressed up in this normal Hollywood style, that you might see in the movies or television, and with their persuasive tones or undertones would sell the idea that they should change their cigarette-vending services to their own. In one instance, one fellow had the gall, or at least the ability and the guts to resist them, and he came to me and asked me what he could do. I said, "Well, you are aware perhaps that this does take guts, and there are going to be threats," and he said, "That is fine." He was willing to go along, and it was only because of insistent intervention by our unit that they gave up trying to change him to take their machines.

They indicated very persuasively and strongly that he would not open his particular restaurant, that they would break the place down, and he might find his body out in the alley, but here was an individual with real guts, and with the real temerity, and it wasn't easy. I will explain here it wasn't easy even for me to get out and harass these individuals with the defense I had at my disposal, it wouldn't be enough for an arrest or conviction. The individual indicated to me, "What do I have to do, be found dead before the police can do something?"

In Buffalo, certainly, the Mafia is well entrenched, and Randaccio's personal touch, in an open and flagrant attempt to "muscle" a restaurant owner, indicates the close attention the leading Mafiosi pay to the details of their rackets. Even a November, 1968, arraignment of Magaddino on charges of international racketeering and conspiracy and a huge tax lien filed against him by the IRS would seem unlikely to shake up Buffalo's Mafia family much.

Randaccio is, according to the Buffalo police department, second-in-command of the Magaddino empire and apparently heir presumptive to the legitimate and illegitimate baronies set up by The Old Man. At the time of the investigation Randaccio's address was given as 562 Richmond Avenue, Buffalo, New York. And since he was born July 1, 1907, in Palermo, Sicily, he is one of the few members of the American Mafia who can claim Italian birth.

Randaccio was first arrested in this country in 1922 for juvenile delinquency. Two years later he was collared for gambling and bootlegging. In 1930 he received a ten-year sentence for felonious assault—reduced from robbery, first degree—when he held up a garage proprietor, but this merely hoisted his personal flag a little higher on the Mafia mainmast. In 1956 deportation proceedings were brought against him by the immigration authorities in the Justice Department, but the legal division of this dedicated branch of the government was horrified to learn that Randaccio had somehow gotten into the U.S. Army in 1945 and served six months—which automatically gave him citizenship. The proceedings were dropped.

Randaccio's interests are varied and somewhat in line with the syndicate *modus operandi* that dictates that money be put anywhere, as long as it becomes legitimate and goes to work somehow. Accordingly, Randaccio and others formed the Delaware Vending Company, which handles all kinds of "slots," the Frontier Lathers, Inc., the services of which are not specified in the Senate records, and the Tur-Ran Builders, operating out of Amherst, New York, a Buffalo suburb.

These legitimate companies, according to Amico, are paralleled by Randaccio's operation of Magaddino's criminal empire, backed by a corps of "muscle men," such as John Cammillieri, who handles labor and union racketeering, Pat Natarelli, Joseph Fino, and Daniel Sansanese, who take care of organization bookmaking interests, and Steven Cannarozzo, who handles the policy, or numbers, racket.

Lupo, who effects a Windsor knot in his conservative ties and a touch of gray at the temples, has no formal education, but the slick gangster with the Palermo label is regarded as a great organizer with ample ability to hold the organization together in times of stress.

Randaccio and his buddies commute frequently between the United States and Canada (Toronto and Hamilton), where the Mafia is firmly established and whence citizen-Mafiosi are branching out throughout what is left of the British empire—especially its remnants in the Caribbean.

Randaccio, who is a young man compared to the oldsters in the syndicate, is waiting for his inheritance to drop into his arms, and it is a safe bet that he will succeed Magaddino, keeper of the keys to the gang treasury in his particular territory—unless a federal court conviction, obtained in Buffalo in February, 1968, for conspiracy to commit armed robbery, alters his plans.

Until recently Randaccio's chief rival for Magaddino's mantle was John Charles Montana, a curious individual who was undercover heir apparent to Magaddino until the Apalachin raid. Born on June 30, 1893, in Montedore, Italy, Montana, who died in 1967, lived to regret that he ever went to that notable gathering in upper New York State. Gray-haired and distinguished-looking, with hard lines that ran down his face to the corners of his mouth, Montana was one of the rarities of the Mafia organization: he had no criminal record until, as a result of his Apalachin appearance, he was accused and convicted of conspiracy to obstruct justice in federal court, and even that conviction was later reversed on appeal.

Testimony at the Senate hearings revealed that Montana lived with his wife at 340 Starin Avenue, Buffalo. His rags-to-riches climb began while he was a messenger boy in a candy shop during his grade-school days. Somehow he made enough money to purchase a taxicab, and somehow he got to know the men who run the Mafia. A cloak of mystery surrounded Montana, and even Amico was forced to admit that until the Apalachin raid, no one, not even the police, suspected that Montana was working with the upper echelon of the New England syndicate. Indeed, his arrest confounded business associates and politicians who had counted him as a friend.

At the time of the Apalachin raid, Amico testified, Montana controlled the largest taxi company in western New York State, formed through a merger of the Yellow Cab Company and the Van Dyke Taxi and Transfer Company. His cabs had a monopoly at preferred taxi locations at Buffalo Airport, the then New York Central railroad station, and the better hotels, including the Statler-Hilton. After November, 1957, Montana's former patrons permitted other cab companies and a host of independents to use the taxi stands, but his cabs continued to do much of the business in Buffalo.

John Montana was elected councilman in Buffalo in 1928 and 1930 and was appointed to other important city posts as the years went by. He was named "Man of the Year" by the local chapter of the National Junior Chamber of Commerce in 1956, in recognition of his services to his home town, where he also was a member of the zoning board and constantly expounded the value of good government. The Elks, the Buffalo Athletic Club, and the Erie Downs golf course, to mention but a few organizations, owe him a debt of gratitude.

Nevertheless, Amico tied Montana in with the notorious Joseph (The Wolf) DiCarlo, a Sicilian-born former Buffalo public enemy No. 1 whose police record includes arrests for assault, coercion, intimidating witnesses, and violation of federal narcotics laws, who is supposedly engaged in illegal gambling in the greater Miami area, and has been reported to frequent the Esquire Smoke Shop, the Carib Hotel, the Tahiti Bar, and the Grand Barber Shop—all in Miami Beach.

In evaluating Montana's contribution to the body politic, Amico was terse and to the point. Then, prodded by McClellan committee member Jacob Javits (R., N.Y.), Amico added:

> I believe I would compare this, that I would say is our great American way of life, that it is such a great nation that anyone, regardless of who he may be, is certainly given an opportunity to succeed and become successful in business. Now it is an apathetic, lethargic public that is enhancing Mr. Montana's position, and maybe a public hearing of this

type might do much toward awakening the public to show that this type of organized crime does exist and some of these people perhaps, it is best not to patronize them and not to go along and not encourage this particular setup. So it is the public themselves that either contribute or detract from such an endeavor.

Incidentally, when Javits took time to deny Amico's charge that an area of crime overlordship was run by "Jewish ties," he must have been unaware that police throughout the country long ago divided the syndicate into Italian and Jewish elements, simply because these ethnic groups controlled the rackets—though the Jewish mobsters have been mostly eliminated over the years. Louis Buchalter, a Manhattan racketeer, his buddy, Bugsy Siegel, the Las Vegas gambling pioneer, Phil (Pittsburgh Phil) Straus, and the notorious Murder, Inc., mobster, Abe Reles, who ostensibly dove to his death from the Half Moon Hotel in Coney Island, were among the so-called Jewish element in the mob for many years. But they were only following in the footsteps of the murdered Arnold Rothstein, Frank Costello's mentor. There were also plenty of Irish mobsters, such as "Peg-Leg" Lonergan, killed by Al Capone in Brooklyn before Capone went to Chicago, and Owney (Owney the Killer) Madden, who died a natural death recently in Hot Springs, Arkansas. Italian, Jewish, Irish, it is doubtful that any one of these gangsters really believed in any god but one: profit.

Lieutenant Amico sounded a clarion call for ordinary people whose accepted norms have to do with the everyday things that affect them: their children, their pots and pans and household duties, their jobs. Such people have precious little time to be concerned about crime and the people who operate the business. It is difficult to rouse them. But as Nicholas Murray Butler once said, the little people are good for a grand splurge of morality if the message can be gotten across to them, even though they return to their own affairs soon enough. Thus, we are not entirely without hope. But it is only a small hope, for even respite from the Mafia is difficult to obtain, as the story of James Delmont shows.

A former bookkeeper for one of the Montana interests, the Madison Cab Company, Delmont witnessed an attempt on the life of another employee, Steven (Flat Top) Cannarozzo. Delmont was present when a volley of shots was fired through a window of the cab company office in Buffalo in June, 1959. Cannarozzo, who has a long record of crimes dating from 1939 to 1950, survived, despite multiple bullet wounds, but his assistant, Delmont, did not wait around to read the medical reports. He had been a witness to the crime —and he fled to California, where he became another "Brother Orchid" inspired by fear to spend the last days of his life along the California mission trail.

Word spread that Delmont was marked for death because he could identify the assailants of Cannarozzo and that the Mafia was out to do the job. In a desperate attempt to square himself, Delmont confessed his past to a brother at one of the monasteries, a priest of Italian origin who in turn contacted the Los Angeles branch of the underworld brotherhood in order to intercede for the worried Delmont.

The naïve holy man, after making what he thought was a convincing argument for the life of his brother, gave Delmont a bus ticket to Los Angeles and a name and address where he said the worried witness would find that his problems were being resolved. Delmont made the trip as instructed and was seemingly cheered by the results, for he then telephoned his wife and told her that all was well and that he would be home in two weeks. But amnesty was not forthcoming despite the façade of forgiveness. At the end of those two weeks—in April, 1960—Delmont's body was found in a field on the outskirts of San Bernardino. He had been shot and tossed from a car a scant sixty miles from Los Angeles and some three thousand miles from his unyielding adversaries in Buffalo.

And Steven Cannarozzo? He stayed mute after the attempt on his life, refusing to tell Buffalo police investigators who shot him, and, at the last report, was a Randaccio "muscle man" in the numbers racket.

Perhaps James Delmont loved his fellow men, if a little late. Seeking surcease, he went from an evil brotherhood, the Mafia, to a blessed brotherhood, but he found that there is really no middle ground between good and evil, and for a resting place he had to pay with his life. In Buffalo, as elsewhere in this country, the Mafia is fully entrenched. It takes real courage either to break out of its tangled web or to resist its encroachments. The Mafia cannot deny anyone the choice, but it often exacts a high price for the privilege of exercising that choice.

FOUR

BOSTON:

Home of the Bean and the Rod

And this is good old Boston,
  Plymouth and Providence, too;
Where the hoodlums talk to no one,
  And even God eschew.

—with apologies to John Collins Bossidy

August, 1961: a hot day on the beach at Salisbury on the
fringe of greater Boston. Edward J. (Punchy) McLaughlin
and his brothers, Bernie and George, were lolling on the
soft sand. A voluptuous female strolled by. Punchy got up,
walked over to the young lady, grabbed her head, and,
apparently in the throes of an oddly directed sexual impulse,
tried to bite off her ear.

The girl in question was a special pal of hoodlum James J.
(Buddy) McLean, who happened to be close by on the
day in question. Not close enough to stop the affront, McLean
ran over to McLaughlin and gave him what newspapermen
called the "beating of his life."

Thus began one of the strangest gang wars in history.
The police are appalled and bemused by it, but in seven
years over forty men—including the two gang leaders,
McLaughlin and McLean, who were murdered within ten

days of each other, Bernie McLaughlin and seven associates, and at least two other members of the McLean faction—have died because of it.

Responsible papers in Boston talk curiously and cautiously about the killings in their town. A headline on the bottom of the first page of the *Boston Sunday Globe*, November 21, 1965, read: "27 Dead—but no one knows why, or how to stop it." Since then, the number of dead has risen; the long arm of the underworld wields a frightening and devastating weapon that may have as its target anyone from a two-bit hood who has stepped out of line to a top law-enforcement official who is dogging the trail of the syndicate.

In its news story, which was cozily wrapped around a blurb about shopping hours, the *Globe* asks: "Why are they killing each other? 'You'll have to give me two or three guesses,' answers a high police official. 'There isn't one basic pattern.' "

The fact that there is "no basic pattern" could well explain the police official's reluctance to talk, but theories are rife. A *Globe* staff writer, for example, expounded two theoretic reasons for the killings thus: "the instinctive reaction of brother to help brother and of gang member to avenge for gang member. The lust for money from two of history's most fantastic robberies, ordinary crimes and the entrapment of loan sharking."

And he added: "There was not a single underlying motive for the deadly series of murders which have generated increasing public demands for not only a solution but firm action by law enforcement officials to end the blood bath."

But to get back to the initial incident, there are divergent opinions as to just who did insult the young lady during the beach picnic. The *Globe* still claims it was Punchy McLaughlin, but in its February 24, 1967, issue, *Life* states that it was brother George who did the biting. It matters little, except that the incident supposedly triggered the greatest destruction of hoodlums over so short a period of time in gangland history. Murder and jail have wiped out the three McLaughlins (George is now on death row in Walpole State Prison); Buddy McLean was gunned down shortly after the beach incident (following an unsuccessful attempt to dynamite his car); and both gangs have been largely decimated in the forty-some killings thus far.

Police and crime reporters have mulled over the possibility that unrecovered funds totaling around $3 million from three

robberies—the famous Brink's robbery in 1950, the 1962
Plymouth, Massachusetts, mail holdup, and the 1966 Brink's
holdup at Bedford, Massachusetts—have somehow got stuck
in the New England gangland financial web. The theory is
that this money has been available, in one fashion or another,
over the years and that the warfare among the Boston
gangs may well concern its final resting place. The tough
boys, the scavengers of the underworld, will always try to
move in to "arrange" the division of any holdup money,
like so many hyenas chivvying a lion seeking to protect its
kill.

Theory after theory has been studied, but seemingly little
attention has been given to the possibility that these killings
might have some connection with the Mafia. Almost all of
the men eliminated as the result of what was, and still is,
called the McLaughlin-McLean feud were non-Italians. But it
is significant that the McLaughlins and McLeans were
enforcers for loan sharks. Bernie McLaughlin was said to
favor a sash weight wrapped in newspaper for breaking the
arms of delinquent debtors; Buddy McLean supposedly did
roadwork to keep in shape for the "muscle" needed in his
business. And loan sharking *requires* the broad base of syndicate financing.

When all the facts are examined, there seems little doubt
that the man behind the scenes, and the murders, is Mafioso
Raymond Loreda Patriarca, sixty-one-year-old hatchet-faced
don of the moderate-sized Cosa Nostra family that embraces
a good share of Massachusetts, Rhode Island, Connecticut,
and Maine. Patriarca's position of power was brought to
public attention at the Senate committee hearings by Colonel
Walter E. Stone, superintendent of the Rhode Island state
police, who labeled him:

> the controlling force behind organized crime in Rhode Island
> and New England . . . Behind the front of his business
> enterprises, Patriarca, through his lieutenants, is still in-
> volved in one of his old specialties, that of strong-arming. Now
> it's being done for unions in the New England area instead
> of for his fellow gangsters during prohibition . . . he has the
> controlling interest in lotteries, bookmaking, dice games,
> and the provision of wire service in this area. Moreover,
> he settles any disputes within the organization working this
> section, sometimes using force or intimidation to accomplish
> his designs.

According to Stone, Patriarca was born on March 17, 1908, in Worcester, Massachusetts. Sometimes using his alias "John D'Nabile," Patriarca, whose headquarters now are in Providence, Rhode Island, began his criminal career as a bodyguard for bootleggers in the early twenties and gained a wide reputation as an effective strongarm man. His police record began while he was still a teenager and includes arrests for hijacking, jail escape, violations of gambling laws, violations of the Mann Act, which prohibits transporting women across state lines for immoral purposes—for which he went to jail—safe cracking, armed robbery, adultery, motor vehicle code offenses, the carrying of firearms, conspiracy, assault, auto theft, and accessory before the fact of murder (two counts). Patriarca, indeed, is no stranger to the charge of murder. He was indicted for this crime by a Rhode Island grand jury for his part in the 1930 Easter Saturday attempt to free two vicious criminals from a prison that resulted in the death of four people.

Until he was thirty Patriarca seems to have been a loser, despite the help of the Mafiosi whose orders he had been following, for he had five convictions and had spent a total of ten years in jail. But his loyalty and persistence, not to mention his excessive nerve, paid off, and today these characteristics are perhaps matched by his influence among top politicians in his area. He began traveling with these high-ranking allies in 1938, possibly through the good offices of his boss, Phil Buccola, who headed the New England Mafia family until he was deported to Italy in the forties.

Buccola, attracted by Patriarca's obvious promise, as indicated by his being arrested at the age of eighteen and breaking out of jail after being convicted of hijacking, took Patriarca under his wing. The young button man soon became a *capo*, a cut much above the soldiers with whom he had been trooping. In 1938 he was convicted of burglarizing a Brookline, Massachusetts, jewelry store and sentenced to five years in prison. This sentence was to run concurrently with two others, the three combined sentences covering convictions for breaking and entering, armed robbery, and arson. But this was no real setback for Patriarca. After only eighty-four days behind bars, he received a full pardon from the Massachusetts governor, who acted on the advice of Executive Councilor Daniel H. Coakley.

The reasons for Coakley's action were hinted at some

twenty years later when a Massachusetts investigating commission found that he was guilty of, among other things, "deceit and fraud" in pressing the petition to free Patriarca. Finally, in 1959, Coakley was impeached and became the first member of the governor's executive council to be removed from office since 1821.

One of the distinguishing features of Don Raymond's career is the lack of publicity he has been given. Somehow he and his organization have, until recently, managed to keep away from the eye of the press—although the appearance at the Apalachin meeting of one of his Boston lieutenants, Frank Cucchiara, a naturalized American born in Salemi, Sicily, embarrassed the whole New England mob to such a degree that Cucchiara, then co-owner of the Purity Cheese Company in Boston and also known as Frank (The Spoon) Caruso, was relegated to a position of relative unimportance in the Patriarca setup.

The theory that the McLaughlin-McLean chain of murders should be tied to the Mafia is further strengthened by the fact that the top man and financier in the New England juice rackets—for which the non-Mafia Irish feuders were strong-arm men—is Gennaro (Jerry) Angiulo, second-in-command to Patriarca and one of six brothers who, according to Senate testimony, are all involved in gaming and loanshark operations.

It is not difficult to believe—and Colonel Stone did believe —that Angiulo, who operates through Mafioso Henry Tamello —both men being insulated by Mafia lieutenant Larry Baioni, who controls some two hundred button men—could have given the word to do away with the troublesome non-Italian McLaughlins and McLeans. The juice racket purportedly provides a million dollars a week to the Patriarca combine and is therefore most sensitive to any sort of interference— from police, journalists, or hot-headed younger gangsters. No well-established Mafioso could stomach the furor caused by the Irish gang leaders.

Indeed, the Mafia move to wipe out the non-Italian opposition in New England may have begun as far back as 1951, with the murder of Carlton O'Brien, an ex-convict and strong-arm man who not only opened several bookie joints in Patriarca territory but also set up a wire service in an adjoining state to bootleg racing information into his own parlors and to other bookmakers. The up-and-coming Patriarca, who owned the Mafia-licensed wire service, moved in fast, and O'Brien was slain early one morning outside his home in a Providence suburb.

In 1956 Patriarca made his next move, into the cigarette-vending-machine business. He followed this up with juke-boxes, cleaning-and-dyeing stores, linen services, auto agencies, drugstores, and garbage-collecting firms. He now controls numerous nightclubs and restaurants, ranging from greasy spoons in the Revere area and the equally seamy Federal Hill district in Providence to some of the top gourmet eating places in New England. His mob owns cemeteries, dude ranches, a New Hampshire ski resort, and a country club north of Boston.

Also, according to Bill Davidson, writing in the *Saturday Evening Post* of November 18, 1967, the Patriarca family had a well-placed Boston drugstore making L.S.D.—"one of the newer Mafia industries"—and distributing the stuff to the many ready customers abounding in three nearby college campuses.

Such enterprises have over the years provided financing for Patriarca's Mafia influence elsewhere, including at one time the Dunes Hotel in Las Vegas—an influence maintained by a front man named Joe Sullivan. Joe did the best he could. He knew the restaurant business and really tried, but Vegas newspapermen who knew Sullivan's backer gave him no peace. One pastime they enjoyed was calling the Dunes switchboard from the house phones in the lobby and having the operators page Raymond Patriarca. Then they would watch while Joe Sullivan, who was usually seated comfortably savoring a drink in the lounge just across the lobby, quietly went into a frenzy. He didn't know whether the big man was really in the hotel or not and would run about frantically trying to find out.

Patriarca, and Sullivan, of course, were not the only targets of newsmen's horseplay in Las Vegas. Pete Licavoli of the Detroit mob, which had a signal interest in the Desert Inn before Howard Hughes took it over, also had his problems with trick paging. Even J. Edgar Hoover's name got some of the play, but that invariably produced a frozen silence that seemed to put the chill on everybody.

In New England there is evidence, on the record, that Patriarca has always played both ends against the middle. For example, Colonel Stone told the McClellan committee that Patriarca was without honor "even among his fellow thieves," having at one time set up the hijacking of the very shipments of alcohol he had been hired to guard. And Stone pointed out that the constancy of the lawlessness of the men who operate within the framework of the syndicate was especially exemplified by Patriarca.

> He is a shrewd, scheming individual as well versed in the ways of crime today as he was in yesteryear. He is as ruthless in the sixties as he was in the thirties.
>
> Another one of the rackets that Patriarca worked was the so-called past posting. This is the placing of a wager on a horserace that has been run and a winner has been determined. These risky but profitable activities were carried on by the goons of Patriarca throughout the East.

Working for Patriarca was John (Jackie) Nazarian, one of the "animals" used by the don several years ago to instill fear in people he wanted to intimidate. Nazarian once killed another triggerman for Patriarca, George (Tiger) Balletto. There were twenty-two witnesses to the murder at the Bella Napoli Cafe in Providence. One man, an ex-boxer by the name of Eddie Hannan, thought he might step up and testify, but he was promptly strangled by Nazarian and left in a local dump. The baling wire Nazarian wound around Hannan's neck added emphasis to the threat to any other potential witnesses.

In this context, the confidence offered to Senator McClellan's committee by Colonel Stone that Patriarca lived in fear, not knowing whether he would also be a victim of Nazarian, was perhaps understandable. If he was, indeed, afraid of the "animal," Patriarca must have been relieved of a great weight in 1962, when Nazarian was murdered while walking the streets of Federal Hill, a short distance from Patriarca's residence.

Nazarian's murder not only freed Patriarca from fear, however, it also demonstrated the attitude of the public to hood killings. Two indictments in the murder were returned, but nothing happened. The public, it seems, feels that mobsters get what they deserve when they are killed, that "due process" is a privilege hoods don't deserve. But by taking the attitude that the killers of killers are not to be bothered with unduly, the public is allowing to go free the very people who not infrequently kill innocent people who stand in their way—a dangerous practice indeed.

The Nazarian type of Mafia terror is exemplified by the

words of a loan shark to whom a bankrupt Boston businessman offered some other kind of collateral than money to
repay, partially at least, a $2,000 loan that had given rise
to an indebtedness of $3,900 in one year. Replied the loan
shark as he slammed a .45-caliber pistol on a table in the retail
store owned by his victim: "Your body is our collateral!"

On the subject of this kind of collateral, Charles Rogovin,
the Massachusetts attorney general's expert on organized
crime, has been quoted as saying:

> All other Mafia families have a tradition which they call
> "stopping the clock." That is, when you're bled dry, they
> stop the clock on the interest and just let you give back the
> principal. They stop short of killing, on the theory that a
> dead man can't pay. But not here. They're totally ruthless
> about loan-shark debts. Two thirds of the murders and
> maimings in New England involve people who have sur-
> rendered the collateral of their bodies to the loan sharks.

The Patriarca family, then, are even more ruthless—if
that is possible—than the ordinary Mafiosi. And yet lacking
in the record on Patriarca are many of the sordid little
details of his "business." However, we do know that having
worked his way to the top of the heap as don of the New
England Mafia family, Patriarca not only commands the
boys who take care of syndicate crime in his territory but
also passes judgment on the "lesser" crimes—bank robberies,
kidnappings, jewel thefts, hijackings, arson, and the like—
committed by the younger punks who will perhaps join
the big-time someday, if they survive. And we also know
that he has any number of non-Mafia allies, representing
at least a dozen different nationalities, who operate as
executive-class silent partners with some of his own boys in
various enterprises involving bookmaking, loan sharking,
and illegal wire-service operations.

Even when this kind of information is made available to
the public—as is finally happening, little by little—it is difficult to determine whether there is any real fight left in the
citizenry against such criminals as Raymond Patriarca;
whether the slow and easy way of life, replete with the
pleasures such as those provided by men of Patriarca's ilk
in the gaming palaces of Las Vegas, the Bahamas, and other
such meccas—has stultified all resistance. We can only hope
that perhaps the cupidity and ego of the Mafia chieftains

themselves may somehow lead to the downfall of the syndicate and to the beginning of the end of the secret society.

An example of just such a slip is found in the story of Al Agueci, who got into trouble with the law but was not given the help he had been promised by Don Stefano Magaddino. His subsequent pursuit of vengeance against Magaddino was the first link in a chain of circumstances which led to his death, to his brother's vendetta, and finally to the Valachi testimony exposing the modern Mafia to the world.

In New England Agueci has something of a counterpart in hoodlum Joe Barboza, a young man of Portuguese descent who came under Patriarca's influence in 1959 after he had served a series of jail terms for various offenses.

Barboza, who had met Mafia members at the state prison in Walpole, Massachusetts, was on a Mafia assignment on October 6, 1966, when he and three friends were stopped by traffic police in the heart of Boston. In their car were found a fully loaded Army M-1 rifle and a .45-caliber pistol. The four were arrested for illegal possession of firearms, and Barboza was held in the unusually high bail of $100,000, probably because at the time of his arrest he was already out on bail on a stabbing charge.

After Barboza had waited in vain for the Patriarca group to bail him out once again, two of his friends, Thomas DePrisco and Arthur Bratsos, decided to raise bail for him on their own. DePrisco and Bratsos collected $60,000 and then sought further funds from an important Mafiosi named Ralph (Ralphie Chiong) Lamattina, who owned a café in the north end of Boston. Chiong asked the pair to wait until the café closed and then invited them into a back room. Next day both men were found shot to death in a black Cadillac in south Boston.

Tipped off by an informant, the police arrived at Chiong's café and found Ralphie mopping up bloodstains in the back room and covering up bullet holes in the wall with a mirror. They therefore arrested him and put him on trial for murder. A few weeks later Patriarca and his Rhode Island executive officer, Henry Tamello, decided that in order to avoid publicity Chiong should plead guilty to being an accessory to the murder. He was told he would get only two years in prison and be rewarded with a profitable Mafia enterprise when he emerged, but he apparently got the wrong judge. Instead of a light two-year term, Ralph Lamattina received two concurrent maximum sentences: eight to fourteen years.

The heavy sentences gave newspapers an opportunity to play up the story—which they did. Joe Barboza, who was by then serving a four-to-five-year sentence on the gun charge and faced life imprisonment as a habitual criminal, read about the case and began to realize its significance: that Patriarca not only had abandoned him and killed two of his good friends but also was so determined to keep Barboza in jail that he had lost the trusted services of Mafioso Lamattina in the process.

Barboza was visited in jail by FBI agents who confirmed the newspaper stories and gave him additional evidence about his betrayal. They added insult to injury by stating that the Mafia had tipped off the police to pick him up on the gun charge. They played a tape made from a "bug" planted in Patriarca's office, and Barboza heard the Mafia chief say: "Barboza's a _____ bum. He's expendable."

It was then that Barboza decided to tell everything he knew, and another thread of truth was stitched into the net with which lawmen hope to catch, and put out of action, the Mafia leaders.

Barboza apparently never took the oath of silence and fealty to the secret society, as Valachi had done, but it probably would not have made any difference once his fear and anger made him decide to talk.

With the information given to authorities by its newest canary, the government, represented by U.S. Attorney Paul Markham, went to the federal grand jury in Boston on June 20, 1967, and obtained an indictment charging that Patriarca and Henry Tamello conspired with Barboza and another man to commit murder—a charge that arose from the shooting of William Marfeo, a relatively unknown forty-one-year-old gambler who had the nerve to run an unauthorized crap game in Providence.

Patriarca was charged with causing Barboza to travel interstate for Marfeo's "hit." Tamello was charged with an additional count alleging he made the interstate phone call that brought Barboza from Boston to Providence. Another hood, Ronald Cassesso, who is now serving a term for armed robbery, was also tried. The three men were convicted on March 8, 1968, and later sentenced to five years in prison and fined $10,000 each. Defense attorneys immediately filed appeals and continued Patriarca free in $25,000 bond, so any or all of them may be in the clear by the time this book sees print. But at least some progress is being made in getting through the insulation to a few of the bigger Mafiosi.

If the police are making progress, the New England junior Mafia are not. First, there appears to be little effort to supplant Patriarca, despite the rumor that Larry Baioni would like the job. And, second, Patriarca's second-in-command, Jerry Angiulo, is in trouble with the law—once again as a result of Barboza's testimony—over the 1967 killing of an ex-boxer, Rocco DeSeglio, who planned to hold up a Mafia floating crap game in Boston.

Thus in New England it's three down for the top Mafia command, and no one knows for sure where it will stop. If Larry Baioni, whose real name is Ilario Anthony Zannino but who is carried on most police records as Larry Zannino, manages a take-over when Patriarca's throne is empty, he will bring with him the necessary prerequisites for a Mafia don. He was born in Boston on June 15, 1920, which makes him old enough to have learned the game but young enough to maintain power. In his many pickups by police over the years since 1938, for questioning on traffic, weapon carrying, gambling, assault and battery, mayhem, extortion, armed robbery, and murder charges, Baioni has variously described his occupation to police as that of a clerk, laborer, salesman, farmer, chauffeur, nightclub manager, and truck driver. In 1960 he was given two four-to-seven-year sentences for extortion, to be served concurrently in the state prison at Walpole. During the 1963 McClellan hearings on organized crime in Boston, Baioni, who was still serving time, was described as a "favorite of Raymond Patriarca." Small in stature—5 feet 7½ inches, 170 pounds—the black-haired, dark-complexioned Mafioso, who carries a small scar on the outer rim of his left eye, may yet become a big man among his confreres.

As a result of all these eruptions, it seems certain that the usually serene Patriarca faces an uncertain future because he disobeyed an unwritten Mafia law that requires reciprocal aid for all members in case of any need whatsoever. And in disobeying the law, he sold his New England organization down the river—just as Magaddino did in Buffalo over the Aguecis. The six brothers of William Marfeo are sure to want revenge and will no doubt wait for Patriarca to get to a quiet spot where the job can be done. In June, 1968, two of them supposedly tried to kill him on the day his indictment was announced.

There are many, however, who would not bet against Patriarca, protected as he is by the wall of insulation and insurance he has built over the years. One well-documented strip of tape made during three years of FBI eavesdropping in Patriarca's Providence office indicates that "in the bag" for the Mafia chief are, among others, a high-ranking court administrator, a top state official, a police chief, two licensing officials, and a few powerful state senators and representatives.

In fact, although he is running out of time and appeals, it is likely that Raymond Patriarca will spend many more pleasant hours, replete in white turtleneck sweater sunning himself on the doorstep of his Nu-Brite Cleansers, on Atwells Avenue in the Federal Hill district of Providence, over which he has built the bug-proof apartment he calls home—pleasant hours, perhaps, but somewhat less carefree than in the past.

FIVE

DETROIT:

Body by Mafia

On February 21, 1962, Frankie Gerlando, owner of a bar in Detroit, heard a noise. It was 2:00 A.M., chilly, damp. The sound came from outside the rear door of the bar. Gerlando tried to push the door open and found it blocked by something piled against it. He pushed harder and the object gave way. Frankie stepped outside and looked down. He saw a dead pig. The porker's legs were bound with rope, and later examination disclosed it had died by asphyxiation.

Frankie walked quietly back into the bar. A dozen patrons swiveled heads toward him. He nodded to the door, and one by one they filed out to take a look at the pig.

The message was obvious: "Squealers Die."

To the bar patrons the real squealer was a man named Ubal (Roy) Calabresse, their former drinking buddy. Calabresse was in the rackets. He had been arrested a couple of times, found guilty at least once, and flashed more money than the top Mafiosi thought proper for a person at the level of operation assigned to him.

Calabresse's mother told police that he had disappeared a week earlier, after receiving a phone call, telling her he had "an appointment with one of Capone's boys."

Several days later, on February 19, Calabresse was found by police in St. Clair Shores, a suburb of Detroit beyond

Grosse Point. He had been garroted, and the arms of a coat were still wrapped around his neck. Calabresse died about two hours after he had eaten dinner at his mother's home on St. Valentine's Day, according to testimony by Detroit Police Commissioner George Edwards before the McClellan committee.

The fate that stalked the two men was set in motion years before, partly because of a vast dissatisfaction felt by three youths who sat in a field outside Palermo, Sicily, one day in 1915.

All three belonged to a class known as "The Green Ones," meaning people who live on Sicily's broad latifondi where herding and farming are the main occupations. They were junior members of the Mafia, of the *Stoppaglieri* faction, and as they sat there, they made up their minds to try to get to St. Louis, in America.

The boys were Vito Giannola, his brother John, and a friend, Alphonse Palizzola. They obtained money from a Palermo banker at stiletto-point, and three days later were in the steerage of a ship bound for the New World, Vito became leader and principal don in St. Louis, where he gathered a few Sicilians together into a gang called by the police of that city The Green Ones.

Alphonse was the enforcer who brought "Little Italy" in St. Louis under the thumb of the gang and collected a tax on every item of food sold to the Italians. Bananas, for instance, were taxed five cents a bunch and bread two cents a loaf. The first murders began in 1923, when Vito went into the wholesale-meat business and signed up Italian butchers. Alphonse was the front man in this deal. When one butcher was recalcitrant, complaining that the gang price for meat was much higher than what he was paying his regular wholesaler, Alphonse pointed out quite truthfully that the extra money was insurance for continued good health. The butcher remained adamant and shouted at the Mafioso: "No orders for you!"

Alphonse stalked out. At 3:00 A.M., two days later, an auto pulled up beside a man walking slowly down the street. There was no moon on that cool September night, and the butcher who had refused to buy meat from the Mafia never saw the men who ran toward him. St. Louis police department records show that on the morning of September 16, 1923, the body of Angelo Pastori, of 1914 Hereford Avenue, was found beneath the Kingshighway Viaduct. He had been stabbed once in the heart and twice in the head and beaten with a couple of baseball bats, which were found nearby. Pastori left a widow and two children.

The most vicious killing performed by The Green Ones was that of two men who were buried in the same grave near one of the stills owned by the gang at Horseshoe Lake.

Deputy Constable Homer Hockett and another officer and friend, John Balke, who had been deputized by the older man, were stationed in nearby Edwardsville when the pair decided to go out and shake down the gang on the night of January 29, 1926. Hockett and Balke walked straight into an ambush. Knocked unconscious as they entered the farmhouse where the still was located, they were bound with baling wire and dragged outside at dawn. Then the frightened men were forced to watch while members of the gang dug a large pit in the ground.

Balke panicked. "For God's sake," he screamed, "what are you going to do?"

"That's all right," came the answer. "We're not going to hurt you, we're just going to kill you."

Then a man came over to the trussed officers and smiled. "We were only fooling, fellows," he said. "Stand up. It's all right."

He cut their wire bonds, and they stood up, rubbing their arms and legs to restore circulation. Then both men started to walk away. As they went by the hole in the ground, two men in the gang drew their guns and began firing. Balke and Hockett fell to the ground, one of the gravediggers ran up and kicked both of them into the pit, and four shovels went to work to level the ground. If the earth heaved a little as the two writhed in their death throes, no one noticed.

The killings put the seal to the power of The Green Ones; the Mafia took over St. Louis' rackets. Then they looked toward Detroit.

Early in 1927 a man named Pete Licavoli left St. Louis for Detroit. He had the proper credentials and did all the right things. First, he married the sister of a fairly well-established hoodlum, Joseph (Scarface Joe) Bommarito, and Joe married Pete's sister, Mamie. Over the years intermarriage between various gang factions in Detroit created a monolith of crime that the authorities have not been able to dent. Indeed, sons and daughters of the criminal combine in Detroit have been tossed out, like bait to sharks, for marriage within other crime factions throughout the country. The resulting unions have forged a steel net in which law-enforcement officials swim blindly, like so many anchovies.

The next thing Pete Licavoli did was to get into the business of rum-running, and while his brother, Yonnie Thomas Licavoli, and a brother-in-law, Frank Cammarata, were in prison, he took over a group known as "The River Gang." Licavoli then formed a union with a hoodlum named Joe (Misery) Moceri and ultimately gained control of the smuggling of Canada's liquor into Detroit's East Side.

Licavoli gave the business his personal touch. Armed with a pair of binoculars, he would get out in the "field—either the blue waters of Lake Erie or those of the smaller Lake St. Clair to the north—and direct rum-running boats to snug harbors.

Pete's modern approach to gang organization soon dissipated the power of "The Purple Gang," which was comprised mostly of Jewish mobsters. Several of these went to Reno, Nevada, and bought into the Riverside Hotel on the Truckee River, which bisects the town. Meanwhile, an East Side gang combined with a West Side gang in Detroit. And the Italian dons who joined with Licavoli soon controlled gang activities in most of the Great Lakes section and branched out as far to the southwest as Las Vegas and Arizona.

The ruling council in the Detroit area, as the police intelligence chart submitted to the McClellan committee shows, consists of Pete Licavoli, Joseph Zerilli, John Priziola, the elder of the group, Angelo Meli, and William Tocco.

Of the ruling council, four were born in Italy: Priziola, Meli, Zerilli, and Tocco—the latter two in the same year and the same town, Terrasina. Licavoli's parents also were born in Terrasina, as were the parents of Joseph Bommarito, Pete's brother-in-law and heir apparent prior to his death.

All five Detroit leaders have been under fire at one time or another, but mostly they try to avoid getting directly involved—except in such high-level meetings as the Apalachin. Usually they send emissaries when minor Mafia business is to be disposed of.

Meli and Tocco learned this technique early in the history of Detroit's gang wars. A few years after Licavoli came to Detroit, the portion of the West Side mob not yet taken over by the Mafia was operated by a man named Chester LeMar. LeMar thought he would pull a fast one and called for a meeting with Meli and Tocco at a fish market at 2739 Vernor Highway, on the near East Side—a place that had previously served as a rendezvous for gang leaders.

Meli and his pal thought things smelled more than a little fishy and sent representatives to the meet. Thus it was Sam Parino and Gaspare Sibilia, known as a peacemaker in the troubled city where gangland murders even today average two a year, who were ambushed and shot to death by LeMar henchmen. The LeMar men were subsequently arrested, tried, and set free by a jury, but shortly thereafter LeMar was killed by his bodyguards, who had made a deal for their own lives with the Licavoli gang.

LeMar was the last really potent underworld figure to oppose the Licavolis. But there were others, not in the underworld, who fared just as badly, and the fate of Gerald Buckley, in particular, seemed totally inconsistent with the rules and regulations of the Mafia.

Buckley, a crusading radio news commentator who had threatened to reveal the identity of the overlords of crime in Detroit, was shot to death in the lobby of his hotel on July 23, 1930. His demise threw the city of Detroit into a turmoil, and four men were indicted for the crime: Joe Bommarito, Theodore Pizzino and Angelo Levecchi, two of Licavoli's pet assassins, and Licavoli himself. Pete didn't wait around. He fled Michigan and did not return until the other three had been tried and acquitted. The prosecution found that none of the witnesses it had counted on were willing to tell the court the same thing they had recounted in the district attorney's office.

The police did not give up, however. In July the home of hoodlum Joe (Cockeyed Joe) Catalanotte was raided. Police found fifty-four firearms, one of which was identified by ballistic tests as the murder weapon in the Buckley case. But the only punishment for Cockeyed Joe was his deportation to Canada, where he settled down in Windsor, Ontario, just across the Detroit River from his pals. There he still sits, apparently as deeply involved in Mafia affairs as ever. The Royal Canadian Mounted Police seem unconcerned, and though he has visited Detroit many times, the local police have yet to collar him.

Perhaps after all the Buckley murder is not so strange. Licavoli's predeliction for murder has always hewed close to the Mafia method and tradition, which is aimed at producing terror as well as results. A man is not just murdered—especially if he is a Mafia hoodlum who has squealed or double-crossed his associates—he is held up as an example. Buckley's murder, like Calabresse's years before, offered a clear warning, but in his case it was: "Stay Away."

The tactic of fear was, and is, very successful. For example, the old Black Handers, the Italians who terrorized their fellow countrymen in America around the turn of the century by chopping up the bodies of people who defied them, produced an atmosphere of terror around their operations that won many battles before they had begun.

Today the dead pig, the lime pit, and mutilation are most commonly used methods. But the mobsters are making continual improvements in their methods, especially when they are dealing with defectors from, or opponents in, the syndicate. Thus, a few years ago several dead Mafiosi were found in New York: shot but with their genitals cut off and jammed down their throats. There is speculation as to whether the mutilation occurred before or after death.

Licavoli's overlordship of gambling in Detroit requires that he inject himself personally into the everyday mob affairs, and he does it with much the same dedication he evinced when in Prohibition days he directed his rum-runners into Michigan harbors. But his job is not too hard, for the fate of the attackers of one of his principal lieutenants, Max Stern, serves as a constant reminder to those who would undermine Licavoli and his circle of dons that something more than a bullet awaits them.

Stern was shot one day after Licavoli had called a conference to clear up some arguments about the handling of gaming operations in Detroit. The malefactors seemed to have been hoodlums Peter Lucido and Sam Scroy. In any case, Licavoli had specifically asked that they be present at the conference, but they did not show up. Then, on June 12, 1948, both Scroy and Lucido disappeared.

Sam Scroy had a brother named Chris, and he got angry, grabbed a gun, and fired a couple of shots at Stern, only wounding him. The attack lead to Chris Scroy's arrest, and he was sent to prison, where he served seven years. Scroy was freed on July 14, 1955, and on April 10, 1959, he disappeared, only to reappear in the suburbs—in a lime pit. Scroy's body had been chopped into seven pieces. The lime had been spread too thinly—probably a habit developed during the mob's "alky" days—and Chris was identified from both fingerprints and a belt buckle. Licavoli, the natural suspect, was in federal prison for income-tax evasion when Scroy disappeared, so he easily avoided the investigative hook, and Scroy's death became another unsolved murder.

When Licavoli got out in the fall of 1960, he decided to celebrate, so he financed an elaborate wedding for one of his daughters. Actually, the wedding served as a sounding board for his ego. The underworld had heard, while Pete was in prison, that he was going to be retired and put out to pasture by the Mafia. The big party indicated not only that Pete had power but that he still had money—access to the honey pot the Mafia makes available to working dons.

Soon after, moreover, Licavoli had a chance to display his talents and, at the same time, to prove that the Mafia believes in the segregation of Negroes but does not object to deriving financial benefit from them.

The Gotham Hotel is a nine-story fleabag with 174 rooms located in the Negro section of Detroit. Just about every citizen in town knew that it was headquarters of the numbers racket. When a reform spree had swept Detroit several years before, the former mayor, prosecuting attorney, sheriff, superintendent of police, and 250 police officers had gone to jail for the acceptance of graft from the gamblers. It seemed that only Licavoli and his boys did not go to jail. They continued to flourish, at the Gotham and elsewhere.

Police raided the Gotham on November 9, 1962, but only eight people knew where the action was going to take place right up until 112 policemen were herded on buses. In fact, the policemen were given their raid instructions only *after* the bus doors had been closed, and Police Commissioner George Edwards used a federal search warrant.

Michigan state police and the intelligence unit of the IRS accompanied the raiders and found a numbers factory in full operation. The raiders seized 160,000 betting slips and $60,000 in cash. Forty-two Negroes were arrested, but as the raiders fanned out through the rooms of the hotel, they found not a single white person.

Commissioner Edwards discovered that Licavoli's outfit supplied all of the "working" apparatus in the hotel, which housed seven major numbers banks representing districts apportioned by the Mafiosi to servile Negro gang chiefs, and controlled the whole operation from the outside: the Mafia supplied the number, based on mutuals payoffs at races on various tracks or on a lottery; the Mafia supplied the numbers pads used by the sellers who took pennies, nickels, and dimes from Negro customers; and the Mafia supplied the dream books so essential to the Negro numbers bettor.

Licavoli was clearly implicated by the raid on the Gotham Hotel. For example, about ten thousand dream books, which are sold for two dollars each, were seized in a raid on his house prior to the Gotham incident, but because of a faulty search warrant—so the court ruled—no prosecution was possible. In addition, the operator of a dice game found going full blast at the Gotham, one Johnny White, had Licavoli's private phone number in his office.

Thirty-five hundred dollars were lying on the crap table when raiders broke into the Gotham, and of the eighteen pairs of monogrammed dice seized, fifteen were crooked. Even the decks of cards on nearby tables were crooked, and they demonstrated that Licavoli was not only a crook but also a student of at least one opthalmological phenomenon: the card decks looked like any others, with the name of a reputable manufacturer on each wrapper, and the police thought nothing of them until an officer in another room found a set of contact lenses with which it was possible to read the backs of the cards. The suckers never had a chance. "Who cares if we are cheating ourselves?" asked Johnny White, rather ambiguously.

Police also found that if there were too many hits on a particular number, the operators at the Gotham merely changed the number.

Commissioner Edwards estimated that the operation at the Gotham yielded about $21 million a year, with the overall illegal Mafia enterprises in the Detroit area probably netting the mob $150 million annually.

Despite what must be some profitable investments in Las Vegas, where gaming is legal in a free and open atmosphere —in swank casinos where the plushest carpets and the finest materials and woods are used in lavish interiors—Licavoli and his Mafia boys hang on to methods in Detroit that are reminiscent of oldtime movies about the sin dens of the Volstead era.

For example, one entered the Lesod Club, which now operates outside the jurisdiction of the Detroit city police, through a locked door at the bottom of a flight of stairs leading up to a gambling room. There was also a locked door at the top of the stairs and a peephole. Buzzers and buzzer controls draped the doors. A guard at the bottom of the stairs screened all who wished to enter for a little action.

The guard was most gracious to police who came to look around. On one such visit, Commissioner Edwards escorted a justice of the U.S. Supreme Court on an inspection tour. They were wafted airily through the first door. The guard stepped on a hidden button, and the sound of scurrying came from above. When the probers got upstairs, they found a mob of people gathered around tables on which hot checker games were being played. At nearby billiard tables dedicated players were stroking the ivory spheres across the green felt. One of the players was addressing a billiard ball with the butt end of the cue. The judge was rather taken aback by this newest method of playing until Commissioner Edwards explained that the man wasn't being stupid. He was merely showing contempt.

Afterward Edwards ordered his men to interview all who went into the club and to take photographs of the more sensitive types. Operators of the club sought relief by asking for an injunction to halt the police harassment. Edwards went into the same court, filed a petition for abatement of a nuisance, and then subpoenaed every person who had been interviewed. All took the Fifth Amendment, and the judge was convinced that something was amiss. He issued a search warrant, and on the same day the club closed, Licavoli took the operation a few miles away, outside city limits, and carried on business just as before.

Licavoli's success is due in part to his generosity to other hoodlum types who seek to settle down in Detroit. He remembers when he came to Detroit from The Green Ones' wars, found the right people, and married into the right family. He, in turn, extended the hand of friendship to Joseph Barbara, Jr., who had left New York State after the Apalachin raid on his father's home on November 14, 1957. Young Barbara went west and married the daughter of Detroiter Peter (Bozzi) Vitale. He then promptly became secretary, treasurer, and resident agent for an outfit called Tri-County Sanitation Company, subsidiary of a company with the same name in New York City.

In February, 1962, Joe Barbara's father-in-law, Peter Vitale, and Peter's brother, Paul, formed the Tri-County Leasing Company to provide motorized equipment for the sanitation firm. The mob had moved into a new field of endeavor, and the take-over was rapid.

The new corporation purchased the most modern rubbish-collecting equipment available, and Tri-County launched itself into the highly competitive refuse-hauling business. Its Detroit rivals were companies of long standing, but they couldn't match Barbara's outfit in the equipment area. Hydraulic units purchased for Barbara cost upward of $20,000 each, were highly mobile, and could haul twice as much as the average competitor's truck. Advance assurance of success apparently inspired the layout of the necessary money, for almost immediately Tri-County became big business and took over several of the most lucrative contracts held by competitors.

Strangely enough, Barbara's truck-drivers, who earned an average of $40 a week less than drivers hired by the competition, were never organized by the Teamsters Union in Detroit, home of Jimmy Hoffa.

Barbara's rabbit foot must have been worked overtime. Just a year after he went into business, twenty-nine employees of the Detroit public works department and five employees of rubbish-hauling companies were indicted for defrauding the city of legal dumping fees at city incinerators. It developed that the rubbish companies bribed the public works employees to cheat on the weight and volume of rubbish dumped.

Testimony at the McClellan hearings by Inspector Earl Miller of Detroit's criminal intelligence bureau showed that the companies involved—all defendants pleaded guilty on April 4, 1963—were Variety Trucking Company, Michigan Business Hauling, Les's Trucking, A. N. Reitzloff Corporation, and the Roulo Trucking Company.

Tri-County Sanitation employees were also observed by probers in the act of paying bribes, but none of the recipients were willing to testify against the Barbara outfit. Curiously, the city ordered the private rubbish haulers barred from city incinerators pending the outcome of the court case, and Tri-County, for whom a warrant could not be issued, thrived on its competitors' misfortune.

In addition, legitimate businesses in Detroit, fearful of adverse publicity, canceled contracts with the offending rubbish companies. Tri-County had further insurance in the fact that it was able to use the facilities of the municipal incinerator in a nearby suburb controlled by a Licavoli henchman.

From rubbish collecting to the sport of kings is a jump the Mafiosi take with almost aristocratic aplomb. The Hazel Park Racetrack, just outside Detroit, is, Police Chief Edwards testified, a state-licensed monopoly operation "subject to in-

fluence by the Mafia." On August 26, 1963, the officers and
directors were listed as Anthony J. Zerilli, the son of Joseph
Zerilli, a member of the ruling council of Detroit dons; Jack
W. Tocco, son of Black Bill Tocco, also on the ruling council; Anthony J. Tocco, another son of Black Bill; and Dominic P. (Fats) Corrado. Relatives of a strange Mafioso
named Santo (Cockeyed Sam) Perrone also held stock.

The Michigan racing commission started to probe the track
and came up with an exposé that, in spite of its rather surprising findings, brought about no action. There was quite
a fuss at the beginning, especially when a deposition in the
Wayne County circuit court established the fact that Anthony
J. Zerilli, at age twenty-one, made an investment of $50,000
in the track. Zerilli explained that this was a loan from his
father, and the probe failed to provoke continued interest.
Perhaps nobody cares. The operation nets a million dollars a
year, and the horse-racing devotees seem to like it.

Santo Perrone, one of the old so-called Moustache Petes,
is a big man in Detroit Mafia circles and a very rich man,
with assets that include auto washes, scrap-metal firms, and
real estate developments. He is worth well over $1 million
and can afford to insulate himself from the work of the rank-
and-file Mafiosi, but he insists on keeping a hand in the
"business" as though he were a mere button man in the organization.

District Inspector Vincent W. Piersanti testified at the Mc-
Clellan hearings that the criminal intelligence bureau of the
Detroit police department has developed evidence that Perrone was responsible for a series of five bombings in Detroit
in 1960. Santo had put a new twist on an old Mafia technique. According to police, instead of asking for protection
money first and, if refused, bombing afterward, Santo bombed
victims *before* trying to shake them down.

A case in point, related by Piersanti, is that of the Victor
Oil Company in Detroit, where a bomb went off near a rear
door at 7:45 P.M. on October 17, 1961.

Perrone's "pilot fish," Richard Lambert, listed by police as
a long-time associate of Perrone, "cased" the oil company for
several days before the bombing. He reported back to Perrone, who then called a meeting with his two favorite bom-
bardiers, Paul Tendiglia, who has a police record showing
twelve arrests with two convictions for burglary dating back
to 1932, and Peter Guastello, whose criminal record includes

arrests for armed robbery, burglary, and Office of Price Administration violations.

All four men were observed meeting in St. Clair Shores at the Village Supermarket owned by Guastello. After the meeting on September 13, 1961, police observed Perrone, the millionaire mobster, going to a gun shop, where he purchased a one-pound can of gunpowder before returning to an auto-wash establishment he owned.

On September 30, police observed Perrone and Lambert again investigating the oil company at Warren and St. Jean Streets. The bombing followed on October 17. Early the next morning the owner of the oil company, Eugene Epstein, received a phone call. The caller did not identify himself, but he warned: "The next bomb will blow your place out of business and you into your graveyard."

That afternoon a private citizen, John Harness, reported to police that he had observed the perpetrators of the Victor Oil bombing. He said that during the evening of October 17, he had parked his car in the Chrysler employees' parking lot behind the oil company building as another vehicle had driven up. Two men got out of this car and walked to the Victor Oil Company property. A short time later they came back to their car.

"You don't have to move the car," Harness heard one of the men say, "because the fuse is long enough to give us plenty of time to get away." Their car, however, left the parking lot at a high rate of speed, and Harness, also, decided to leave. When he stopped for a traffic signal half a block away, he heard an explosion from the direction of the Victor Oil property.

Harness went to the police, he said, because he felt a sense of outrage. His life had been placed in jeopardy, and he wanted to testify. As a result of the descriptions supplied by him, police arrested Perrone, Lambert, Guastello, and Tendiglia. Specifically, Harness identified Lambert and Tendiglia as the men he saw in the parking lot. Nitrate tests showed a positive reaction on Perrone, Lambert, and Tendiglia. Guastello's test came up negative.

It was at this point that Harness learned whom he had identified. Police, to allay his fears of reprisal, took maximum security measures to ensure the safety of Harness and his wife and children. In October Harness testified at a preliminary examination held in Recorders Court in Detroit and repeated the facts he had previously given the police. Perrone, Lambert, and Tendiglia were bound over for trial. The case against Guastello was dismissed.

After many delays the trial was set for September 27, 1962. Police were still guarding Harness' family, but the witness' personal guard was discontinued at his request. At about the same time startled police learned that Harness had visited the office of the defendants' attorney, Joseph Louisell, and signed an affidavit stating that he had been at the scene of the bombing in the company of a girl friend. He said he had observed the two men he had previously identified but now could not with assurance make a positive identification.

Police had not been aware there was an additional witness. The girl was questioned but would not describe or identify anyone. It developed that Harness had been ridiculed by friends and acquaintances, including his union steward, for getting involved with the powerful Perrone.

The trial started on schedule, but Harness recanted the testimony he had given at the pretrial examination. The defendants were acquitted, and Perrone went home, all grains of guilt apparently cleansed from his hands.

So goes Detroit, seat of Mafia power and criminal nepotism second to none in the history of the world, where the dons sift gold or gunpowder through their fingers, depending on whom they want to influence.

Detroit Police Inspector Earl Miller testified at the McClellan hearings as to the extensive infiltration of Mafia elements into legitimate business in and around the city, and he put into evidence a chart prepared by his department's criminal information bureau listing businesses that, currently or at one time, were "owned, infiltrated or influenced by" the Detroit Mafia. Placing the names of the firms in proper context with regard to the Mafiosi who either own them in their entirety or have a part of them posed a difficult problem for the law-enforcement group, but it is quite clear that the Detroit Mafia leaders exercise an amazingly diverse influence over the people of Detroit and of the United States, as a study of the list below makes clear (the addresses refer to Detroit unless otherwise indicated). The Detroit Mafia controls or has interest in hundreds of other business interests —in the United States, Mexico, and Canada. Indeed, there are many top businessmen in every big city in the country who owe their financial well-being to Licavoli and his associates. How so? Because the mobsters are interested in anything that can make a dollar.

Peter Licavoli
Lakeshore Underwriters, Inc., 16135 Harper
Office building, 16135 Harper
Lakeshore Insurance, Inc., 16135 Harper
Gold Cup Coffee Co., 6353 W. Vernor
Fototronics, Inc., 6230 John R.
Apache Nickel Surplus, 6230 John R.
Grace Ranch, Tucson, Arizona
Casa Catalina Motel, Tucson, Arizona
Riding stable, Tucson, Arizona
Tanque Verde, property, Tucson, Arizona
Tucson Printing Co., Tucson, Arizona
  (*with Joseph Bommarito*)
Apache Realty, 15126 Mack
Michigan Mutual Distributing Co.
Hart Center, 1135 Beaufait
Chrysler Office Bldg., 6230 John R.

John Priziola
Harper Metro Park subdivision
Moravian Acres subdivision
Rental property, 16905 to 16915 Harper
Tocco Wholesale Food Co.
City Barber College
Balmoral Gardens
St. Clair Terrace Corp., 830 St. Clair
Motel and Bar, Gratiot and Masonic Blvd., Roseville, Michigan
Starlite Motel, 19021 Florida, Roseville, Michigan
  (*with his sons-in-law, Frank and Joseph Matranga*)
Papa Joe's Restaurant, San Diego, California
Tropics Bar, San Diego, California
La Mesa Bowl Corp., San Diego, California
Bar of Music, San Diego, California
Cactus Bar, San Diego, California

Angelo Meli
Flint Cold Storage, 925 S. Dort
Pure Oil Co., gas station, 2970–98 E. Vernor
Income rental property, 13127 Harper; 19565 Mack

Meltone Music, 2971 Grand River
SC & CC Trucking Co., 1640 E. Six Mile Road
Ace Automatic Music Co., Saginaw, Michigan
Bel-Aire Lodge Motel, Saginaw, Michigan
480-acre farm, Marine City, Michigan

William Tocco and Joseph Zerilli
T & M Construction, 11896 E. Outer Drive
Grocery store, 710 Jos. Campau
Hazel Park Racing Association
Pfeiffer Macomb, distributors
Melrose Linen Service, 4630 Crane
Lakeshore Coach Lines
Detroit Italian Bakery
Jarson-Zerilli Co.
Income property, 4120 Woodward
South Branch Ranch, Roscommon, Michigan
Elias Big Boy, Ann Arbor, Michigan
    (*with Peter Licavoli*)
Office building, 16135 Harper
Muller Foods, Jersey City, New Jersey
Deer Valley Citrus Association, Glendale, Arizona

Tucson, Arizona, has for years been a favored spa for a number of misplaced and displaced eastern mobsters, including Pete Licavoli and Joe Bonanno, a resident since 1943 when not on the move, and Anthony Tisci, son-in-law of Sam Giancana of Chicago. However, an increasing number of bombing and shooting incidents, beginning in 1968 and involving the homes or properties of these three and others, may tend to cool the welcome Tucson has given such syndicate investors in the past.

While Licavoli, an Italian-American and therefore not subject to deportation, has generally been considered to be the Detroit don for many years, the combined power of Joseph Zerilli and William Tocco would seem at present to hold the ruling votes in the council of five that rules Detroit, and together they probably wield the upper hand.

Intertwined with the top dons are the men who actually look after the various income-producing properties. They, in turn, are given fiefs of their own. Men such as Mike Polizzi and Anthony Giacalone and his brother Vito operate, according to McClellan committee testimony, on a lower level of command in such firms as Michigan Metal, Garomot Corporation, Roseland Club, and the Home Juice Company, which distributes soft drinks and exchanged hands, police claim, via an Italian craps game called Barbudi.

The junior Mafiosi's level of activity is not insignificant, however. For example, Tony and Vito Giacalone were arrested and arraigned in October, 1968, along with five others, on conspiracy charges stemming from a loan-shark racket allegedly resulting in at least two violent murders in the Detroit area. A six-month investigation by the state crime commission led to thirteen grand jury indictments, involving thirty-two defendants including known Mafiosi, and exposed, among other things, an illegal interstate horse-race betting ring.

The Sport of Kings is kept up, at the race-horse level—as against the business-office level—by Mike (The Enforcer) Rubino, one of the big men reported to operate the Double "D" Farm at 8351 McKinley Road, Algonac, Michigan.

Men such as Dominic and Anthony Corrado, pals of Black Bill Tocco and Joseph Zerilli, ran a variety of businesses in Detroit, among them, according to testimony, the Grecian Gardens, Kozani Bar, Selco Management Company, Gunn Dairies, vending-machine outfits, and income property including a one-hundred-acre farm in Price, Ontario.

The bakers of the Detroit Mafia seem to be confined to the Cavataio family. Nine members of this family headed by Julian, Peter, and, until his death, Dominic run a variety of business enterprises in addition to their many bakeries, including, according to testimony, four auto-wash companies, the Chesterfield Lounge at 4721 John R., Eastland Court apartments at 10410 Cadieux, Prince Macaroni at 3261 Belleview, and several dry-cleaning establishments.

Of course, it's no crime to be interested in anything that can make a dollar. In fact, it's a typically American pastime. But the devious methods used by the mob in the making and dispensing of the green stuff, as evidenced by the testimony at the McClellan hearings, should give pause to those who say that when a mobster goes into business and turns "honest," he ought to be left alone by the lawmen. The four speakers in the following testimony from the McClellan hearings are Jerome Adlerman, general counsel to the permanent subcommittee on investigations; Senator John L. McClellan, Chairman; and Commissioner Edwards and Inspector Miller of the Detroit police department:

MR. MILLER. . . . The logical belief that Hart Center, Inc. was in fact a three-way partnership between Licavoli, Scarface Joe Bommarito and Matthew "Mike" Rubino, was confirmed when the property was sold on March 26 of this year to a New York City investor.

Wayne County records indicate a sale price of $620,000; after indebtedness of about $125,000 was satisfied leaving proceeds of $495,000, the president of the corporation purchased a total of 36 cashiers' checks made payable to Licavoli, Bommarito, and Rubino.

MR. ADLERMAN. The last three you mentioned are on your chart?

MR. MILLER. Yes, sir.

MR. EDWARDS. Yes, and these are very high-up figures.

Mr. Chairman, it might be desirable at this point for me to point out that Peter Licavoli, who has run through this whole presentation, is at this point in debt to the people of the United States by official court decree to the tune of $411,000 for income tax not paid and penalties for failing to pay income tax.

THE CHAIRMAN. I wonder why these checks could not be impounded and money collected?

MR. EDWARDS. We have a unit of the Intelligence Division of the Department of Internal Revenue for whom we have a great respect. I am sure if they knew that those checks were going to be issued at a given time, they would have been there.

I am also reasonably sure they feel they have already levied liens which will protect the people in relation to the collection of that $411,000.

It is just interesting to note that here is a fellow who has been operating this way for all these years, he owes $411,000 on income taxes up to 1951, Senator. I don't have any idea what he owes from that point forward.

THE CHAIRMAN. You mean that was prior to 1951 that he owes that much?

MR. EDWARDS. Yes, sir, this indebtedness concerning income tax evasion prior to 1951.

MR. MILLER. The cashiers' checks rendering each of the principals $165,000 for a total of $495,000.

THE CHAIRMAN. I assume there is no lien placed on that building. Maybe the Revenue Department did not know it. They were able to conceal that ownership.

MR. EDWARDS. The record ownership was indeed concealed until actually after the transaction was over.

THE CHAIRMAN. As I point out, it is not always the fault of the officials.

These folks are cunning. They are very resourceful in evading not only the law but in evading taxes.

It is perhaps time the powers that be among our various law-enforcement and crime-detection and prosecution agencies put their collective heads—and information—together and begin to heed the wisdom of the esteemed Judge Learned Hand, who said in 1923:

Our dangers do not lie in too little tenderness to the accused. Our procedure has always been haunted by the ghost of the innocent man convicted. It is an unreal dream. What we need to fear is the archaic formalism and the watery sentiment that obstructs, delays, and defeats the prosecution of crime.

SIX

FLORIDA:

Fun in the Sun

All Florida has been divided into two parts, insofar as the Mafia is concerned. One part is the west coast of Florida, the center of which, from the standpoint of mob influence, is Tampa. And the west coast was the first to be exploited. The men of the Mafia have been in that area for a long time, sharing the loot with, and the lawless endeavors of, the adjoining, widespread New Orleans Mafiosi. In fact, the two families have been so successful that together they have brought the whole southern tier of the United States under control.

The other part is the lush east coast, which came into its own in 1933 when a jockey-sized tough known as Little Augie Pisano, a henchman of New Jersey gambling boss Joe Adonis, went south to establish a beachhead for Adonis in the form of lush "carpet joints," establishments that were copied from some of the lavish gaming houses operated by Adonis in New Jersey.

A carpet joint is several cuts above a "sawdust joint," where that stratum of society known as the middle class is wont to gamble, and Adonis saw his future in the richer rooms even though the less pretentious places and their customers were the backbone of his gambling empire in the thirties. Today, most of the gaming salons, in Las Vegas and elsewhere, are carpet joints, but the clientele, a far richer middle class than existed in Adonis' salad days in New Jersey, is the same; it is still largely made up of "grinds," one-dollar bettors. When a carpet joint "busts out" a member of the jet set, credit, established by consulting the hieroglyphics imprinted on a card in the cashier's office, is usually forthcoming. The grinds, however, must wire home for money when they go broke in Vegas, as they did in Joey's New Jersey joints once upon a time.

To Adonis it seemed that if the wealthy jet set of the thirties flocked from New York City across the Hudson River to his pleasure palaces—the chief of which was Ben Marden's Riviera at the west end of the George Washington Bridge—it would also flock to new establishments in Florida. Events proved him right.

When Joe's advance man, Pisano, went to Florida, his first move was to make peace with the brotherhood in Tampa. There sat such members of the Mafiosi as Ignazio Antinori, later assassinated, James Lumia, a Mafia chief killed in 1950, and Santo Trafficante, Sr., who had arrived much earlier and laid the foundations of the narcotics trade. Once he had done this, Pisano was free to set up the eastern Florida operation, and the fact that it was to be primarily a carpet-joint operation showed that Adonis was out to take the rich. But Adonis and his henchmen were not so stupid as to try to freeze out the old guard, Trafficante and his friends. There was plenty for everyone.

Trafficante, who had been born in Sicily in 1886, arrived in Tampa in 1904 and became a naturalized citizen in 1925, at a time when the notorious non-Mafioso Charles M. Wall was acknowledged boss of most of the illegal gambling in Tampa and central Florida. Wall called himself "dean of the underworld," but he made the mistake of cutting Trafficante in on the proceeds and of opening the newcomer's eyes to gambling profits tnat made blackmail and extortion money from Italian businessmen seem small potatoes indeed.

In 1954, after experiencing three unsuccessful attempts on his life, Wall announced that he was retiring, without saying exactly what he was retiring from. But in April, 1955, he really retired: his brutally beaten body was found in his own home; his throat had been slashed.

Wall had provided valuable information to the Kefauver committee in 1951, at which time he was one of the few non-

Mafia gamblers who talked about the organization and its operation in Tampa. This action probably sealed his death, but he was able to speak even from the grave: in 1960 Sergeant Jack de la Llana of the Tampa police department's criminal intelligence unit obtained a report made by Wall in 1945 about the Mafia, naming some of the members of the national board including Brooklyn's Vincent Mangano, Detroit's Joe Massei, and Chicago's Frank Nitti. Wall also put the finger on Joe Profaci.

The line of influence from Joseph Profaci of Brooklyn, where Adonis got his early start, to the Trafficantes, Senior and Junior, is laid out on police blotters for all to see. Trafficante, Sr., got a leg up and a lot of ideas from Little Augie Pisano, who was backed by Adonis. Adonis, in turn, gained ascendancy in the New York—New Jersey area with the help of Profaci, lifetime friend of Trafficante. The circle, though plated with murders and hard cash, seems always to be completed on the graph paper used by the Mafia, whether it begins in New York, Florida, or some unpronounceable city in a far corner of the earth.

As Trafficante and his Tampa thugs watched with undisguised interest, Adonis worked with the members of the Detroit mob on many of his financial forays at the Mafia level. For example, Adonis' top gaming place in east Florida was the Colonial Inn, near Hallandale, which he started in the late thirties with Mert Wertheimer, Detroit gang wheel, Meyer Lansky, who gravitated to gambling from New York City's industrial racketeering, and Vincent Alo of the Bronx. The Inn's gross profit for the year ending October 31, 1946, after many years of police-free operation, was $685,538.76, which was split between the partners.

It has been estimated that within a few years, up until the time that gambling was outlawed in the Miami area following a public outcry, Adonis had banked over $13 million in cash, using the Merchants Bank of New York. Trafficante and others really blinked when the total was racked up by accountants for Manhattan District Attorney Frank Hogan, who probed Joe Adonis and all angles of his gaming activities.

Adonis' now-defunct Greenacres Club, in Hollywood, north of Miami, was a forerunner of what was to come in Las Vegas in the early forties, and experience garnered in the gambling tourist traps of east Florida was to prove invaluable when Bugsy Siegel opened up Las Vegas for the syndicate.

So it was that Florida gangdom gained through the know-how of Adonis. Adonis' success, however, did not help his pal, Pisano, whose real name was Anthony Carfano. Little Augie was slain in New York City on September 25, 1959, probably as the result of the Vito Genovese take-over—but, then, not even Mafiosi win them all.

When Adonis left Florida, he centered his activities on his old stamping ground in the north and seemed able to get along with everyone, including public officials, and even with the aspirations of Genovese. Joe's hobby was riding to hounds on Shore Road in the Bay Bridge section of Brooklyn. In the full regalia of a fox-hunting *aficionado* he would pound the bridle path, the pride and joy of his hoodlum pals. Finally, however, he made an error, or perhaps his time for playing and being a big man was over. False testimony before a Bergen, New Jersey, County grand jury to the effect that he had been born in Passaic at an address that turned out to be a vacant lot once occupied by a livery stable led to his deportation in 1956. Adonis then joined his pal, Lucky Luciano, as crown prince of "displaced" Mafiosi in Italy: both had come home again.

Adonis' Florida associate, Santo Trafficante, Sr., died on August 11, 1954, leaving behind six sons, one of whom bears his name and wears his Mafia garments with pride.

During his formative years Santo Trafficante, Jr., had been rewarded by his father with control of the numbers racket in central Florida and ownership of the Sans Souci gaming casino in Havana—a casino formerly owned by Gabriel Mannarino of Pittsburgh, Pennsylvania, a fellow delegate with young Santo Trafficante at the Apalachin crime convention in 1957.

Trafficante, Jr., was a pioneer in Cuban gambling and shared the proceeds of the Sans Souci casino with Cuban dictator Fulgencio Batista y Zaldivar for many years. Indeed, so powerful did Trafficante eventually become in Cuba before the advent to power of Fidel Castro that four gunmen who arrived on the island from America to kill him, probably on the instruction of an envious Albert Anastasia, were told by Cuban police they would have to accomplish their purpose on American soil—if they could.

Young Trafficante publicly ascended his father's throne a year after the latter's death when he was introduced to "polite society" in Brooklyn at the wedding of the daughter of Don Joe Profaci to Anthony Tocco, son of Detroit mobster

William Tocco. On June 4, 1955, Santo, Jr., was among the guests at a reception following the ceremony at the Hotel Commodore in Manhattan and was greeted with "royal" deference by such gangsters as Frank Livorsi, Thomas Dioguardi, his brother John—"Johnny Dio"—Albert Anastasia, and Three Finger Brown Lucchese. It is, of course, highly unlikely that Trafficante knew then that Anastasia had an eye on his gambling interests in Cuba.

The slick road Adonis laid out in Florida for a short time helped put Trafficante, Jr., on the way to a kind of wealth very different from that amassed by such earlier Mafiosi as his father and Lumia and Antinori, Mustache Petes who were connecting links between the first wave of Mafia immigrants to this country and Joe Adonis. But Santo Trafficante, Jr., did not inherit the easy life. Another legacy was a quarrel born of an incident created by Cuban narcotics smugglers who had sold Antinori a shipment of tainted drugs. Antinori had carried the drugs to the Midwest and peddled them to distributors for the crime cartel. But when it was found that the drugs were tainted, Antinori was not able to make restitution to the distributors and was eliminated, leaving a lot of bad blood between the distributors of the Florida family.

It was probably Little Augie Pisano, a veteran of New York City gang wars and one of the least publicized of the New York-New Jersey Mafia gang, who ironed out the feud between the Cuban mob element and the syndicate brotherhood. At any rate, Pisano certainly stirred up the Floridan criminal waters. During Little Augie's Florida years there were fourteen murders and six attempted assassinations in and around Tampa; Adonis' strong-arm man was keeping the Tampa crowd on a friendly basis and paving the way for his boss's entrance into Florida.

In testifying before the McClellan hearings as to the domination of Santo Trafficante, Jr., over Tampa's criminal organization, Tampa Police Chief Neil Brown presented a chart showing the interrelationships of the boys under Trafficante's thumb and stated:

> It is our considered conclusion that the Mafia exists in Tampa, that it controls most illegal gambling in Tampa and central Florida, and that its members have interstate and international ties to other Mafia groups.

That Trafficante's power extends over more than merely the Tampa area is clearly indicated by his presence in the hotel suite of Albert Anastasia in New York on the night of October 24, 1957, during what appeared to be a showdown discussion about Albert's attempt—despite the fact that concessions had already been handed out by the syndicate, not only to Trafficante, but also to men such as Meyer Lansky and his brother Jake—to move in on Trafficante's gambling operations in Cuba. Trafficante moved out of the hotel approximately one hour after Anastasia was murdered in a nearby barber shop the next morning. He had been registered under the alias "B. Hill," and neither the local police nor federal officials knew of his presence until much later. Trafficante, in fact, may well be the one who gave Anastasia the traditional Mafia kiss of death.

Trafficante showed up again at the famous Apalachin conference, which was held, partly at least, to discuss the division of Anastasia's rackets "estate." And he has never parted company from the Mafia leaders since. Moreover, Trafficante, who has been busy building his own empire, maintains his ties with the organization throughout the country in entirely typical fashion, depending largely on the movements of various couriers. There are few phone calls made, and no mail is sent. Word of mouth—away from all possible recording devices—is the principal mode of communication.

Trafficante and the syndicate depend upon couriers to carry not only information but also cash around the country in order to balance accounts. The couriers are, therefore, extremely important cogs in the Mafia wheel. And the gang leaders make their selections carefully, sometimes even choosing women—such as Virginia Hill, former sweetheart of both Adonis and Bugsy Siegel, who was established in a penthouse atop the Hotel Flamingo in Las Vegas when Bugsy was kingpin in town.

Certainly, the courier method of communication has its advantages. In spite of the fact that well-known gangsters are always subject to being stopped and questioned by the police, by keeping their mouths shut or using their imagination to say the "right" things, they can often turn the officers' probing into a reverse asset. False information can tie up the police longer than trustworthy facts.

For many years the chief courier for the Mafia was Gaetano

Ricci, alias "Tony Goebbels," who twenty years ago made his headquarters at 5 Court Square, Brooklyn, in a restaurant beneath the local Democratic party headquarters. Goebbels, who is six feet four inches tall, has been picked up by police in every large city in the country and in many of the smaller towns, but he has now dropped out of sight and is presumably living in retirement in Florida—although his reported appearance in Chicago with other crime bosses in November, 1968, makes his "retirement" questionable.

One of his replacements appeared to be Louis Coticchia, alias "Lou Brady," who came into prominence in April, 1962, when members of the Tampa police department spotted him in the company of veteran Tampa Mafioso Frank Diecidue and a pal, Augustine Primo Lazzara. It is thought that Coticchia served as a trusted courier until he did "something bad," as Tampa police surmise, because a year later he walked out of his house in Miami bound for a luncheon date with Santo Trafficante, Jr., and was never seen again. His wife told police Coticchia received a phone call just before leaving the house.

Coticchia may well have been the victim of foul play because he had taken a contract to collect money due Tommy Eboli, acting boss of the Genovese family. The funds represented interest due on a juice-loan advance to the operator of a New York tractor company. Police believe that the courier may have collected the money but failed to pass it on to Eboli—thus losing not only his job but also his life.

Coticchia is a good example of how a Mafioso works his way up in the world of crime. Born on February 25, 1920, in Cincinnati, Ohio, Coticchia was first arrested in 1936, for robbery in Ohio. In 1937 he was arrested in Miami for investigation of a "shakedown," but after being held for four days, he was released without having charges filed against him. Arrested again and held for investigation, this time in Hot Springs, Arkansas, a noted center of Mafia activity, he was released with the understanding that he would leave the city. A few weeks later, in Cleveland, Coticchia was picked up and charged with assault to commit rape. He was convicted and received a sentence of from one to fifteen years. He served four years and was released in 1941.

Coticchia's next arrest was in Los Angeles. Police arrested him there in 1942 on a warrant issued in Baltimore for grand theft. Tried in Baltimore for receiving stolen goods, he then served five years in prison. Thereafter, for almost fifteen years, Coticchia virtually dropped out of sight, but apparently he was exceedingly active on behalf of the syndicate, cementing ties and contacts throughout the country, and learning new and important duties. He had graduated from soldier to button man in the organization and was picking up the experience needed by a courier. His last arrest came in Tampa, in January, 1963, when he was picked up and booked in connection with a charge of grand larceny, but the charge was dropped for lack of evidence. At the time of his arrest Coticchia had $1,775 in cash on him; he was a trifle shorter than usual because a few days earlier he had plunked down $3,625 in long green for a new car.

Also found on Coticchia were papers indicating that he had lived for a while at the Aloha Motel in Miami under the alias "Luiz Paulino Bailey," of Rio de Janeiro, Brazil. Another paper listed gambling equipment and the statement: "Empress Lines, Ltd., Nassau—via Wappen Von Hamburg—German boat loading pier No. 3."

An investigation indicated that Coticchia had worked as a pit boss in gaming casinos in Las Vegas and Havana and had contacts that would enable him to buy gambling equipment. The cargo listed on the paper included fifty slot machines valued in excess of $65,000. The equipment had been shipped air freight from Las Vegas to Nassau and placed in the German vessel. The information received indicated that the German ship was to travel between Miami and Nassau as a floating gambling casino, but the chances are the cargo finally wound up in the gaming casino of the Lucayan Beach Hotel in the Bahamas, which opened a few months later.

Phone calls are of course frowned on by the Mafia, for obvious reasons, but a record of at least one of Coticchia's long distance calls does exist. The record, submitted to the McClellan hearings by Sergeant de la Llana of the Tampa police department, indicates that late in 1962 Coticchia phoned from Tampa to Sonny's restaurant in Miami Beach, which was owned by Thomas Altamura, reputed Mafia member and an associate of Santo Trafficante, Jr. Coticchia was no doubt well acquainted with Altamura, "The Enforcer," who was killed five years later, on October 30, 1967, as he entered another restaurant in Miami. One of Altamura's lieutenants, Anthony (Big Tony) Esperti, who had fallen out with his boss, has been charged with the murder, and

both men have weighty files in the intelligence division of
the Los Angeles police department. One question not answered by the files, however, concerns the presence of a
$10,000 cashier's check found on Altamura's bullet-ridden
body, drawn on a bank in Sherman Oaks, a Los Angeles
suburb.

While couriers are essential to Trafficante's successful
operation in Florida, his success can be credited even more
to his adherence to the Mafia code of *omerta* and to his
ability to maintain himself as the power behind the throne
in Florida with none of the accoutrements of power: the
creature comforts that usually are associated with powerful
and financially successful men the world over.

To the syndicate, Trafficante must seem to be a model.
Thus, on October 14, 1968, Trafficante once again found
time to illustrate to the syndicate the value of *omerta*: he
merely coughed and guffawed politely when questioned by
counsel for a Florida legislative committee probing lawlessness. Santo took the Fifth Amendment when asked if he
was a member of the Mafia. No one knew precisely why he
laughed. But then he is a secretive man. Authorities, for
example, know of no legitimate businesses, not even of any
real estate, owned or controlled by Santo Trafficante. His
house, car, and other possessions are held in the names of
others. If the rules of humility and austerity, in the old
tradition of the Mafia, are thus observed by Trafficante, he
must be one of the few true Mafiosi left in the United States.
And whatever the motivation behind Trafficante's simple
mode of life, it seems to keep him healthy. The downfall of
the more polished members of the secret society in Florida
over the years has often come through their violation of
the old concepts of the Mafia. When a Mafioso gets away
from the traditions, he runs into trouble.

Take, for instance, the case of ex-convict Harry I. Voiler,
who founded a newspaper, the *Daily Mail,* in Miami in
1949—years before Trafficante, Jr., emerged as a power. A
woman witness close to the Mafia testified at the McClellan
hearings that the purposes of the paper "were (1) to provide
prompt dissemination of racing results and (2) to create a
favorable atmosphere toward out-of-state racketeer elements
to be found in Miami." Chief backer of the paper was
Martin Accardo, brother of Chicago mobster Tony Accardo,
who invested $125,000. Voiler said that no money had come
from the mob, but Mrs. Oretta Y. Carroll, who had once

been married to Martin Accardo but was obviously not bound to a code of silence, produced documentary proof that Accardo had indeed been the money man behind the journal.

Everything went down the drain for the *Daily Mail*, however, when, no doubt in a burst of loyal feeling, the paper published an editorial welcoming the notorious Frank Costello to Miami when the big boss went south one year to take the sun. It was a momentary visit, to say the least.

The old-time racketeers who had a finger in the pie of Miami have now all gone by the board. One was Samuel (Gameboy) Miller, who had been a partner in the Island Club in Miami, from which he gleaned, he said, $15,000 a year. Another Miami stalwart, now out of business, is John Angersola of Cleveland, a member of the old Mayfield Road gang, which operated the Desert Inn in its early days in Las Vegas. Angersola, an associate of Mike Coppola, used to own the Grand Hotel in Miami and a piece of the Wofford Hotel in that area. At present Angersola is reportedly an organizer for the Cleaners and Dyers International Union in Florida at a salary of $100 a week, but he is somewhat vague as to what his duties are. He is also employed by the "23" room, a Miami Beach establishment, at $100 a week. No work is involved here, either, but, as Angersola puts it, "they may need me."

While Angersola awaits his call to duty, Trafficante awaits his greatest opportunity. A windfall of refugees from Castro's Cuba may be providing the wherewithal to launch Trafficante into a truly golden financial orbit. Besides the usual requirements of food and lodging, the Cuban refugees hanker for daily knowledge of the main gambling activity on the island: Bolita or Cuba.

> Bolita is a numbers lottery where the winning number is drawn daily. Cuba is a numbers lottery where the winning number is drawn weekly. Bettors can place bets on any number from 1 to 100 and receive a 60-to-1 return if they win. The Cuba winning number is the last two digits, from the Cuban national lottery number, which is five digits, and is broadcast over a Havana radio station each Saturday shortly after 2:00 P.M.

Thus testified Sergeant William Branch of the Orlando, Florida, police department at the McClellan Senate hearings. The public—over three hundred thousand Cuban refugees have swelled the fertile fields of the lottery boys to incredible proportions—is contacted by peddlers or sellers who receive a commission of 15 per cent of their sales. Pickup men who take the bets from the sellers to the checkup houses receive 20 per cent of what they collect. Employees such as checkup men, adding-machine operators, and supervisors usually receive salaries for their duties.

Mafia watchdog of the lush Bolita-Cuba dough is Sam Cacciatore, cousin of Santo Trafficante, who with another Trafficante relative, Armando Rios, was picked up in a raid staged before the current influx of Cuban refugees and found even then to be doing a business of $160,000 a week in Orange County, Florida—a mere segment of the Trafficante operation.

Santo Trafficante, however, seldom makes mistakes. One is constantly confronted with evidence of his canniness; for example, his tolerance of non-Mafia men in his organization. One such non-Mafioso is Harlan Blackburn, a convicted felon born in Sand Lake, Florida, in 1919. Blackburn was convicted in 1935 of forging a U.S. government check and served four and one-half years in prison. He was arrested again, in March, 1956, for operating a lottery in Polk County, Florida, and received a five-year prison sentence. Released in 1959, Blackburn has since remained active in Trafficante's operation.

When he testified about Blackburn's operations, Sergeant Branch referred to the chart of the Mafia organization in the Tampa area and pointed out that of the twenty-seven people listed as working on the Florida lottery under Blackburn's supervision only five were without criminal records or arrests for gambling and other crimes.

In view of the records of even comparatively unimportant members of the Mafia organization in Florida, it is interesting to note that while the police have solved all but 4 of the 145 murders of "ordinary" people occurring between 1958 and 1962 in the Tampa area alone—a solution ratio of better than 97 per cent—and all 83 "regular" homicides occurring between 1960 and 1962, only 1 of 23 gangland murders has been solved.

With the departure from the syndicate scene in Florida of such elite members of the Mafia as Joe Adonis, Frank Costello, who had more important gold mines to pursue in New Orleans, Joe Massei, who owned cheese companies, and others—all of whom wanted to escape the limelight after a sudden upsurge of morality on the east coast of Florida—it became easy for Trafficante to impose his special brand and organization on many people. Thus while the carpet-joint Mafiosi have moved on, preferring to deal with some of the pushover public officials in the Caribbean's expanding gaming *boites de nuit* as well as with those in Nevada, the diehard Mafiosi who remain are well established, determined, and well organized.

Trafficante's personal touch is best exemplified by the division of organization between the "dirty dollar" boys, who handle the narcotics trade, and the soft-sell fellows, who ply the gambling trade and are finding the refugee Bolita enterprise a fantastic treasure trove. But, according to the Tampa police department, Trafficante has been ably assisted by Salvatore (Sam) Scaglione, now dead, and Gaetano (Joe) Mistretta, both classified as Mafia elders and as old friends of Trafficante's father, who himself started the wholesale take-over of Florida gambling as the carpet-joint boys moved out.

Directly under this local board of directors are other influential Mafiosi, as linked on a chart submitted to the McClellan committee by the Tampa police department: Frank Diecidue, member of a pioneer Mafia clan whose hand was weakened by the demise of Brooklyn's Vincent Mangano some years ago; Angelo Bedami, whose specialty is receiving stolen goods and bootlegging. Trafficante's under-boss, Augustine Primo Lazzara, who liked to bribe public officials and assault people who wouldn't go along with him, died in 1968.

The Diecidue clan was given a rather loosely woven barony in Florida when, in 1929, Frank Costello called a meeting in Atlantic City to try to unite warring Mafia groups throughout the United States and to form a cohesive Mafia, subject to its ancient rules and regulations, to take advantage of the huge treasure pot in America that dwarfed the combined riches of all the countries of the world.

Costello was able to integrate the warring factions, and, through the influence of Vincent Mangano, the Diecidue family was able to maintain its power in Florida for some time. The power of the Trafficantes, Senior and Junior, was locked in, however, in 1952 after Mangano, a member of the Mafia governing board, disappeared from sight and became part of the concrete foundations of a well-known housing project in Nassau County, New York.

A current handhold on the rackets for the Diecidues is James (Jimmy) Costa Longo, a gambler who likes to tell the judge off when he stands before the bench—a real loud mouth.

Working with and for these men are the usual assortment —records indicate that forty Mafia members and affiliated hoodlums operate in south Florida—of button men and soldiers who have helped to make Florida a fruit just ripened for picking by the syndicate of crime, which never seems to run out of harvest. In Dade County (the greater Miami area) alone crime investigator Richard B. Wallace estimated in 1966 that organized vice—bookmaking, lottery operations, prostitution, and abortions—was grossing $50 million a year.

Wallace also strongly urged the creation of a state crime commission, and the war on organized crime in Florida was in fact stepped up recently because of developments stemming as much from crusading zeal as from a desire to make the state appear politically and ethically acceptable, both to its own citizens and to the tourists who wonder whether Florida is a better place than Las Vegas to take the kiddies during vacation.

In a report to Governor Claude Kirk climaxing a six-month probe into syndicate activities in Florida, Director Ed Yarborough of the Florida sheriff's bureau claimed that information developed by his staff indicated that hoodlums, with the aid of eighty-seven corporate structures, control forty-five hotels and twenty-five cocktail lounges and restaurants in the Miami area. Also, in his report, delivered to the governor's office in March, 1967, Yarborough asked for more money to continue the investigation, which came to a close after six months of gumshoeing by three full-time agents.

In the meantime, in December, 1966, a new Dade County sheriff was appointed: E. Wilson (Bud) Purdy, a former FBI agent in New York and Florida who, among other jobs, headed Pennsylvania's state police for the three years prior to his Florida appointment. Purdy has a special interest in the movements of Santo Trafficante, Jr., and believes that every time Santo is picked up by police, there is a corresponding hole knocked in the Mafia's confidence in the Florida hood.

"Santo wants to have the confidence of the New York Mafia," Purdy told a reporter for *Time* magazine in April, 1967, "but how can he control this town when he can't even get past the Miami airport without being picked up?"

Purdy also seeks a boost in his department's $8.6 million budget. He would increase his 1,101 man force by 223 and raise salaries. He says he wants a "damn good" department— the best trained, best equipped, most efficient, and most honest anywhere.

Reflecting another facet of Florida's war on crime, quite apart from Sheriff Purdy's efforts in Dade County, was Governor Kirk's attempt, immediately after his January, 1967, inauguration, to establish a privately financed war on criminals. Kirk hired and utilized the men and files of a private detective agency known as the Wackenhut Corporation, headed by former FBI man George R. Wackenhut.

Wackenhut, according to reporter Jack Nelson of the *Los Angeles Times* bureau in Atlanta, met Kirk in 1964 when both men were staunch backers of Barry Goldwater in the presidential race, and the two became fast friends.

Kirk said that he personally solicited funds for the 1967 "private" crime probe from business and industry and that "money was pouring into the war chest" even before his solicitation began.

According to reporter Nelson, this particular war on Florida crime was called many names, such as "Gestapo, Kirk's private police force and Wackencops, among others," by persons who questioned its acumen. And, Nelson added, some Democrats in Florida, a state with few Republican office holders, fear that "if information developed by Wackenhut's men cannot be used to convict them in court, it can be used to convict them in political campaigns."

Claude Kirk is Florida's first Republican governor in ninety-four years, and the feeling was that his private probe could be a two-edged sword. However, on November 8, 1967, Kirk announced that the Wackenhut probe was ended. There was a $300,000 debt remaining, Kirk said, and the files that had evolved were being turned over to a new state crime-fighting agency, the Florida Bureau of Law Enforcement, which was created on October 1, 1967.

"My investigators are zero, zero, zero," Kirk said. "We don't have any money."

Consequently, when all the chips are down, Sheriff

Purdy, along with the new state agency, may have the last word after all. But Santo Trafficante doesn't seem to be the least bit worried, in spite of the listing of forty-five Miami hotels and twenty-five restaurants as being Mafia-owned. The mob still finds its own kind of fun in the sun. And it will take more than a little effort to shift it.

SEVEN

BAHAMAS:

Hoodlum Sea

Columbus didn't know it, but he did find a pot of gold at the end of the rainbow when he steered his little ships into the heart of what has become one of the greatest crime syndicate enterprises since Al Capone left Brooklyn and discovered Chicago.

Capone had no connection with Columbus, of course, but their descendants share one thing in common: a place at a trough of gold where pigs and paladins are born, weaned, and grown to maturity—the West Indies. Laved on the north by the Atlantic Ocean and on the south by the warm waters of the Caribbean Sea, this ancient haunt of pirates is the new playground of the mob.

The Caribbean can be blue or green, according to weather conditions, but for the gamblers who rarely give it a second glance the sea generally glints gold. Just a scant ten years ago these almost tropical waters harbored a pearly string of tranquil islands, stretching from the Bahamas, seventy miles off the coast of Florida, to Barbados and Trinidad, off the northern coast of Venezuela, South America—a thousand-island crescent of peace and pleasure providing retreat for tired tycoons, wound-up executives, and more or less lethargic but happy natives, many of whom thought voodoo was the closest they could get to the devil. Places with names such

as Bimini, Nassau, Virgin Islands, and Martinique were
shrines dedicated to those who liked to take the sun every
now and then.

If there was a devil in the area, he didn't make himself
manifest until Fidel Castro unlocked the Cuban Pandora's
box and drove out a segment of the American crime syndicate that had obtained a foothold in Havana—long a way-
stop, as we have seen, in the dope traffic that flows through
the Caribbean via Florida and New Orleans into the veins
of addicts in the United States and, during the years of
Batista's regime, a gambling hot spot as well.

Castro, who sought no piece of the action in the country
he took over, banished the gambling operators, pimps, and
dope pushers from the Cuban littoral. American law-enforcement officials were impressed by Castro's efforts to clean his
nest, but Cuba's loss was America's unfortunate gain, for
the hoods drifted back into the underworlds of the cities
that had spawned them: Miami, Tampa, Biloxi, Gulfport,
New Orleans, and Las Vegas.

Thwarted only temporarily by Cuba's rejection, the hoods
soon regrouped, returned to some of the smaller islands in
the Caribbean, and began to discover more riches than
Columbus ever dreamed of. In outflanking Castro on the
Spanish Main, they became part of a milieu that combined
many talents—the know-how of financiers, lawyers, legislators,
politicians, construction men, show-biz nabobs, gamblers,
and plain "ordinary" greedy people—and came up with what
in financial and real estate parlance is called a "real business
boom."

There is little doubt that Castro has since taken note of
this "capitalistic" influx of money just a few blue waves from
the shores of Cuba, where, under his guiding hand, com-
munism is making its play under a somewhat marginal
economy. But one of the first to note the potential in the
Bahamas and get the ball rolling for the entry of the syndicate boys was a man named Wallace Groves, "Boy Wonder
of Wall Street." Groves did not throw himself out of a window when the financial crash of 1929 tumbled fat cats and
golden calves throughout the United States, and he now has
just about everything a man could want—a man such as
Groves, that is—though he'd no doubt like to expunge from
his record a 1941 conviction involving a $750,000 stock
swindle for which he was sentenced to two years in prison.
In fact, he served only five months in durance vile, in the

federal penitentiary at Danbury, Connecticut, and was released in December, 1942.

The conviction arose through Groves's pyramiding company on top of company until he had built up $10 million in assets at a very small cost to himself, though this success could hardly have changed the flavor of the federal food allotment at Danbury. At the time of the conviction the Securities Exchange Commission said: "Almost all of the companies which came under the control of Mr. Groves suffered severe losses." Yet a friend said of Groves, who owned substantial pieces of twenty-three corporations, "He had a good reputation on Wall Street. He wasn't one of those sharpshooters."

In January, 1967, after trying to dig out the facts about Groves, *Parade* magazine reported: "There is one area in which Groves's friends and enemies agree: He is shrewd, quick and perceptive—'a natural genius at making money.'" Groves is also credited with having extrasensory perception when it comes to business deals and has said that he receives "vibrations" during business negotiations.

Groves's vibrations were apparently unhampered by his short vacation behind bars, for he went to Grand Bahama Island in the mid-forties to cut timber and found natural beaches, a frost-free climate, and convenient proximity to the tip of Florida—whence the scent of tourists wafted across the surging sea waters. Since then, the sixty-seven-year-old Boy Wonder has managed to wolf down half the island for himself with the help of two other men peculiarly suited to the task of helping him build up what is now a one-hundred-and-fifty-thousand-acre barony plus substantial pieces of outlying enterprises. The two associates have been fifty-six-year-old Louis Chesler, a 256-pound, blue-eyed son of a Lithuanian immigrant to Canada, and sixty-seven-year-old syndicate gambling chief Meyer Lansky.

Groves provided the land; Chesler, through his Canadian connections and financing, helped smooth the way for the construction of a beautiful hotel and subsequent permission for gambling therein; and Lansky came up with the syndicate know-how of casino operation to entice, cater to, and gauge the financial limits of the tourists—thousands of them— that was the main prerequisite to the money-making dreams of all three men.

In 1955 Groves managed to wangle property from the Bahamian (British) government for £1 per acre (at that time £1 equaled $2.80). Certainly, Groves couldn't complain. Some of the original $2.80-acres he purchased from the Bahamian government were reportedly later sold at $50,000 each. Critics of the Bahamian hierarchy say Groves was given a blank check. His domain on Grand Bahama Island includes a 211-square-mile slice of the 430-square-mile island.

All Groves's holdings are the legal property of various Groves corporate entities: the parent organization, Grand Bahama Port Authority, Ltd., set up for the supposed purpose of creating a deep-water port to enable Groves to bring industrial and commercial establishments to his barony, which is named Freeport; the Grand Bahama Development Company, established for the management and sale of real estate; and Bahamas Amusements, Ltd., a subsidiary organized to take charge of the gambling casinos to be brought to the island.

No branch of the Bahamian government seems willing to tangle with Groves, yet the big man loathes descriptions of his operation as a "kingdom" or "dictatorship." "That's a lot of bunk," he scowls. Nevertheless, if you went to live—or play—in Freeport, you would use Groves's airport, Groves's harbor, Groves's roads, Groves's schools, Groves's land, Groves's supermarket, and Groves's electricity and water. The Port Authority is a private tax-exempt super-corporation, and its subsidiaries affect Freeport's twelve thousand residents from birth to death.

Freeport has no income tax, no profits tax, no real estate tax, and no sales tax. Indeed, Groves's long-term contractual guarantees build in these privileges, which are almost impossible to find elsewhere. Consequently, wealthy businessmen looking for business outlets are quick to take advantage of such favorable opportunities.

These advantages were probably what first attracted Toronto tycoon Lou Chesler to the sunny Caribbean. Chesler was no novice at the business of making a fast dollar. Starting as a customer's man for a brokerage firm, he had piled up $4 million on Toronto's version of Wall Street almost before he was weaned. With his $4 million he built up a paper profit of $70 million by stalking small U.S. companies with big potential. His perception was uncanny. For example, he accurately presaged the coming boom in electronics, Florida land, and leisure activities, including horse racing.

In fact, he gave all such industries a boost up to the starting gate.

Chesler was also something of a *bon vivant*, building up a large and what, in June, 1964, the *Wall Street Journal* called "somewhat incongruous circle of friends and acquaintances." Among these, the *Journal* pointed out, were such respected business figures as publisher Gardner Cowles, investment banker John Weinberg, and bank president Gabriel Hauge, onetime economic advisor to President Eisenhower. Others listed were such former Eisenhower administration officials as Robert Anderson, who served as Secretary of the Treasury, and cabinet secretary Maxwell Rabb, who in 1964 was one of those trying to secure the Republican presidential nomination for Henry Cabot Lodge.

Chesler, who fed $12 million into the Bahamas before Groves ousted him with a clever squeeze play in May, 1964, has been a prime mover behind many important companies in the United States, including General Development Corporation and Universal Controls, Inc. Universal makes electronic equipment, and General Development is a huge mail-order merchandiser of Florida houses and lots. Banker Weinberg went on the General Development board of directors in 1959 at about the same time publisher Cowles became interested in the organization. Cowles later succeeded Lou Chesler as chairman and became the company's second largest stockholder.

Chesler's guiding hand has also functioned in Canada's Lorado Uranium Mines, Ltd., and in the entertainment complex called Seven Arts Productions, Ltd., which has made its mark on the Hollywood movie-making scene. Incidentally, it was Maxwell Rabb who, as a board member of Seven Arts, came to Chesler's defense in 1963, when the management was being attacked by stockholders for investing $5 million in Chesler's and Wallace Groves's Grand Bahama Development Company—a squabble resulting in an announcement that Chesler would liquidate his holdings in Seven Arts and resign as chairman and director of the board after Seven Arts had disposed of its investment in the Grand Bahama Development Company.

The circle of Chesler associates and friends was not limited to Wall Street or Capitol Hill. He had a well-known love of horse racing, which may have prompted him in 1965 to secure, with the help of millionaire cronies such as Baltimore Colts' owner Carroll Rosenbloom, an outfit known as Baltimore's American totalizator, which owns and leases most of the racetrack "tote" systems that figure odds and winnings based on bet totals of individual horse races. Another Chesler associate, who had no business connections with the Canadian but was a friend, according to the *Wall Street Journal*, was Trigger Mike Coppola, whose activities were detailed in the chapter on the Mafia in New York.

Looking back on his Caribbean adventure in April, 1967, Chesler classified himself as "probably the biggest loser in the Bahamas" and admitted that he had paid huge sums of money to the "Bay Street Boys," the ruling clique at the time in Nassau, to buy permission to bring big-time gambling into the British colony. The story began in 1960 and 1961 when Chesler entered the picture as Groves's partner in the Grand Bahama Development Company, which was then selling real estate in Freeport.

Chesler arrived on the scene at a time when Groves's initial ideas were undergoing change. What had originally been planned, ostensibly, at least, as an industrial boom— seen in terms of harbor development, hotels, golf courses, shops, homes, and various private businesses—was beginning to take on a new aspect. The Groves enterprises apparently needed a few additional inducements for the growth their creator had envisioned, something to bring in the fun-loving, rather than just sun-loving tourists with money in their pockets. Gambling, therefore, was put on the agenda for the Grand Bahama Island, and in the winter of 1961 construction was begun on the lavish, 250-room Lucayan Beach Hotel—for which Chesler, as part of his agreement with Groves, had to raise and invest $12 million—containing, among other conveniences, a room with nine thousand square feet of floor space designed officially as a convention hall and privately as a handball court.

Since gambling was, and still is, specifically forbidden by law in the Bahamas, some legal maneuvering was necessary. But getting the needed certificate of exemption was easy, providing the right lawyer was on hand. And he was. Sir Stafford Sands—the leader of the Bay Street Boys and of the primarily white, long-standing governing party—had helped Groves all along the way in setting up his numerous interlocking firms in the island and was just the man for the job.

Louis Chesler, being a Canadian, would supposedly carry

none of the onus of American gangster influence with him into the hallowed halls of a casino and thus was another essential party to the scheme. Finally, all was ready. In March, 1963, Groves and Chesler went to the Bahamian government to seek an exemption from the anti-gambling laws. They went specifically to the governor's executive council, and their case was presented by Sir Stafford, who just happened also to be a member of the council. The certificate of exemption made out in the name of Bahamas Amusements, Ltd.—whose shares were then split equally between Chesler and Groves's wife, Georgette—was granted in April. The gambling license was ordered prepared for issuance, and the boys were in business.

The initial contract stipulated that casino employees be British, Irish—no one could have been more surprised than the Irish!—or European citizens and specifically excluded American executives and personnel. It provided that company casinos could be operated anywhere on Grand Bahama so long as they were in, or in the vicinity of, a hotel having at least two hundred rooms. What a happy coincidence that the newly built Lucayan Beach Hotel had not only the necessary guest rooms but also a sizable "convention hall," which could be, and was, quickly transformed into a casino!

The hotel opened in January, 1964, with all the glitter and gold its social director, Mrs. John McLean, could muster. The plan had been to operate gambling on the highest level —a white-tie-and-tails copy of the ornate gambling palaces of Monaco. But the great experiment proved a complete bust, at first, as the fickle phonies of the jet set failed to show. The Monte Carlo room remained as empty and cold as a pit boss's heart.

Chesler and Groves, however, quickly learned what the big-time operators of Las Vegas and Reno, Nevada, spent millions to find out: that a successful casino must in the long run grind its dollars from the pockets of little people, simply because there are so many more of them than jet-setters. Accordingly, plans were changed, and the boys in the know—Meyer Lansky and crew, who had made a life-long study of gambling within the framework of the crime syndicate—were brought in. The avant-garde of the gambling fraternity, with the love of warm climes already in their blood, turned their hawk noses to the Spanish Main, and things began looking up in the Bahamas.

Early in 1967 Chesler blandly told a four-man investigative Royal Commission of Inquiry headed by Sir Ranulph Bacon, former assistant commissioner of Scotland Yard, that he sought Lansky's advice on gaming potential in the Bahamas because he considered him a "dean of gambling." "It was no easy job," he told the probers, to organize a large-scale gambling operation, and he needed the advice of an expert.

A smooth and profitable route for the gaming industry always seems to require the Lansky types and their know-how, but sometimes you wonder what keeps their noses to the grindstone. Is it the result of a sort of force-feeding hoodlums have to put up with? Or perhaps the Lanskys of this world have nothing else to do with their days? Whatever the reason, apparently no one ever really *retires* in the crime syndicate, although a few have claimed to have done so when investigators were on their trail.

For example, witness the current career of eighty-year-old George Sadlo, time-honored gaming Sancho Panza for Lansky, who, it appears, thought nothing of launching a new project such as the Bahamian enterprise.

In the early days Lansky had been a murder partner of Las Vegas pioneer Bugsy Siegel when Siegel was strong-arming it for Louis Buchalter. Years later Lansky provided—through George Sadlo, his "insulation"—the wherewithal for the late gambler Marion B. Hicks and Cliff Jones when they decided to build the Thunderbird Hotel in Las Vegas. In fact, Jones himself is another example of how old friends stick together and of how men connected with the Mafia never seem to give up. A former Lieutenant-Governor of Nevada, Jones now has his fingers in various financial and gaming pies in and out of the Caribbean and is a good friend of top airlines officials, who also have a vast financial stake in that tropical playground.

But to return to Sadlo, Lansky thought nothing of bringing his old crony out of semiretirement. And when Louis Chesler was asked about Sadlo's duties by the investigative commission, he said: "George Sadlo was in complete control of the hiring and firing of employees" when the casino got started. In fact, Sadlo's activities in Grand Bahama merely illustrate the beginning of another operation featuring the competence and talent of the men who make up one side of the seemingly endless war of attrition waged by the syndicate against legal authority. There was, and is, a specific ban on the employment of American personnel in the big

Freeport casino. Yet at first it was not enforced; it was forgotten, as is made clear by the following list, which appeared in the April 6, 1967, *Wall Street Journal*, of just a few of the syndicate workers, American born or naturalized, who moved in, along with Sadlo, as gambling aides in the Monte Carlo room of the Lucayan Beach Hotel:

Frank Reiter, alias "Frank Ritter"	credit manager
Max Courtney	general manager
Charles Brudner, alias "Charlie Brud"	floor manager
Dino Cellini	craps supervisor
James Baker	craps supervisor
David Geiger	craps supervisor
Al Jacobs	craps supervisor
Roy Bell	craps supervisor

Max Courtney and Frank Ritter first made their marks as close associates of Dutch Schultz, a leading bootlegger in the New York-New Jersey area who unsuccessfully plotted the murder of Thomas Dewey, prosecutor in Manhattan during the vicious Prohibition days of open gang warfare. When Dutch Schultz died—he was machine-gunned by his rivals—Ritter and Courtney decided to take up a less violent occupation. In the fifties they appeared in Montreal as operators of a huge layoff bookmaking operation. To relieve the pressure of large bets made in Las Vegas, Chicago, New York, and other fast-buck areas, the two men set up their operation in Canada outside the reach of U.S. law-enforcement agencies. But somebody must have snitched to the Royal Canadian Mounted Police, for they soon galloped into Montreal and arrested the two bookies. Expelled from Canada, Courtney, who is also known by his real name, Morris (Moishe) Schmertzler, and Ritter, who often moved around under the alias "Red Reed," spent a number of years taking bets in the salubrious atmosphere of various gaming centers in the United States, finally showing up as executives of the Monte Carlo room in Freeport. Which all goes to prove that though a good hood may be down, he's never out.

Cellini, Baker, Geiger, Jacobs, and Bell were eventually investigated by the Bahamian government and expelled from the Bahamas in March, 1964. Apparently it had taken some of the more conscientious officials that long to discover that the whole crew—including Sadlo and Lansky's brother Jake—

had been the main-stem of the Lansky gambling combine in Havana under Batista's rule before Castro threw them out in 1959.

Ritter, Courtney, and Brudner, who also had done time with Lansky's gang in Havana casinos, escaped pressure in the Bahamas until January 15, 1967, when it became clear to the Bahamians that they were fugitives from justice in the United States, having been charged with evading income taxes while allegedly running a bookmaking operation in New York. But at least the three fugitives were still on hand when the new El Casino opened in Freeport on January 1st and had two weeks in which to give a high-level, graduate course in running the place to the new boxmen, stickmen, and pit bosses—also, of course, Lansky associates from way back.

Miami Crime Commission Director Dan Sullivan, on an "Open End" television program, said that Courtney and Ritter, before they left the country, were probably the "two biggest, heaviest bookmakers and sports bookmakers in the United States." Yet, though officially banned from the Bahama casinos along with Brudner, all three men have been granted asylum "as residents" in the Bahamas despite their fugitive status. In this connection, too, it is interesting to note that Sir Ralph Francis Alnwick Grey, Governor of the Bahamas by appointment of Her Majesty Queen Elizabeth II, said in relation to the hard lines tossed at the Lansky boys running the gambling details at Freeport: "The mere giving a dog a bad name ought not to be cause to have him hanged. If you go into the tourist business, all sorts of strange people with strange proclivities come in."

Testimony before the Bacon investigative committee revealed that banishment of Courtney, Ritter, and Brudner from the casinos did not exactly leave them out in the cold. An agreement was made that the three men will, over the next ten years, receive $2.1 million for a credit-card file they apparently brought to the island when gaming first began. Thousands of well-heeled American gamblers are listed on the cards, and Keith Gonsalves, president of Bahamas Amusements, Ltd., and former head of Barclay's Bank in the Bahamas, told the commission that the purchase was made so that the casinos would "continue to function smoothly." As Gonsalves said, the men "could have left us with a completely sabotaged organization."

While the hoods in the Bahamas have had to put up with

certain inconveniences, the operators of the casinos cannot complain about their profits, although their initial expenses were not negligible, either. For example, in 1965, its first full year of operation, the Lucayan Beach Hotel casino on Grand Bahama Island laid out $490,000 for chartered flights to bring in free-loading "high rollers" from the United States, people with blue-chip credit ratings meticulously provided by Lansky and his associates. And, according to a *Life* exposé of the Bahamian gaming idyll, another $930,000 was spent to provide hotel and ship accommodations for the pampered guests.

Rumors are that close to $500 million have been sunk into Wallace Groves's island empire, and, according to *Parade*, Groves calls profits from his gambling casinos "peanuts." For Groves's information, Meyer Lansky has *never* settled for peanuts, and it is estimated that by 1970 more than half a million tourists a year will be visiting the Lucayan Beach Hotel and others like it, some still to be built. And syndicate ledgers prophesy that each tourist will leave at least $25 on the tables. Some peanuts!

The *Life* article went on to point out that U.S. lawmen are convinced the mob is getting a big cut of casino profits, so perhaps their harassment is not too onerous. In January, 1967, the El Casino, a new carpet joint also owned by Bahamas Amusements, Ltd., opened to swell the total take, and 30 per cent of the sum is going, *Life* claimed, to such Lansky confederates in the Mafia as Stephen Magaddino of Buffalo, Angelo Bruno of Philadelphia, Frank Costello of New York City—this is disputed by Mafia buffs in Manhattan—Santo Trafficante of Tampa, and Joe Adonis in Italy.

Newsman Clarence Jones of the *Miami Herald* reported in July, 1967, that so much money was being raked in by the casinos that "it had to be mailed, parcel post, to New York banks in cardboard beer cartons." He quoted records of the Royal Commission of Inquiry and said the cartons full of money also "hinted at wholesale skimming from the casinos."

If this is true, and there is little reason to doubt it, it is also true that the gambling operation is having a profound effect on the whole economy of Grand Bahama and neighboring islands. Some fringe "benefits" of wholesale gambling have already become manifest: the local, comparatively unskilled, and certainly confused police on Grand Bahama are, for the first time, up against organized prostitution and narcotics, traditional enterprises of the Mafia. Three Americans were recently deported for trafficking in whores and drugs. Two of them had police records and Mafia affiliations in New York City and used Las-Vegas-trained girls in the old "badger game," housing them, according to the *Saturday Evening Post*, in the King's Inn, one of the island's plushest hotels.

The periodical also recounted the inauguration of a Mafia-type extortion enterprise in which local businessmen were threatened with physical harm if they did not pay protection money to the gangsters. To the Bahamian government it seems to be of little concern. In response to such allegations Sir Ralph Grey said: "We can't police the world. No one has yet shown me any clear-cut evidence of wrongdoing."

Evidence is, however, not unavailable. Under oath, Keith Gonsalves, who apparently was third in the Groves hierarchy before Lou Chesler moved out of his post as president of the Grand Bahama Development Company in 1964, named a dozen Bahamian government officials who had been receiving largesse from the Groves operation, and he pointed out that Chesler negotiated most of these deals. One deal Gonsalves referred to involved Sir Etienne Dupuch, editor of the *Nassau Tribune*, who took "5,000 or 6,000 pounds a year" for two years "to assist us with our public image," which "locally has always been poor." Gonsalves also testified that former Bahamian Premier Sir Roland Symonette had a road-building contract with one Groves company that paid him over $16,000 a year. Symonette's son, a jet-setter named Bobby whose yachting prowess got him on the cover of an issue of *Sports Illustrated*, was hired by Groves to act as adviser on marina construction at $14,000 a year.

The big man behind the men on the islands, however, was Minister of Finance and Tourism Sir Stafford Sands, the highest paid lawyer in the playground of pirates. Sands will deny it, but testimony indicates that his fees for guiding Groves through choppy legal waters over the years may run well over $1 million, so it was not surprising that Sir Stafford was said to be "ill in Spain" when the commission of inquiry first met in the Bahamas in May, 1967, and did not make an appearance.

When Gonsalves was asked by the commission about a $500,000 check reportedly given to Sir Stafford in April, 1964, the witness said it was an "omnibus fee," related to "obtaining an exemption certificate [to operate gambling casinos in Freeport] from the government." Gonsalves said

the size of the check "didn't stagger me" and added that
Sir Stafford performed many duties for Bahamas Amusements.

An additional $50,000 a year, for ten years, was promised
to Sands, Gonsalves testified, for advice in "advertising,
publicity and promoting all phases of the development company." In addition, Gonsalves listed "political contributions"
by the Groves group to the United Bahamian party totaling
$320,000, which were said to have been funneled through
Stafford Sands as legal fees.

Thanks to the absence of a conflict-of-interest law in the
Bahamian government, Sir Stafford and some of his other
Bay Street Boys had functioned for years both as legislators
and private lawyers, a combination that has enabled them
to accumulate and manipulate considerable power and
wealth.

Apparently 1964 had been a very busy year for all concerned. According to the *Wall Street Journal* of October 19,
1966, Lou Chesler "resigned" in May, 1964, because he and
Groves "didn't see eye to eye." "There was a lot of emotion
built up," Chesler stated. "It got to the point that I wanted
out."

"Groves hates inefficiency," said one person who had
worked in the organization, belittling Chesler's administrative abilities. "So he made it clear to Lou he'd have to go."

The exact circumstances of the split are somewhat clouded,
but in the obvious clash of personalities Chesler was apparently the one to yield and allow himself to be bought
out. And he did it at a time when the development company was apparently becoming financially shaky and the
ownership of the Lucayan Beach Hotel was undergoing
some complicated legal shenanigans—the understanding of
which would take a battery of Philadelphia lawyers.

The hotel itself, a separate entity from the Monte Carlo
room casino within its walls, has run in the red almost since
its opening. Officially, this is the result of overstaffing and
poor management; unofficially, of the usual "tax write-off"
or "robbing Peter to pay Paul" reasons. At any rate, while
being subsidized to the tune of $500,000 yearly from the
Monte Carlo room, which is raking in the money hand
over fist, the hotel has gone from Chesler's sponsorship
through the hands of another Canadian entrepreneur into
the control of a Canadian holding company that had numerous other investments in Freeport but defaulted on $104

million in debts in June, 1965, declaring bankruptcy and causing what was called an "international financial scandal." The hotel then went into receivership.

The story goes on and on. But it is enough to say that Louis Chesler played his part well, spent his, or somebody's, $12 million, and left his mark on Grand Bahama. He brought money, his "good name," and—despite the protestations of a Seven Arts publicist who said, in defense of his company's $5-million investment in Chesler's Bahama interests, that jurisdiction over the gambling licenses there had been given to Bahamas Amusements, Ltd.: "to make sure no improper elements infiltrated the operations of the exclusive gambling licenses"—the syndicate to the island.

The first competitive challenge to the Groves-Chesler-Lansky triumvirate came in 1963 from grocery-chain, model-agency, theater-arts magnate Huntington (Hunt) Hartford, who tried to fire a legal torpedo from his own little domain a few miles away across the blue sea at the Freeport empire a-building.

Hartford had control of a smaller island a short sail from Freeport on Grand Bahama Island, and just across the harbor from the Bahamian capital of Nassau. Hartford's island is listed on navigation charts as Hog Island, but, as a step to converting it into a tourist paradise, Hunt renamed his floating platter of earth Paradise Island. Between 1959 and 1963 Hartford said he poured $25 million into Hog, trying to change it into a silk purse, and originally he protested the introduction of any form of gambling to the Bahamas.

Hartford apparently assumed he had the right to speak for the islands, and he still had a substantial part of the A & P fortune to back him up. But he must have reckoned without the ABC's of modern economics, especially since his attempt to buck both the gambling-eating-sunning-carousing splendor of Las Vegas and other tourist traps and the rapidly developing Grand Bahama Island right in his own back yard was made from an off-the-track island: Paradise.

Finding that a marina, hotel rooms, golf course, and continental restaurant weren't enough of a lure to tourists, Hartford made an about-face in 1963 and said he would like to put a gaming casino on Paradise Island and build a bridge to get the tourists across the bay from Nassau. In a press release issued at the time, making a public plea for the issuance of a gambling license, Hartford declared that he thought it would be of benefit to the natives on Paradise Island because

> babies are occasionally being born blind, and worms and amoebic dysentery and tuberculosis are prevalent due to poor sanitation and overcrowding. If gambling would be permitted on Paradise, it goes without saying that there will be employment for thousands and I trust that my past record in giving employment will confirm the responsibility of my statement.

Hartford's seemingly good intentions, however, came to naught, for neither the gambling license nor the bridge-building permit could be secured. It appears that Hunt had failed to hire the able Sir Stafford Sands as his lawyer and, to add insult to injury, had even contributed $15,000 to the opposing political party: the largely Negro Progressive Liberal party, which scored heavily in the January, 1967, elections and gave the islands their first black premier.

The A & P heir eventually decided to bail out, and, in a flash, a buyer showed up for the former Hog Island. Hartford announced in January, 1966, that for $3 million in cash, the assumption of a $9-million mortgage by the buyer, and the retention of a 25 per cent interest in the entire operation (to include the building of a five-hundred-room hotel with casino), he had sold Paradise Island and its facilities to the Mary Carter Paint Company.

Since 1962 the Mary Carter Paint Company, a Delaware corporation recorded in October, 1958, with headquarters in Tampa, Florida, had been exceedingly active in swallowing up businesses, increasing her paper assets, and assuaging her thirst in various ways in the Caribbean. There were, by 1964, some one thousand Mary Carter dealer and company paint stores spread throughout much of the United States and in Puerto Rico and the British West Indies. A subsidiary operated National Biff-Burger System (drive-in restaurant) franchises together with a manufacturing plant that produced everything needed to operate one of the drive-ins, including the portable building-units themselves. Another subsidiary, Bahamas Developers, in 1963 acquired some thirty-five hundred acres of land within the Groves domain on Grand Bahama Island, part of which was developed in 1965 into a residential community called Queens Cove.

In 1966, therefore, when Mary Carter—she doesn't really exist, but it's a good feminine handle on which to hang one's company hat—made her deal with Huntington Hartford, she was no virgin in island commerce and already had a more-than-platonic interest in her future playmates. Shortly after Mary disposed of Hunt, she proceeded to make a marriage of financial convenience with the Groves group in order to accomplish something that Hartford had been unable to do: secure permission for gaming on Paradise Island. The Mary Carter Paint Company was able, through the representations of none other than Sir Stafford himself, to purchase for $750,000 the certificate of exemption covering the Bahamian Club, a conservative gaming parlor in Nassau owned by Groves's interests.

The agreement, according to *Life* magazine of February 3, 1967, called for the Bahamian Club permit to be transferred to the Paradise Island casino when it opened on condition that Mary Carter relinquish a reported four-ninths of the casino's profit as well as management of the entire casino to Wallace Groves's Bahamas Amusements, Ltd. Lansky and his crew, who were at the time managing the Bahamian Club for Groves as well as the Monte Carlo room on Grand Bahama Island, were slated to run the Paradise Island casino when the change of ownership was made, for a flat 15 per cent of the gross gaming profits.

In reporting the details of the arrangement to her jet-set readers, syndicated gossip columnist Suzy spoke of "nice fresh money" being brought in by Hartford's new partners to alleviate the $50,000 monthly losses he had been suffering. "That's expected to stop," she surmised, "because the new group has acquired the gambling permit once owned by Nassau's Bahamian Club. Now they can play with the big boys." How right she was!

Since then, Mary Carter's Paradise Island has joined hands with Nassau on New Providence Island via a $2-million toll bridge. It seems that, miraculously, Mary Carter was also able to get the bridge-building permit denied Hartford in 1963. The new $15-million Paradise Island hotel and casino was opened in January, 1968, in typical gala fashion. Columnist Eart Wilson reported that Lady Astor, Lady Sassoon, Carol Channing, Serge Obolensky, and Huntington Hartford—apparently still comfortably ensconced within his 25 per cent retained interest in what Wilson called the "Paradise Island, Ltd., Complex"—together with others of the jet set, made quite a night of it.

"It's all run by James M. Crosby, head of the Mary Carter Paint Co.," Earl reported, "and they tell me there never was any Mary Carter but this paint company thought it sounded like a sweet name."

Business on Paradise Island has been booming ever since, and plans are going ahead for the building of houses, apartments, a shopping center, and more hotels. Consequently, it is interesting to note that the Paradise Island casino is managed by none other than the brother of the ousted Dino Cellini, Eddie.

Dino Cellini, moreover, although out of sight is anything but out of action. After he was ousted from the Bahamas in 1964, he ran a school in London to train European croupiers for work in the Bahamian casinos. Then, when the British got wise and banned him at the same time as they gave George Raft his walking papers, Cellini returned to Miami to become a highly successful organizer and promoter of international gambling junkets—affairs involving the bringing in of planeloads of "high-rollers" to a hotel-casino, to be lavishly coddled, catered-to, entertained, and deprived of their money.

According to Keith Gonsalves' testimony before the Royal Commission of Inquiry, two-thirds of the Bahamas' casino profits come from junkets, each of which reportedly costs the casino operators about $50,000. It is therefore not too difficult to picture the brothers Cellini working hand-in-hand, "doing their thing" for the mob.

At any rate, it now would appear to be a toss-up between Groves, Lansky, Mary Carter, and the local Bahamian government—officially represented by its newly elected premier, thirty-eight-year-old Lynden O. Pindling, whose vociferous campaign against allowing the Bahamas to become a "lucrative center of international crime" had resulted in the royal commission—as to just who will roll the vital seven that loses the game and shifts the dice to the next man at the table.

Groves lives in a blue-green tile palace valued at $1 million; Lansky lives in a modest $25,000 house near Hollywood, Florida; and Mary Carter's J. M. Crosby is rather comfortably situated—when not in Paradise—in Great Neck, Long Island, where, cozily enough, Lou Chesler also maintains equally elegant lodgings. The question at the moment is what kind of residence Pindling is planning for himself.

Pindling's drawing boards are currently covered with designs for a new approach to the gambling free-for-all—for Groves and friends, that is—espoused by the former Bahamian administration. The new approach is somewhat obscure, however, because the Nassau-born, London-educated Pindling plans to reject the royal commission's ruling barring Americans from casino employment on the ground that "some taint" seems to cover anyone connected with organized gambling in the United States, even persons with no criminal records.

According to Pindling's enemies, his Progressive Liberal party has accepted money from syndicate sources; in fact, they say that the party must have received payments because gamblers always insure their bets. But Pindling is not alarmed at the reports or criticism, nor does he seem to have to be. Apparently, his philosophy is: if you're going to have a gambling casino, you need gamblers to run it. The skilled labor needed for such an enterprise will therefore stay.

Pindling has, however, stated that there will be no more certificates of exemption granted for new casinos—which eliminates the competition, at least—and that he will honor a previous law prohibiting Bahamian residents from playing the games. New schools and housing tracts are planned for the impoverished native residents, but Pindling is apparently moving toward ghetto-style living for his people—Negroes represent 80–85 per cent of the Bahamian population—through his efforts to keep the gambling environment off-limits to the local black electorate.

Appeasement, in the form of a flat $500,000 fee charged annually against each casino and increased taxes on a graduated scale for all revenues above $5 million, has done little to demonstrate that things will be easier for the locals. The cost of living has gone sky-high, and the Bahamian chamber of commerce has warned that a family of three needs about $10,000 a year to live reasonably, an altogether impossible prospect for the people who voted Pindling into office.

Regardless of politics and the changing of the guard, it would appear that the syndicate holds most of the gaming aces in the Bahamas. After his election Pindling, who demands the islands' eventual freedom from Britain, apparently not only changed his mind about the facts of gambling life and related aspects of international crime but also showed up in full dress at the January, 1968, opening of the Paradise Island hotel and casino with a big welcome for the guests. He danced a wild rumba with actress Janet Leigh and reportedly kept asking orchestra leader Meyer Davis for more of the same. It seems that Pindling, too, is "playing with the big boys," and it remains to be seen just who is hustling whom.

There are hundreds of sunny islands in the warm sea around the Bahamas, and it could be that Lansky and his cohorts may one day spread themselves too thinly. The key point perhaps, is just how far his associates in the States will let him go. A big head is an easy target, and the Mafia is not quite as racially integrated as it may seem. Meyer Lansky is still the kid on the corner who shines the shoes of the boys in the Sicilian brotherhood. They know without question that he handles the shinola with a dexterity second to none and that he takes a goodly cut for his services, but they aren't likely to let him climb to the top of the stool himself and pretend he's really one of them.

The Bahamas, however, do not stand as the only gemstones in the Caribbean crown of the syndicate; there are other diamonds in the rough operated by the slick-suited professional gamblers. To the south are numerous other islands, stretching down to Aruba in the Dutch Antilles, where the Mafia boys have decided to settle.

In Port-au-Prince, Haiti, the depression-ridden voodoo capital of the Caribbean, a gaming casino has been established by Mafia hoodlums. Run by the Canadian branch of the syndicate and controlled locally, according to U.S. Immigration Department files, by the Volpe brothers, Paul, Albert, and Eugene, the Carib-Haiti was established with the help of Haitian dictator François (Papa Doc) Duvalier.

Also connected with the Volpe operation in Haiti is John Pasquale Tronolone, alias "Salvatore Tronolone," also known as "John Rich," and intimately known to his Mafia colleagues as "Peanuts." Tronolone is known to have represented Mafia chieftain Frank Costello's interests in Las Vegas. Some of his more odious associates, in addition to Costello and the Volpes, have been syndicate hearties Joe Massei, John and George Angersola, Joseph DiCarlo, Fred Felice, and Frank Caruso.

Wherever you pry the lid off a Caribbean vacationland nowadays—with the possible exception of Puerto Rico, where government-run gaming casinos are in the experimental stage—you generally find that if there are casinos, the cashiers of the mob are in charge. An even more disturbing fact, however, is—as the next chapter shows—that Caribbean gambling is not just a syndicate operation. Representatives of the U.S. government, union officials, executives of American financial institutions, as well as Las Vegas gambling operators—all have set out on their own treasure hunt for the buried gold of the Spanish Main.

EIGHT

THE CARIBBEAN:

Las Vegas Sharks

Take Eddie Levinson, one of the country's top gambling entrepreneurs from Las Vegas and "leg man" for Joseph (Doc) Stacher, elder in the Jewish Mafia. Add Sam Giancana, Chicago underworld chief until recently, Cliff Jones, former Lieutenant-Governor of Nevada, and Bobby Baker, onetime handmaiden of the U.S. Senate. Stir them all together in the Caribbean. What you come up with is something less than a fragrant bouillabaisse, but it is somewhat fishy: a sort of Alliance for Progress syndicate-style.

Ed Levinson's involvement in the Caribbean first came to light in 1957, with the accidental discovery of two of his canceled checks made out to a casino in Havana totaling $50,000.

Bryant R. Burton, the Beverly Hills attorney then listed as secretary of Levinson's Fremont Hotel Corporation in Las Vegas and long a legal front man for Stacher, is usually an extremely cautious man. He always exercised great care in the protection of the private records of the hotel and the boys connected with it. But in November, 1957, he slipped up. As he boarded a plane at McCarran Field, port of entry and exit for the starry-eyed tourists who keep Las Vegas operational, he left behind a bulging briefcase.

Officials of the airport opened the briefcase in an effort to establish ownership, but what they found sent them scurrying to the FBI. Mob faith in the airport hierarchy began deteriorating from that point on. Among the more interesting items the investigators dug out of the leather case was a bank statement of Ed Levinson showing that he had a current cash balance of $24,582.33 in a local bank, but they also found several canceled checks recently written on the account, three of which were rather sizable. One for $350,000 was payable to the First National Bank of Nevada; the other two totaled $50,000 and were payable to Compañía de Hoteles La Riverside de Cuba. All three checks were dated October 18, 1957.

Levinson remained calm when the find was announced. After all, it wasn't his fault. But Stacher chewed out everybody until the briefcase was returned to Burton. Whatever significance the FBI attributed to the findings was officially filed away, but it was apparent to those in the know—in Las Vegas and Havana—that the $50,000 represented Levinson's (Stacher's) share of expense money for the newly established Cuban hotel-casino.

The Stacher-Levinson relationship began in Las Vegas years earlier and resulted in Ed Levinson's becoming top dog in the multi-storied Fremont Hotel and casino in downtown Las Vegas. Levinson, in fact, had come a long way along the many-dimensional road of crime. From his birthplace in Detroit, he traveled to Las Vegas via the twin cities of corruption, Covington and Newport, Kentucky, and Miami, which he left after Kefauver's rousting of illegal gambling. Levinson finally arrived in Las Vegas in 1952 as part-owner of the Sands Hotel—a Stacher interest and the shrine of one of Frank Sinatra's best efforts to maintain status among gambling *aficionados* until he relinquished his 9 per cent "piece" after a hassle with Nevada gaming control officials over his close friendship with Sam Giancana.

Levinson's record of some forty years of hustling his way up through the world of illegal gambling already showed five arrests, four dismissals, and one $1,500 fine. But he had a wife and family, including a couple of grandchildren he adored, and apparently couldn't do anything about his own future. The mob had locked him in.

By 1955, Levinson had acquired interests in the Flamingo and Dunes Hotels but was ready to give them all up for his coming involvement—a 20 per cent interest in Doc

Stacher's Fremont Hotel, which was built with the help of substantial Teamster loans.

Joseph Stacher is a former New Jersey gangster whose charmed life transcends all common concepts held by the public and even by law-enforcement officials about just how long a man in the business of giving the business to the law can survive. Little known, Stacher nevertheless has been in and out of trouble throughout his life and has more aliases than J. Edgar Hoover has enemies. His police record, however, is scattered, its availability depending on where he has been able to have it expunged. But pick just one alias—such as "Joseph Rosen," the name under which he is listed in Newark, New Jersey—and in the six years between November, 1924, and November, 1930, you find ten arrests for breaking and entering, larceny, atrocious assault and battery, robbery, and interfering with an officer guarding a still for the federal government. Stacher's consistency in being arrested in those days was matched only by his consistency in securing a dismissal—or at least in avoiding a disposition. In nine of the above arrests he secured a dismissal; the only disposition was a $50 fine.

Using the same alias in New York City in 1931, Stacher who put together the Jewish Mafia at about the time people were beginning to accept that the syndicate was a fact, was rousted from a hotel room in the company of eight other mobsters, including Bugsy Siegel, Louis Buchalter, and Harry (Big Greenie) Greenberg, who was murdered in Los Angeles eight years later. In fact, of the eight men in the room that day, Stacher is the only one still living, having survived the men who helped him along the way in his early days in New York.

Doc Stacher came to this country from Russia in 1912. As a youngster he shined shoes, sold newspapers, and peddled fruit from a pushcart. Settling in Newark, he met Longy Zwillman, New Jersey syndicate chief for many years, and was introduced by him to such men as Willie Moretti, who was murdered in a Palisades, New Jersey, tavern in 1951, and Jerry Catena, both of whom became Mafia leaders in New Jersey.

Stacher has what might be called a certain mystique. Certainly he has something that keeps him immune from punishment and was no doubt instrumental in his being left a criminal heritage by Zwillman, who was New Jersey's version of underworld Prime Minister Frank Costello. In

1965 Stacher left for Israel—because he chose to be deported rather than to serve a jail term for income-tax evasion imposed by a federal judge—where, apparently, he passed part of his heritage along to Jerry Catena, who was named in 1966 by the *Chicago Sun-Times* as a secret part-owner of the new Caesar's Palace in Las Vegas.

The Levinson-Stacher interest in the Hoodlum Sea was revealed at a time when the dope-smuggling activities of the Florida Mafia were being conducted through Cuba with the help of corrupt government officials operating with a free hand under Batista. Castro's subsequent take-over in 1959 resulted in the exclusion of syndicate gambling. However, New York City narcotics agents seized more Cuban cocaine in the fall of 1962 than in the entire year of 1961, which indicates that Cuba's liberator has increasingly had to fall back on the old system to raise money and is, through the well-used pipelines to Tampa and the Trafficante mob, reaping a harvest other than sugar cane.

It is interesting to note, moreover, that Cuban narcotics smugglers, within the framework of the Cuban Navy and the fishing fleet, have also been using Cozumel and the Isle of Mujers as smuggling bases. These Mexican islands, off the east coast of the Yucatan peninsula, are becoming popular American tourist areas. In 1965 native hotel proprietors on the islands complained to the Mexican government that Cuban seamen were insulting and beating up U.S. tourists, but all indications are that their protest was quietly filed away in Mexico City.

Whatever the current developments, Levinson had staked his claim in Havana with his $50,000 and probably much more, and after Castro's housecleaning apparently thought he still had squatter's rights in the Caribbean. He joined the other displaced gamblers and their Mafia associates— some of whom reestablished themselves in the Bahamas— who were soon to turn their Cuban failure into a monstrous success. And the monster is still growing.

The mob is firmly entrenched in the vast sweep of Caribbean islands and intends to stay there, using the time-tested techniques of bribery, graft, intrigue, and unkept promises. The boys make friends and promote goodwill among the local governments, whose island economies are in the developmental stage, by corrupting businessmen, lawyers, and politicians through the promise of wealth more easily acquired than through the dubious potential of milking U.S. development loans.

Part of the syndicate Caribbean money structure is represented by the Bank of World Commerce, Ltd., which was incorporated in 1961 under British law in Nassau, Bahamas, where, as has been pointed out, taxes are no problem. Ed Levinson and Nevada's Cliff Jones were listed as stockholders. Tied into the whole structure was an outfit known in 1961 as Allied Empire, Inc., formerly Allied Television Films, Inc., of Beverly Hills, California. At that time Allied Empire was listed as a corporate stockholder with ten thousand shares of Bank of World Commerce stock, and was the holding company for the bank. In 1964 Allied changed its name to Riverside Financial and moved its offices to Riverside, California.

The financial structure had myriad connections. For example Jimmy Hoffa, through Allied Empire investments, and a score of Las Vegas gamblers and politicians were involved in the setup through Anjon Savings and Loan, Account Number 804, and Merritt Savings and Loan of Baltimore, Maryland, which was bought out by Anjon Account Number 804. By means of a bewildering network of American and British corporate laws, Account Number 804's list of depositor-stockholders (the complete list of names can be found in the Epilogue) includes not only the Bank of World Commerce—$23,000—but also a number of Las Vegans. And when all the records are put together, we find that the names of a number of individuals involved show up again and again in the complex web of gambling operations in various places on the North American continent—inland and offshore—and form compass points with which patient investigators are attempting to chart a course to the truth, and the enormity, of the operation.

Take, for instance, the persons holding office and stock in the Bank of World Commerce at the time of its inception. Corporate papers filed in Nassau listed the following officers: John Pullman, president and director; Edward Dawson Roberts, vice-president and director; Gerald Nelson Capps, secretary and treasurer; N. Roberts, director; Alvin I. Malnic, director; and Philip J. Mathew, director. In addition, stockholders and the number of shares indicating their initial investment were listed as follows—each share representing £1 British, or, at that time $2.80 American:

Stockholders	*Shares*
Edward Dawson Roberts	1
Margaret Elizabeth Roberts	1
Alexander Pericles Maillis	1
Margaret Rose Malone	1
Gerald Nelson Capps	1
Philip J. Mathew	82,500
Thomas A. Shaneen, Jr.	30,000
James H. Adams	10,000
Joseph Fendel	10,000
Henderson, Holton & Company	5,000
Elwood Linde	5,000
Kenneth D. Mann	5,000
Harvey Glen Leason	5,000
Charles L. Holton	10,000
Sydney V. Levy	10,000
Leon C. Bloom, Jr.	10,000
Philip Nasser	11,786
Mr. and Mrs. Irving J. Leff	10,000
Clifford A. Jones	20,000
John Pullman	2,000
Irving Devine	1,000
Edward Levinson	1,000
Alvin I. Malnic	1,500
Aaron Magidow	11,800
Allied Empire, Inc.	10,000

On September 8, 1967, two of the individuals involved with the Bank of World Commerce and Anjon Savings and Loan, Account Number 804, were named by *Life* as "bagmen" for Meyer Lansky in the syndicate's far-flung gambling kingdom. A third, an alleged "bagwoman," is the wife of one of the Bank of World Commerce stockholders. Cash was carried by these people and others, the article stated, via the Bank of World Commerce into the financial arteries of an organization in the Bahamas known as the Atlas Bank, a working subsidiary of yet another financial institution, the International Credit Bank in Switzerland. All three of the boards of directors and staffs of these money entities were what *Life* described as "studded with both skimmers and couriers" for the mob.

Among the bagmen listed was Ben Sigelbaum (Seigelbaum), sixty-five years old, political adviser and a long-time associate of Ed Levinson in many of his business endeavors. Sigelbaum was also a business associate and confidant of Bobby Baker when the latter was secretary of the Democratic Majority in the U.S. Senate. Also named was John Pullman, sixty-seven years old, original president of the Bank of World Commerce who once served a prison term for violating U.S. liquor laws and gave up his American citizenship in 1954 to become a Canadian. He now lives in Switzerland. Another alleged bagman was Sylvain Ferdmann, a thirty-three-year-old Swiss citizen described as an international banker and economist and, by U.S. authorities, as a fugitive accused of interfering with federal inquiries into the skimming racket in Las Vegas and elsewhere. In addition, *Life* charged, Ferdmann was once approached by Teamster boss Jimmy Hoffa to raise money for union officials' surety bonds.

Ida Devine, wife of Las Vegas gambler Irving (Niggy) Devine, supposedly traveled with Sigelbaum from Las Vegas to Miami with skimmed money for Lansky; Ferdmann is said to have carried the skim from the Bahamas to Lansky; and Lansky supposedly counted the money in Miami, took his own cut, and dispensed other sums, via different couriers, to a few syndicate chieftains in the United States. At that point, the story went on, Ferdmann and Pullman carried the remainder of the funds to the International Credit Bank in Switzerland and deposited them in numbered accounts in the Swiss haven for secret-money banking.

The most mysterious part in the whole affair seems to have been enacted by Ferdmann, who organized the Atlas Bank as the Bahamas subsidiary of the International Credit Bank. *Life* contended that Ferdmann's contacts in this country included members of the Communist party in New York and functionaries of the Czech delegation to the United Nations. Probers are said to have drawn conclusions that the International Credit Bank enjoys strong ties with communist countries and that there was a flow of communist money coming to this country through the Ferdmann conduit. At least, his money bags seemed to be as full each time he returned to the United States as when he left.

Ferdmann made one blunder, on March 19, 1965, when he dropped a piece of paper from one of his pockets while loading satchels into an auto at the Miami airport. A parking attendant turned it over to authorities, who identified it as a letterhead of the International Credit Bank. The memo beneath the letterhead read as follows:

> This is to acknowledge this 28th day of December, 1964, the receipt of Three Hundred and Fifty Thousand ($350,000) Dollars, in American bank notes for deposit to the account of Maral 2812 with the International Credit Bank, Geneva, the said sum being turned over to me in the presence of the named signed below.

Life states that John Pullman was listed as a witness on the note and that the cautious Ferdmann had added the following postscript: "The above is subject to the notes being genuine American banknotes." Thus, here was a document not only proving the receipt of the syndicate's skimmed money by a Swiss bank but also identifying the account number under which it was deposited.

To sum up, it appears that the Hoodlum Sea is at present split into two areas of money-making syndicate endeavor tied into the mainstream by Meyer Lansky: the northern regions, which reach into the blue waters of the Atlantic, where the Groves enterprises hold forth in the Bahamas; and the islands to the south, which fall under the domain of Stacher, Levinson, Cliff Jones, and their associates.

In 1962 an attempt was made by another branch of the Mafia to "muscle" in on the Caribbean domain of the Trafficante-Lansky combine. Chicago's chief Mafioso, Sam Giancana, who was last reported looking after the shop from faraway Argentina, had watched Albert Anastasia's attempt to carve out some of the Caribbean for himself with great interest. Undoubtedly he thought that he would be more successful than the murdered head of Murder, Inc., and therefore, despite weak protests from the Florida branch of Cosa Nostra, which considered the Caribbean its private preserve in spite of the infiltration from Las Vegas, Sam and his associates began making overtures to government officials in the tropical islands.

Giancana first arranged to meet a top man from Dominica in a neutral area—France—to discuss gaming potential, but the FBI scotched the meeting by tailing Sam on an around-the-clock basis. Sam then invited a member of the Jamaican government to Chicago for discussions regarding gambling on Jamaica. An emissary, displaying an abundance of greed, perhaps, but a great lack of wisdom, flew to the Windy City to confer with Giancana. But since the Chicago boys demanded 70 per cent of the Jamaican take, the good people whose home is in the midst of the Hoodlum Sea decided instead to limit their tourist attractions to horse racing, steel drums, calypso singing, and tall rum and Cokes.

However, although Giancana was not wanted in the Caribbean, the syndicate members already entrenched were not averse to calling on people for help. Among those who contributed their talent to syndicate efforts in the Hoodlum Sea was Bobby Baker, the country boy from Pickens, South Carolina, who started as page boy in the Senate and ended as secretary to the Democratic Senate Majority. In his sixteen years in the Senate, Baker became an influence peddler par excellence, the most successful—while the going was good—since the days of Albert Fall, U.S. Secretary of the Interior under President Harding. Fall, who secretly peddled oil-rich lands at Teapot Dome in Montana to the highest bidder, was a piker compared to Bobby. Fall put his fist into only one honey pot before his exposure and downfall; Bobby was grubbing into many enterprises with both hands when he was finally caught. Baker was found guilty on January 29, 1967, on seven counts of tax evasion, larceny, and conspiracy and sentenced to serve one to three years in prison, but he is at present free on bail pending appeal. Among other things Baker was charged with stealing at least $80,000 from a fund totaling $99,600 that represented payment from some savings and loan companies in California, presumably to be used to influence Senate legislation to give tax benefits to savings and loan organizations.

The syndicate boys may have made a mistake when they chose Baker to help them in an attempt to strengthen their power structure in the Caribbean, but it could be called an "honest" mistake inasmuch as they couldn't have foreseen that he was headed for a fall. And Bobby was a persuasive man. He had a habit of running off at the mouth and dropping the names of important people he claimed could—and they often did—help him in his various moonlighting business deals, and he could produce glowing testimonials.

Senator Alan Bible (D., Nev.), for instance, coyly referred to Bobby as "Lyndon, Jr.," and Lyndon Baines Johnson, who was Senate Majority leader at the time, proudly claimed that Baker was his protégé: "One of my trusted friends, and a man who will go far." He was so right.

Baker took time out from his busy schedule in April, 1963, to charter a plane of Riddle Airlines to fly a group of eighty

Washington lobbyists and congressional employees to Las Vegas to attend a $100-a-plate dinner at the Flamingo Hotel in honor of Senator Howard Cannon of Nevada. Later that summer Riddle Airlines, in what seemed to be an after-thought, billed Baker, but he made no payment. In January, 1964, after a Civil Aeronautics Board investigation, the airline offered to pay $750 as a compromise fine for failing to charge, and press collection of, scheduled fares—a violation of the Federal Aviation Act. The $750 was accepted by the CAB after Riddle's veteran airline officials claimed a "misunderstanding" of CAB rules.

Two months after his Vegas charter junket, Bobby Baker began to concern himself with a chain of resort hotels that had three casino operations in the Caribbean. Bobby's interest had to do with the possibility of moving one or two friends in on two of those operations—and perhaps, himself, as well, for later investigations showed that he had a habit of "taking his cut" when profitable business deals were made for buddies. He aimed his influence, and the know-how of his syndicate friends, at Intercontinental Hotels Corporation, which is a 100-per-cent-owned Subsidiary of Pan American World Airways. Intercontinental operates twenty-three hotels in nineteen foreign countries, three of them resort hotels with carpet-joint gaming casinos located in Curaçao, the capital of the Dutch Antilles, Santo Domingo, in the Dominican Republic, and San Juan, Puerto Rico.

Incidentally, Puerto Rico has nine casinos in San Juan and five others throughout the island, all located in major hotels. The gaming is strictly regulated by government control, which includes security checks for all personnel, casino licensing by the economic development administration, and low bet limits. The government philosophy is, according to the head of its tourism department: "Gambling must only be another attraction for tourists and not a main reason for their coming."

The movement of Pan Am into the gaming business through its hotel chain was outlined to the Senate committee investigating Bobby Baker in 1964 by John Gates, chairman of the board of Intercontinental Hotels. For competitive reasons, Gates maintained, his company had to have casinos in the three Caribbean hotels as an attraction for tourists—the same people, of course, that Pan Am conveniently dropped into the lap of the tourist-hungry Caribbean community. The inference was that tourists—the "right" types, that is—just would not be enticed unless there was a crap table handy as a pleasant change from water skiing, skin diving, sun-bathing, and the other usual approaches to fun in the sun.

Gates went on to explain that Intercontinental had no wish to operate the gambling casinos itself and that, while it was forced by law to do so in Puerto Rico as the owner of the hotel, the casinos in Curaçao and Santo Domingo were treated as concessions and let out to "acceptable" gamblers.

Pan Am was gearing to bring in thousands upon thousands of tourists and "grinds" a year to the Caribbean playground, and the responsibility apparently fell to Gates to help find the knowledgeable—yet acceptable—syndicate men who could handle the elite, "high-roller" clientele they hoped would be included among those seeking to lose their money with little effort.

What obviously was needed were men with years of experience in dealing with the credit end of gambling together with the knowledge of how to collect the "lost" money afterward. But such "inside" knowledge was manifest only in the experience of the men of the syndicate who meet and memorize a thousand faces and bank accounts every week.

For Bobby Baker, apparently, with his influence on Capitol Hill and important contacts throughout the Caribbean, the situation was fraught with wealth. He saw an unbeatable opportunity to squeeze himself into a big-time operation and wheeled his motive out into the open for all to see in the summer of 1963.

On June 20, the "101st Senator"—a title Washington newsmen often used when referring to Baker—appeared in the New York office of John Gates with an associate. The appointment had been arranged, at Baker's request, by Samuel Pryor, a Pan Am vice-president. Baker's associate that day was introduced to Gates as Ed Levinson, owner of the Fremont Hotel in Las Vegas, and John Gates was asked about the possibility of Levinson's becoming associated with either the Santo Domingo or the Curaçao gambling concession.

Gates, who had not previously met either of the men, asked Baker if he was interested for himself, or for both himself and Levinson, or what. Bobby quickly explained that he himself had no interest in the concessions. Levinson was his friend and client, and he was merely trying to pave the way for him as a favor. This was no more than the truth. Levinson, along with Ben Sigelbaum and others, had made substantial and complicated investments in various Baker enterprises, including stock shares in the District of Columbia National Bank and the Serv-U Corporation, entities that figured prominently in the Baker investigation.

Gates accepted Bobby's explanation, apparently unconcerned with a most unusual situation in which the Majority secretary of the U.S. Senate was openly representing a major gambling figure in a request for interests in two rather small casinos, and at the time when, in the words of Wallace Turner in *Gamblers' Money*, agents of the executive branch of the U.S. government "were watching Levinson's every movement and checking carefully on all his financial transactions." But, then, as Turner concludes: "The flood of money that powers the gambling empire in Las Vegas creates many ironies of this sort."

Levinson himself, a squat man with a strong jaw and heavily-lidded eyes, slow-moving except when Doc Stacher or one of his hirelings is on the other end of the wire, is supposed to have said little in Gates's office, evidently satisfied with Bobby's representations. At any rate, Gates explained that the existing lease on the Curaçao gaming concession would soon expire and that other potential bids were already under consideration for it—including one from Cliff Jones and his partner, Jake Kozloff, whose Caribbean American Investment Company, Inc., already had four small casinos in the Caribbean.

Ed Levinson assured Gates that the Jones-Kozloff bid created no problems by saying, "We're all very close," and indicating that they could all work together. As it turned out, Jones and Levinson were a great deal closer than Gates realized, and Bobby Baker must have known it from his previous relationships with the two gamblers. The meeting ended with Gates's agreeing to write the Curaçao hotel owners about another possible bidder on the casino lease, since the owners were responsible for letting out the concession.

A second meeting was held a month later, with Bobby Baker present, during which Gates told Levinson that if his brother, Sleep-out Louie, were involved, their bid could not be considered. At a third meeting, also in August, 1963, and again arranged by "Baker's office" but unattended by him, Levinson showed up in Gates's office with Jones and

Kozloff in tow. According to Gates's testimony to the Senate committee, Levinson told Gates that he was dropping out of the picture but that Jones and Kozloff were prepared to submit their bid.

Oddly enough, the letter written by John Gates to the Curaçao hotel owners on August 13, the day after the above meeting, stated: "Messrs. Jones, Kozloff and Levinson called on me yesterday in regard to the casino contract. They are going to present a joint bid." The actual bid submitted to the Curaçao hotel board for its September meeting and decision was signed only by Jake Kozloff and Clifford Jones for the Caribbean American Investment Company, Inc., probably for the very good reason that Levinson, under a Nevada law passed in 1958—of which, one suspects, Mr. Gates must have been aware—would have had to give up his Nevada gaming license if he officially went into the gaming business in any other part of the world. Nevada claims its own with the fervor of a mother elephant, and Levinson was obviously not about to relinquish his 20 per cent interest in the Fremont Hotel setup or an additional reported 27 per cent interest in another downtown casino, the Horseshoe Club. But Jones and Kozloff, having officially divested themselves of any gaming interests in Las Vegas, were in the clear.

On September 12, after perusing the two bids submitted to the Curaçao hotel owners, Gates wrote them that the Jones-Kozloff bid would seem to be preferable "from a strictly objective, business point of view," in that it "provides a more favorable guaranty and the quality of their entertainment is well known." Gates went on:

> Apparently there is some problem about Jones and Kozloff insofar as the Government of Curaçao is concerned, and they may have compelling reasons for preferring Sweet [the former casino operator who was also bidding] but I am in no position to judge or evaluate the reasons since I do not know what they are.

In a postscript Gates added: "I have made inquiry in the United States regarding Jones and Kozloff because we have asked them to make a bid on our casino in Santo Domingo. Everyone I have contacted gives them a clean bill of health."

One of Gates's inquiries was directed at John Scarne, "gambling detective," so-called nemesis of crooked gamblers and staunch defender of Las Vegas gaming. Scarne replied that Levinson ran honest gambling. Scarne's concern apparently is only that the tourists get a fair shake. The government's share is of no interest to him, it seems: in 1968 Levinson pleaded no contest to charges of skimming in that eventful year of 1963.

On November 7, 1963, another letter was written by Gates to the Curaçao hotel owners, and he enclosed articles from New York papers regarding the Bobby Baker case, which was beginning to receive a good deal of public attention. With references to Ed Levinson's probable involvement with Baker, Gates said:

> As for Levinson, you will note that Jones is quoted as saying [in the articles] he is not involved. I recommend you write Jones asking whether Levinson is associated with him since my sources of information about Levinson may have been wrong.

Further inquiries were put to Jones at that point. Jones replied in the negative, but the Curaçao people kept postponing a decision on the letting of the new casino lease. On November 20, Gates wrote once more to Curaçao, pointing up Jones's explanation that Levinson withdrew his interest when it was learned his brother would not be acceptable and that "Levinson took the attitude he would not be a party to a bid against Mr. Kozloff and myself . . . In declining to bid, he did decline in our favor." Gates enclosed more newspaper clippings and added: "I believe this should be the end of any mention of the Bobby Baker episode so far as Intercontinental and Curaçao are concerned."

On February 27, 1964, when John Gates appeared before the Senate investigating committee, he said that the decision of the Curaçao hotel owners as to the letting of the new gaming concession lease had still not been made. In August, 1968, however, when questioned by the author, Gates revealed that four months after the Senate hearings, in June, 1964, the Jones-Kozloff bid for the Curaçao Intercontinental Hotel casino lease was accepted. In addition to the Curaçao concession, Jones and Kozloff have the casino leases at the Embajador Intercontinental Hotel in Santo Domingo, Dominican Republic, and the Quito Intercontinental Hotel in Quito, Ecuador—all three hotels being Pan Am affiliates. The two casinos in Puerto Rico, San Juan and Ponce, are run by Pan Am personnel with local help, in keeping with government regulations there. They are "not particularly profitable," according to Gates. Indicating that he was "alarmed" at the thought of a possible Jones-Kozloff tie-in with syndicate gambling elements, Gates said both men would be "further checked out."

Gates won't have to delve too far back into history to find the truth. In 1954 Clifford A. Jones, Nevada's Lieutenant-Governor and Democratic National Committeeman, was an 11 per cent owner of the Thunderbird Hotel casino. After the *Las Vegas Sun's* exposure of connivance between the gambling fraternity and state politicians, the Nevada tax commission began proceedings against the Thunderbird, charging that it was unfit to hold a gaming license. Jones denied before the commission that Meyer and Jake Lansky had hidden interests in the hotel, in spite of the fact that his own law partner had told of Lansky backing in "bugged" conversations subsequently published in the *Sun*. The commission produced, for Jones's enlightenment, a copy of the federal income-tax returns of George Sadlo and Jake Lansky showing that the two of them had paid taxes on $200,000 worth of income from the Thunderbird. The hotel's gaming license was subsequently revoked by the tax commission, but the state Supreme Court then came to the boys' assistance by reversing the commission's decision. However, the proof of the pudding was in those tax returns. Perhaps the only question John Gates needed to answer for himself is whether or not a leopard can change its spots.

An interesting addendum to the Pan Am Caribbean story occurred at the end of 1968, when the Mary Carter Paint Company, under its new name of Resorts International, bought a sizable chunk of Pan Am stock. In May of the same year, Mary Carter had sold its paint division for approximately $7 million in cash and $2 million in 6 per cent notes. The new company, Resorts International, decided to limit its interest exclusively to land development in the Bahamas—probably for the very good reason that its earnings as a paint company had decreased steadily over a four-year period and then, in 1968, showed a substantial upturn after the January opening of the Paradise Island hotel-casino operation.

The Resorts International purchase of Pan Am stock, although not nearly large enough to give it control, gave certain Pan Am officials food for thought. Their concern was not only as to how much more stock might be picked up by

Resorts International but also, and particularly, as to how much influence such men as Meyer Lansky might have on the future of Pan Am.

All these complications make one wonder what there was, prior to 1963, that had already made Bobby Baker an old hand on the Hoodlum Sea as well as in the murky waters of stateside political-business negotiations. The fact is that Bobby had been "pooping" around the Caribbean for some time, with Levinson and other pals, and had become involved with highly placed Puerto Rican and Dominican public officials in the process. Consequently, he had built for himself a tall ship and had a star by which to steer when he later plunged into more dangerous waters. The boys from Puerto Rico and the Dominican Republic were small and rather innocent fry, however, compared to the syndicate sharks for whom Bobby played pilot fish in the Pan Am-Intercontinental-Hotels caper.

One of Bobby Baker's first big deals in the Caribbean involved him in the highly lucrative import-export meat business. At the 1952 National Democratic convention in Chicago he became acquainted with a free-wheeling politician named Jose Benitez, who was the chairman of the Puerto Rican Democratic party. The friendship flourished, and Bobby soon became a part-time commuter to Puerto Rico—collecting people, as always, who would be useful to him over the years in the exchange of small favors. Thus by 1960, when Bobby was firmly entrenched as Majority secretary to the Senate, the Benitez-Baker exchange was in the making.

Benitez had discovered through a friend, Puerto Rican meat importer Andres Lopez, that there were many people in his country who had never tasted fresh beef, a luxury item only the rich could afford. Lopez explained to Benitez that the high cost of beef resulted from the necessity of having to buy it in Central America and then ship it to Puerto Rico, a fourteen-hour trip by air. The freight time plus the need for expensive refrigeration on the long trip put the cost of fresh beef beyond the reach of the poor people on the island.

Lopez, a shrewd businessman concerned over his limited market, had searched for other sources of supply and happily stumbled across the answer to his needs: a slaughterhouse and packing plant in Haiti barely two air hours from Puerto Rico. But there was a fly in the ointment: the U.S. Department of Agriculture had denied Lopez a license to import

meat to Puerto Rico—an American possession—because of
unsanitary conditions in the Haitian slaughterhouse. Lopez
told Benitez that he was willing to give a finder's fee of one
cent per pound of beef imported to anyone who could clear
up the matter and secure for him a contract with the Haitian
company. Benitez assured Lopez that he knew someone who
might be just the man for the job, and within days Benitez
was winging his way to Washington for a meeting with
Bobby Baker.

This was when the seeds of influence Bobby had so carefully planted in earlier days effected a kind of cross-pollini-
zation that resulted in hybrids that will probably haunt the
ex-Senate version of Paladin and his pals for years to come.

The slaughterhouse and packing plant in Haiti's capital
city, Port-au-Prince, were a new investment venture called
HAMPCO—Haitian American Meat Packing Company—
which had been set up by the Murchison brothers of Texas.
The Murchisons' holdings in oil, construction, real estate,
and cattle were so vast and complex that they maintained a
staff of attorneys, public relations men, and lobbyists in
Washington second to none. But the Murchisons and their
lawyers were generous and made it a point to include Bobby
in many opportunities.

Spurred to action by Benitez' story of a finder's fee for the
solution to Lopez' predicament, Bobby Baker made one
phone call and parlayed it into a substantial income for three
years, manipulating the situation eventually to a point where
he was in the unusual position of collecting dividends from
both buyer *and* seller.

Bobby called the Murchison brothers' Washington attorneys, Webb and Law, explaining that he had an interested
buyer in Puerto Rico for HAMPCO meat. They apparently
indicated that if Bobby was interested in the deal, they were.
Shortly thereafter, therefore, Benitez made another trip to
Washington, with his wife and Andres Lopez. Baker referred
them to the offices of Webb and Law, where, on the same
day, according to Senate testimony, a HAMPCO-Lopez ex-
port-import deal was made. The agreement included Lopez'
paying the one per cent per pound finder's fee to Baker and
Baker's subsequent distribution of the money: "one-half cent
to Webb and Law and one-quarter cent each to Baker and
Mrs. Benitez."

The deal, of course, hinged on obtaining Department of
Agriculture approval for the shipping of meat from the Hai-

tian slaughterhouse to Puerto Rico, or into the United States. Law, according to the Senate report, "thought the conferences with representatives of the Department were in progress when the first meeting was held with Mr. and Mrs. Benitez and Lopez and when the agreement was made about the compensation of the 'finders.' " At any rate, by the time the contract was ready to go into effect, the Department of Agriculture had found conditions in the slaughterhouse to be adequate. Everything was in order for a smooth operation. What voodoo couldn't do, Bobby Baker apparently did. He may even have made a second ten-cent phone call to earn his finder's fee.

By the end of 1961 Lopez was getting his meat from HAMPCO, and Bobby was happily counting his pennies and making distribution of same. Before the two-year contract was up, however, Lopez had become disenchanted with the deal and wanted out. Instead of the fine beefsteaks he wished to sell to his fellow Puerto Ricans, he complained of receiving inferior meat, some of which had to be disposed of back in the United States for conversion into bologna.

At this point Irwin Davidson, a registered lobbyist in Washington for the governments of Haiti and Nicaragua—and also for the Murchison interests—contacted William E. Kentor, an official of The Packers Provision Company, Inc., with headquarters in Chicago. Kentor's firm, which had been a buyer of some of Lopez' meat shipped to the United States, also had a meat-processing plant in Puerto Rico. Kentor subsequently made a deal with HAMPCO to take over the Lopez contract, importing the HAMPCO beef to the Puerto Rican plant for processing into bologna and sausages, mostly for local sale. When Kentor was informed of the one cent per pound finder's fee arrangement, which he was expected to continue, he balked. Then he made a compromise offer of one-half cent per pound—which, after much dickering, was accepted.

What Kentor didn't realize was that, as a result of his re- luctance to pay the full one cent per pound, Baker and his co-finders had persuaded HAMPCO to give them 10 per cent—up to $30,000 a year—of HAMPCO's net profits from the Kentor contract. Thus Kentor, the buyer, and HAMPCO, the seller, were both paying off Baker and his pals.

Bobby Baker netted himself approximately $12,000 as a result of one or two ten-cent phone calls, and even those were paid for by his employer, the U.S. government. It would not seem too illogical, therefore, to assume that Bobby had clearly explained his finder's fee method of operation to the Levinson-Jones-Kozloff combine when making their representations to Pan American and John Gates in the summer of 1963.

Obviously, then, Baker was well known in the Caribbean, but his influence in the Hoodlum Sea may have been far greater than has yet been generally recognized. In fact, it may even have a bearing on some of the political upheavals in the Dominican Republic.

Diego Bordas, an exiled Dominican revolutionary whom Bobby had met in 1956 or 1957 through Jose Benitez, had been exporting cement from Dominica to the United States with Benitez in a partnership arrangement. When a group of American cement companies complained to the U.S. Department of Customs that the pair were in violation of America's anti-dumping laws—especially at cut-rate prices, with which they could not compete—Benitez took his problem to his friend Bobby. The upshot was that Baker walked into the Department of Customs with his arm around Diego Bordas' shoulder while the matter was pending and pointedly announced: "This is Diego Bordas. He is a friend of mine." There is no record of any further consideration of the complaint.

Bordas and Baker began spending a great deal of time discussing the turbulent Dominican political situation. When Trujillo was assassinated in May, 1961, Bordas paraded for Baker's benefit his friend Juan Bosch, a historian and self-taught political scientist. Bordas told Bobby that Bosch could become the first freely elected president of the Dominican Republic in over thirty years.

It all happened as Bordas said it would, and, at the end of 1962, for his loyalty to President-Elect Bosch, Bordas was in line for a top cabinet appointment in the new administration. Before Bosch was inaugurated in February, 1963, however, Bordas suggested that he make a trip to New York to meet his friend and intimate associate of the then Vice-President, Lyndon B. Johnson, Bobby Baker. United States support for Bosch had to be won, and the Baker pipeline could be used.

In December, 1962, a meeting between Bosch and Baker took place in the luxurious Hampshire House Hotel, overlooking Central Park in New York City, and the following month Bobby received an invitation to the Bosch inauguration. He flew down to the ceremony in February with Johnson and the then senior senator of Minnesota, Hubert Humphrey. Pictures were taken of Johnson happily embracing Bosch, and Dominicans interpreted this as an official blessing of their new president by the United States.

Within a year, however, Johnson had become president through the tragedy of John Kennedy's assassination, Bobby Baker's situation of power and influence had greatly changed, and the 101st Senator had been publically dumped by many of his former friends, including Lyndon B. Johnson. Bobby was described as a wanton opportunist who used his Senate position for personal gain, and when he resigned from his job as secretary to the Senate Majority in October, 1963, Baker's former business associates scurried to protect themselves from the publicity that was to come from the exposé of his wheeling and dealing.

That Bobby Baker's questionable elbow-rubbing with, and influence-peddling for, Dominican politicians and would-be politicians had a part in effecting a subsequent change of official U.S. attitudes toward the Dominican Republic is perhaps in the realm of speculation. Still, the complete turnabout toward Juan Bosch made by President Johnson, after the Baker scandal had erupted in Washington and all hands were being washed of him, makes for interesting reading and consideration.

Although the Kennedy administration had fully endorsed and supported Juan Bosch after his victory in the free elections of 1962, the Johnson administration, despite much criticism from Congress, sent U.S. marines into Santo Domingo in April, 1965. Presumably this was to protect U.S. citizens there, help restore order, and "avoid another Cuba," but it occurred at a time when revolutionary elements were trying to return Bosch to his rightful position as president, a post from which he had been ousted by a military coup in September, 1963, just seven months after his inauguration.

In commenting on this shift in policy, Senator J. W. Fulbright said:

> In 1963, the United States strongly supported Bosch and the PRD [Bosch's party] as enlightened reformers; in 1965, the United States opposed their return to power on the unsubstantiated ground that a Bosch or PRD government would certainly, or almost certainly, become Communist-dominated. Thus the United States turned its back on social revolution in Santo Domingo and associated itself with a corrupt and reactionary military oligarchy.

The role played by Baker and the syndicate in Dominican affairs is of course unclear. But almost certainly the Alliance for Progress that Bosch saw exemplified in President John F. Kennedy's inauguration gift to him—an ambulance for the use of the people—is dead. As Bosch said: "Although the machinery of the Alliance for Progress survived him, the vitality and spirit of reform with which he imbued it when he created it, died with him in Dallas on November 22, 1963." But a syndicate Alliance for Progress remains, solidly entrenched in the Caribbean under Meyer Lansky's watchful eye. And for Bobby, perhaps, it now makes little difference; he "has it made." According to an *Esquire* article in July, 1967, Baker still has considerable financial worth and shows few signs of tightening his personal purse strings to cut expenses. He also is said to command no small amount of attention and respect from headwaiters, hatcheck girls, restaurant proprietors, and like admirers in Washington, where, as the article says, "obviously, Bobby Baker is somebody."

While speaking to writer Milton Viorst about his reaction to the jury that found him guilty—the verdict is being appealed—Baker may well have voiced not only his own outlook and self-serving philosophy but also that of the syndicate itself when he said:

> I feel sorry for the members of that jury, even if they convicted me. They were all just little government workers, putting in their time, filling out their forms, waiting for their pensions. There's none of 'em ever made more than $7,000 a year in his whole life, maybe $10,000 at the most. They just couldn't understand how anybody who worked for the government, like me, could get his hands on so much money. They figured it had to be crooked. It just never occurred to them that it could be honest.

Bobby Baker's appeal could eventually reach as high as the Supreme Court, where justices receive an annual salary of $39,500. But it's just possible that even the justices would take a dim view of a man who apparently got more than an honest baker's dozen out of every deal he ever made.

NINE

NEW ORLEANS:

Bayou Buccaneers

"Oh, Billy, Billy, they have given it to me and I gave them back the best I could!"

New Orleans Police Chief Peter Hennessey had six chunks of lead in his body when he mumbled these words to a detective friend, Captain William O'Connor, at about eleven o'clock on the Wednesday night of October 15, 1890—a balmy, peaceful night filled with the scent of the flowers that strewed Hennessey's front lawn. He died in Charity Hospital after eleven hours of physical anguish.

It was a sweet night in New Orleans, but it signaled the advent of the terror, of the indelible hue that always comes with the Mafia, of the ground-color on a horror-splashed canvas that is never finished. And in the Bayou City it has been added to each year, each month, and each day since the night Hennessey put the key in the lock of his front door on Girod Street and a shotgun blasted him from behind.

Hennessey was a good policeman and a fine man but, nevertheless, a minuscule stopgap against an almost classic disease. In its essence the story of Hennessey is much like that of any town engulfed by the Mafia in those early days when no one felt the terror of the secret society—no one, that is, until Hennessey took six slugs in him.

Hennessey had been checking into several murders that

had no validity, as ordinary murders go, from the standpoint of motive. An in boiling them down, he came up with an answer that sealed his doom. What the good police chief had stepped into was a feud between two Mafia brotherhoods, the Camorra and the *Stoppaglieri*, whose U.S. contingents, dedicated to a way of life Hennessey would not have believed if the chapter and verse were thrust down his throat, had freshly arrived from Sicily.

Hennessey's death could have been a hallmark in the understanding of the criminal mind and what it can do with a little organization, but the truth is often hard to come by—especially when details have to be provided. Nevertheless, two grand juries in New Orleans studied the situation that had led to Hennessey's murder, and one of them came up with the fact of the existence of the Mafia, seventy-five years before Valachi's testimony.

The other grand jury returned indictments against nineteen persons in connection with the Hennessey murder. One of those indicted was a fourteen-year-old boy accused of running ahead of Hennessey as he approached his house on the fatal night and whistling, thereby earning himself the dubious title of "fingerman," one of the first in the history of organized crime in New Orleans.

All of the accused were put on trial for their lives on November 29, 1890, but, unaccountably, the state asked for an order of severance, with the result that only nine men were left in the dock facing what was to become a thoroughly confused and botched-up trial. The defense, among whom were some of the ablest attorneys in the city—chief counsel for the Italians was Thomas J. Semmes, former attorney general of Louisiana—drew on a $75,000 defense fund raised by the Mafia in New Orleans and other cities. Sixty-seven witnesses gave testimony for four days, and then, dramatically, one defendant, Manuel Polizzi, said he wanted to confess. Amazingly, the district attorney turned down the offer and proceeded with the prosecution of the nine defendants, including Polizzi, whose lawyers refused to handle his case further after the confession offer was made.

Local newspaper accounts of the trial told of Polizzi's testimony about a drawing of lots among the Mafiosi to see who would murder Hennessey. And the trial jury was shaken during the proceedings by reports that efforts had been made to bribe its members. These reports were so strong that a detective was given a seat behind the press table in view of the jury to discourage "telegraphing" between spectators and members of the jury panel.

On March 13, 1891, after nine hours' deliberation, the jurors found that in the cases of three defendants they were unable to reach a verdict and that the six others were "not guilty."

The citizens of New Orleans were jolted by the unexpected outcome of the trial, and pandemonium followed. An investigation by yet another grand jury resulted in charges that one lawyer had indeed attempted to bribe panel members. An indictment was handed down, but nothing ever came of the charges. The people formed a "Vigilance Committee" and began the purchase of shotguns, rifles, and revolvers from the hardware shop of A. Baldwin & Company. A public meeting was organized and exhorted by concerned citizens to denounce an attorney for the defense as a "suborner and procurer of witnesses and a briber of juries."

The meeting on March 14, the day after the verdict was delivered, soon became a mob, and a horde of armed men rushed from the town square down Bienville Street to the local prison, where the Italian prisoners were still under custody. The captive Mafiosi gibbered in terror as they heard the roar of the approaching crowd outside. A giant Negro picked up a huge paving stone and smashed it through a wooden door at the side of the jail, about 150 feet from the main gate. The crowd was momentarily awed and stilled by this feat. Then thirty men rushed through the wooden shards of the door into the prison, like a wolf pack hunting its quarry. The leaders of the mob decided to bring the prisoners outside and hang them publicly. The boy who whistled and signaled Hennessey's doom was found and left unharmed, but the others were herded under a grove of trees. The first to meet his doom was a dark little man named Manuel Polizzi.

The *New Orleans Picayune's* reporter on the scene quickly filed a story that reflected the goggle-eyed horror with which he watched the massacre. He later wrote that a "stalwart public official" had dragged Polizzi into St. Anne Street from his hiding place on the ground floor of the prison and carried him in one hand to the corner of Treme and St. Anne, where a rope lifted Polizzi off the ground to the top of a lamp post. A group of armed men were said to have riddled him with bullets, the power of the Winchesters jolting his body and making it wriggle "like an angle worm on a hook."

Some even were hanged from tree limbs and then shot. Finally, they hung limp in a pal of blue smoke that brought the stink of burning powder to the frenzied executioners, who screamed, again and again, "Shoot! Kill the Dagoes!" The crowd was estimated at eight thousand, and so tightly did it pack around the scene of carnage that there was scarcely room for the executioners to bring their guns to bear on the cowering victims. Eleven men finally lay dead, including two whose trial had been severed from the others'—of no matter to the mob. One man escaped by hiding in a barrel of trash in the women's quarters of the prison, curled up like a child about to be born.

One local newspaper, *The Item*, viewed the whole proceeding with satisfaction. Next day an editorial pronounced:

> The military precision, skill and rapidity with which the prison was stormed and taken, the care exercised to do no harm except to the guilty parties, the wonderful forbearance of the angered populace, all are commended: while no complaint is uttered against the officials for their failure to interpose resistance to the avengers of outraged justice.

The *St. Louis Post-Dispatch*, which many years later was to engage in a deadly editorial crusade against The Green Ones, scolded New Orleans with the words: "It is hoped that the leading citizens will get the same punishment they meted out to the Mafia."

The *London Times* declared that "Italy's indignation is shared by the whole civilized world." In Rome, the *Don Chisciotte Delta* said:

> Italy ought to demand that instant measures be taken to protect the Italian colony in New Orleans. . . . It is just also to recognize the fact that similar incidents would not occur if the towns of the Atlantic littoral were not infested with the ex-galley slaves of Europe.

A lot of hell was raised by Italian officials in the United States, and veiled threats to take some sort of action by deploying the Italian Navy in U.S. waters were voiced. Secretary of State James G. Blaine maintained that the protesters were off base and declared: "The Sicilian who comes here must become an American citizen and subject his wrongs to the remedy of the law of the land, or else there must be no place for him on the American continent."

Money was furnished by Congress for more ships, and the U.S. Navy was really the chief beneficiary of the squabble, for it was brought home that the Italian Navy consisted of twenty-two first class ships while the United States had only one first-class battleship, and an uncompleted vessel at that. This realization led to a great deal of shipbuilding, so that seven years later, when the Spanish-American War broke out, the U.S. Navy found itself in excellent condition, with much new equipment.

In the meantime, the Italian government, which was having money problems, decided against war, and eight Italians suspected of complicity in the Hennessey murder were freed and promptly vanished. The stir caused by the Mafiosi massacre was smoothed out by time and some soothing words from President Harrison, who offered $25,000—the offer was accepted—to the Italian government as compensation for the victims of the New Orleans affair.

It is evident, however, that some of the descendants of the same Mafia factions that spawned the murderers of Chief Hennessey are today in control of the rackets surrounding New Orleans, so much so that the original $25,000 largesse from the U.S. government has multiplied a million-fold for the secret society.

The man currently spinning the syndicate wheel of fortune in New Orleans is hoodlum Carlos Marcello, Louisiana boss of bosses, the midget Midas of the Mafia who, upon the deportation in 1947 of Mafia chieftain Sam Corollo, inherited the bullet-drilled mantles of the men who died at the hands of vigilantes.

The story of Marcello can be recounted with the same kind of tedious but telling facts that typify the histories of others of the Mafia hierarchy who brought its terror to the United States and who siphon off the money in every direction and under every guise. Carlos Marcello, according to the considered judgment of top U.S. law officials, was born in Tunisia as Calogero Minacori on February 6, 1910, after having been conceived in Sicily. Tunisia was merely a way-stop in his parents' emigration to the United States, for they soon proceeded to New Orleans. During Carlos' childhood in New Orleans, the family shared its home with another Sicilian family. They, too, had crossed the ocean with the Marcellos, and they could, but for the Mafia code of silence, give witness to the fact of Carlos' Sicilian heritage, which he denies.

In his early days Carlos committed more obvious, though less sinister, offenses against society than now, one of the first being assault and robbery of a Chinese grocer. This caper he paid for, serving four years in prison. A practice skirmish, apparently, was a bank robbery a year earlier in the Algiers section of New Orleans. Carlos, then nineteen, his brother Peter, and his father Joseph were arrested as accessories, but the charges were dismissed.

After his release from prison, Carlos tied up with the Frank Costello-Phil Kastel combine, which had moved operations to Louisiana after their slot machines had been outlawed in New York by Mayor LaGuardia. In 1935, at the relatively tender age of twenty-five, Carlos received a full pardon for the 1930 assault conviction from Governor O. K. Allen, stooge of the Kingfish of Louisiana politics, Huey P. Long. The record shows two more arrests of Carlos—for assault, beating, and attempt to murder and for violation of the U.S. Internal Revenue Code—in the same year. But the charges were again dismissed. Carlos had obviously learned well his lessons from his seasoned Mafiosi tutors and was entering into the more sophisticated echelons of crime where "the handcuff was replaced with the handshake."

However minor these charges may have seemed, at least in underworld circles, Marcello became a real target for lawmen when he pleaded guilty in 1938 to selling more than twenty-three pounds of marijuana in association with the largest narcotics ring in New Orleans' history. He had left himself wide open and was sentenced to a one-year stay in Atlanta's federal prison and fined $76,830—a sum that he was permitted to settle with a token payment of $400 on the plea he was a pauper.

The U.S. Immigration Department subsequently found that Carlos had never become a naturalized citizen. This fact made deportation for a narcotics conviction feasible, and in 1951, after Marcello had appeared as a reluctant witness before the Kefauver hearings and refused to answer questions, Senator Estes Kefauver recommended that he be deported. Thus, from 1953 until 1961, when Robert Kennedy finally turned the trick, Carlos was under a continuous order of deportation and had to do battle with every legal weapon available to him in order to stay in the United States.

When approached by U.S. immigration officials, both Italy

and Tunisia turned thumbs down on taking Marcello back.
It seemed no one was interested in the boy who had left
town and made good. Besides, from Carlos' point of view
these places were thousands of miles away, and he was the
kind of man who liked to insure his bets. If he was to go
away on an enforced vacation—and he hoped this would
never happen—he wanted both a friendly welcome and a
salubrious atmosphere.

Finally, therefore, Marcello dispatched an aide to Guatemala to dig up evidence that there, in a country of many
friends, Carlos Marcello first saw the light of day. The attorney, ensconced in a chauffeured limousine thoughtfully
provided by Guatemalan government officials, toured the
country examining birth records in remote villages. Large
document books are kept in these sparsely populated, mahog-
any-forested areas, and anyone handy—the parish priest, the
local clerk, the farmer-mayor of the town—could and would
make the necessary birth entry. Blank spaces were sometimes
left between names and could well be used for the very
purpose Carlos had in mind.

Finally, in a jungle city called San Jose Pinula, there was
found the kind of blank space needed in the local record
book. The name of Calogero Minacori was inserted, in water-
mixed ink so that the scrawl would match those already
there, and Carlos Marcello was born again—in Guatemala,
a scant three-and-one-half-hour trip by air from New Orleans.
To make doubly sure of his new identity, Marcello also succeeded in getting the best mob counterfeiter, who was at the
time in jail—such is the power of Marcello—to make him a
Guatemalan passport. If worse came to worse and Carlos
had to take that "vacation," he would at least be in fairly
close touch with his business associates.

Meanwhile, according to the New Orleans crime commission, which had compiled an extensive file on Marcello's
past, Marcello has not been neglecting his affairs. At one
time or another his varied business operations have involved
banks, truck dealerships, motels, housing subdivisions, bars,
restaurants, finance companies, linen-supply services—a traditional syndicate interest—beer and whiskey distributorships,
shrimp fleets, shipbuilding firms, taxi and bus companies,
souvenir shops, gas stations, ceramic-tile companies, phono-
graph-record wholesalers and shops, and electrical-appliance
stores. The evidence points to the fact that Marcello interests
are not confined only to Jefferson and Orleans Parishes

(counties). His many enterprises are scattered through surrounding states and include thousands of acres of oil leases on federal land. In one section, Marcello purchased land for 50 cents an acre; a few years later, he sold a thirty-acre parcel for $7,500,000 for the development of a shopping center.

Marcello's financial successes, however, had little effect on the Justice Department. The Attorney General, Robert Kennedy, and his staff greeted with hilarity the news of Carlos' rebirth in Guatemala and decided that they would oblige.

On April 4, 1961, Carlos Marcello left his white marble two-story home overlooking a well-trimmed golf course in Metairie, a suburb of New Orleans, to make his quarterly visit to the New Orleans immigration department. Kennedy and his aide, Walter Sheridan, had already collaborated on the script. As Marcello extended his arm across the desk at the department's headquarters to sign a statement of appearance, instead of being offered the customary pen he was quickly handcuffed by two officers and hustled out of the office into a waiting car. Within thirty minutes he was the only passenger aboard a giant Immigration Department jet plane whistling its way toward Guatemala.

Apocryphal stories have been published about the great outcry Guatemalan citizens were supposed to have made over Marcello's presence in their midst. One such story relates that eight government secret agents "redeported" him by depositing him at the El Salvador border, the whereabouts of which have always been in dispute. In turn, the El Salvadorians are supposed to have taken him and deposited him on top of a mountain in the wilderness on the Honduras side of the border. From here Carlos is supposed to have walked seventeen miles to the nearest village, fainting three times on the way. Actually, Carlos was wined and dined by the aristocracy of Guatemala. He was flown to the finest resort areas in the private plane of the country's president, Miguel Ydigoras Fuentes, who was forced to flee Guatemala in 1963.

Carlos' exile was short-lived. He was photographed at the Guatemala City racetrack with Felice Golino, once the biggest shrimp-boat fleet operator in the Gulf of Mexico and a long-time friend of Marcello sometimes identified in newspapers as his uncle and certainly a partner in various enterprises. Then in May, 1961, just one month after his abrupt deportation to Guatemala, Carlos was escorted from his "native land" to neighboring Honduras, then a British colony but claimed by Guatemala and therefore looked upon by Guatemalan citizens for immunity. And in Honduras, it is said, Marcello soon set off for home from the capital city, Belize, in one of Uncle Felice's shrimp boats. Carlos was supposedly taken to a spot off the Mexican port of Chetumal, a few miles to the north, where one of the shrimpers waited for him in the dead of night to carry him back to New Orleans.

This version of Carlos' return with Golino's help—given by Carlos himself to close friends—is somewhat discredited by lawmen, who say that Golino disposed of his shrimp fleet long before Marcello's deportation difficulties began. Golino, moreover, has denied any part in assisting in the reentry to this country of one of the underworld's brightest stars. However, both Marcello and Golino had connections with shrimpers and their boats, a connection that would have made both easily accessible to Carlos, and on a shrimp boat Carlos could have arrived in Louisiana via any number of the secluded bayous that weave mysteriously from the gulf coast almost into the heart of New Orleans.

In any case, on June 3, after getting his business affairs in order, Carlos surrendered voluntarily to immigration agent Bruce Hemstad, spent a few days at the federal alien detention center in McAllen, Texas, and was released on bond. He was subsequently indicted for conspiracy to commit fraud by obtaining a fake Guatemalan birth certificate, for committing perjury in swearing he had nothing to do with obtaining the fake certificate, and for unlawful reentry as a deported alien. However, nothing ever really happened to untangle the legal flim-flam. A conspiracy trial resulted in a not-guilty verdict, and Marcello went back to his men and his properties, and business went on as usual—except for one thing: the vendetta with the Kennedys, Robert in particular, was sworn.

Business as usual has meant dispensing income. And if a portion of Marcello's money has an eventual resting place in the pockets of mysterious and powerful higher-ups, or in the seemingly sacred vaults of the Alps-girdled Swiss banks, or in Panamanian money houses, he has spread at least some of the wealth among a huge and prospering family, many of whose members are planted in key positions in his Louisiana investment honey pot.

Most of Marcello's interests in illegal activities are carefully screened by the practice of having the business officially listed in the names of others, but his finger is in whatever pie he feels a fondness for at any given moment. The big questions are: Why does a family constantly pile up wealth when it already has plenty? And, who holds the big purse into which the net profits finally find their way?

Robert Kennedy may have been close to the answer when he was Attorney General, but even he must have been puzzled by Marcello's rapid climb to fortune up the ladder provided by the Mafia—a criminal talent machine oiled by pure gold. To be sure, it is difficult to make too many mistakes when you have Mafia backing, especially when one considers its resources. Thus, a former collector for Marcello's music company, convicted in 1943 of bribing a witness to help two mobsters, was identified by *Life*, September 8, 1967, as being at that time a chief investigator on the staff of the district attorney of Jefferson Parish—a story confirmed to this author a year later by Aaron Kohn.

Perhaps the secret of Marcello's success lies in the fact that his organization is tight and laid out according to the oldest and, apparently, best Mafia tradition. In the opinion of Aaron Kohn, managing director of New Orleans' metropolitan crime commission, Marcello's underboss is his brother, Joseph Marcello, Jr., who operates handbooks and gaming casinos and has had minor brushes with the law. A *caporegime* in the outfit is Peter Marcello, another brother, who is blind in one eye but can see enough to be able to run strip joints such as the Sho-Bar on Bourbon Street. Peter has been arrested for crimes of violence and has served time on a narcotics conviction.

Marcello's six younger brothers—Peter, Joseph, Pascal, Vincent, Anthony, and Sammy—maintain control of many of the operations of the boss of bosses. Having been born in the United States, they, unlike Marcello himself, are not subject to deportation, which is usually a most helpful weapon in the armory of government lawmen trying to rid the country of pestilence. The brothers, according to the crime commission, are the guiding forces behind a variety of business partnerships, including a wire service, a music company operating slot and pinball machines and juke boxes, and a gambling casino.

Marcello's lieutenants come and go, for it is apparently a rule that if one gets caught cold, he takes the rap and thereby, it is hoped, gets a little smarter. One such lieutenant is Nick Nuccio, for years a chief lieutenant with a $4-million-a-year bookie business. Like others of the Mafia hierarchy, Nuccio could not keep his hand out of relatively minor matters, and thereby he provided one more look at the baffling facet of the Mafia character. Nuccio was caught in the act of burglarizing the safe of a large dairy near Baton Rouge in 1963, captured after a gun battle with police, sentenced to ten years in the state penitentiary for the burglary, and fined for illegal possession of burglar tools and narcotics. Why risk such punishments when you are already a chief lieutenant to a boss of bosses? Perhaps because most Mafiosi have a fatally flawed character. They always want more.

Known in the New Orleans underworld as "The Little Man," Carlos Marcello stands only five feet four inches in his elevator shoes, but he is infinitely more polished than such slick Mafia worthies as Chicago's Sam Giancana and New York's Vito Genovese. He sets himself apart with the well-tailored $300 suits he has made with a triple-sized pocket sewn into one pants leg to accommodate the huge sums of cash he usually carries with him.

Crime fighter Aaron Kohn, an ex-FBI man, figured that in 1964 Marcello was directly providing the syndicate with about $400 million a year, of which $100 million came from Uncle Sam in the form of underpayment—or nonpayment—of taxes. Actually, the overall annual take for the mob in the city of New Orleans and environs is something like $1.114 billion in Kohn's estimate, and the sum compares favorably, from the viewpoint of Mafia accountants, with the calculated $2-billion racketeer rakeoff in Chicago, an area with more than five times the population of metropolitan New Orleans.

The local boys, under the astute guiding hand of Carlos Marcello, have become so adapt at high finance that their combined annual income makes them and their business the state's largest industry. As if that weren't enough, they seem to have become the nucleus of an "investment center" for the whole Mafia organization. Their legitimate real estate acquisitions, together with partnership and other involvements in countless thriving businesses, add up to what is an unbelievable total worth.

Thus Frank Klein, chief assistant district attorney of Orleans Parish, has said:

> In fact, we think there's too much money here. We feel that it's flowing in from other Cosa Nostra organizations in other parts of the country for investment by the local mob.

This could be their financial center, with a lot of nice safe places where campaign contributions and outright bribery have pretty well insulated them from the law.

The heart of Marcello's territory is Gretna, the "Cicero of the South," which lies directly across the Mississippi River from New Orleans in Jefferson Parish. New Orleans itself, in Orleans Parish, is comparatively clean, but of Jefferson Parish, wherein prostitution, gambling of all varieties, and narcotics are apt to be found with ease, Kohn has said, "Not even in Tangier was there ever a cozier arrangement between the mob and the law." The customers who throng to the many pleasure palaces in Gretna would seem to have a death wish, and Marcello has a ready-made guillotine for them. Louisiana's version of Las Vegas wears a suit that badly needs laundering, but it has the same big back pocket.

Possibly the fun seekers who troop to syndicate-provided pastimes, not only in Gretna and Las Vegas, but also in the hurly-burly of the casinos being built up in the Caribbean, feel somewhat as Lincoln Steffens suggested all Americans do:

> The American people don't mind grafting, but they hate scandals. They don't kick so much on a jiggered public contract for a boulevard, but they want the boulevard and no fuss and no dust. We want to give them that. We want to give them what they really want, a quiet Sabbath, safe streets, orderly nights and homes secure.

Steffens was quoting a Tammany Hall politician who operated in old New York at about the time Marcello was changing his diapers for real pants. The Tammany brand of serenity was fine for the politicians, but apparently it did not produce enough money for a group of killers who kissed your hand as they killed you. The mobsters therefore pushed south to Florida and Louisiana to find a breed of moneyed swingers who prefer a violent whore over and above a willing but indentured Lady Chatterley; for the swingers pay well for their fun.

Apparently immune from the law, Marcello cleverly operates with an arrogance that brooks virtually no opposition, and the good people of Louisiana appear to be unimpressed by the menace of his power. "Our biggest problem is the attitude of the people," New Orleans Police Superintendent Joseph I. Giarrusso has said:

We closed up half of the mob-operated strip joints on Bourbon Street and elsewhere in the city because tourists were getting drugged or getting their heads bashed in and robbed in them. But we can't close up the rest because certain businessmen feel that, with no place to sin, the tourists won't come to New Orleans anymore. The bookies come across the line from their main base in Jefferson Parish, and we raid them; the prostitutes come across the line from Jefferson Parish on a call-girl basis, and our Vice Squad makes arrests nearly every night. But the courts tend to give out light, slap-on-the-wrist fines and they're back again. Our people just can't understand that what seems to them to be a little harmless gambling is really tied in with far more serious crimes. They can't understand that these are not just local boys they've known all their lives and that they really *are* tied in with the national crime syndicate.

Given such attitudes on the part of the people of Louisiana, it is not surprising that Marcello is not often opposed now by the so-called lawmen who back up the sovereignty of the people in the area, but reporter Bill Davidson tells of at least one rebuff given The Little Man by New Orleans District Attorney James Garrison, who is trying to remake the Warren Commission report by proving a conspiracy in the assassination of President John F. Kennedy. In the fall of 1963, Garrison is reported to have turned Marcello down on a $3,000-per-week offer for his help in opening up the city to hoodlum slot-machine operators. The idea was to have the district attorney seize two illegally placed slots so that a test case could be brought for the purpose of having the machines declared legal. And thereafter Garrison was to get $10 per machine per week for this favor.

Another reverse occurred on September 22, 1966, when Carlos Marcello was arrested in the company of twelve other Mafia chieftains during a luncheon meeting in a private basement dining room at La Stella's Restaurant in fashionable, tennis-oriented Forest Hills, New York, just across the East River from Manhattan. The thirteen Mafiosi, among whom were leaders of the Genovese, Gambino, and Colombo New York Mafia families, were charged with "consorting with known criminals" but had little difficulty in putting up the $1.3-million bail—$100,000 each—that set them free the next day.

Police theorize that the New York luncheon was merely one of a series of top-level Little Apalachin meets, one of which had taken place in Las Vegas two weeks earlier and another in Palm Springs in October, 1965. Among other items on the agenda, it has been suggested that one involved Santo Trafficante, Jr., who early in 1968 visited Singapore, Hong Kong, and South Vietnam and has had his eye on portions of Marcello territory in the South for some time. Since Trafficante lost a good slice of revenue when Castro dumped gambling in Havana and is being given a hard time by lawmen in Florida, he needs new ground. He made frequent trips to Louisiana prior to the La Stella meeting and may very well have been presenting his case for a piece of Marcello's rather substantial pie.

Upon his return to New Orleans after his arrest and release by the New York police, Marcello was met at the airport by inquiring newsmen and photographers and by FBI agent Patrick Collins. Apparently thinking this an invasion of his privacy, Carlos reportedly said, "Don't you know I'm the boss around here!" and took a poke at agent Collins. As a result of his action, Carlos was charged with, and found guilty of, assault in September, 1968, fined $2,000, and sentenced to two years in prison. Of course, Marcello is free on bail, and the sentence is being appealed.

After all his troubles, Marcello should know better, but he remains fond of using the telephone, and even his experience at the restaurant in New York did not prevent him from keeping in touch with the boys. The result was predictable. His calls were monitored. And in its issue of September 29, 1967, Life laid some details bare. Via a complicated series of "cheesebox" phones—used by bookies to hide their location—Carlos made calls until March, 1967, from his office in the Town and Country Motel near New Orleans, the first of two such motels built by the mobster. Some of these calls, Life claims, went into the governor's offices in the state capitol at Baton Rouge after being diverted from a nearby motel owned by a Marcello henchman.

Other calls, according to Life, outlined a plan for bribery in connection with an effort to spring Jimmy Hoffa from federal prison at the behest of syndicate and Teamsters Union officials in the East. The scheme was to offer $1 million to a

Baton Rouge Teamster official, Edward G. Partin, in order
to "encourage" him to change or recant his testimony as a
prime government witness at Hoffa's trial. The bribe was
turned down, according to *Life*, but the stench is still
floating through the state capitol.

Marcello also used the phone to contact other Mafiosi.
At least six Mafia figures—Mike Miranda and Thomas Eboli
of New York City, Nick Civella of Kansas City, Joe
Civello of Dallas, James Lanza of San Francisco, and Santo
Trafficante of Florida—were called during the period the
bribery deal was being considered. And it is interesting to
note that Miranda, Eboli, and Trafficante were all at the
La Stella luncheon meeting.

Unfortunately, under the law it is impossible to use
testimony derived from tapped telephone calls. While the
listings of toll-call records can be secured, the resulting
dialogue has been placed in limbo insofar as legal action is
concerned. However, Marcello's protection is not without
weak spots. Thus a surprising hole in his layer of criminal-
activities insulation, which generally keeps his name from
public mention, was made in August, 1968, in East Chicago,
Indiana, when a thirty-three-year-old Chicago truck driver,
who allegedly claimed to be representing Marcello, was
picked up while collecting $6,500 from a Chicago stock-
broker as part of what was said to be an extortion plot.

The victim, who worked with the FBI in setting up the
arrest, admitted a legitimate debt of $2,000 owed to a
former New Orleans business associate, but he said the
young collector more than tripled the amount to be collected and threatened bodily harm, saying he was representing the New Orleans Mafia boss. If the truck driver did in
fact represent Marcello, it is a good indication that the
long reach of Marcello's power extends far beyond the
bayou country he chooses to call home. Indeed, an incident
that occurred at Churchill Farms, the plantation Marcello
owns on a soggy piece of land near New Orleans, suggests
that Carlos Marcello is mixed up in some extremely murky
activities.

September, 1962: a great blue heron had just speared a
frog from the pond beside a dusty road. The huge bird
looked up suddenly, pumped its great wings, and sailed
away as a black Cadillac bumped smoothly along the road
that flanked the marsh, plowing furrows in the powder, tracks

that filled in as fast as the bubble of air behind the car sifted the dust again.

The marsh is flat, and streaks of silver—seen best at evening—trace the waterways that thread the rough grass to the Mississippi, muddy pathway to the Gulf of Mexico traversed by shrimp boats, catfish, and waterfowl.

In the air-conditioned car were four men. At the wheel was Carlos Marcello, "the most powerful, most influential, most sinister racket boss in Louisiana." Carlos stopped the car outside a small shrimp packing plant. A man came out and handed him a crate of frozen, packaged shrimp, which was placed in the car. The signal was clear: no one had preceded Carlos down the lonely road. The car started off again, this time along damp ruts through the rank marsh growth, and in a few minutes two buildings came into view.

One was a typical country barn. It served as a shelter for chickens and goats. Swallows had plastered their light-gray mud nests against the angle of eaves around the barn. Bottle-green flies were everywhere. The other was typical southern lower-class Americana—narrow windows, a tiny porch, no pretense—but it served as a retreat and secret meeting place for Marcello and his business associates.

Carlos braked the car to a halt at the farmhouse. He led his guests into the kitchen, sat them down on comfortable chairs next to a refrigerator and large freezer, and poured Scotch all around.

The kitchen led into a hall flanked by sparsely furnished bedrooms. One door, however, opened onto a room about twenty-five feet long, completely alien to the simple farmhouse with its ramshackle façade. Down the middle of this room was a long table of polished wood, and placed around it were executive-type, black leather chairs. It was a room set aside strictly for business, and the business discussed was not a matter of pigs and cows.

The conversation began with the usual badinage of men of the underworld—sex, money, sex, money. Later, as the Scotch brought more familiarity and relaxation, the dialogue turned to serious matters, including the pressure law-enforcement agencies were bringing to bear on the Mafia brotherhood.

It was then that Carlos' voice lost its softness, and his words were bitten off and spit out when mention was made of U.S. Attorney General Robert Kennedy, who was still on the trail of Marcello.

"*Livarsi na petra di la scarpa!*" Carlos shrilled the Mafia cry of revenge: "Take the stone out of my shoe!"

"Don't worry about that little Bobby son of a bitch," he shouted. "He's going to be taken care of!"

Ever since Robert Kennedy had arranged for his deportation to Guatemala, Carlos had wanted revenge. But as the subsequent conversation, which was reported to two top government investigators by one of the participants and later to this author, showed, he knew that to rid himself of Robert Kennedy he would first have to remove the President. Any killer of the Attorney General would be hunted down by his brother; the death of the President would seal the fate of his Attorney General.

No one at the meeting had any doubt about Marcello's intentions when he abruptly arose from the table. Marcello did not joke about such things. In any case, the matter had gone beyond being mere "business"; it had become an affair of honor, a Sicilian vendetta. Moreover, the conversation at Churchill Farms also made clear that Marcello had begun to plan a move. He had, for example, already thought of using a "nut" to do the job.

Roughly one year later President Kennedy was shot in Dallas—two months after Attorney General Robert Kennedy had announced to the McClellan committee that he was going to expand his war on organized crime. And it is perhaps significant that privately Robert Kennedy had singled out James Riddle Hoffa, Sam Giancana, and Carlos Marcello as being among his chief targets.

It is impossible to assert that any syndicate member organized the assassination of President Kennedy without further proof. But Lee Harvey Oswald did live and work for a time in New Orleans, could have been connected with Jack Ruby—a small-time ex-Chicago hood—and could well have contacted displaced American mobsters in Mexico during the crucial five "lost" days in September, 1963. Certainly many mobsters had every reason to want the Kennedys out of the way.

Of course, as District Attorney James Garrison is certain he can prove, other interested parties also had reasons for wanting to eliminate John F. Kennedy. Perhaps the truth will emerge one day. Meanwhile, Marcello remains in the country, no longer pestered by the Kennedy brothers. His fate is no longer in their hands. In fact, to return to his more "ordinary" affairs, whether he will be permitted to exercise continued control of the mob's money machine, in New Orleans and points north, east, and west, is up not to officials but to the citizenry that comprises the hoards of suckers who play the syndicate games in one back room while their pockets are picked in another.

TEN

CALIFORNIA:

Malice in Wonderland

The Mafia came to California almost as soon as the golden dawns had faded for the Spanish grandees and the Conestoga wagons of those who rushed westward had blotted out the sun. The pueblos and missions and land grants fell before the invaders who brought what was known as law and order—though the law was designed largely to make things easy for the new native sons.

The lawyers obliged and begat judges, the judges begat decisions, the decisions begat protection of a sort, for the Mafiosi, and the Mafiosi begat a monster of terror capable of hypnotizing anyone. The terror, of course, is not always needed, for the Mafia can also use another kind of enslavement—the enslavement wrapped up in the hallucinogenic and pacifying products that have begun to twitch the minds and bare feet of a generation of young people. But, in any case, a tea party has begun, and it may never stop in the Mad Hatter's personal preserve: California, U.S.A.

California's nine-hundred-mile littoral features archetypes who would almost make you believe Lewis Carroll had explored the American West for his material. It is as though the looking glass Alice stepped through was simply a doorway to California, for there can be found almost anything.

Almost everyone in California has his own looking glass,

but deep in the heart of America's movieland-wonderland each finds himself being upstaged by Cheshire Cats, Red Queens, and such assorted bad men as Humpty Dumpty, the White Knights, and the Jabberwockys. Everybody seems to have gotten into the act, and some of the money-grubbers and their bosom-buddy, mob-connected politicians have never had it so ruthlessly good. As in the rest of the country, so in California: the men with the money are out to make more of it, and the men without it are hoping for a chance to make it. The Mafia casts a long shadow on what once was an Eden, and there appears to be few left to cry or care. There is little left of that garden, and that little will be saved only if a real effort is made to drive out the crooked businessmen-politicos and the syndicate boys who helped put them in their positions of power.

Police records show that by the turn of the century the Mafia had firmly entrenched itself in southern California, chiefly by using its dreaded terror tactics on those of the Italian element, within and outside of the secret society, who didn't go along with its demands. A review of suspected gangland murders and mysterious disappearances in this early era, prior to Prohibition, shows a consistent pattern to the method of operation used by "The Black Hand Society," as it was then called by lawmen and frightened citizens. Only the motives—intimidation, extortion, revenge, jealousy—varied.

The police investigation reports on these cases invariably contained such phrases as:

Italian fruit peddler ... shot in back on street. Believed to be long standing feud of Sicilian origin.

Victim killed by shot through window of his barber shop. Definitely a "Black Hand" killing as a letter was found in victim's pocket written in Sicilian. Letter also bore crude drawing of a clown and a policeman, evidently referring to victim as a stoolie.

Victim wounded after being shot by unknown person with shotgun on street . . . stated he did not see who fired as his back was turned (although he received wounds in front of his body). Victim stated he had received Black Hand letters demanding money under threat of death. Letters later found in his room.

Victim shot in back of head and hand. Aftermath of a Sicilian mob feud . . . believed at time to be Italian Black Hand killing.

This killing was the outcome of bad blood between Italian elements and also from "muscling" of different factions.

The four words, "no prosecution to date," that terminate a large majority of these reports are a good indication of the high degree of skillfulness that the Black Handers had achieved.

A second era of organized crime began in California, as it did all across the country, with the enactment of Prohibition as of January 29, 1920. The bootlegging of illegal liquor gave the Mafia an opportunity to make larger amounts of money in a shorter time than ever before. But simply because there were more profits to be made, Prohibition also initiated a divisive power struggle within the organization. Brother was pitted against brother, one faction of the society against another, in a joust for the plunder and the spoils. And while the Roaring Twenties became in one stratum of society, the era of Flapper Girls, raccoon coats, and female emancipation, in another they were a decade of criminal violence involving smuggling, hijacking, and murder.

A typical twenties incident occurred in California on November 25, 1929: a person was reported missing to the authorities.

The incident was typical in that people were always being reported missing. However, this particular incident led to nailing into place one of the many rungs in the ladder of organized crime in California, and it also served to introduce the name of gangster Jack Dragna to California police files at a time when orange groves and vineyards were paving the hills with gold once again.

The official record can be found in a Los Angeles police department report entitled "Gangland Killings—1900–1951," a partial recitation of what is known of man's inhumanity to man in Los Angeles and environs.

The man in this case was Frank Baumgarteker. Baumgarteker, who was partly bald and about fifty years old, was a well-known winery owner, and he was also part-owner of the Western Grape Corporation, 279 North Avenue 19, and owner of the Union Motor Transport, 633 Gibbons Street, Los Angeles, three ranches, and the Cucamonga winery near that city.

Baumgarteker was suspected of large-scale bootlegging and transportation activities in connection with the bootlegging, and it was reported that he owed over $200,000 to creditors and that he was unable to pay them. It is almost certain that Baumgarteker's winery was being used to manufacture illegal alcohol, and it became apparent to investigators that the vintner did not exactly like the idea and wanted out. His debts were not being taken care of by the men who had forced him to use the winery to manufacture moonshine.

In September, 1929, Baumgarteker had an argument with the mob representative in charge of the "alky cooker," Jimmy (Schafer) Fogarty, whose true name was Zorra. Somehow Baumgarteker summoned enough courage to order the bootleg installation out of his winery. It was removed the same day, and on his way out of the office that evening the vintner made it plain to his secretary, a Mrs. Day, that the Italians could no longer use his winery for the making of illegal alcohol. And he added: "I have signed my death warrant."

Shortly thereafter three up-and-coming hoodlums—Jack Dragna, titular head of the Mafia in California and president of the Italian Protective League, Joe Ardizzone, treasurer of the League, and Eddie Rollings, about whom little is known—dropped in to talk to Baumgarteker. But the vintner was adamant, and the trio left the winery.

Baumgarteker was last seen on November 25, 1929. At 11:30 A.M. he finished eating lunch with his partner, Bob Demateis, and his attorney, Walter Hass, at the Hoffman Cafe, 743 South Spring Street, Los Angeles. He had also spoken that morning with John Vai of the Padre Wine Company, Los Angeles and Alameda. The vitner left the luncheon appointment in his purple 1926 Cadillac touring car after telling his friends that he was going to Wilmington, California, where his Union Motor Transport organization had an office. That night, at 10:50 P.M., his car was left at the Sixth Street Garage, 745 Sixth Street, San Diego, California, by a man described as being about 40 years old, weighing about 160 pounds, and wearing a short leather coat, khaki pants, and leather riding boots.

The missing man's wife received a letter from her husband postmarked San Diego, 7:30 A.M., November 26, and the handwriting indicated that the writer was under great mental strain. An intensive search made in southern California and Mexico yielded many leads, much publicity, and no results. A $1,000 reward was posted, to no avail. Baumgarteker's auto, lab tests revealed, carried the type of peculiar dust and dirt found at a place called Riverside County Wells—in those days a place of bubbling springs and deep mineral water where a skeleton would be washed free of its enclosing flesh in a matter of days, especially if weighted and lowered into the gushing water.

The last line in the missing man's folder at police headquarters reads: "To date, no indication or evidence of victim's whereabouts. No prosecution."

As Alice said, after she read the poem "Jabberwocky" in the White King's castle: ". . . only I don't exactly know what they are: However, *somebody* killed *something*: that's clear, at any rate. . ."

Jack Dragna had made his mark. And while he hadn't exactly established himself as the leader, at least he had impressed others that he was the man to look up to in the California underworld—a process that would require a great deal of neck-twisting under any circumstances.

The Italian Protective League, which had its offices on the eleventh floor of the Law Building in Los Angeles, was, according to police intelligence reports:

> strictly a "muscle" outfit, preying on various business activities, such as produce, cleaning establishments, barber shops, etc.; also had its fingers in gambling, bootlegging, smuggling, and was suspected of many "Black Hand" killings and some "sudden disappearances" of Italians, bootleggers and others.

And its president, Jack Dragna, was the man who, floating on a river of illegal alcohol, led the big-time Mafiosi into California by smoothing the way for Frank Costello's boy, Bugsy Siegel.

The story of Dragna's career and infiltration into the heart and soul of a great land should be documented even though it is a long and typical one. Dragna died in 1957. He stumbled out his last days in Las Vegas browbeating cashiers whose courage fronted for the fear of their bosses. He had even been ordered deported a couple of years before he died, but the order had never been carried out. Presumably it was on appeal. It is all a rather dreary story.

Dragna, whose real name was Anthony Rizzoti, was born in Corleone, near Palermo, Sicily, before the turn of the century. He came to the United States with his brother Tom about 1908. The family settled in California. Although arrested many times on vaious charges, Dragna served only one term in jail, going to San Quentin in 1915 on a three-year sentence for attempted extortion.

Released from prison in time to get into full swing with syndicate Prohibition activities, Dragna soon worked his way to the top of California's criminal hierarchy and, eventually, into the Mafia's ruling council. However, he was never all powerful. For example, even if he had wanted to, he was unable to prevent the disappearance in 1931 of Joe Ardizzone, his fellow officer in the Italian Protective League who had helped him try to "muscle" Frank Baumgarteker two years earlier.

Ardizzone's fate also illustrates once again how the syndicate will use the vengeance on its own men, when necessary, that it uses on outside competitors. The police report on Joe Ardizzone, missing since October 15, 1931, reads as follows:

> Ardizzone shot and killed George Maisano, July 2, 1906 . . . was apprehended and charged with murder, but on February 9, 1915, case dismissed, insufficient evidence, no witnesses that would talk.
>
> Ardizzone was wounded in a gang war deal in February, 1931, when he was supposedly taking Jimmy Basile for a "ride." Friends of Basile saw them in a car in Downey and opened fire on Ardizzone, wounding him. It's always been a question of whether Ardizzone had already killed Basile or if the bullets intended for Ardizzone got Basile. Three men with sawed off shotguns did the job, but Ardizzone crawled away only wounded, and later while in the hospital another attempt was made to get him, but was unsuccessful.
>
> Ardizzone [had] an argument with Jimmy Basile, "Little Jimmy," and his partner in the "bootleg" business, Domenico Di Ciolla, "Danto," a power in "Little Italy." These two men had invested $1,000 in a "still" to start making alcohol. Ardizzone tried to "muscle" in but was repulsed. Ardizzone is supposed to have told Di Ciolla that he [Ardizzone] had killed 30 men and he would make Di Ciolla the 31st, if the partners didn't "cut him in." Ardizzone [was] suspected of killing Basile, by taking him for "a ride," and then putting Di Ciolla "on the spot" because of fear that Di Ciolla would "squeal."
>
> Ardizzone was known as one of the wealthiest of local Italians, and was mixed up in the bootleg wars between local factions and Eastern gangsters who were attempting to "Muscle" into local territory . . . [He] was called "Iron Man" because he wanted to be king of the Sicilian gang; he

claimed to be the "strong man." . . . [He] was a suspect in the disappearance of Tony Buccola and Joe Porrazzo and others, as he was trying to gain control of the local scene, the "bootleg wars" having disrupted the status quo of the local Sicilian Mafia. He had made many enemies, and many there were who would like revenge.

In 1926, Ardizzone was listed as an executive officer of the "Italian Protective League."

Ardizzone left his residence at 6:30 A.M. on October 15, 1931, to go to Joe Cuccia's ranch near Ettiwanda, California; never arrived. At time was driving a 1930 Ford Coupe SR W7653 and carrying a 41 Caliber Colt Revolver #323. Victim was a cousin of Frank Borgia . . . and was going to pick up another cousin Nick Borgia, who had just come from Italy, at the ranch.

On December 3 1931, four suspects were arrested. "All were released; insufficient evidence; no prosecution."

Thus goes the last memory—on the police blotter, anyway—of a missing person last seen October 15th at 6:30 A.M. at his home, 10949 North Mount Gleason, Sunland, California. It was not for Joe Ardizzone that the sun shone brightly that day. What matters the year?

The repeal of Prohibition on December 5, 1933, came, in the words used to summarize the Los Angeles gangland killings report,

> as such a shock to the Los Angeles underworld that for half a dozen years, an uneasy peace prevailed. Many of the big shots of the Twenties went legitimate and bought into wineries, distilleries, and other comparatively respectable businesses. To their great surprise, they found going legit could be as profitable as bootlegging. Others just couldn't face respectability and went in for other violent pursuits which marked the underworld's reconversion period. It wasn't long, however, before the cagiest of the racket boys struck it rich with the biggest bonanza in the history of crime—organized gambling. It wasn't long before the guns came out, professional killers were again taking rubout orders from here to Brooklyn, and organized crime introduced sound business doctrine at gunpoint into what had been a penny ante racket.

Again, it was Jack Dragna who set up the gambling operation when Prohibition went down the drain and the Mafia bosses began to seek diversified sources of income. In the process, however, he had to deal with Benjamin Siegel, reputed West-Coast representative of the eastern gang, Murder, Inc., who arrived on the Los Angeles scene in 1937.

Bugsy Siegel was a graduate of the "Bug and Meyer" mob, which was formed when he joined forces on the Lower East Side of New York with Meyer Lansky to execute "contracts" —murders—for the New York and New Jersey gangs during Prohibition. Siegel and Lansky, who were friendly with all of the top eastern syndicate mobsters, traveled across the country doing their "jobs" and eventually sat as equal members on the board of directors with Lucky Luciano, Frank Costello, Vito Genovese, and others.

While at the zenith of his power in New York, where he lived in a suite of rooms at the Waldorf Astoria Towers two floors above Luciano, Siegel was "given" California during the division of territory undertaken by Costello and other gang bosses in 1931. His mission was to form a coalition of the top West-Coast mobs, which previously had no working arrangement between them, and to help Mafioso *capo* Jack Dragna establish, for the use of bookies, the Capone-controlled Trans-America wire service in California and, later, in Nevada.

Bugsy's reign in California, with Dragna as his chief lieutenant, blossomed as he played around with George Raft and many other of Hollywood's early stars, including Jean Harlow, who was having a Pygmalion-type romance with Longy Zwillman, one of Joe Adonis' mentors in New Jersey and political fixer of note. Siegel was handsome, liked sharp clothes, and found it necessary to have his initials monogrammed on everything he wore or carried, even down to his tailored silk shorts—which put Bugsy, in his own mind, in the echelon of real class.

There was, however, nothing foppish about his power or the syndicate weight he brought with him from the East. In September, 1937, the year in which he arrived on the West Coast, Siegel held a meeting of the top mobsters he was about to organize and laid down the rules of the game. Only one hood stood up to protest: Les Brunemann, a Redondo Beach gambler who had hopes himself of controlling gambling activities in southern California. Less than a month later, on October 25th, Brunemann, who was still recuperating from gunshot wounds inflicted during a previous attempt on his life, was shot to death at the Roost Café in Redondo Beach by two gunmen, who also wounded his nurse and others and killed a bystander.

There is some difference of opinion in law-enforcement circles about the relationship between Bugsy Siegel and

Jack Dragna. To talk in terms of elegance about two people
with few social graces may seem stupid, but Dragna
needed Siegel in the overall plan the mob had worked out
ultimately to get deeply involved in the free-gaming town of
Las Vegas. Dragna was a "plug-ugly" who needed a silk
purse, and "Glamour Boy" Siegel provided the come-on for
the Hollywood-Beverly Hills crowd who were the first to
rush to Las Vegas and be "busted out." On the other hand,
Siegel needed Dragna as his California contact man, especially at first. Perhaps it was a marriage of convenience in
which both partners thought himself the leader.

In any case, many authorities believe that Bugsy was the
first one to recognize the mother-lode potential of Las
Vegas. It was Dragna, however, who unintentionally moved
big-time gambling into Vegas when he attempted to "muscle"
into the bookmaking activities in Los Angeles of the then
Los Angeles police department vice-squad officer Guy McAfee
and his gambling partner, Tutor Scherer.

"Who the hell is Jack Dragna?" McAfee wanted to know.
He soon found out. Stick-up men raided his books, runners
were roughed up, and the Italians demanded in. McAfee
folded his gambling tent, took Tutor by the hand, and went
east to Las Vegas, where together the two put together the
Golden Nugget, two blocks from the railroad station at the
north end of Fremont Street.

Charlie King, auditor for the Golden Nugget, told the
author that McAfee was not driven out of Los Angeles by
Dragna. "McAfee saw a great opportunity in Vegas and
decided to get in on it," said King, formerly a group
chief for the IRS in southern California. But however it
happened, McAfee and Tutor soon were reaping such a
golden harvest that Jack and his pals began blinking their
eyes.

Perhaps engulfed by his unexpected good fortune, Tutor
Scherer, who affected flowing white locks, married a Las
Vegas girl and had a son by her. For some reason, he
named the child Lord Bacon Scherer, and everyone figured
that Tutor was a secret devotee of the art of poesy. Scherer,
however, was far less flamboyant than the first legitimate
"California" Italian Mafioso in Las Vegas, Antonio Cornero
Stralla. Tony, a sort of maverick member of the brotherhood
who was born in Italy at the turn of the century, had made
a million dollars as a bootlegger before he was thirty years
old. He therefore went to Las Vegas looking for money and

trouble, and the extravagance of his dreams made even Siegel's look like two-bit nightmares.

Tony started a place called the Green Meadows and staffed it with girls, slot machines, and waiters. It was actually the first "class" joint in Las Vegas, and he built it after he had served two years on bootlegging charges arising out of his arrest when his gambling ship, the S.S. "Lilly," was boarded by the Coast Guard off Long Beach, California. Four thousand cases of bootleg liquor were found on board. Bad luck seemed to follow Tony, in fact. The Green Meadows burned down one hot night. Cornero then sold out his remaining piece of interest in Las Vegas gaming, a chunk of the Apache Hotel casino at the corner of Second and Fremont Streets operated by the Silvagni family.

Tony Cornero died on July 31, 1955, while shooting craps at the Desert Inn in Las Vegas. Before he had his fatal heart attack, he had begun work on the Stardust Hotel, a glittering place that he thought might cater to the little people, and the plan called for hundreds of rooms for them. It remained for many other people to complete the Stardust, and today the glittering facade of the hotel is his tombstone. Everyone remembers.

Cornero's dream came true some years after Siegel started construction on the Flamingo Hotel, drawing on the Frank Costello-Joey Adonis bank in New York and New Orleans. It was evident that Siegel had the proper formula in spite of many troubles: he was the elected, true, and legal representative of the syndicate in Las Vegas, by way of California.

Since Siegel enjoyed such backing, Dragna was stuck with him. Left with what he could dig out of California, Dragna found that the boys had sent him, in the person of Siegel, someone he couldn't even understand. In fact, the golden age of gambling in Las Vegas left Dragna far behind, and in so doing, it unglued the eastern mobsters. The big men of the East suddenly realized that many people had moved into Los Angeles, along with the kind of industry they had feasted off for many years in New York City. Las Vegas was a lemon-cream pie. Even when dished out in small wedges to members of the Cosa Nostra families, there were suddenly more relatives coming to the tea party than anyone could imagine. But California was a different matter. In Los Angeles and the other cities were pickings for many jackals. Consequently, eyes turned back to California. There one could await the call to Las Vegas and yet still get immodestly—if not filthy—rich.

Some of the first to try and move into Los Angeles were garment racketeers from New York City's garment section. Supposedly, a fellow named Louis (Scarface) Lieberman led the assault, and the records indicate that John Ignatius Dioguardi, the hood believed by the FBI and others to be at the bottom of the conspiracy that resulted in the blinding of labor writer Victor Riesel, followed Scarface into California.

The suave Dioguardi, who escaped a conspiracy conviction in the case involving the acid-blinding of Riesel after prosecution witnesses refused to testify, was, in September, 1957, sentenced to two years on conviction of extorting money from an employer in return for labor peace. In pressing his case against Johnny Dio in the Riesel blinding, U.S. Attorney Paul S. Williams said that a twenty-one-year-old thug named Abraham Telvi had, for a fee of $500 from Dio, splashed sulphuric acid on Riesel's face. Incidentally, in the way of many mobsters, Telvi signed his own death warrant by going back for more money and by talking too much. After receiving another $500, according to Williams, Telvi was shot and killed on Dio's orders.

Scarface Louis Lieberman, alias "Louis Green" and "Louis Martin," has a criminal record that started in 1931, when he was sentenced to a prison term of fifteen years. The prison term lasted the legal minimum period, and it was followed by a long series of arrests and convictions. Finally, on February 20, 1951, Lieberman was sentenced to Sing Sing for a term of three to four years for attempted extortion. Shortly after the completion of that sentence, which marked his graduation from the lower to the higher echelons of the mob, Lieberman migrated to California, where his internship began. He started something called the Lucky Trucking Company.

Among the mass of testimony in a 1959 report of the Senate committee on rackets concerning organized crime in California is one most inviting morsel. The Lucky Trucking Company, it seems, was financed by the sale of two kilos of heroin, apparently provided by a prospective partner, Louis Fiano, who eventually wound up in a federal penitentiary after conviction on July 18, 1958, on a charge of selling the heroin. No conviction has deterred Lieberman, however. His interest in the garment trade has not altered. Bombings and acts of violence have been directed against legitimate garment firms such as the D'Amico Coat Manufacturing Company of Fullerton, Vogel and Weiss of San Gabriel, Jack Kramer of Los Angeles, and Mike Silvers, a dress manufacturer in Los Angeles.

At Mike Silvers' place on November 17, 1953, Gene Burg, a U.C.L.A. student and member of the varsity football squad, helped two thugs break up the machinery with crowbars. Burg eventually pleaded guilty and served a three-year sentence in a state penitentiary. He was "hooked" on narcotics, it was learned, and refused to answer questions put to him by the state rackets committee.

One of Burg's two accomplices in the wrecking of the plant was Rocco Guiliani, who although only twenty-four at the time already had a long criminal record, both in New England and California. A few weeks after the Silvers incident he was convicted of grand theft in San Francisco and sentenced to a ten-year penitentiary term. Later he was brought from the penitentiary to Los Angeles to plead guilty in the Silvers case and received a three-year sentence. The third accomplice has not been apprehended.

Guiliani, a smug, smirking hoodlum, was interviewed at San Quentin but would give no information beyond saying that he "got Burg into the deal—Burg does not know the persons" who hired them to do it. This could have been a grandstand play to impress officials with Guiliani's importance, for it had been established that Burg had called James Fratianno and his long-time associate, John Battaglia, alias "Charles Batts," many times before the Silvers incident.

The late Captain James Hamilton of the intelligence division of the Los Angeles police department called Guiliani a lieutenant or "right-hand bower" of Battaglia prior to the incident. Therefore, it would appear that the action was not an independent act of Burg and Guiliani but an ordered job by the Fratianno-Battaglia combination.

The East Coast-West Coast connection enabled the boys in Three Finger Brown's section of New York to try their luck in California, and the new association was cemented at a meeting between Louis Lieberman and Louis Tom Dragna, nephew of the now-deceased Jack Dragna, held in Room 101 at the Sands Hotel in Las Vegas on January 18, 1957. Louis Fiano and other soldiers were present, and the future of the Lucky Trucking Company was mapped. The target was to secure for the company the delivery work in the Los Angeles garment section.

It would reasonably be deduced that such an array of experienced talent from the East was not welcomed by the relatively untrained hoodlums of California, especially by the young ones who had been shouldered out of the lush Las Vegas melon patch by such elders as Emilio (Gambo) Georgetti, who moved from San Mateo County, California, to Las Vegas in 1947 when his friend, San Mateo County Sheriff James McGrath, was defeated after a twenty-six-year tour at the helm of the county law-enforcement office. Their jealousy is understandable. Georgetti bought a piece of Benny Binion's Westerner Club in Las Vegas and in six weeks controlled the whole operation.

The garment boys had high hopes of breaking into Las Vegas when Jack Dragna took over in Las Vegas after Georgetti died of cancer. But despite Dragna's ties to Johnny Dioguardi in New York through a mutual friend, Sam Berger, the boys in the garment rackets on both the East and West Coasts made very few dents in the behind-the-scenes Las Vegas economy. Legalized gambling seems to have fallen primarily into the hands of the Jewish element of the mob—the old-time gamblers from the Detroit, Cleveland, New York City, and Chicago areas who, in later years, were accused of sending a share of the skimmed profits back east to their Italian Mafiosi brothers-under-the-skin.

While it is true that the mob looked increasingly to other money-making opportunities after the repeal of Prohibition, the liquor industry remained a fruitful source of Mafia funds. In addition, the mob's involvement in liquor shows how the boys exercise, with the help of their friends in office, political power. The story of the California alcohol beverage control board, born in 1939, might well be a case in point, for it came into being after the syndicate's Prohibition dream had gone down the drain and many former bootleggers had become legitimate distributors.

The Alcohol Beverage Control Act gave the control board and the state board of equalization responsibility for the licensing of every cocktail lounge, liquor retail store, and restaurant or nightclub serving wine and the headier stuff. Appointed by the governor, the members of the board were given the authority to determine not only who should be licensed but also which licenses should be suspended or revoked.

Meanwhile, during the rather turbulent aftermath of the

state of California's attempt to get a grip on the liquor industry, a man named Artie Samish became top dog in the dark halls that house the lobbyists who plague the state capitol in Sacramento. Samish often called himself the "unelected governor of California" and represented himself as the man who controlled the state board of equalization while fronting for major breweries on the West Coast. Certainly, in his heyday Samish was immensely powerful in California.

The portly Samish had a number of clients for whom he lobbied, including the California State Brewers' Institute, which paid him $30,000 a year in salary and expenses and gave him control of a $153,000-a-year slush fund. In addition, merely for being "on call," Samish received $36,000 a year from Schenley Distillers in New York. Samish's brewery funds, which were supplied by the eleven-member Institute "for so-called political purposes" and "to establish good will" or protect the industry, totaled $953,943 over a six-year period—all in cash, a fact that later led to problems with the tax men. And lack of information was not confined to the IRS. In 1951 the Kefauver probers had trouble getting at the facts of the Samish operation. Finally, however, the big man admitted that the special funds given him by the Institute were spread around among "good, honest, outstanding officials that subscribed to the temperate use of beer, wine and spirits."

If that is the case, it is equally true that mobsters Mickey Cohen, Joe Adonis, and Phil Kastel were among the seamier people Samish called friends. Telephone company records indicate that Cohen, former non-Mafia operating member of the syndicate's bookmaking and strong-arm departments in California, called Samish frequently.

Samish was fond of saying that he was "the governor of the legislature and to hell with the governor of the state," and he made no bones about thinking he was the power behind the political throne in California. Perhaps he was— for a while. But in 1956 the federal government clipped Artie's wings when he was sentenced to three years in prison and fined $40,000 for failure to pay taxes on income of $90,000 between 1946 and 1951.

Samish served twenty-six months on McNeil Island and was released on March 17, 1958. A stockily built man weighing over three hundred pounds when he went to prison, Samish emerged much slimmer, insisting that the "stretch" was good for his health. Samish had always had a Lucius Beebe-like instinct for fine meals and a very real understanding of the value of good food even at the bargaining table. In his lobbying days he believed more in plying a man with succulent wild ducks flown a thousand miles to a well-placed table in a fine restaurant than in confounding him with mere words. An army travels on its stomach, and Samish was an army.

The year Artie Samish decided really to swing with the pendulum of the power he claimed was 1947, when he decided to promote a man named Fred N. Howser for the post of State's attorney general. Samish thought his boy Howser would be a shoo-in because his lobbying cabal would be able to trade on the good reputation of a man with a similar name: Fred Houser, who had been elected Lieutenant-Governor of California and was remembered for his great integrity.

The stratagem, however elementary, was successful. In January, 1948, Howser took office as attorney general under Governor Earl Warren, now Chief Justice of the U.S. Supreme Court. Fortunately, however, the results were not all bad for California. Because there were rumors of a certain lack of ethics in the conduct of Howser's campaign, Warren established a commission to study organized crime in the state, with the initial request that Howser investigate bookmaking organizations operating with the use of Western Union wires in Palm Springs, a sunbathed winter resort basking not only in the direct rays of a cruel orb but also in the reflected heat of the limestone slopes of 12,000-foot Mt. San Jacinto.

Howser sent to this palm-fringed clot of desert one Wiley H. (Buck) Caddel, who was to be aided by an investigator named John Riggs. Riggs did his job. But it was found that doctored, negative reports had been sent to the commission, and Riggs in defense said he had been ordered to do so by his chief, Caddel. Warren then ordered that his group send their own investigator to Palm Springs. The new findings resulted in a ruling by the state Public Utilities Commission that when a telegraph or telephone company was notified by law-enforcement units of illegal use of its wires, it must immediately cancel the leases involved.

The rule set up by the Warren group was first used by Pat Brown, California's governor from 1958 to 1966, who was then district attorney of San Francisco County. A publicity release announced that "bookie drops," the places where bets are made, had been shut off from service by the telegraph and telephone companies. Apparently District Attorney Brown had located a network of bookies in short order and really surprised the more conservative elements in San Francisco, who wondered why the bookies had been allowed to operate for so many years. The final scenes were played out later when Howser's Wiley Caddel was convicted in 1948 on charges of bribery and conspiracy to violate gambling laws. The case and the details eventually disappeared in a flurry of appeals, but the point had been made. The bookmakers would no longer have such an easy time.

What did not appear at first, however, was Samish's part in the affair. Those details appeared later. In July, 1956, Bernard P. Calhoun, executive secretary of the Southern California Spirits Foundation, was charged with others of conspiring to collect illegal political funds from liquor dealers. In reply Calhoun said that $5,000 was contributed in 1950 to Howser, who was defeated in the June primaries that year for reelection as attorney general, and an additional $5,500 was paid the same year to "various candidates." Several other politicians were named by Calhoun, who also recalled that a check for $5,000 was sent to the Los Angeles Jefferson-Jackson Day dinner in 1954. It seems almost certain that Samish was the channel for those moneys, and there is no doubt that Howser was Samish's man.

In fact, as is well known, the 1950 election resulted in Democrat Pat Brown's defeat of Edward C. Shattuck, who had defeated Howser in the Republican primary election. And of course Brown went on from attorney general to become governor, without the overbearing influence of Artie Samish but with the ever-present specter of corruption in the liquor and illegal-gambling industries plaguing him—which brings us back to Western Union.

It seems that California gamblers, and those to the east in Las Vegas, received a little better service from Western Union than did honest citizens. John Doe came second to the gambling nabobs who leased lines from Western Union. This was made clear when a small plane attempting an emergency landing near Bakersfield, a San Joaquin Valley town later to be included in the investigation by Howser, tore down the Western Union hot line to the bookies and other salient points and wiped out itself and its crew. Within half an hour all the leased wires of Western Union in use by bookies were in operation, but the U.S. Army Western Defense Command had to wait more than two hours before service was restored to one of its lines.

The story of liquor-bookmaking interests in California is interminable. But one more brief interjection into the California history is worthwhile since it brings the chain of corruption closer to a current analysis and the inevitable conclusion that things are getting worse instead of better.

In March, 1949, a grand jury in San Bernardino was convened to hear the testimony of a Mrs. Earl Wilson. Mrs. Wilson flatly accused State Senator Ralph E. Swing of soliciting an under-the-table cut for using influence to obtain a midget-auto racing concession for her and her husband at the San Bernardino County National Orange Show.

Swing was a director of the Orange Show, which turned into a real lemon for Mrs. Wilson when another 5 per cent kickback for the concession was demanded by W. C. Shay, then chief agent for the board of equalization, which Artie Samish boasted he controlled. Denials of any graft were quickly voiced by the accused. But the accusation remained.

The total cut demanded by Swing and Shay was 20 per cent, 15 per cent to Swing, 5 per cent to Shay, and negotiations for the graft came, according to Mrs. Wilson, through a Mr. Edward J. Seeman, known throughout southern California as the slot-machine king of San Bernardino.

Checking records for the grand jury, probers discovered through the California division of corporations that Seeman and Senator Swing were two of four partners in a liquor business known as Alfred Hart Distributing Company of San Bernardino and Riverside—an association confirmed by C. H. Palmer, Los Angeles attorney for the Alfred Hart Distillers, Inc. The third partner was Al Hart, who has since divorced himself from the liquor business and now is head of City National Bank of Beverly Hills. The fourth partner listed by Palmer was a Miss E. Mack, who helped organize the liquor outlets.

Apparently all the male partners were on good terms with Artie Samish. Profits of hundreds of thousands of dollars had resulted from an initial capital investment of $2,000, through know-how and know-who, the testimony revealed. But the grand jury apparently found nothing amiss and returned no indictment. The testimony, however, is on the record. And though it was shortly after these revelations that Attorney General Howser announced he would run for reelection, he was probably aware that both he and Samish might soon be found out. And so it came to pass. Even the bad guys finish last occasionally.

Today, rule of the burgeoning Mafia in southern California is vested in several men who have long histories of criminality. They are, in the order of their importance: Nick Licata, an elder whose advice is much sought after to settle quarrels among the Mafiosi in most of the western states; Louis Tom Dragna, a much younger man and nephew of Mafia West-Coast pioneer Jack Dragna; Frank Bompensiero, former strong-arm man for the San Diego organization; Anthony Pinelli, an elder facing possible deportation who often hosts Mafia chieftains at his home in Sierra Madre, near Los Angeles; John Roselli, former labor racketeer who also may be deported; and James Fratianno, "muscle" and "trigger man" who supposedly was the "hit" man involved in the last of the big Mafia murders in Los Angeles—the still unsolved 1951 murder of two toughs, Anthony Brancato and Anthony Patrick Trombino, killed in an auto on North Ogden Drive in Los Angeles following their holdup of a Flamingo Hotel cashier in Las Vegas.

Nick Licata, whom *Life* magazine has labeled "one of the top leaders of criminal groups in California," lives in Torrance, California, and his position as chief don is not exactly of his own doing. He became top man on January 10, 1968, on the death following a heart attack of the California boss, Frank DeSimone of Downey, California, who had taken over southern California after the 1957 death of Jack Dragna.

DeSimone, convicted of conspiracy to obstruct justice in connection with the 1957 Apalachin meeting, was sentenced to four years in jail, but the conviction, along with those of two dozen other Mafiosi at the meeting, was later reversed. DeSimone, in fact, was a strange man. Apparently he exemplified the terror that has played such a large part in the viability and success of the Mafia.

The hoodlums have always prided themselves on their respect, not only for their family boss, but also for the women of the family. There are, however, any number of exceptions to the rule. And one such occurred in 1956, when DeSimone, according to a police informant, raped the wife of Girolamo (Momo) Adamo in the presence of the shocked husband, who had served the Mafia longer and in more diverse capacities than DeSimone.

DeSimone's action, according to the informant, was under-taken to show Adamo who was boss. The outraged and dis-illusioned Adamo seriously wounded his wife shortly there-after, then shot and killed himself with a .32-caliber pistol in their home in San Diego. DeSimone had broken a pri-mary Mafia law relating to the inviolability of the women within the society, but there is no record that he was ever brought to task for it.

Incidentally, children find no protection, either, when they can be used to further the terror that permeates the Mafia structure. Thus, an eleven-year-old boy was killed by the mob to silence his brother, a government witness in a narcotics case in Kansas City. The witness, Carl Cara-mussa, was a member of a narcotics ring, and despite the terror of his brother's murder he later testified against hood-lums associated with the tough Kansas City Mafioso Joe (Scarface) DiGiovanni. After he had testified, Caramussa tried to elude his former associates and start a new life. But in June, 1945, while attending a wedding party, his head was blown off by a shotgun. City detective Louis Olivero also was shot and killed as he probed the ramifica-tions of the Kansas City dope ring.

DeSimone's underboss and family heir had been Simone Scozzari who also was at the Apalachin meeting, until Scozzari's deportation to Palermo, Sicily, in 1962. Scozzari reportedly still receives large sums of Mafia money from the United States, and he is apparently trying to arrange for his reentry to the country.

Meanwhile, Nick Licata not only has the last Mafia word from San Diego to Los Angeles and points north, but his domain also reaches Dallas, Texas, where he shares the rule with Joe Civello. In Dallas, Licata and Civello have replaced a hood known as Sam Maceo, the iron hand in the velvet glove who ruled the southern tier of states for many years with Carlos Marcello of New Orleans and Santo Trafficante, Jr., of Tampa, Florida.

Born in Camporeale, Italy, in 1897, Licata presumably took over the California business interests of another Mafioso, Tony Mirabile of San Diego, who was murdered in 1959 and left control of twenty-seven bars and taverns to Licata and the organization. Mirabile, who came from Alcoma, Sicily, typified the father-type don whose hands are kissed and to whom the Mafiosi genuflect when they come to pay court. He operated a club known as the Midnight Follies in Tijuana before establishing permanent residency in San Diego. He set "true" Mafia patterns of conduct: over the years he was arrested on various charges, including one of assault with intent to kill—a charge dropped when a prosecution witness took fright—and one of grand larceny—which was not pressed.

Mirabile's interest in bars served a good purpose. He sought control of the local bartenders' union in San Diego through the simple process of hiring men for his union shops, then firing them and hiring others to increase union membership. Finally, the weight of the votes was carried by employees and former employees who knew and feared the don.

The San Diego locale is most useful to syndicate members because of its proximity to the border, where illegal crossings, into and out of Mexico, can be implemented with relative ease.

For all his advantages, however, Licata seems to be more penurious than Mirabile, who maintained $50,000 in the San Diego Security Trust and Savings Bank for the use of friends, who merely had to say, "Tony sent me," in order to get a loan.

Licata's record includes a small fine for refilling liquor bottles. And he was also questioned about the murders of the two Tonys, Brancato and Trombino. Later, during a probe of California racketeering by a state assembly subcommittee, Licata denied any knowledge of the Mafia and was cited for contempt upon refusal to answer other questions, but charges were dismissed in November, 1959.

Despite his silence official police records indicate that Licata's interests have included gaming operations in Mexico with hoodlums Joe Sica, Pete Licavoli, and a couple of relatives of noted Mafioso Frank Garofolo; gold and silver smuggling from Mexico City; and a variety of legitimate businesses including fruit-juice vending machines and dairy-products companies. Licata has also invested in subdivision developments near Los Angeles, which reportedly involved James Fratianno and Jack Fox, a Chicago hoodlum. Mortuaries and such mundane businesses as delicatessens have also attracted his organizational zeal.

In 1949 Licata was associated, according to law authorities, with Louis Tom Dragna, the late Girolamo Adamo, and three others in the operation of the Prairie Club in Hawthorne, California, just outside Los Angeles, and he also controlled bookmakers in nearby Burbank with tough Mafia enforcers.

Licata's sense of decorum and adherence to the old-time principles of the Mafia have won him a revered position in the secret society—insofar as the criminal society may be said to understand reverence—but, at seventy-two, he is perhaps too old to last much longer in the highly competitive world of the Mafia.

Louis Tom Dragna of Covina, who was listed by the McClellan committee as a "criminal associate" of hoodlums, seems gradually to be grasping the reins of ultimate, supreme rule of the California Mafia. Forty-eight years old, Dragna is directing his racketeering efforts with the help of the clan, which sees a potential gold mine on the West Coast.

Dragna, according to McClellan committee records, is closely associated with Harold (Happy) Meltzer, a product of the New York City rackets who has been tracked on various occasions, during weird but apparently profitable wanderings, through New England, Canada, Mexico, Cuba, Hong Kong, Japan, Hawaii, and the Philippines, to mention but a few way-stops. Meltzer, who, like Meyer Lansky, the ex-husband of his wife Doris, is Jewish and therefore a non-Mafia syndicate power, has two federal narcotics convictions. The McClellan committee called him "an international drug trafficker closely allied with top Mafia racketeers," an associate of top labor organizers, especially those affiliated with Dragna—who owns or has interests in a number of dress-manufacturing concerns in Los Angeles—and "head of a large bookmaking and prostitution syndicate in California."

The McClellan report also listed Dragna and Meltzer as partners in the California Sportswear Company of Los Angeles. And it was no doubt Meltzer who, along with Jack Dragna, helped Louis Tom Dragna's climb up the ladder of Mafia hierarchy in the early 1950's when police records point to the latter's involvement in bookmaking and a wire-service operation—Trans-America—to provide betting information to bookmakers.

Louis Tom Dragna has had many brushes with the law, including arrests on charges of burglary and conspiracy to commit murder, and he was picked up for questioning in 1941 about a ring that counterfeited $10 bills. In 1959 he was indicted with four other men for extortion; they were allegedly attempting to shake down welterweight fighter Don Jordan. Subsequent conviction, however, was reversed as Dragna's lucky charm held.

Louis Tom is not without influence in Las Vegas, either, having in October, 1967, according to police intelligence files, placed an associate as a pit boss in the Thunderbird Hotel casino in Nevada's sanitized, legitimatized, and glamorized version of Sin City.

Frank (The Bump) Bompensiero of Pacific Beach in San Diego is sixty-three years old and has an impressive roster of past and present criminal playmates. A paragraph in the listing of Los Angeles gangland killings indicates that on February 28, 1938, Bompensiero and a fellow hood forced one Phil Galuzo

> into an automobile and drove him to the vicinity of 1674 E. 83rd Street where he was severely beaten, pushed out of the car and shot several times. Victim taken to Maywood Hospital and on March 7, 1938, died. Frank Bompensiero was arrested on June 21, 1941. However, as there was insufficient evidence to prosecute on kidnapping and murder charges, suspect released. At this time Bompensiero was wanted for three felony counts of robbery by San Diego police. Disposition unknown. Bompensiero is now located in San Diego operating a cafe bar and poses as a legitimate businessman. He is a partner of Tony Mirabile and an associate of Jack Dragna.

By 1955 Bompensiero was reported by informants to be the head of the Mafia in the San Diego area, "an organizer . . . feared by all who know him." But in April of that same year he was convicted on three counts of bribery and sentenced to serve five years in the state prison—a slip that may have prompted Mafia elder Anthony Pinelli three months later to call Bompensiero a "dumb hoodlum."

Paroled in May, 1960, The Bump, whose wife, Marie, is rumored to be Momo Adamo's widow, apparently remained on relatively good behavior until his release from parole in June, 1965. Since then police surveillance records indicate that he "has become increasingly active in the bar business in the San Diego area" and that he has been observed on numerous occasions in the company of such former hood buddies as James Fratianno, Louis Tom Dragna, Leo (Lips) Moceri, Joe Matranga, and Detroit's Papa John Priziola, Joe Matranga's father-in-law. The *El Centro Press* believes him to be the "head of the Mafia in San Diego." Bompensiero's messenger boy appears to have been Julio Petro of Van Nuys until Petro was shot and killed in the front seat of his car at Los Angeles international airport the night of January 12, 1969. The forty-six-year-old Cleveland-born safe burglar received a twenty-five year sentence in 1952 for a $71,000 bank robbery and was released on parole in 1966. Petro was considered by police intelligence to be the southern California contact man for eastern hoods, and his murder added more fuel to the Mafia fire developing in California.

Anthony (Tony) Pinelli was born in 1899 in Calascibetta, Sicily, and came to New York in 1913 as an immigrant. He has never applied for citizenship and years later was named by the U.S. Senate rackets committee as "a top figure in the Cosa Nostra and associate of Anthony Accardo, heir to Al Capone's Chicago crime empire." Madeline, Pinelli's wife of forty-three years, was born in the United States. They have five children and twenty-two grandchildren. Pinelli has a business record that, as outlined by his attorney, would raise no eyebrows whatsoever:

> He has lived in Sierra Madre since 1949, headed Century Distributors, a juke box business, from 1956 to 1962, and was in the grape business for 16 years as Northside Grape Distributing Co., which operated in the Chicago area. Pinelli sold out in 1963 and has since been in retirement.

In fact, Pinelli has kept out of the limelight for the most part, but in 1960 he was intimately linked by the Senate rackets committee with the gambling, prostitution, and other rackets around Gary, Indiana, as a sort of absentee landlord. Robert Kennedy, the committee's chief counsel, charged that Pinelli used profits from the rackets to acquire valuable real estate in southern California.

The Senate committee's chief investigator at the time was Pierre Salinger, later press secretary to President John F. Kennedy and an unsuccessful candidate for the U.S. Senate in California. According to Salinger, Pinelli used profits from gambling and other rackets activities in Gary and Chicago to acquire $443,000 in real estate and to set up his son in the motel business.

Salinger charged that Pinelli—in a kind of reverse version of the skimming operations recently charged to Las Vegas casinos—often exchanged thousands of dollars in cash for checks issued to him by Las Vegas gambling casinos, making it appear the money came from legal dice-game winnings. Salinger introduced as evidence a series of canceled checks from the Desert Inn, ranging from $5,000 to $15,000 and totaling $74,000 up to December 31, 1958. Obviously, this kind of procedure merely returned Pinelli's own money to him, but instead of being illegally gotten syndicate money, it became legitimate gambling winnings, which merely had to be included on his income-tax report. Moreover, the casino was able to show the same amount as a business loss, thereby lowering its reported income.

Eventually, however, tax men caught up with Pinelli. On June 17, 1960, he was fined $1,470 and placed on two years' probation for failing to file a California State tax return on earnings from 1955 to 1958.

Pinelli's home has often been used to entertain rackets figures. And when, in the past, Tony Accardo of Chicago went to Las Vegas via Los Angeles, it was Pinelli who met him at the Los Angeles airport. One of Pinelli's special pals is Gabriel Mannarino of New Kensington, Pennsylvania. A labor racketeer and gambler who was at the Apalachin meeting, Mannarino owns slot-machine, vending-machine, and jukebox privileges in New Kensington and was formerly part-owner of the casino at the Sans Souci Hotel in Havana.

In July, 1966, the government began making efforts to deport Pinelli by arresting him at his home on grounds of "moral turpitude." The charge was based on a record of two convictions in connection with defrauding the government of alcohol taxes (bootlegging) and of two income-tax convictions. He pleaded guilty to evading $4,315 in federal income taxes for the year 1959 and was fined $2,000 and put on probation for two years. Pinelli won a delay in the deportation case, however, by filing with the Immigration Service an application for permanent residence and was released on $10,000 bail.

John Roselli, sixty-three-year-old Italian-born Mafioso, is "righthand bower" of the fast-rising Louis Tom Dragna. In fact, he might have been top man in California but for a threatened deportation—which may yet come off—and a recent court case involving him in a card-cheating ring at the "members only" Friar's Club in Beverly Hills, where he was sponsored for membership in 1963 by Frank Sinatra and Dean Martin.

Roselli arrived in the United States under his real name,

Filippo Sacco, with his mother on September 16, 1911. They
were to join his father, who was then living in East Boston.
In 1921 Filippo Sacco was arrested by federal narcotics
agents in Boston. Released on bail, he left town, and it was
probably at that time that he changed his name to John
Roselli.

Through his early associations with the Longy Zwillman
mob in Brooklyn and Newark, and later with Al Capone,
Roselli became prominent in bootlegging and illicit liquor,
and by 1936 he had a percentage of Nationwide News, the
only bookmaking wire service at the time.

After Prohibition was repealed, Johnny Roselli went west
from Chicago and, as an associate of Jack Dragna, became
known as a labor racketeer and "muscle" for the movie
studios. These activities, however, led to his conviction in
1944 on charges of racketeering and conspiracy to interfere
with interstate trade in connection with the 1941 Bioff-
Browne movie extortion case. Sentenced to ten years in
prison, he was released on parole forty-three months later,
on August 13, 1947.

After his stint in prison, Roselli was given the green light
from the eastern boys to run Jack Dragna's wire service
while using his position as "public information and contact
man" with the Eagle-Lions movie studio as a front. Roselli
began spending a lot of time traveling between Los Angeles,
Palm Springs, and Las Vegas, associating extensively with
Mafia members. In 1951, in fact, he testified at the Kefauver
hearings that he knew Jack Dragna, Momo Adamo, Tony
Accardo, Frank Costello, Joe Sica, Bugsy Siegel, Joe Adonis,
Anthony (Little Augie Pisano) Carfano, Joe Massei, Meyer
Lansky, Louis (Little New York) Campagna, Frank Milano,
Joe Profaci, Sam Maceo, and Lucky Luciano, among others.

Although he answers to Meltzer and Dragna, Roselli is
reputed to be a *capo*-Mafioso and the Mafia's western
power and mouth-piece in Las Vegas. He lives in Beverly
Hills and is said to have among his closest associates a man
once employed by the Sands Hotel as "muscle man" to
collect bad debts from debtors living in the Los Angeles
area, a onetime public relations man for the New Frontier
Hotel who has arrests for bookmaking and was once in the
bail-bond business, and an attorney who has a lengthy and
rather successful record of defending pimps, gamblers, and
hoods.

On October 20, 1967, John Roselli was indicted by a federal grand jury on one count of failing to register and be fingerprinted as an alien and five counts of failing to notify the U.S. Immigration and Naturalization Service of his address for the previous five years. The indictment charged that Roselli is really Filippo Sacco, born in Esteria, Italy, in 1905, although Roselli has always maintained he was born in Chicago. It is interesting, too, that Roselli claims that he is a Los Angeles-Las Vegas real estate developer, and that he has nothing to do with former gangland associates.

Roselli took the Fifth Amendment in declining to answer the questions put to him by U.S. District Judge Warren Ferguson in Los Angeles. Mrs. Barbara Crosby, wife of singer Gary Crosby, was more talkative, however. She told the grand jury investigating Roselli's citizenship status that she knew of him as "a nice man. He has been like a father to me."

"Dear Old Dad" Roselli took a trip to Washington, D.C. in November, 1967, and upon his return was quoted as saying that the purpose of his visit was to make contact with certain influential persons who could help him win his case with the U.S. Immigration and Naturalization Service. He did not identify anyone by name but made the statement that he had many friends in Washington, "including two ex-FBI agents who are now practicing attorneys, an inspector of police who accompanied him to the airport on his return trip and several senators, one of whom he described as an elderly statesman with a great deal of experience." Roselli reportedly said he had been told by his friends not to worry, that everything would be taken care of.

Nevertheless, Roselli lost out to the government in his attempt to prove he was born in Chicago and, as a result, may face deportation plus a fine of $2,000 and eleven months in prison. Oddly enough, if he had admitted to being an unregistered alien and then registered within thirty days after his indictment, the government probably would not have had a case, according to an Immigration Service spokesman. But if he was so advised by his attorney, James Cantillon, Roselli apparently paid no heed, trusting his luck to his eastern contingent.

The Friar's Club incident arose out of a summer, 1967, Los Angeles federal grand jury probe into charges that electronic devices were being used by a ring of conspirators to cheat wealthy club members who had a penchant for gin rummy and used the exclusive show-business hangout for their card playing.

The roster of disgruntled losers who testified about their mysterious losses and their suspicions of peepholes in the ceiling included the following: Harry Karl, millionaire shoe-man and husband of actress Debbie Reynolds; singer Tony Martin; television's famed Sergeant Bilko, Phil Silvers; Zeppo Marx of the Marx Brothers; Ted Briskin, former camera manufacturer and onetime husband of Betty Hutton; Richard Corenson, real estate investment banker; and Hollywood actors' agent, Kurt Frings.

There were obviously no problems of poverty among the players. Subsequent testimony brought out evidence of indi-vidual losses for one day's play ranging from $5,000 to $50,000—with one individual's total loss over a period of ten months going as high as $220,000. One key witness who participated in operating the cheating apparatus—peep-holes in the ceiling that allowed the observer to signal a confederate player with an electronic shocker attached to the player's leg and concealed by his trousers—testified that the swindlers took in "about $400,000 in a period of less than a year."

The grand jury investigation led to the indictment in December, 1967, of five members of the club, including Johnny Roselli, who allegedly participated in a five-year con-spiracy of card cheating, primarily at the Friar's Club. All five faced charges of conspiracy to violate federal statutes, punishable by five years in prison and/or a $10,000 fine; interstate transportation to aid racketeering, five years and/or a $10,000 fine; and interstate transportation of funds ob-tained by fraud, ten years and/or $10,000. Three of them faced an additional tax-violation charge of failing to report what they won in the crooked games.

The four men indicted with Roselli were Maurice Fried-man, onetime part-owner of the New Frontier Hotel in Vegas whose application for a 2 per cent share in the casino ownership was subsequently turned down by the Nevada gaming commission; Manuel (Ricky) Jacobs of Beverly Hills, a professional gambler; Benjamin J. Teitel-baum, manufacturer of movie-studio equipment and owner of an art collection valued at $3 million in 1962; and a prominent Beverly Hills physician whose name was later dropped from the list. A sixth indictment named a non-member of the Friar's Club, T. Warner Richardson of Las Vegas.

Included among nonindicted "co-conspirators," whose testimony at the trial gave them immunity and helped put the others on the spot, were Beverly Hills restaurateur Al Mathes and ex-convict George Emerson Seach. Seach manned the peepholes and gave the necessary signals to the card players down below. Edwin N. Gebhard, the Miami electronics engineer who allegedly installed the cheating devices in the club, was convicted on fifteen counts of perjury during the grand jury hearings that led to the indictments.

The card-cheating trial, held in U.S. District Court in Los Angeles, makes rather interesting reading—if you don't have a sensitive stomach and want to see to what lengths some men will go to "make a buck." On December 2, 1968, four defendants in the conspiracy case—Roselli, Friedman, Jacobs, and Teitelbaum—were found guilty on 49 felony counts. Richardson was acquitted. A later date was set for sentencing and hearing arguments on motions for acquittal. Whatever the outcome for the others, it would appear that Filippo Sacco (or John Roselli, or "Don Giovanni," as he is known in the Mafia family) may have an opportunity—at government expense—to return once more to the old homestead in Esteria, Italy, in the not too distant future.

James Fratianno is last, but possibly not least, among the top Mafia powers in southern and central California. Based in Sacramento and named in California's 1959 Assembly committee report as the "West Coast executioner for the Mafia," Fratianno may even rank in syndicate hierarchy above his pal Frank Bompensiero. If so, however, it is probably only because of his ability to reflect and transmit the terror on which the Mafia feeds and profits. At any rate, his press notices are not improving, unless he takes pride in newsmen's frequent references to him as "The Weasel."

Captain James Hamilton credited Fratianno with at least sixteen gangland executions, including the 1951 mob execution of Tony Brancato and Tony Trombino. Hamilton, as well as others, was convinced that The Weasel was the calm killer who fired four shots each into the heads of the two Kansas City thugs who had the audacity to pull off the only successful armed robbery of a Strip casino in Las Vegas history.

Fratianno was arrested and questioned regarding the murders. But later he was reluctantly released by the police for lack of witnesses and evidence.

Fratianno was subsequently sentenced to five years in prison for extortion and, after his release, resumed associations with his former Mafiosi playmates. But he was not forgotten by at least one member of the fourth estate. On July 8, 1966, *El Centro Post Press*, a little newspaper in the lettuce belt at the foot of California's Imperial Valley, broke a story by reporter Mike James. James reported that James Fratianno, alleged gangland executioner, and his buddy, Frank Bompensiero, had started a trucking firm in Sacramento, the Fratianno Trucking Company. The story also noted that the firm had "managed to obtain a contract to haul fill for the last 15 miles of freeway into Las Vegas" and was in the process of zeroing in on El Centro, where Fratianno and Bompensiero had taken up residence in a local motel.

Both men, wrote reporter James, became interested in the Imperial Valley, the most fertile in California, after a meeting in 1965 at the Beverly Wilshire Hotel in Beverly Hills with Frank Liparoto, alias "Frank LaPorte." James pictured LaPorte as a mystery man who lives in a closely guarded home worth $100,000 in Flossmoor, Illinois, and is reported to control mob-ridden Calumet City, Illinois. Frank LaPorte was identified at the McClellan hearings as a "terrorist once in the employ of Tony Accardo" and listed by the U.S. Attorney General as one of the top ten Mafia figures in the United States.

The Fratianno-Bompensiero trucking gimmick was that the Fratianno firm leased tractor-trucks to drivers as subcontractors on an earth-removal project on two sections of Interstate 8, south of El Centro, totaling 12.3 miles. Reporter Mike James claimed that the unusual leasing deal included eventual purchase of the equipment and stipulated that the driver "agrees to lease tractor exclusively to the Fratianno Trucking Co., Inc. Driver and tractor to be under complete control of Fratianno Trucking Co., Inc. Buyer agrees to work whenever and wherever jobs are offered by Fratianno Trucking Co., Inc." But as it turned out, none of the drivers was ever able to make enough money to cover all the monthly payments, and upon default each forfeited to the Fratianno Trucking Company his equipment and any equity he thought he had built up in it.

The *El Centro Post Press* story named Leo Moceri, former member of the Detroit Purple Gang and a convicted blackmailer, as a big Mafia power in California and an associate of Fratianno who had accompanied The Weasel on several mysterious trips to Mexico. The *Post* article also states that Moceri was present at the 1957 Apalachin conference—although this has never been verified—and charged that the Mafia is seeking control of "all trucking operations from San Francisco south."

Reaction to the James story followed quickly. Fratianno and Bompensiero, among others, threatened to sue the *El Centro Post Press* unless a retraction was made. The *Los Angeles Times*, playing it safe, waited a month to pick up the story and then did so only after Fratianno, the Fratianno Trucking Company—owned in the name of Fratianno's wife, Jewell—Bompensiero, and several associates were charged with fraud by Imperial County District Attorney James E. Hamilton, who had been investigating the matter.

A month prior to the *Post*'s story, a Fratianno associate, forty-three-year-old Nick Diacogianis, who has a record of convictions for auto theft, burglary, forgery, and white slavery, had been convicted of assault. He had slugged a truck driver who had complained about the system. The Mafia implications in the trial of Diacogianis were on the record for all to see, but it was left to a relatively tiny paper, one of a small chain, to brazen it out with the boys.

The felony case, based on twenty-eight counts, against Fratianno almost went out the window when Imperial County Superior Judge Victor A. Gillespie dismissed charges because of "lack of evidence and jurisdiction." However, Hamilton and the state attorney general's office appealed, and on January 11, 1968, the Fourth District Court ruled that Fratianno, his wife, and the Fratianno Trucking Company must stand trial on sixteen counts of "conspiracy and aiding and abetting the making of false reports on payrolls" during the 1966 period of highway construction. The Merced trucking firm, which shared Fratianno's contractual responsibility and had been accused of overloading dump trucks—apparently one reason drivers could not meet their quotas of two loads per hour—paid a $25,000 fine after the initial charges had been dismissed.

A month after their convictions on June 28, 1968, of conspiracy to defraud the federal government through false statements, Fratianno was fined $10,000, and his wife and the Fratianno Trucking Company were ordered to pay fines of $4,016 each. Although the maximum penalty could have included five years in prison, U.S. District Judge Edward Schwartz handed down no prison sentence for Fratianno but placed him instead on three years' probation.

In the meantime, on July 8, California Democratic floor leader George N. Zenovich presented a bill to the state Senate that would, in the words of the *Los Angeles Times*, "remove dump truck operators from State Public Utilities Commission regulation and control while working on state public works projects such as highways." The bill is supported by the California Trucking Association and the Teamsters Union. Opponents say that, if enacted, the bill "could directly benefit Sacramento trucking contractor James Fratianno," who faces yet another trial, in Los Angeles County, on several charges stemming from public utilities' violations.

Fratianno's troubles continue. On July 19, 1968, James and Jewell Fratianno (and others) were sued for $645,000 in Sacramento Superior Court by the Mercantile National Bank of Chicago. It was charged that the defendants "fraudulently transferred and hid assets and used various subterfuges, including the corporate form, to veil individual dealings, to prevent [the bank] from securing proper payment." In addition to the $645,000, the bank is asking 7 per cent interest on the money and the return of seven truck-tractors.

All in all, 1968 may well have been in Mafia circles, "The Year of The Weasel." Then, in January, 1969 Fratianno was found guilty of conspiring to commit petty theft and to violate the state public utilities commission and labor codes. He was sentenced to spend one to three years in prison and his company was fined $85,000.

Not all things go well for the Mafia all the time. But in California the Mafiosi have spread their poison widely. The rootlets of the good things in California are slowly dying. And like barracuda circling a swarm of anchovies, the mob follows the public with a cradle-to-the-grave malevolence.

Consider the arteries of the airlines, crisscrossing the

country, dropping customers by the millions at every important city. The International Airport Hotel located on Century Boulevard, the gateway to the Los Angeles airport, would seem to be a product of the malevolence that is reaping a harvest for the boys.

Two of the individuals who appear to be involved in the hotel corporation out of which the Los Angeles hotel developed are Ed Levinson, whom we have already mentioned as a front man for syndicate vice king Joseph Stacher, and Benjamin Sigelbaum, partner of Levinson in numerous business deals, truly one of the mystery men in the Levinson entourage, and, as reported in the Caribbean chapter, an alleged "bagman" who carried skimmed money for the mob.

When the airport hotel corporation decided to go public in 1962, the names of Levinson and Sigelbaum probably would have made a stock offering somewhat unattractive for several reasons: Sigelbaum had declared bankruptcy many years ago in Florida; Levinson was associated with Las Vegas gambling interests; both men were deeply involved in financial transactions with the fast-stepping Bobby Baker, whose downfall was already in the making.

In any case, Levinson's name was not listed among the officers and directors of the company when the Los Angeles International Airport Hotel saw the light of day. Nevertheless, he is reported to have been able to keep an eye on his interests, and to make some pocket money on the side as well, through his control of the drugstore concession there.

The airport hotel system originally got under way in Miami in 1958 as Airway Hotel, Inc., and in 1959 it obtained a lease from the Dade County Port Authority and constructed a 264-room hotel atop the Miami International Airport terminal building.

The green light from the flight-control tower was apparently activated by Jimmy Hoffa, for the company received a $2-million loan from an "institutional lender," which was quickly assigned to the Teamsters' central states, southeast, and southwest areas pension fund. This, of course, occurred in the early days of Hoffa's power climb up the ladder of Teamster pension fund loans, well documented by Gene Blake and Jack Tobin in a series that appeared in the *Los Angeles Times* in the summer of 1962.

One of the next jumps on the flight schedule of the airport hotel boys, who in 1961 changed the company name to

International Airport Hotel System, Inc., was the leasing from the city of Birmingham, Alabama, property within the airport compound. From Birmingham, the same company made a fast move to Houston, Texas, which was to become one of the best-known airports in the country when the N.A.S.A. program was based there

Almost simultaneously, the hotel group made application to build airport hotels in Minneapolis, Minnesota, and at the Dulles International Airport in Chantilly, Virginia, which serves Washington, D.C. In February, 1961, it negotiated an agreement for a Dulles hotel, including a forty-year lease, between Airway Hotel of Washington, Inc., a wholly owned subsidiary, and the director of the Bureau of National Capital Airports, Federal Aviation Agency

The Justice Department is said to have expressed great shock upon learning that Airway Hotel group, several of whose members were under the probing eye of congressional committees, had managed to obtain the Dulles Airport hotel lease. The Minneapolis lease application had been short-circuited, at last reports, inasmuch as a preliminary check into the reputations of some of the corporation directors gave pause to the city officials who authorize such leases.

In Houston, however, the airport boys were successful. And while the Houston operation was under way, the company pushed westward in a frenzy of activity, and the hotel at Los Angeles airport began to take shape in 1962.

In its efforts to raise money to purchase the land for their Los Angeles hotel, the company decided to offer stock for public sale. Securities division officers in California and Illinois, however, had some serious reservations about sanctioning the stock offering. They questioned in particular the company's showing no profits for the previous three years of business. Other misgivings concerned the proposal that the stock price to the public be $10 to $12 per share while the directors, officers, and promoters of the company would continue to hold their 68.8 per cent of total shares acquired at anywhere from 2¢ to 34¢ per share. The applications for public sale in those states were eventually withdrawn, and the shares sold instead to a group of seventeen underwriters.

In the corporation's 1962 annual report, the following officers and directors were listed:

President	Saul S. Cohen
Executive Vice-President	George M. Simon
Vice-President	Bryant R. Burton
Secretary	Burton M. Cohen
Treasurer	Solomon Levine
Director	Bryant R. Burton
Director	Burton M. Cohen
Director	Saul S. Cohen
Director	Solomon Levine
Director	David Lubart
Director	Roy Perry
Director	Maxwell M. Rabb
Director	George M. Simon

Not listed, but reported to be behind the company along with Levinson and Sigelbaum, was Jack Cooper, a former vice-president of the Miami Marlin's Baseball Club and the West Flagler Kennel Dog Racing Club. Certainly, Cooper's wife, Gertrude, held considerable stock in the airport hotel firm.

A sort of Miami-Los Angeles-Washington, D.C. axis seemed to be in the making. A probe of the city officials involved might be very revealing, and it might also provide an embarrassing, or at least interesting, contrast to their more conservative counterparts in other cities where similar proposals by this company must have been turned down. After all, the officers and directors of the International Airport Hotel System, Inc., do have interesting backgrounds.

Bryant R. Burton is a Beverly Hills attorney who pops up periodically in many deals involving big money and the mob boys, like a pit boss watching out for the house dough. Burton, who was secretary of Ed Levinson's Fremont Hotel, Inc., in Las Vegas, is also an acknowledged representative of Levinson's boss, Doc Stacher. In fact, Burton made the association official for any disbelievers when he testified in February, 1962, before a federal grand jury investigating underworld gambling figures that he managed properties for Stacher, including the Moulin Rouge Theater-Restaurant in Los Angeles.

Solomon Levine figured in the 1959 Senate committee hearings on improper activities in the labor or management field. As a vice-president of the Manhattan News Company in New York, wholesale distributor of magazines, he took the Fifth Amendment when asked whether he had made payoffs to a union official representing fifty union drivers employed by Manhattan.

In 1959 Levine also held stock in the Manhattan News Company in trust for the children of his brother-in-law, Henry Garfinkle, president of the American News Company. And Garfinkel's Union News Company, a division of American News, has an exclusive lease for the restaurant and cocktail lounge concession in the Miami Airport Hotel.

Maxwell M. Rabb is a New York City attorney. He served as secretary to President Eisenhower's cabinet from 1953 to 1958 and as special assistant to the controversial Washington Svengali, Sherman Adams, Ike's political mentor for many years. In 1956 Rabb was accused of leaking confidential information about the cabinet to a writer, much to the chagrin of Senate investigators who had previously been unable to get the same information. Rabb declined an invitation to come in and tell the probers about the situation.

In 1962 Rabb was listed as a director in the Gotham Bank, the American News Company, Seven Arts, Ltd.—of which we have previously spoken—and other corporate entities. An interesting addition to his circle of business influence and affluence was his appointment as a director of the Struthers Wells Corporation, a company licensed in Maryland. On April 26, 1966, George E. Reedy, onetime press secretary to President Lyndon B. Johnson who in July, 1965, had been moved for reasons of health over to the post of Special Assistant to the President, announced that he would be leaving to take a job as an executive in private industry, though the name of the specific firm was not mentioned. *Standard and Poor's Annual,* which lists industrial corporations throughout the country, had in its 1966 edition a listing of the Struthers Wells Corporation officers and directors showing George Reedy as a director.

Struthers Wells and a subsidiary, Titusville Iron Works of Titusville, Pennsylvania, manufactures of welded carbon and alloy products and of high-pressure vessels, have been on the receiving end of numerous U.S. government contracts for equipment to be used in its space and underwater research programs.

Max Rabb, born in Boston in 1910, took a law degree at Harvard in 1935. He is now a partner in the firm of Stroock, Stroock, and Levan at 61 Broadway, New York City. He lives at 145 Central Park West, one of the few places in Manhattan where you can see trees from your front window over the tops of luxury cars, cabs, and ambulances transporting the strained heart and bleeding ulcer cases in that odd suburbia of New York's financial district.

Two years after acquiring his law degree, Rabb became administrative assistant to Henry Cabot Lodge and served in varying capacities to that wandering minstrel of several administrations. He served with Lodge from 1937 to 1952, then jumped to the White House in 1953, where he became right-hand man to President Eisenhower until 1958.

Finally, in 1965, Rabb became Chairman of the Board of Directors and the Executive Committee of the International Airport Hotel System.

George M. Simon is the accountant for Levinson's buddy, Sigelbaum, and for the International Airport Hotel System, Inc. It was he who testified before a congressional committee about Bobby Baker and a junket Baker took with Jack Cooper, Levinson, and Sigelbaum to the Dominican Republic. Together, Simon and Cooper invested $91,889.30 in Baker's controversial Serv-U Corporation at the request of Eddie Levinson, who invested some $64,000 in the company himself.

As of December 31, 1965, the International Airport Hotel System listed the following officers and directors, indicating a slight shuffle in the three-year interim, but the mixture was much as before:

President and Treasurer	Solomon Levine
Vice-President and Secretary	Burton M. Cohen
Vice-President and Director	Bryant R. Burton
Director	David Lubart
Director	William Ash
Director	Jerome Molasky
Director	George M. Simon
Director	Maxwell M. Rabb
Director	William Levine
Director	William Werfel

William Levine figured in the McClellan rackets committee testimony. There it was revealed that American News Company president Henry Garfinkle set Levine up in the trucking business in Queens County to force a competitor out of business—almost in the fashion of Detroit's Joe Barbara, Jr. Of course, Levine was in good company in Queens. There Jimmy Hoffa ran things, with the cooperation of his enforcer, Tony Corallo, a noted mobster who helped get a New York State Supreme Court justice into trouble as well as the assistant U.S. attorney in Brooklyn and later a commissioner in Mayor Lindsay's administration.

Jack Cooper was revealed on the company's stock prospectus as a promoter, having been paid $75,000 for his services in connection with securing the lease and construction financing, through the $2-million Teamster loan, for the Miami airport hotel. His name would hardly be ideal on the roster of officers and directors, however, inasmuch as in 1962 he was convicted of income-tax evasion totaling $259,-000 for the years 1953–1954, sentenced to three months in prison (plus nine months' probation), and fined $15,000. He was thus, in the lingua-Vegas, "eighty-sixed" out of corporate respectability.

Cooper, who is in his fifties, is a short man, a product of the Oak Street section of New Haven, Connecticut. He can often be seen visiting the come-as-you-are places in Las Vegas in black mohair slacks and matching shirts and slippers with red linings.

During his tax-evasion trial in federal court in Miami, Cooper admitted that he and Rafael Trujillo, Jr., son of the dictator, garnered $744,000 from the Dominican Republic in an airplane deal involving the purchase of U.S. fighter planes delivered to Sweden and resold to Papa Trujillo's country. When Cooper was later summoned to the Bobby Baker hearings, however, he lost his tongue, took the Fifth Amendment, and admitted only to having been born in New York City.

Cooper is the happy tour conductor for the airport hotel group, arranging charter flights that scoop up gambling men from all over the country and drop them down on the rather hard sod of Las Vegas, where the routine of booze, twenty-four-hour-a-day companions, and the eternal sound of clicking roulette wheels somewhat softens their landing. Silver dollars in Vegas are passé; plastic chips and souvenir coins enthrall at the moment. But the gold is still there—for the bosses, who find its keening command in paper money, a rare gift of hearing, indeed.

These then are the sort of men who run International

Hotels. Why? Why do they involve themselves in such affairs? Perhaps we can find an answer by looking at Ed Levinson, the man behind numerous operations across the country, some yet to be detailed. Very possibly Levinson is the heir apparent to Doc Stacher and the dynasty, now spread across the United States, that Doc took over from Bugsy Siegel and Jack Dragna. What makes him tick? Certainly not a vibrating spring in a commanding hoodlum clock.

Are the men of the Mafia in the thumbscrews of a power that overwhelms them, that promises only two variations: a life of happiness if they are capable of achieving it under the conditions that prevail, or a life that becomes nothing the moment they slip out of the vortex of mob influence that pushes them on? Are they truly the other side of the coin that matches the sucker prototyped by Phineas T. Barnum when he said, "There's one born every minute!"?

Who are the suckers? The suckers themselves, or the men born to bleed the suckers white? Perhaps the answer lies in a simple concept: the mob boys have reduced their lives to such common concepts of eating, drinking, and sleeping that they go along with each day, doing the accepted job but really serving as slaves to bigger people about whom they know nothing, like so many ears of corn in a willing windrow ready to be chopped down at the first sign of insurrection or ripeness.

Who really bosses the crime syndicate?

Maybe Eddie Levinson is a product of his time. Not yet ready to die, he lives each day hoping that it will bring one more good thing—a step up on the ladder of the next day. But believe it, *he* is getting *his* orders, too!

Obviously, the presence of large numbers of men of Levinson's ilk in California and elsewhere has a considerable effect on ordinary citizens. In California, in fact, the citizen can find anything he wants in the long state that encompasses and supports the flora and fauna of every known level of geologic time—and many things he may not want. But there are signs that an enormous lethargy is setting in, while very few of the public officials who have the power to act seem to care that the state is being undermined from within.

Take the case of ex-Governor Edmund G. Brown, for example. Of the Samish-Howser-Brown trio, only Brown remains on the public scene. And Brown has very carefully avoided trouble ever since 1947, when a body was found in the trunk of a new convertible.

The body in the trunk was that of Nick De John, who had been killed in the basement of the Alouette Restaurant in San Francisco. There was a hemp rope around his neck, and the car was parked in a quiet corner of the Marina, a sacrosanct section of town noted for its tidy lawns and very fine view of the steel harp that is the Golden Gate Bridge.

The auto Nick's body was found in could be considered a hearse, for he wasn't placed there by choice. His killers had apparently planned to take the corpse across the bridge and leave it on a lonely mountain back-road, where play miniature iguanas and the small blue butterflies such as *Brephidium Exilis*, the smallest of them all, which floats on gossamer wings over the driest of salt flats and loves it when the tide goes out.

As the murderers neared the approach to the bridge, however, a motorcycle policeman warned them against speeding. Taking fright, they left the body in the car at the Marina, and as the tide went out for Nick, they found no butterfly hovering over him. Instead, a penny—that's all it was worth to his killers—had been stuffed into his rectum: a Mafia mark of derision for a double crosser.

Nick De John was a member of the Chicago mob who tried to become a big shot too fast. After being threatened on several occasions by some of the mob's tough guys, he suddenly took off for the San Francisco area. He left in such a hurry that his wife had to remain in Chicago to make arrangements for packing their household goods while De John tried to find a place for them to live in California.

One theory behind his hurried exit was that he had squandered mob money on extracurricular gambling and betting on the races—things that had no relation to mob economy. But in any case, he hardly had time to settle down and contact a few of his Mafia friends before it was all over for him. The San Francisco police, answering a citizen's request to remove a parked car, opened the trunk and discovered De John's mutilated body.

Two dedicated inspectors of the San Francisco police department, Frank Ahern and Thomas Cahill, began an investigation of the murder and soon had narrowed a long list of suspects down to a very important few. Leading the list was Leonard Calamia, alias "Benny Leonard," who had served two terms for narcotics peddling. Calamia admitted to having been with De John and, in fact, proved to be the last known person to have seen De John alive.

Calamia denied any knowledge of the crime and insisted he was merely an employee of the Sunland Oil and Cheese Company of San Francisco. The car he drove was registered to Frank Scappatura of the oil and cheese company. Scappatura was a native of Italy and had served two years in federal prison for counterfeiting. Two other Italian-born men were also partners in the olive oil business: John Franzone of Tunisia and Italy and Michael Abati, a part-time bartender.

At this point Ahern and Cahill had a lot of evidence tying their suspects to Nick's death, but not enough to make an airtight case against them. Then, from out of nowhere, came a big break. A local woman who was an admitted abortionist complained to the two police officers that she was being shaken down by a former bootlegger in the Bay area named Gus Oliva. In return for protection, she calmly announced to the amazed policemen that she had overheard the plot to kill Nick De John.

The woman, Anita Venza Rocchia, said she was willing to testify in court that she had been in a basement card room in the Italian North Beach section of San Francisco, and that the men playing cards—Barbuta—were Scappatura, Abati, Tony Lima, a food broker from Lodi, California, and Sebastiano Nani, an international dope smuggler born in Sicily. Anita said she had heard the complete details of the plan to murder De John; when the news of her evidence sifted down to the underworld, all four of the men mentioned disappeared.

Scappatura hid out in Seattle until the case cooled; Lima, who was convicted in 1956 on charges of grand theft and embezzlement, took off for Johnstown, Pennsylvania, but is once again very active in the produce business in California's Napa Valley. Calamia was picked up in Albuquerque, New Mexico; Nani was arrested in New York; and Abati was arrested when he tried to return to San Francisco.

The San Francisco grand jury voted indictments for murder against the men, and on February 1, 1949, the trial of Calamia, Nani, and Abati began. The case went through the usual court procedures, with testimony from, among others, Anita Venza Rocchia, and finally went to the jury on March 8. Then, when the jury was still undecided after more than thirty hours' deliberation, District Attorney Brown asked that the indictments be dismissed without prejudice. Brown told Cahill and Ahern that there were implications of perjury and that it would be better to drop the case at this stage rather than take the chance of losing it and closing it forever. Brown said he would aid them in the case and resolved also to reopen it as soon as they were ready. That was twenty-two years ago, and it has never been mentioned since.

In the interim, Pat Brown became governor of California and made his prosecuting attorney in the case, Tom Lynch, state's attorney general. Both have moved up many places, like the Mad Hatter, to get to cleaner cups. Frank Ahern and Tom Cahill did likewise. Ahern was jumped over dozens of other officers with seniority into the top spot as chief of police, and Cahill moved nearly as far to become his assistant.

The point, of course, is that everything went down the drain. But perhaps another point is that when Frank Ahern died, Cahill inherited the mantle of a very important job along with the responsibility for the safety of many people.

When legal action on the De John murder was pulled out of court, Ahern and Cahill said to Pat Brown: "We'll keep working on the case. Nobody is going to get away with murder on our beat"—an ironic statement, in view of later events. But those very events make clear the reasons behind Cahill's failure to return the phone calls the author made in 1966 to inquire about progress in the case.

Somebody got away with murder, and Pat Brown never mentioned it again. Perhaps he felt no different from one witness who became fearful and dropped out somewhere along the line. No names were ever put into the hands of newspapermen, but Ahern dropped a few hints about the frightened man:

> He was afraid of them. They are Sicilians. He is a Sicilian. They stated they wouldn't only get his wife. They would get his family. He got down on his knees; he said he would do anything but tell. He doesn't mind facing anybody, but he would be walking down the street someday and somebody would step out of a dark doorway—and they would all get it.

Of course, it did all happen a long time ago, but even twenty-two years can't erase the memory of a job unfinished.

As governor of California, Pat Brown had an annual salary of a mere $44,100, knew a lot of people, and seemed bitten by the celebrity bug. His political and moral acumen may be challenged on many fronts.

For instance, the *Los Angeles Times* of April 11, 1966, turned out a very fine story about the governor's spending a quiet Easter with his family at a desert estate near Palm Springs, "despite demands that he meet striking grape workers at the end of their 300-mile march to the state capitol in Sacramento."

The grape workers staged a protest rally in downtown Palm Springs—to be accommodating, no doubt—but failed to budge the governor from his previously announced "family" commitments. Imagine their surprise, then, when it developed that Governor Brown and his wife, their four children, and eight grandchildren had spent most of that Easter Sunday at the home of singer Frank Sinatra, six miles southeast of Palm Springs.

Frank Sinatra lost his gambling license at Lake Tahoe and relinquished his points in the Sands Hotel in Las Vegas because he was overfriendly with Sam Giancana, alias "Sam Mooney," alias "Sam Flood," etc. But the governor apparently dismissed the implications of the association, which had been monitored through every step of the way by the FBI, as a bad dream, the nightmare of the Nevada gaming control board.

To grab the throne once occupied by Al Capone, Giancana, who became boss of the Mafia's Chicago fraternity and one of a dozen members of the grand council that controls syndicated crime in the United States, had to work his way through the ranks of pimps, burglars, bootleggers, dope pushers, and varied assassins. This was and is Sinatra's buddy, along with numerous other known mobsters, and Sinatra apparently had Governor Brown's approval—or was it vice versa?

Behind most organized crime is not only the thinking, the buying of votes, and the allegiance of learned lawyers with dubious morals, but also the lack of any real comprehension of the problem on the part of the public—the people who call the shots on their own future, depending on how they think in the voting booth. California voters seem not to be aware of the soaring crime rate in their state. Thus, when in 1965 a fighting assemblyman, George Deukmegian (R., Long

Beach), introduced bills to put into effect the demands of a
Republican crime task force to increase the minimum penalties for armed bodily-injury crimes, the governor used his
veto. Likewise, Brown's successor, Governor Reagan, has
yet to come to grips with the problem of organized crime,
though current legislative efforts may soon put him on the
record.

Perhaps Governor Brown's indifference to organized crime
and influence peddling and their repressive effects on his
constituents' lives can best be illustrated by an incident
having to do with the alcoholic beverage control board.

As has been mentioned previously, the board was created
to probe the characters and records of applicants for liquor
licenses, determine the true ownership of prospective licensed
premises, and see that license fees are collected. Late in 1965,
however, while presumably performing the above duties,
two investigators from the A.B.C. were lavishly wined and
dined by certain notorious members of the Matranga family
of San Diego, California, who are part of the family of
Mafioso John Priziola of Detroit.

The Matrangas were having difficulty in obtaining a liquor
license for their La Mesa Bowl, the bowling alley in which
Teamster President Jimmy Hoffa sank $1,250,000 of his
union members' pension funds. The original license had
been revoked on the grounds it was obtained by subterfuge:
a dummy corporation had been set up. Probably the Matrangas thought a party was a good way to win friends and
influence people. Unfortunately, for the Matrangas, publicity
given to the dinner for the A.B.C. men resulted in the investigators' resignations. Governor Brown hastily assured the
press that he thought there was nothing wrong with the
situation and that he felt the men had merely made a
mistake. In getting publicity?

The result of the whole affair shows that justice is occasionally allowed to rear its head. On April 8, 1966, the
financially troubled owners of the Bowl lost a court fight
for their liquor license. A writ was sought by Frank (Big
Frank) M. Matranga, president, Leo M. Matranga, vice-
president, and Joseph Matranga, secretary-treasurer of the
bowling alley, but without success.

Troubles mounted. The Teamster loan was in default—as
are, at present, a number of similar loans throughout the
country. But in July, 1967, a company headed by prominent

San Diego land developer Irving J. Kahn used a $1.2 million loan from the Teamster pension fund to bail out the bankrupt bowling alley, which was already in debt to the union for $1.1 million.

Kahn's group could afford to be generous, for seven months later the outfit received a $35-million loan from the pension fund, the largest in the union's history. The loan did not list as a trustee Teamster President James Hoffa, who has been convicted of conspiracy to divert $1.7 million from the union's pension fund. But the Teamsters have invested a total of $55 million in Kahn enterprises.

Meanwhile, Frank Matranga has succeeded in getting himself in trouble by violating the probation order he had acquired as a result of a 1965 fraud conviction. On February 15, 1968, he drew a sentence of from one to ten years in Superior Court, San Bernardino, California, after adding insult to the fraud injury by getting indicted in nearby Orange County late in 1967 on charges of grand theft, conspiracy, and obstruction of justice.

Indicted with Matranga was Robert B. Salerno, former City of Commerce councilman. They were charged with taking $3,500 from a Newport Beach man on a promise they could arrange for his acquittal in a case involving the use of an electronic device to circumvent telephone toll charges. Upon hearing the case, Superior Judge George Dell said: "I think Mr. Matranga and Mr. Salerno perpetuated a 'con' job on a 'con' man." Judge Dell found Matranga guilty as charged in June, 1968, and scheduled Salerno's trial for later in the year.

Big Frank Matranga is another example of a hood who stooped for pennies in the shadow of millions—in terms of syndicate operations—and got himself caught. And his confreres in the secret society have surely written him off by now as having fallen from grace.

It is one thing for a mobster to overreach himself. It is, however, quite another for him to be apprehended by law-enforcement agencies before he overreaches himself. And in California the latter seldom happens.

The lack of consideration for the citizens' protection on the part of public officials found in so many offices in the state is not paralleled by a complete indifference to all things, however. The officials give great care to some things. Recently, for example, a committee of the Los Angeles city council recommended salary increases ranging from 47 to 85 per cent for 18 city officials, including: mayor, from $35,000 to $52,592; city attorney, from $32,000 to $47,333; city controller, from $25,000 to $36,814; and city councilman, from $17,000 to $31,555.

Los Angeles should not be singled out over much, however. In San Francisco, where the elite meet to eat, police intelligence has determined that packages of cash are finding their way from syndicate strongboxes right into well-manicured fingers at City Hall itself—as usual via a circuitous route. The couriers are said to be a long-time Cleveland hood now based in Los Angeles and an associate who is a convicted safe cracker. The two have been observed carrying the money more than once, and some careful police work could put on the record the name of the ultimate beneficiary and the reason behind the transfer of funds.

The outlook is not entirely bleak, fortunately. Announcements made recently by California Attorney General Thomas C. Lynch and his chief deputy, Charles O'Brien, seem to indicate an increasing concern over organized crime, their prime targets being the boys who are investing racket money in legitimate businesses through the state. According to O'Brien:

> These fellows are not making their money in California. They make it from rackets in New York and New Jersey and from gambling in Nevada and other places. Then they "wash" the money or invest it in legitimate businesses here. That way they can put the profits on their income tax reports.

Although the businesses may be legitimate, O'Brien explains, the methods of operation used by the boys seldom are:

> For example, recently crime operators have invested in the vending-machine business. Instead of asking a bar owner or a cafe owner if he wants a vending machine in his store, they tell the proprietor he will be roughed up if he doesn't install a machine.

In June, 1967, announcing the formation of a special unit within his Department of Justice to study organized crime, Attorney General Lynch said: "Our state has become the favorite investment area of the veiled finance committee of organized crime." And he went on to point out the following major danger areas of such activity: hidden interests on state licenses; the intrusion of criminal cartelists into our sensitive world of finance; the layoff of huge sports bets into the Los Angeles area; loan sharking and the reported moves of remnants of the old Mickey Cohen mob to control it, together with some new tough boys; and the conspiracy of silence that so often meets enforcement agencies, grand juries, and courts when investigations are undertaken.

It will be interesting to see what inroads are made into these "major danger areas" by law-enforcement agencies when the flames fanned by such enthusiastic announcements have died away. In July, 1968, just one year after the new crime fighting unit went into operation, Charles O'Brien, its overall chief, told the author that slow progress was being made and that a larger staff and budget were needed, and that there was much to be done.

In the meantime, the land of milk and honey curdles day by day, racked by scandals that arise through abuse of responsibility the perpetrators should never have been given —from some of the corrupt city assessors in the north (three have been convicted to date for taking bribes on behalf of clients of tax consultants) to the mob boys and their bankers who prefer the crowded cities in the South while on the waiting line for Las Vegas, killing time and doling out dollars to developers who chop down the land into squat, house-crowded obelisks with chipped-in terraces going up to nowhere.

Meanwhile, too, another matter is becoming even more important and occupying Mafia interest to an even greater degree: drugs.

One cannot annihilate the image and importance of a big city or of the state in which it exists by bewailing the moral degradation of a segment of its youth. It is a fact, however, that over the past few years the people who have swept across the United States into California—only, like jewels in a strongbox, to be trapped against the backstop of the Pacific Ocean—have tolerated thus far the growth of a new morality. And by this concept, born of a new revolutionary spirit in youth and moving in a direction that is as baffling as it is unprecedented and dangerous, is the reputation of the state imperiled. How so? Because the Mafia is able to use the art workings of this morality to penetrate, in yet another way, the armor of the people inhabiting our largest state.

The Mafia in California has had its successes in the past. But until recently free and easy gambling in Nevada has served as a safety valve against Mafiosi greed. While in the past many hoodlums have merely waited on the Coast for an opening in the gambling structure of Nevada, recent events in the big coastal cities may have changed the direction of their interest. Youngsters queuing up in ever-lengthening lines for a dip into the fast-rising river of dope flooding across our southwest borders provide a tempting prospect.

The police in California like to say that there is no true Mafia organization operating on the West Coast. In Los Angeles, for instance, the belief that a known lawbreaker, Mafia member or not, will call the police before he visits the city to see whether he would be stepping on any toes is enough for them. Perhaps their faith is justified. But it is hard to say what is gained by such social amenities; possibly the hood is only out to protect himself from enemies.

In 1967, in a speech given in Los Angeles, U.S. Deputy Attorney General Warren M. Christopher made a statement to the effect that organized crime had not gained a foothold in California "because of the quality, honesty, and integrity" of law-enforcement agencies in the area, and he added that those organized crime figures who do live on the West Coast do not have major ties into the secret organization.

While this writer has no wish to question the quality ascribed to California's law-enforcement agencies—particularly in Los Angeles, where the late Police Chief William Parker built up a superb department—it would seem that the host of names, associations, and activities outlined in this chapter refute the accuracy of the remainder of Christopher's statement. But perhaps Christopher was the victim of ignorance.

A lack of cooperation between police and intelligence units throughout the country, at the local, state, and federal levels, is certainly one of the reasons for the scattered and incomplete knowledge about organized crime in California. And while ignorance may be bliss, the facts indicate that the bliss could be short-lived: the criminal syndicate on the West Coast is perilously fluid and quite capable of becoming one of the largest organisms in the whole structure of North American crime.

If the revolutionary spirit in California is typified by its bearded and beaded hippies and their miniskirted molls, as the news media imply, then the populace is being offered a dangerous and comic approach to what must be considered in a more serious vein in areas of the country such as Chicago, Cleveland, and Detroit, where blood rather than just youthful spirit is beginning to bubble to the surface. The widespread and growing use of drugs is a door to unlimited ecstacy—for the Mafia. And they are quickly learning to make the most of it.

If one assumes that no gangster organization now operates in Los Angeles, San Diego, and other southern California cities despite the some-fifty documented gangland killings in Los Angeles alone in the first half of the century—not to mention other syndicate activities—how can one dismiss with total equanimity the fact that while in 1964 only two tons of marijuana were seized by customs officials at the Mexican border, in the year ending April, 1968, twenty-four tons were seized? And, it must be remembered, these quantities must represent a very small percentage of what actually got through.

There are as many methods and kinds of couriers—"mules" —used in bringing the stuff into California as there are varieties of youthful users. Often the mules are solicited below the border to drive a car containing hidden marijuana into California, park the car at a designated spot, and leave it. They never meet the pickup man, who has been forewarned that the shipment is on its way, and are therefore unable to identify him for California lawmen. One U.C.L.A. student used this system, with the help of some good contacts below the border, to bring in one hundred kilos of marijuana a week for a number of months (for profitable and widespread distribution) before he was finally caught and sent to prison.

Another young man, newly arrived in San Francisco's Haight-Ashbury hippie haven and anxious to help his roommates pay the rent on their pad, passed around the hat for contributions to buy some marijuana in order to sell it at a profit for rent money—saving just enough to keep everyone hazily happy for a time. He drove down to Tijuana, where it's as easy to get marijuana as it is to get a girl, but was caught by border guards while bringing the stuff back. He doesn't have to worry about rent money anymore.

California's braceros, the agricultural workers who go back and forth across the border with relative ease, can be used for smuggling. American tourists, too, are sometimes victimized while unknowingly carrying marijuana or other narcotics in the hubcaps and other hard-to-get-at places of their cars. No, mules are not hard to come by.

Along with an ever-increasing volume of marijuana being brought across the border, there has been a corresponding increase in the amount of heroin seized by authorities. Over thirty pounds of Mexican-manufactured heroin fell into the hands of customs men in the year ending April, 1968—again, just a fraction of the heroin that must have been smuggled in. This potent, chocolate-colored dope made of poppies cultivated in hidden fields on the Mexican mainland is so powerful, and therefore so profitable, that the lighter-colored heroin made in Red China, Europe, and South America is often tinted with powdered coffee to give it a darker color and make it more salable here.

Thirty pounds of heroin will go a long way, depending on how it is cut, and its increased flow over the border indicates that the marijuana users are probably moving on to the more potent dope. And there lies the danger. There is scarcely a single victim of the strong heroin-derivative drugs who did not start on the dope kick by experimenting with marijuana.

Most of the Mexican contacts who handle heroin and marijuana—weed, tea, pot, as it is variously called—are well known to U.S. authorities and Mexican lawmen as well, but they operate with almost total immunity south of the border. As one U.S. narcotics agent told the author: "It almost seems to us that arrests down there are made only to impress upon the peddlers that control can be exerted upon them, control that is then translated into 'mordeda' or graft paid to certain Mexican policemen to keep hands off the traffic."

The apparent lack of Mexican law-enforcement cooperation is not the only difficulty, however. The U.S. Treasury Department has only forty customs agents to do the job of curtailing the circulation of marijuana and other drugs in eight western states, and the intrigue used by the smugglers together with the necessity of coping with vast numbers of people crossing the border every day make detection a chancy kind of thing.

The fact is that California is the victim of a poverty of body and spirit in the area just south of the boundary between the United States and Mexico, where the demarcation has left geography behind and the black lines representing latitude have come to mark the smudge of dope spreading across the southwest.

The Mafia has moved in on every source of easy money to be found in America, and the dreamers who see social revolution in the smoke curlicues of marijuana cigarettes offer a perfect opportunity to the patient artisans of the Mafia. Mafiosi are always looking for a larger foot in the door—whether it be the entrance to a college dormitory, an expensive split-level home in one of the finer suburbs, or the rat-chewed egress to a hovel in a ghetto.

Official awareness of the seemingly sleepy cat that is the Mafia in California has always been manifest in a low key. The men of the syndicate have rarely been sought behind the façade of so-called legitimate business or even official corruption. One statement made by San Francisco's Mayor Joseph L. Alioto in July, 1968, however, at least indicated official recognition of the existence of organized crime in the illegal business of peddling narcotics.

After one of the hippie riots in his city, the mayor said that the long-haired, blue-jeaned youths and their female counterparts were inspired to go on the rampage because the mob was taking over the sources and distribution of marijuana and making things tough for the flower children. He clearly inferred that the hippie influx had created a huge market for pot and heroin and that the increasing revenues were being diverted to the pockets of mobster narcotics vendors.

Two murders in August, 1967, in the Haight-Ashbury district of San Francisco have been attributed to the new "muscle." The victims were John Kent Carter, aged twenty-five, and William E. (Superspade) Thomas, aged twenty-six, both known narcotics dealers. Thomas was found in a sleeping bag at the bottom of a cliff. He had been stabbed in the heart and shot in the back of the head. Carter's body was found in his apartment. He had been stabbed many times, and his right arm had been cut off above the elbow. Missing was about $3,000 in cash he was known to have been carrying. The arm was later found, wrapped in a suede cloth, in a car belonging to a twenty-three-year-old motorcycle racer who said he killed Carter in self-defense after having been cheated in the sale of some L.S.D. during a "bad trip."

A hippie newsletter put out by a group called the Communication Company deplored the killings and said that "the dope business has been like that lately. Lots of burns. Lots of guns. Lots of power games." The newsletter went on to state that some of the most "beautiful" people in the San Francisco hippie community are moving out, and it also reported that Negro gangs have begun to attack hippies despite the operation of a free store for the blacks and the staging of weekend festivals with free food, rock music, and flowers.

The Mafia's role in promoting the importation and distribution of narcotics in the United States has been well established and documented over the years. Anyone only vaguely aware of the existence of a criminal syndicate knows that profits from narcotics have always been one of the basics of mob economy and have helped finance their more recent entry into the so-called legitimate fields of endeavor that are proving even more lucrative.

In refuting rumors of organized crime's infiltration into the mushrooming marijuana traffic across the Mexico-United States border, police authorities regularly fall back on such standard arguments as:

> It takes no talent, no organizational ability, no brokers, no middlemen to drive to Mexico to arrange for a purchase of drugs. Anyone who has an automobile and ambition to be a peddler can drive to Mexico and pick up narcotics. These people who peddle in California are private entrepreneurs.

These arguments could be applied as well—and even better, in fact—to prostitution, where some talent may be needed but certainly no organizational ability, no brokers, and no middlemen. And you don't even have to drive to Mexico! Yet organized prostitution in its heyday undoubtedly put enough money into syndicate coffers to rebalance the current national budget.

The Mafia has the power and the means to organize *any* kind of activity and will do so if there is promise of sufficient return to make the effort worthwhile. And although California's marijuana traffic may have been little league a few years back, all reports indicate that marijuana is continually reaching greater numbers of users and filtering down into younger age brackets. And all of these pot smokers are potential buyers of the syndicate's stronger stuff a few months or years hence; for while the smoking of marijuana does not *necessarily* lead to drug addiction, it does, in the words of the McClellan subcommittee report on the investigation of narcotics, "tend to cultivate the 'fertile soil' of addiction—the state of mind and the environmental influences that lead to the use of addictive drugs." As if to substantiate this theory, narcotics officials are currently checking the suspicion that, in some cases, heroin is being mixed into marijuana by the pushers to "hook" people who might otherwise not go on to the stronger stuff.

In short, it would behoove all those charged with the responsibility of keeping an eye on the activities of organized crime in California to recognize the possibility that the criminal syndicate may have, or take, a hand in pushing the use of marijuana to proportions that represent an even greater menace to the citizenry than that already reached by private entrepreneurs.

At the same time, law-enforcement authorities should also look to another drug source: the Chinese. Though powerful and well-entrenched Chinese "families" exist in San Francisco and elsewhere on the West Coast, probably some of the disparaging remarks made about the California Chinese can be attributed more to the opium-oriented legends of the early Chinese tongs, which flourished in New York City at the turn of the century, than to any substantial participation in this generation's narcotics picture. But a real Chinese interest in narcotics can almost certainly be found in the mind of Red China's ruler, Mao Tse-tung, whose heroin factories are turning out the white powder in wholesale lots.

In May, 1968, for example, six Chinese seamen believed involved in a huge heroin ring were arrested in Long Beach, California. Federal agents discovered heroin worth $12 million in concealed pouches strapped about four of the seamen. The Dutch-registered cargo ship, S.S. "Zeeland," on which the seamen had arrived in this country, was searched, but no more heroin was unearthed. Narcotics agents determined that two of the seamen were natives of the Kowloon district of Hong Kong and that the other four came from Kwangtung Province and the city of Canton in Red China. They carried what was called the "very finest type of Far Eastern-grown heroin."

When Harry J. Anslinger, who served for thirty-two years as U.S. Commissioner of Narcotics before becoming U.S.

representative on the narcotics commission of the United Nations, testified at the McClellan hearings, he presented evidence, according to the subcommittee report, to show that

> the Soviet Union believes the Red Chinese are actively engaged in fostering the narcotics traffic as a national economic measure. An article in *Pravda*, dated September 15, 1964, charged Red Chinese officialdom with active support of the growth of opium poppies in Yunnan Province. The newspaper's correspondent, on an official tour of the Province, saw vast fields of poppies under cultivation. The article made the following charge: "About half a billion dollars every year comes into the hands of the present leaders of China from the illicit sale of narcotics." The article stated that the traffic was encouraged in order that the resulting opium would find lucrative dollar markets outside Red China.

Drugs, corruption, gambling—syndicate activities seem to reflect the eventual ending of California's reputation as a recreational and dwelling area. The politicians have demonstrated their ineptness, corruption, and lack of interest in minorities and have invoked a sense of frustration in the people who crowded west with their dreams. The fine, tall trees that once blanketed the surrounding mountains are mostly gone—leaves, conifer needles, wilted by a host of automobile exhausts and the gaseous dregs of careless industry, by people who already outnumber the struggling saplings in the summer campsites of California's national and state forests. Soon, possibly, the people themselves will be driven out.

In the long history of California's involvement with the Mafia there is precious little on the record about anyone or any local group really trying to lock horns with the secret society, although Los Angeles police department's Captain Hamilton could have claimed much of the credit for thwarting the attempted take-over of the garment industry by the invaders from New York and for harassing Mafiosi in his domain whenever, wherever, and however possible.

Even the famous shakedown of the Hollywood movie industry in 1941, which saw half a dozen mobsters, including Johnny Roselli, go to jail for conspiring to extort $1 million from Loew's, 20th Century Fox, and Warner Brothers, was a cross-country affair. Arrests, indictments, and prison sentences were arranged by the government, not by the state, with the help of informers Willie Bioff and George Browne.

The ancient code of *omerta* still holds, and any infraction of the rule of silence is followed by the old Mafia terror tactics that reinforce the meaning of *omerta* for others. Thus Bioff was killed November 4, 1955, when he stepped on the starter of his pickup truck at his Phoenix ranch and a load of dynamite blew up under his seat. Or take the case of Chicago hood Gerald Covelli. Covelli made a deal with law authorities in 1962. In exchange for a short prison sentence on a major charge, he exposed mob secrets to federal officials. Later he was quietly released from an obscure Texas prison, given a face-lift that was supposed to throw any pursuers off his trail, and moved with his family to Encino, California, just outside Los Angeles. However, there, on June 18, 1967, forty-five-year-old Gerald Covelli was blown in half when a bomb exploded under the front seat of his aquamarine Thunderbird.

Yet the mob, in California as elsewhere across the nation, is changing. The post-Prohibition era, which saw the syndicate turn its efforts from bootlegging to gambling and book-making, is now itself giving place to a new approach to illegal activities, involving infiltration and subversion of seemingly legitimate business. This new sophistication represents a change from the forceful, often violent seizures of the past, but it is change of technique, not of philosophy. No matter what color you try to paint it, the Mafia story always comes up red—blood red.

ELEVEN

LAS VEGAS:

Teamstertown, U.S.A.

The beginnings of Las Vegas are found in the land itself—split open in a cataclysm that an aeon ago produced a gigantic spring of water athwart a wide, mountain-rimmed valley, gouged out by the turbulence of mountain storms that snapped gigantic whips of white foam and rocks down across the desert, smoothed clean by howling winds, and haunted on hot sunny days by dust devils swaying in their own weird ballet as they twist, counterclockwise, forever to the northeast.

Vegas itself had its beginning at about the time the Declaration of Independence sounded the death knell of British rule in the American colonies. In 1776 a small band of Spanish soldiers carrying the banner of King Charles III camped beside the sweetly flowing spring around which Las Vegas later sprouted.

The Mormons further tamped down the dust in 1855, when Brigham Young sent a mission from Salt Lake City to the area to convert the Indians and cultivate the land, a dream that disappeared as quickly as water in the hot sun. The Indians idled away the hours stealing and starving and almost ate the Mormons out of house and home, and the experiment was abandoned.

A reputed cannibal, Bill Williams, a Baptist preacher

turned mountain man, organized a band of Indians and made Las Vegas and other western "spas" the headquarters for a group of horse thieves that terrorized ranchers from Cajon Pass, near Los Angeles, to the big spreads in Arizona.

Williams had guided the explorer General John C. Fremont through California's Mojave Desert and the country split by the Grand Canyon of the Colorado. On one occasion a detachment of men was threatened with starvation, and it was during this rough time that Williams was thought to have had a fling at "long pig," much as had members of the ill-fated Donner party in the Sierras. Of him, Kit Carson is reported to have said: "In starving times don't walk ahead of Bill Williams."

Carson himself fought the horse thieves and Indians and made a reputation in the country with Jose Antonio Carillo, who once led a posse from San Gabriel mission toward a lair of horse thieves and routed them, seizing clothing, saddles, and cooking utensils. Fifteen hundred horses dead from lack of food or water were counted during the chase.

Squaw men by the hundreds wandered the countryside, and every settlement had its gambling halls. Everywhere gamblers used their skills and their special type of squaws to lift the pokes of the horse thieves, who, in turn, retrieved their losses by charging exorbitant prices to the prospectors and ranchers for the very nags that had been stolen from them.

Fortune-hunting miners drilled still-to-be-seen stopes and holes into the rocky mountains around Las Vegas, branching out to every point of the compass and taking the "high grade from the grass roots" until it was all gone. Thirteen million dollars came out of one major lode in Searchlight, Nevada, to the south of Las Vegas. That was real success, and today a couple of gaming joints maintain the high-grading tradition there, moving tourists, however, instead of mountains.

The Union Pacific Railroad threw spurs into the gold country, extending one to Las Vegas in 1905 and maintaining service until the gold disappeared. The line was renewed when Las Vegas came to life again, but automobiles and airlines now supply the gold-plated maw of the gambling town with the necessary tourist grist for its money mills.

In 1931 Nevada legalized gambling, and the gaming parlors, which had run openly though illegally since 1910, really began to flourish. The next decade saw Las Vegas'

Fremont Street become the still-touted Glitter Gulch, with its carnival atmosphere of flashing neon lights, block after block of open-doored casinos, and a beckoning din of frenetic merriment.

In the process, gambling became refined. Sawdust joints gave way to multi-hued, carpet-swathed halls of chance flanked by tiers of handy rooms, flickering numbers of Keno games, mahogany-and-walnut-veneered crap and 21 tables, and crystal glasses laced with amber booze doled out to the players by sleek cocktail waitresses. Cheering sections comprised of pay-as-you-go broads stacked around the tables lent simple solace to winners and losers alike.

The gamblers' playground soon expanded from Fremont Street to a strip of land lying conveniently just outside the Las Vegas city limits on Highway 91—the Los Angeles-Las Vegas artery that for years has carried to and from Las Vegas a steady stream of weekend players who are about as talented at the game of chance as they are at dodging one another in the traffic lanes.

Appropriately called the Strip, the gamblers' mecca had its beginning in 1941 with the building, right on the county line, of El Rancho Vegas. Legend has it that the owner stopped to water his horse at a windmill there, liked what he saw, and stayed on to usher in what was to become the Golden Age of Las Vegas gambling. The Last Frontier Hotel followed, adding to El Rancho's western flavor, which lent a come-as-you-are invitation to fun-seeking travelers.

However, the present-day flashy counterpart to the coruscating mountains that parallel the Strip was really pioneered by hoodlum Benjamin Siegel, a Jewish Don Quixote in reverse who faced many strange windmills in the new land, aided by Tony (Hard Way) Cornero, of California gambling-ship fame. Siegel and Cornero came into Las Vegas from two different directions but with the same objective. Tony had even bigger dreams than Bugsy, but his money-making dreams were largely for the benefit of himself and a few of his hoodlum-gambler associates back in California. Bugsy, on the other hand, was obviously bringing mob organization from the East to the do-it-yourself gaming entrepreneurs who had arrived in Las Vegas ahead of him.

In 1941 Bugsy, who was getting his California business pretty well in hand, sent a disciple to Las Vegas to extend the Siegel barony via the wire service, which was in ever-increasing demand as the state of Nevada began licensing casinos with a free hand. In fact, many of the downtown casinos had "race books" for bettors, to attract daytime patronage, while the nearby gaming tables provided a handy pastime between races. A year later Siegel himself paid a brief visit to Las Vegas and "sewed up" his cut from all the casino bookmaking operations using Trans-America's wire service—a total take for Bugsy of something like $25,000 a month.

Ben Siegel—his friends never called him Bugsy—soon began to dream of bigger things. He envisioned himself as *the* impresario of American gambling, with a luxurious gambling casino surrounded by a plush hotel with all the elegant trimmings: nightclub, restaurant, bars, swimming pool, fine service, and exotic landscaping. Finally, he packed his bags and went to Las Vegas in 1946, taking with him not only his dreams but also backing, financial and otherwise, of the syndicate bosses from New York, Florida, Louisiana, Detroit, Cleveland, Illinois, and points west such as Minneapolis and Kansas City.

Bugsy hired the Del E. Webb Construction Company of Phoenix to build his hotel—the "fabulous" Flamingo—on the Strip, out in the open spaces beyond El Rancho Vegas and the Last Frontier. After he had experienced numerous troubles in getting not only the building materials he wanted but also additional funds to cover the ballooning costs—he sold hotel "stock" to hoodlum pals in the East and raised $3 million—Bugsy finally had a white-tie opening of the still-unfinished hotel on December 26, 1946. The casino went into the red from the start, with few of the expected Hollywood celebrities showing up. Within two weeks $100,000 had gone down the drain, so Bugsy closed the hotel until all construction could be completed.

In the meantime, the Capone mob had taken over its wireservice competition in the West, Continental Press Service, after killing its owner, gambler James M. Ragen, in Chicago in June, 1946. With the extensive apparatus of Continental Press in its grasp, the boys no longer needed Trans-America, and they so informed Siegel. But the budding impresario's ego had become so inflated by then that he talked back to the mob, informing them that his hard work in California—with Jack Dragna and Mickey Cohen—and in Nevada, and the efforts of his pal, Gus Greenbaum, in Phoenix, had together made Trans-America vastly profitable and that it could therefore only be bought off for $2 million.

Bugsy went ahead with the completion of his hotel. But the conflict was still unsettled, and bookies in Los Angeles began to scream at the $150 weekly charge for each telephone of both the wire services they were now forced to use.

The Flamingo reopened on March 27, 1947, and after three nervous weeks, Bugsy was somewhat calmed as the money began to roll in. His little domain was graced by a number of women, chief among them being Virginia Hill, busty messenger for the syndicate and former sweetheart of Joe Adonis. Ensconced by Bugsy in the Flamingo's penthouse, Virginia helped work things out for him through the troublesome times and probably kept him alive longer than the mob thought necessary. But Bugsy seemed unaware of the favor and attributed his syndicate seaworthiness to his own talents. By early 1947 Bugsy was still deep in debt, and he had been told by Lucky Luciano in Havana, during a hasty visit there to plead for time, that the $3 million he owed the boys was long overdue and that the wire service had better be turned over to them in a hurry.

On the night of June 20, 1947, in the Beverly Hills home of Virginia Hill, the matter was settled—in a way the secret society has been settling such disputes for years—when Bugsy was shot to death through an open window by an unknown killer.

Bugsy's dream, the Flamingo Hotel, was entrusted by the syndicate to the care of Gus Greenbaum, who soon put the hotel in the black. But seven years of gambling, booze, and women—all of which interested him personally—took their toll on his health, and Greenbaum tried to bow out in 1955. He moved back to Phoenix, but a new Strip hotel, the Riviera, had opened in March of that year and was losing a lot of money. Gus still owed a large debt to the Chicago mob from his high-living Flamingo days, and he was compelled to return to Las Vegas to put the Riviera on its feet. He did his work, and the old habits were taken up once more. His gambling debts increased along with his liquor and drug consumption, to the point where his backers wanted him out. The casino books were showing unexplained losses, and Gus was suspected of doing some skimming on his own. But by then he was well hooked on Las Vegas ways and had no intention of retiring. He hired a couple of bodyguards and stood his ground.

In November, 1958, Gus Greenbaum went home to Phoenix for the holidays. The mob permitted him a pleasant

Thanksgiving dinner with his family, but on December 3, the society did its work once more: Gus and his wife, Bess were found at home, their throats slashed with a butcher knife from their own kitchen.

It is significant—if anyone cares about *why* the mob murders its own—that both Siegel and Greenbaum were thought by the syndicate to have misused funds entrusted to them. Gus, perhaps, had little excuse when he got his mob deserts—his wife, apparently, just happened to be there at the time—but Bugsy was up against a stone wall of postwar priorities in the building of the Flamingo and was "stolen blind" by dealers in supplies and by the unions. Consequently, the costs of the Flamingo had risen, and so had Bugsy's dollar demands on the boys back east.

In the period following Bugsy Siegel's glorious entrance to Las Vegas, the mob had pretty much of a free hand. Its emissaries thronged the Strip. In ten years there was built an equal number of luxurious hotel-casinos, with the building splurge taking a temporary halt after the completion in 1957 of the Tropicana Hotel, which was backed by Frank Costello and his pal, Phil Kastel of the Louisiana mob.

The Lansky-backed Thunderbird Hotel opened in 1948; Cleveland's Mayfield Road Gang opened the Desert Inn in 1950; Doc Stacher's Sands Hotel made its debut in 1952; the same year the Sahara Hotel, which had its backing in the Portland, Oregon, gambling-horsebook organization headed by Al Winter, opened its doors. The year 1955 saw the opening of the New Frontier Hotel, which was the Last Frontier, restyled and renamed, with a strictly "non-pro" by the name of Warren (Doc) Bayley at its helm. Later, Bayley, who has since died, built the Hacienda Hotel at the far end of the Strip, and it, too, was a kind of amateur operation—by mob standards. Three other hotels opened in 1955: the Riviera, which Gus Greenbaum took over for the Chicago boys; the Dunes, backed by Rhode Island's Mafia boss, Ray Patriarca; and the Royal Nevada, which went broke and closed on New Year's Eve, to be taken over later by the Desert Inn crew as a convention center.

The Las Vegas entrance of Moe Dalitz and his Mayfield Road Gang buddies, whose notoriety has been detailed in *The Green Felt Jungle* and other places, signaled an era of predominantly Jewish operation of *the* Mafia's money business: legalized gambling. Dalitz and his pals bailed gambler Wilbur Clark out of debt and made possible the completion of "Wilbur Clark's Desert Inn" by cutting themselves in for 74 per cent of the take. They arranged financing, satisfied gangsters elsewhere who wanted "in" on hidden percentage points, and greased the palms of various local politicians who had their own two-way-stretch scoops in the money pot. The only remaining barrier was the Nevada tax commission, which had declined to issue licenses to Moe and his boys because of an alarming report from Virgil Peterson of the Chicago crime commission.

In spite of Peterson's detailed outline of the previous criminal activities of Dalitz and his friends, opposition began to melt away when Mafioso Sam Maceo, top syndicate man in Texas at the time, showed up at the Riverside Hotel in Reno to talk things over with Nevada's Senator Pat McCarran. The necessary licenses were issued post haste. With a Sicilian running as quarterback and an Irishman providing interference, the game was a pushover for the Cleveland team. Today both McCarran and Maceo are dead, and most of the Mayfield Road Gang have limped away, their ranks somewhat thinned by punitive government measures and by the greenback offerings of Howard Hughes, the walking Fort Knox, to take over their holdings and lure them out of Las Vegas.

A perusal of trends in Las Vegas, and of the vanishing powers behind various thrones, shows that the Jewish members of the syndicate, who lived through and brought about the Strip's Golden Age, have been edged slowly, very slowly, out of the picture. Meyer Lansky stands today as perhaps the last of the big-time Jewish gambling racketeers with a vested interest in the Vegas Temples of Mammon, though he long ago abandoned his belief in the moral concepts that have shed greatness through the centuries of the race that produced him. Needless to say, his turn will come when he stops producing.

If the barbarians conquered Rome, then it could be assumed their descendants built today's Las Vegas Strip and have withstood the onslaught of the millions of Americans who for years have rushed headlong with rubber-tired, gasoline-propelled chariots toward a financial cancer that happily consumes their purses at about the same speed as that with which it divests them of their reason.

There are two dooms in Vegas, doomsday and doomsnight. The latter is merely an artificial extension of the former occurring when the sun goes down. If, however, you can manage to stick it out in a casino for twenty-four hours—Nick the Greek did it once for seventy-two, betting on the no-pass line at a crap table, without ever going to the men's room—you begin to wonder what are the normal waking and sleeping hours. One thing is certain: the doom is inevitable, whatever the hour.

There is no point in going outdoors at night since it is opthalmological suicide to expose the delicate retina of the eye to the didactic rhythm of the incredible, blinking spectrum that burns up desert moths long before they get to the alluring electric inferno. When daylight comes, the gambler finds he is handcuffed, a prisoner of the heat and the bright flame of the sun, which crawls into his head and drives him back to the air-conditioning, the pastel-tinted cards, and the polka-dotted dice.

So it was with a considerable amount of squinting and brow-wiping that a slight, fiftyish, balding man, dressed more for the Kriendlers' "Club 21" in New York than for Kit Carson's sandy acres, looked out one day in 1958 over a mesquite-lined dry wash jutting north from U.S. Highway 91 and decided that he was going to be a really big man.

The name of the dreamer was Max Field. He was a laundromat distributor in Los Angeles. He placed machines in stores, hired a couple of hostesses, and then sold or leased the properties to people who figured soap and water and a little bluing was a clean way to make money.

As he looked out over the sand and mesquite and even beyond to the geological phenomenon that is Mount Charleston, Field visualized a highrise hotel to be called the Tower. He could see it, even taste it: a pristine white mass of air-conditioned cubicles that would give shelter to thousands of tourists and joy to the least inhibited of them, greenbacks fluttering to the floor of the counting room where a man could stand hip-deep in security.

Field's vision was shared by other people with more violent histories and ideas—by men such as Joe Sica, scion of a multi-murder family that has been the scourge of California since Joe and his brothers, Fred, Frank, and Angelo, went west from New Jersey and boiled a pot of hell for one and all.

Another visionary was Roger Leonard, a partner of Joe Sica with somewhat less vision than either Sica or Field. Leonard once trotted around Mexico under the name of "Kallman de Leonard" but was booted out as an undesirable, probably because of a U.S. arrest record that included charges of rape, burglary, robbery, murder, and assorted bookmaking that he had racked up in thirteen years of activity starting at the age of twenty.

Leonard won a lot of popularity with the right people, one of whom was Mickey Cohen, pal of Joe Sica in many forays where knuckles and muscles played a counterpoint to demands made on Los Angeles businessmen by racketeers. Leonard, in fact, had some winning ways. For example, he tickled Cohen's risibilities by laughing fit to bust when Mickey draped his pet bulldog with a napkin in Rondelli's restaurant in California's San Fernando Valley and fed the beast ground round.

Roger Leonard and Joe Sica tickled Max Field's back with a gun and declared themselves in on his desert dream. What can a man do under these circumstances? Field probably knew that a man once walked into Cohen's favorite private kennel club in Rondelli's and all of a sudden crumpled up, stone dead, with a bullet in him. The bullet ended the life of bookmaker Jack (Jack Whalen) O'Hara, and it was discovered that a man who called himself Kallman de Leonard had purchased the murder gun in a pawnshop in Phoenix, Arizona.

The start of what appears to be a troubled existence for the little strip of Max Field's desert seems to have been initiated the day Sica and Leonard tried to move in on the dreamer. But the mobsters at least got results. Today, a concrete pterodactyl called Caesar's Palace stands astride the sands, financed by an army of partners and $10 million from Jimmy Hoffa's Teamsters. Caesar's Palace is Las Vegas' latest entry in the ever-running hotel derby, and though its wings—unlike the desparate arms of the crap shooters within its gold-spangled, statue-flanked casino—do not beat the air, Max Field may have provided for it the beginnings of the same kind of continually eroding extinction that erased the flying reptile aeons ago.

Perhaps Field should not have erected the giant sign on his property, calling attention to the fact that the Tower Hotel would be built on the spot and outlining a few of the coming attractions. Perhaps he did make a mistake, but it was an honest one. He just hadn't counted on the two gangland minstrels, Sica and Leonard.

Of course, to attempt to do what Field's new partners tried required an okay from the boys who give the okay to

come into Las Vegas. This permission has nothing to do with
the governor's office, the gaming control board that operates
out of the state capital, or the local county offices encom-
passing the sheriff and county commissioners. Consequently,
Field could turn nowhere. Everywhere he was told that Sica
and Leonard had the "fix" in with the politicians who run
Nevada, and the heartless racketeers milked the little man
dry with the promise that his gambling license was a sure
thing.

The fleecing of Max Field did not go unnoticed. Captain
James Hamilton of the Los Angeles police heard the story,
and when Sica, Leonard, and Field stopped at the Sands
Hotel during a visit to Las Vegas, the Clark County sheriff's
office stepped in and arrested both mobsters. Sica was on a
list in a "black book" issued by the gaming officials in Nevada and was therefore "eighty-sixed" out of all Vegas casinos. In the pockets of the two mobsters were found checks
made out by Field for hundreds of dollars plus credit cards
with Field's name on them.

Incidentally, use of a man's credit card is a tried and true
racket with Mafiosi. Instead of asking for cash from businessmen who are "under the muscle"—cash for which the businessmen must account—the mob boys take their credit cards
and bleed them for all they're worth. Indeed, the syndicate is
involved in a thriving trade in stolen credit cards.

Sica and Leonard soon dropped their relationship with
Field when they found they had drained his resources and
that he had, in fact, not even enough money left to pay for
the sign he put up on the Strip in Las Vegas to announce his
dream.

Las Vegas, then, is a constant source of misery for others
than the "busted" gamblers. And in particular an aura of
sadness and doom seems to curse what were to become the
future Caesar's Palace grounds. An especially haunting episode
concerns one Myford Irvine, heir to a multi-million-dollar
estate in Orange County known as the Irvine Ranch which
was originally a Spanish land grant, contains 88,256 acres,
and includes the posh, oceanside city of Newport.

Irvine somehow became involved with Vegas gamblers
who had their eyes on his millions. They pointed him toward
the same property Max Field had woven his illusions around
a few months earlier, and they had high ambitions late in
1958, when Irvine's gilt-edged two-reeler began.

No one who will tell knows what really happened to

cause Myford's death "by suicide" on January 11, 1959. We can, however, piece together some of the story. Irvine apparently had made commitments to a gambling group in Las Vegas. The result was that the sixty-year-old protagonist in one of Las Vegas' oldest and most repeated plays got deeply involved and had to produce a fantastic sum of cash, in a hurry. Irvine could have done it, given time. He was president of a vast trust left to him by his father, and a brother who could have shared it with him had died of tuberculosis in 1939. However, at first he tried to buck the pressures placed upon him. Then, it seems, he suddenly decided to go ahead and provide the money that would transform everybody's dream into reality.

But by then it was too late. He asked the men who helped him administer his trust to give him the money he needed—reportedly about a million dollars—and for some incredible reason insisted he had to have it almost instantly: on Saturday, January 11, 1959. It was not possible, and Myford cried, "Too late, too late!" when he learned that his trustees would not be able to meet until the following Monday to vote the funds. His niece, Joan, tried to speed the loan but failed.

According to the Orange County police files, on Saturday, January 11, Irvine went into the den of his home on the estate and fired a shotgun blast into his body. Then he is supposed to have secured a .22-caliber pistol and finished the job with a shot in the temple. Why?

Part of the answer to the Irvine mystery may have come in a disclosure made by U.S. Judge Thurmond Clarke and his wife, a former sister-in-law of the dead man whose death was finally listed by law officials as a suicide. Judge Clarke recounted that "Irvine approached Mrs. Clarke and her daughter [Joan Irvine Burt] and said he needed $5 million right away. He said he had to have $400,000 of it by Monday morning.

"He said he was 'sitting on a keg of dynamite' and had been trying to sell some stock to friends," Judge Clarke continued. "One was interested but decided he couldn't set up a company to take the stock in time for Irvine's needs."

Judge Clarke said he asked Irvine why he didn't go to a bank for the loan, and the man replied: " 'I've never had to borrow from a bank before and I don't want to start now.'

"We never did find out what the keg of dynamite was," Judge Clarke concluded.

After his death, Irvine's estate was estimated to be worth in excess of $10 million and his yearly income $100,000. He also had a $325,000 home under construction at Corona del Mar. And although there is some confusion about the total amount of money Irvine needed and the date he had to have it, he evidently needed the kind of money necessary for entree into the more select circles of Las Vegas' gaming gentry. Relatives are still trying to figure it all out, and the answer may lie in the sands of Las Vegas, under dunes flattened by the weight of Caesar's Palace and the pressure of unhappy and unholy memories.

The parcel of land that supports the Palace has been an "in and out" bit of property. Owned and claimed by an assortment of people at one time or another, it was finally wrapped up by one Kirk Kerkorian, a sort of ham-sandwich Howard Hughes. By the end of 1968, Kerkorian had sold his Trans International Airlines, which he had started with the purchase of one war-surplus DC-3 for $12,000, gained control of and was running the Flamingo Hotel, and was planning the building of another hotel and casino near the Strip. He and Hughes were competing for headlines and confusing readers by their respective bids for control of Western Air Lines and Air West.

According to a local magazine, Kerkorian's landlordship of Caesar's Palace was frequently interrupted by his disappearance "in his private jet ($620,000 cost—$15,000 monthly maintenance) to Europe and the Caribbean." It was further stated that Kerkorian negotiated and closed the land deal for Caesar's Palace over a weekend.

An even more important figure in Las Vegas, however, and one who received a great deal of local publicity when Caesar's Palace stuffed the customers into the amphitheater on its opening was a relative unknown, the prime owner of the casino, Jay Sarno, who had a 10 per cent interest.

It was supposedly Sarno's imaginative talents in the architectural world of marble and concrete-over-chicken-wire that helped pace the tourists' path past fountains—replicas of classic originals such as the Rape of the Sabine Women by Bologna, Apollo and Daphne by Bernini, the Aphrodite of Melos, Hebe (powers of rejuvenation were attributed to this young lady) by deVries, and the Three Graces by Antonio Canova in Italy in 1757—into the casino. But then, if Martin Stern, the prominent Los Angeles architect who designed the Sahara and the new façade of the Aladdin (formerly the Tally-Ho) in Las Vegas, will check his files, he may discover that Mr. Sarno has marvelous extrasensory perception. The design of Caesar's Palace is remarkably similar to Stern's own renderings for the aborted Tower Hotel and of a dream once held by a man named Max.

Sarno, however, takes no small amount of credit for the marble and mammary trappings of the Palace. As he told a *West* magazine writer coyly:

> So I don't look like a designer, but see that block outside there through the window, that design that covers the front of the building? That's the Sarno Block. I've had it patented and anybody wants to use it, they got to come to me! . . .
> The new convention hall we're building will be my version of a Roman circus—elliptical. [It opened in October, 1968.] I dreamed up the idea for this whole place, and I designed or supervised everything. It was a team project with Melvin Grossman of Miami Beach and Jo Harris who's an architect and interior designer. I was like the quarterback. I'm a builder and I've always been very impressed by Roman architecture. It's very romantic.

The first of Las Vegas' resident caesars, Sarno added that he has a "fine Roman head" that would "look very good on a bust." But comic Alan King may have said something not nearly as funny as it sounded when, while playing the Sands Hotel in Las Vegas, he joked about Caesar's Palace: "I wouldn't say it was exactly Roman—more a kind of early Sicilian."

Sarno, who owns fourteen hundred shares in the Desert Palace, low-key name for the holding company that controls Caesar's Palace, has a real talent for knowing where the money is. He and his partner, Stanley Mallin, are not new to the hotel game. They put together a chain of plush motels called Cabana, starting in Atlanta, Georgia, and spreading out to Dallas, Texas, and Palo Alto, California. An interesting story behind the Cabana concerns the business merger of two fairly well-known names: Doris Day, America's Number One screen virgin, and James Riddle Hoffa, America's Number One purveyor of labor's pension funds. Doris, with Cabana partners Sarno and Mallin, has benefited greatly from loaned Teamster pension greenbacks, $5 million worth.

Mallin, who lives at 130 Alden Avenue, N.W., in Atlanta,

owns a mere 3.9643 percent of the Caesar's Palace casino end of the deal but is in for a whooping 17.55 per cent of the hotel operation.

In fact, it appears that the real caesar is Jimmy Hoffa. Although he must now reign from a prison cell, his suite at the Palace is lavishly furnished in modish ebony and white. Even the Teamsters' famous "Taj Mahal" headquarters in Washington, D.C. can boast no finer accommodations.

Los Angeles society columnist Cobina Wright could not make the three-day opening celebration of the Palace in August, 1966, but printed a lengthy guest list of the "beautiful people" who attended. On hand, among the bejeweled celebrities, were Governor Grant Sawyer, who later attacked the FBI for trying to pry into the secrets of skimming in Las Vegas and Reno casinos and carried his complaint all the way to the President of the United States; Nevada's junior senator, Howard Cannon; and Andy Griffith, Joe Louis, Prince Puchartra of Thailand, and Melvin Belli, San Francisco legal eagle and onetime defender of Jack Ruby. Belli's nine-year-old son, Caesar, was given a pair of gold-plated dice by the Palace president, Nate Jacobson, owner of a 4.6429 per cent interest in the casino. The boy gave them to his dad, who went down in local history as having rolled the first pair of bones at Las Vegas' newest pleasure dome.

Jimmy (Caesar) Hoffa, wielder of the $10.5 million money mace that kept everyone in line, took the occasion of the opening—and made it official a few days later—to announce that he was tossing another generous $5.5 million loan at Las Vegas' principal phallic symbol, the Landmark Hotel, then a silo-shaped shell. The structure resembles an atomic explosion at the moment that the mushroom cloud umbrellas out. The shaft houses the rooms; the umbrellas encloses the gaming casino and restaurant that goes around and around —but slowly, so that the gourmets can enjoy 360 degrees of Las Vegas between soup and nuts, achieving a gastronomic empathy with all the roulette wheels in town.

With the loan to the Landmark, Teamster participation in Las Vegas, which extends to four other hotels, a hospital, two golf courses, and some hoodlum-connected downtown business property, totals over $50 million.

Clearly, the lines are now drawn between Hoffa and his union, the mobsters who fawn upon him, and the people who figure that Las Vegas should be contained and not

stretch across the trail of East-West travelers. The route
gets longer and fatter along Highway 91, a dollar-studded
booby trap operating for the mob, which roars like a lion
through the electronic verbocity of coruscating signs and
bleats like a lamb when it is asked to come up with a little
extra tax money for the benefit of the stable residents of
Nevada and their children.

The laurel wreaths assumed by the management at Caesar's Palace wilted a bit in January, 1967, when a Miami
bookmaker named Ruby (Fat Ruby) Lazarus was summoned
by a federal grand jury and declined to answer any questions.
He was ordered to jail the following March by U.S. Judge
A. Andrew Hauk, who alluded the biblical story of Lazarus
who died and was entombed but was resurrected by Christ.

"He had no control over his death," the judge said. "Mr.
Lazarus here has control over his fate. He has the key to his
own resurrection."

The judge meant that if Lazarus talked about a Little
Apalachin meeting held in Palm Springs in October, 1965,
he would be let out of jail. Among questions Lazarus refused
to answer, even though granted immunity from prosecution,
was whether conferees at the Palm Springs meeting—
held at a home rented by two Las Vegas showgirls—discussed how ownership of Caesar's Palace was to be divided.

Those in attendance at the Palm Springs meeting were
identified in grand jury questioning as Vincent Alo, Anthony
Salerno—eastern gangsters—Jerome Zarowitz, and Elliot Paul
Price. The latter two assumed positions later at the Palace,
Zarowitz as credit manager and Price as a host.

Lazarus, if he did not talk, could have stayed in jail for one
year or until the life of the grand jury expired. However,
after eight months in jail Lazarus decided to talk and, as a
result of his testimony, was indicted for perjury. Sentenced
on May 28, 1968, to thirty months in federal prison, he is at
present free on a $10,000 appeal bond.

A dramatic aside to the federal probe was an alleged attempt by one of the showgirls, Natalie Loughran, to commit
suicide by jumping out of a car on Wilshire Boulevard in
Los Angeles in December, 1966, after her initial appearance
before the grand jury. Judge Hauk later told her she need
fear no person, "whether he comes from the underworld of
New York or the overworld of Caesar's Palace." The girl,
who uses the stage name of Vickie Lockwood, later told

what she knew about the Palm Springs meeting in a secret deposition given to the U.S. attorney in Los Angeles. Two psychiatrists stood by in an adjoining room.

Earlier scandals in Las Vegas, however, are nothing to the furor that erupted in Nevada just before the Palace opening. In July, 1966, Sandy Smith stated in the *Chicago Sun-Times* that Caesar's Palace, among other hotels, was owned in part by gangsters. Named by Smith were Jerry Catena, a protégé of the late Longy Zwillman of New Jersey, Vincent Alo, boss of the Bronx, Ray Patriarca, New England boss and former money man behind the Dunes Hotel in Las Vegas, Chicago's Tony Accardo and Sam Giancana, and a number of assorted "muscle men" such as Jerry Angiulo, Henry Tamello, and Joseph Anselmo—the latter three members of Patriarca's branch of the Mafia. Anthony (Fat Tony) Salerno and Joe Palermo, supposedly racket bosses in New York City and across the Hudson in New Jersey, also received notice and are probably Alo's soldiers.

Smith also asserted that the take on skimming—the hiding of part of the profits before they are counted for the benefit of Nevada's tax men—totaled $6 million in one year in six Vegas casinos.

The reaction to the skimming exposé followed the normal lines of alarm in Nevada—probably the last state in the Union in which Indians regularly raided the settlers. Governor Grant Sawyer, in a taped interview that appeared on N.B.C.'s inquiry into organized crime a few weeks after Smith's article appeared, came up with a gem:

> Las Vegas, behind the glitter and the glamour that many people see—and that's all they see—happens to be a very stable town that involves a lot of people who are doing all the same kinds of things people in other towns do.

Nobody thought to ask the governor, "Such as what?" And if what happens in Las Vegas happens in towns all over the country, then what could possibly be the great attraction there?

In response to public pressure after the nationwide publicity, Sawyer did order the five-man Nevada gaming commission to conduct hearings into the charges of skimming, although little apparently was said about the even more damning charges of hoodlum ownership. But the hearings didn't

get off the ground until three and one-half months after
FBI testimony in Denver, which resulted in an attempted
extortion conviction for one Las Vegas casino owner, clearly
indicated that "bugging" in some casinos had produced evidence of skimming for the benefit of undisclosed interests.

The governor's foot dragging is perhaps understandable in
view of the fact that Sawyer was facing a reelection campaign for his third term as governor of a state whose main
industry—which is gambling, despite Sawyer's claim that it
is tourism—reportedly grossed $330 million in 1965, employs
35,000 of its people, and provides in the way of gambling
taxes alone 30 per cent of its general fund revenue. But in
any case, nothing happened.

The closed-door hearings, which themselves led, even in
Nevada, to criticism of the commission for not inviting
elected representatives of the people or the press or the public itself to sit in, produced nothing unexpected. Chairman
Milton W. Keefer dutifully called in some of the boys representing ownership of various casinos, asked them a few
unrecorded questions, and said at the conclusion that they
were "very cooperative and friendly" and that all "categori-
cally denied they have been involved in any skimming whatsoever."

Attorney General Nicholas Katzenbach clamped a lid on
the FBI's more than nine-hundred pages of so-called bugging
records—which would have set Las Vegas and other cities
right in the lap of the Mafia-guided gambling syndicate—
although the records could have been used at Keefer's hearing since it was not a prosecutive inquiry. Katzenbach
claimed "executive privilege" in buttoning down the records,
but they were very important. Dean Elson, Las Vegas FBI
chief, stated candidly that his agents hid an electronic listening device in at least one plush hotel-casino to pick up information on "criminal activities."

"In this connection," Elson said, "I would refer to ownership which is not officially recorded with the state of Nevada."

The suspicion that the FBI, who almost certainly "leaked"
their records to Smith out of frustration, really did have evidence that would embarrass casino operators led Chairman
Keefer to indulge in almost Byronesque semantics to defend
the Nevada gamblers: "If the Federal agents have any information we do not have, they are unable to produce it.
Hence, we cannot in any manner proceed upon any unveri-
fied public expression by people not in public capacity."

However, allegations aside, it is a fact that conspiracy-seeking wiretaps were found at the Fremont Hotel in April 1960; at the Desert Inn in August, 1963; at the Sands Hotel on July 2, 1963; and at the Stardust and Riviera Hotels. Don't take the word of the FBI for this; take the word of Fremont chief engineer John Grandi who filed a taxpayer's suit, along with several Strip hotel nabobs, against the FBI and the telephone company when the taps, involving twenty-five phone lines, were discovered.

Former Nevada Lieutenant-Governor Cliff Jones claimed that he, too, was tapped by somebody. According to Jones, on August 15, 1965, he found a microphone and radio transmitter, powered by his own phone lines, hidden in a wall telephone well in his office.

So the hotelmen complained, recalling perhaps the incident of undercover man Louis Tabet. Tabet came to Las Vegas in 1954 and caught key officials with their money pockets open. The men he interviewed talked freely into Tabet's hidden microphone as the author and then Assistant District Attorney Gordon Hawkins worked the tape recorder in a closet. Quoted at hearings later in Carson City were an embarrassed Cliff Jones and various county officials who recommended allocation of gaming licenses. The state of Nevada has the authority to give gambling licenses, but it acts on the recommendations of the county or city that houses the proposed casino; without the approval of these entities, the state is somewhat helpless. One unit has a veto over all the others, which splits up the graft potential into many fine hairs.

While the FBI was never given a chance to lay its facts before the public, casino owners were given full opportunity. And when they were asked if they were skimming and cheating the state out of taxable dollars, they smiled benignly—there were no hurt countenances—and said of course not. That's apparently the way the questioning went—no records were made—just a query into "the truth and nothing but the truth."

An eight-page report by the gaming commission following its "inquiry" indicated, among other things, that: (1) the only discernible results to come from the skimming charges were "indictments by newspapers"; (2) Robert Kennedy was responsible for starting the stories; (3) it had failed to un-cover evidence that substantial amounts of money were being skimmed by casino owners and channeled to the syndicate;

and (4) it would try to devise a means of keeping a closer eye on Nevada gambling, possibly with closed-circuit television and other electronic devices.

The state, however, has its own anti-wiretapping statutes and has claimed that it lacks the authority to deputize federal officers for the purpose of keeping an honest count in the casinos. It has thus pretty well hamstrung itself, perhaps conveniently so.

But the proof of the inquiry pudding lies in the suppressed records of the FBI, the lack of public access to the state hearings, and the political maneuvering—hurried conferences between Nevada officials, Attorney General Katzenbach, and President Johnson, followed by the public outcries of Democrat Governor Sawyer to the federal government to "Give us your evidence, or call off your dogs!"—necessary to send the damning electronic canaries into orbit, out of sight and sound.

Shortly after Governor Sawyer's "Call off your dogs" cry, grim federal officials decided to try for a jackpot themselves. The result was an investigation by a U.S. grand jury in the gaming town, and in May, 1967, three officials of one Las Vegas hotel and four former officials of another were indicted and charged with conspiring to skim money from gaming profits in order to evade corporate income taxes.

Named in one indictment were Ed Levinson, whose age was given as seventy-one, former president of the Fremont Hotel; Edward Torres, fifty-two, former vice-president; P. Weyerman and Cornelius Hurley, former stockholders and employees of the same hotel located in downtown Las Vegas. Defendants in the other indictment were Ross Miller, chairman of the board of the Riviera Hotel; Frank Atol, a stockholder and employee at the Riviera; and Joseph Rosenberg, a stockholder and casino manager at the same hotel for many years.

This was the first time indictments had been returned for skimming money. All four former officials of the Fremont were named in one count of conspiracy. Another count accused Levinson, Torres, and Weyerman of aiding in preparation of a false tax return. A third count accused Levinson of making a tax return he knew to be untrue. All defendants pleaded innocent in June, and U.S. District Judge Roger Foley said the trial date would not be set for at least three months.

A surprise came late in March, 1968, when Levinson and Rosenberg pleaded no contest to the charge they skimmed money in that they "wilfully aided and assisted in the preparation of false corporate tax returns for the fiscal year ending in 1963." But the real blockbuster came when Judge Foley accepted the pleas, despite government objections, and fined Levinson a mere $5,000 and Rosenberg $3,000. The government then moved to dismiss the other charges against Levinson and Rosenberg as well as the five other men originally named in the two indictments.

Just two days later papers were filed in Nevada State Court by Levinson's attorneys dismissing his suit against four FBI agents who had allegedly invaded his privacy by placing "bugging" equipment in his Fremont Hotel office. A related suit against the Central Telephone Company for supposedly aiding the FBI's wiretapping was left pending, but one can safely assume that this matter will be settled out of court.

The swift court action ended a government case that was almost two years in the making and encompassed a six-month long federal grand jury probe during which over one hundred witnesses, including singer Frank Sinatra, were called.

Federal racket busters were "shocked and demoralized by the sudden and unusual end of a major tax evasion case against Las Vegas casino operators," according to the *Los Angeles Times*, which noted that even Henry E. Petersen, chief of the Justice Department's organized crime and racketeering division, didn't know the skimming case was being ended until it was all over. When a reporter later tried to question Petersen about the case, he replied: "I refuse to talk because I don't know anything about this."

Judge Foley's handling of the matter is reflected in a study of tax cases brought before him in the past six years, the *Los Angeles Times* pointed out, quoting Mitchell Rogovin, assistant attorney general in charge of the tax division. Rogovin evinced dismay at Foley's record: only one jail sentence had resulted from fourteen tax cases in six years.

There was much private questioning as to whether the criminal cases were in any way related to the FBI "bugging" suit. And although many denials were made, some Justice Department and IRS people are not convinced, contending, according to the *Los Angeles Times*, that "it is 'just too

coincidental' that the suit against the FBI was dropped
the day after the criminal case ended."

Nevertheless, Edwin L. Weisl, Jr., assistant in charge of
the civil division responsible for defending the FBI agents,
said that the government's handling of the case was proper
and that Attorney General Ramsey Clark and Petersen's boss,
Fred Vinson, who was in charge of the criminal division,
knew in advance of the government strategy. The case
"served notice that skimming will have to stop," said Weisl,
and that "the government is aware and watching."

At least one skeptic remains, however. A "lesser official,"
reported the *Los Angeles Times*, "noted that the investigation cost the government more than $100,000 and thousands
of man-hours." His conclusion: "Now the gamblers and the
mob think they're immune from attacks on skimming."

Possibly this official and others took hope, however, from
a new investigation into skimming reportedly charted at a
June, 1968, meeting in San Francisco of fifteen IRS and
Justice Department officials. The new probe was expected to
take a different approach, with attention being directed at
"credit play" operations. This would involve locating players
who would admit to losing in casino play large amounts of
money given to them on credit. Then, once the loss had been
paid off to the casino by the player, a perusal of casino
records would reveal whether or not that loss had been reported as taxable casino income, the suspicion being that a
number of these debts are reported as uncollectable and
written off casino records although they actually are collected "on the outside" and thereby skimmed.

It might also be noted that money could be handed out as
credit to a so-called player who actually is a management
stooge. He need not bet on the tables at all, yet the money
could be written off as a casino gambling loss while most of
it finds its way back into the pockets, if not the records, of
the casino operator.

Skimming is, without a doubt, the name of the game that
has kept most of the syndicate boys in Vegas, and their Mafia
pals elsewhere, so well fed for so many years. And there
are more variations to this game than a poker player ever
heard of!

However, while skimming is the most profitable pastime in
Vegas, every once in a while "skamming" occurs. A skam at
the Riviera Hotel participated in by almost every dealer in

the casino over the Fourth of July holiday in 1958, just a few months before owner Gus Greenbaum was murdered, milked him of over $250,000. Chips were stashed away in "subs"—secret pockets in the clothing of the house men—until they bulged. The mobsters backing Gus were short a huge sum, and it could be that Greenbaum was framed by deliberate thievery. He certainly wasn't able to answer for the dishonesty of his subordinates, and it could be that he trusted too many people, too many times.

Least known or publicized of Las Vegas' legal money-making schemes are the coins minted by many of the casinos to take the place of scarce silver dollars. They cost the casinos about seventeen cents apiece, and in order to gamble with them you have to put down a dollar for each one. The proposed statute to cover their use at the time of the first minting in 1966 read that they were to be used only in the casino where issued, whose name appears on them, but tourists use them throughout the town in the dollar slot machines and on the gaming tables. The tokens were also used in over one hundred new automatic blackjack machines, until the machines were banned from casinos in December, 1967, by the Nevada gaming commission. And the coins quickly became "legal" tender for tipping cocktail waitresses, bellboys, etc.

So here is a town minting its own money—this time in metal instead of the clay chips used normally. The gimmick is that tourists, in the first few months after the initial minting of the coins, took home with them some $6,000,000 in so-called silver souvenir chips, leaving a profit for the casinos of about eighty cents apiece, depending on the deal they made with the minters.

Somehow the phony dollars tie into a statement made by Palace chief Jacobson, who said that the "nut"—the dollar intake necessary every day to pay running expenses—would be $40,000. He pointed out that gaming would not take over the whole load, as it did in the now-nostalgically-referred-to "old days," so that rooms, food, and beverages would have to pay a profit. In such an atmosphere it is still anticipated that the good gray tourist cannot win at the games; otherwise the hotel would soon go out of business. So what's in it for the tourist? Expensive broads, expensive gambling, and expensive booze.

Jacobson's quarrel with the government was that the

federal government levies $250 a year and the state $300 for each slot machine operating in the casino. But if such demands are too great, why not take the dollar slot machines out, since it is illegal, anyway—in the partnership agreement the gambling fraternity has somehow worked out with the federal government—for the machines taxed by the United States to absorb phony money? The rules state clearly that only genuine coin of the realm be used in the machines.

What's behind it all? Maybe Mr. Katzenbach did not want his men too involved in the intricacies of the gaming in Nevada. There were—and are—after all, more important things, such as the "ten most wanted men" and all those Communists, to catch.

Of course, the men of Las Vegas don't always confine themselves to their gambling interests. For example, Caesar's Palace president Nathan S. Jacobson, an insurance company executive from Baltimore, is also interested in sports. According to a story in the *Los Angeles Times* of July 4, 1966, he was one of the original owners of the Baltimore Bullets basketball team. In this respect, Jacobson's credit manager at the Palace, Jerome Zarowitz, would seem to reflect his boss's interest.

Zarowitz, who attended the Little Apalachin meet in Palm Springs, served nearly twenty months in jail in 1947–1948 on a conspiracy conviction growing out of an attempt to "fix" a National Football League championship game in 1946. In recent years, according to gaming commission files, Zarowitz has operated as a sports bookmaker in Miami. But that is not of much concern in Nevada. Chairman Keefer, in admitting that the gaming commission was aware of Zarowitz' background when it granted Caesar's Palace a license, shrugged and added: "Many licenses are granted to people in bookmaking."

Another money gambit, possibly rather incomprehensible on the part of the men in Las Vegas, was that of Mike Singer, labor racketeer and convicted extortionist who built the International Motor Inn in Palm Springs, California, a few miles south of Palm Springs. In 1965 Singer, a former business agent of Teamsters Local 626 in Los Angeles and close friend of Jimmy Hoffa, paid for a series of advertisements in the Los Angeles papers stating that any guest at his motel would receive a 10 per cent reduction in his bill if he paid in silver dollars.

Then, in the summer of 1966, Singer ran ads in the *Wall*

Street Journal offering five million silver dollars for sale at $1.50 each. Singer said that the silver was stored in a Swiss bank because he could not find space in U.S. banks.

Possibly Singer's advertisements were ill-advised, for in September of that year the IRS filed a $72,927.63 tax lien against him involving undeclared income for 1965. But in any case, Singer died in March, 1967.

Until his death Singer had been active in savings and loan groups. He was listed as a founder of Allied TV, which split up and became Allied Empire and is now known as Riverside Financial of Banning, California. He was also connected with Waikiki Savings and Loan of Hawaii, in which Bobby Baker, Cliff Jones, and their associates invested heavily when the move into the Caribbean was made.

In fact, few things have really changed since the author's last visit to the green felt jungle as far as the general trend of Las Vegas life is concerned. But there have been substantial changes in ownership.

For example, the Fremont Hotel, formerly operated by Ed Levinson, seems to have undergone a financial face-lifting. The hotel was originally financed in part by San Francisco's fabled real estate operator, Lou Lurie, with some substantial help from the Teamsters. But in 1966 an announcement was made that the Parvin-Dohrman Company of Los Angeles was negotiating to buy the Fremont. The company, however, had one minor problem. It was issuing stock to be publicly held, and the Securities and Exchange Commission could find no precedent for granting a permit to a gambling casino—which was one of the stumbling blocks that Tony Cornero ran across when he tried to juxtapose legal gambling in Nevada with other legal concepts in Washington, D.C.

If, as has been boldly proclaimed, casino operators skim money off the top of their winnings, how would a shareholder ever know the true value of his stock or receive a fairly representative dividend check?

IRS agents offered to be helpful and said their department would check around Las Vegas to ascertain just what yardstick could be used to establish the worth of a share of common stock, in any casino. But, strangely, the gambling fraternity was appalled and took appropriate measures to curb any such investigation. Parvin-Dohrman had seemingly rolled boxcars. It was, of course, all straightened out eventually and the government let the matter drop.

Months later, when the Fremont sale had finally gone through and Parvin sat in the driver's seat, his vice-president and treasurer Harvey L. Silbert explained to stockholders at their annual meeting just how the complicated acquisition was arranged.

Silbert said that purchase of Las Vegas gaming casinos by publicly held companies is, in effect, prohibited by Nevada law, so that for the purpose of purchasing the Fremont Hotel a dummy company was set up, with the approval of Nevada gaming officials. The dummy was owned by the Parvin-Dohrman Company, whose officials would be the gaming license holders and would collect profits from the "fictional" company as "rent."

The precedent for this kind of operation had been set when the Del E. Webb Corporation moved into Las Vegas in 1961 with the purchase of a downtown casino, the Mint, and the Sahara Hotel on the Strip.

Obviously such moves were profitable. Silbert described the $10-million deal with five of the Fremont Hotel owners as "so good it's almost frightening."

"Tonight," he told financial editors, "we pay $1.5 million [15 per cent of the purchase price] to Fremont owners and they pay us $1.7 million for 125,000 shares [in the Parvin-Dohrman Company] and thus we get the Fremont and a surplus right away of $170,000." The remainder of the payments on the Fremont were due, he added, over coming years.

Midway through the meeting at the Beverly Hilton Hotel in Beverly Hills, California, a stockholder stood up and asked: "If it's such a good deal for us, why did the Fremont sell?"

"I couldn't answer that," Parvin said. "It's the way the ball bounces sometimes. It amazes us, too."

One reason the Fremont went on the block might be found in the impending government tax action against Fremont officials that ultimately resulted in the indictment of Levinson and others. Silbert said that a $5-million contingency fund had been set up in case the government proved that casino income had been understated. "It could be as much as $3 million," Silbert said of possible government findings. In fact, as has been shown, the actual penalties meted out at the skimming trial of Levinson and the others were puny.

To add to the tax woes of all casino operators, the new governor, Republican Paul Laxalt, has increased taxes on the state's principal industry by 18 per cent to raise $3.7 million in 1969. In addition, he is trying hard to mend Nevada's gambling fences after former Governor Sawyer's blasts at the FBI and the Justice Department for what he felt to be a campaign of harassment aimed at the state. But Parvin was no stranger to the seething gaming pits of Las Vegas and therefore knew what he was letting himself in for.

In 1955 Parvin, formerly an interior decorator, purchased the controlling interest in the Flamingo Hotel. Five years later he dumped it into the laps of a group of Miami Beach hotel operators, including one Morris Lansburgh.

The Flamingo history is one of constant change. On January 13, 1967, it was announced that a Japanese hotel firm had purchased the former Bugsy Siegel ménage for at least $20 million—subject, of course, to approval of the casino deal by the Nevada gaming commission, recently restaffed by Nevada's new governor, and other local agencies. The Fujiya Corporation did their negotiating with Flamingo major stockholders Morris Lansburgh, who shortly thereafter returned to his Eden Roc Hotel in Miami Beach, Sam Cohen of Miami, and Al Parvin.

However, the Japanese bid for the Flamingo Hotel was turned down by the gaming commission. And one therefore wonders if there is any connection between the gaming commission's authorization of Howard Hughes, former owner of Trans World Airlines, to purchase the Desert Inn Hotel and Casino and the seizure by its Japanese owners of Conrad Hilton's Tokyo Hilton Hotel—because of their objection, they said, to the Hilton merger with T.W.A. Hilton's hotel company has been eyeing with interest the profits being made by Las Vegas hotels every day.

Another incident that may have helped trigger the Flamingo upheaval occurred on December 8, 1966. Morris Lansburgh and a group of syndicate-connected men from the Philadelphia, Pennsylvania, and Short Hills and Trenton, New Jersey, areas were called before a New York federal grand jury probing gambling sprees on chartered trips from New York to London. Nothing really came of the probe, but the Flamingo was eventually taken over and is being run by Kirk Kerkorian. And so the trail goes around and around. But if there is a mystery man in Las Vegas now, it could well be Al Parvin.

Among the directors listed in 1966 for the Parvin-Dohrman Company are names that indicate interesting relationships.

Along with Parvin, the directors' list shows: Harvey Silbert, Maxwell Rubin, and E. Parry Thomas.

Harvey Silbert was in 1954 an attorney for the group of Miami businessmen who built Las Vegas' Riviera Hotel, the first high-rise hostelry on the Strip. The Miami men went broke—or were "busted out," whichever you prefer—and Harvey acted as their representatives when Gus Greenbaum took his old group from the Flamingo to the Riviera. In fact, Greenbaum headed the men who had sold the Flamingo to Al Parvin. For his work in representing the Miami group, Silbert wound up with a fairly good-sized chunk of the operating side of the Riviera.

Silbert's name didn't show up at first on the gambling license of the Riviera, but he nevertheless maintained an expensive suite at the hotel and took part in many executive, usually secret, meetings there, and to give him an official, but harmless, title—so he could keep an eye on things—he was made chief "talent buyer" for the Riviera shows. Now that the Fremont has changed hands, moreover, Silbert's position at the Riviera seems solid. He is a four-thousand-share stockholder.

It was in the Bank of Las Vegas that the Teamsters placed their security when they first loaned money to the Fremont Hotel, and E. Parry Thomas, vice-president of the bank, also appeared as a director in the Parvin-Dohrman Company, which was supposedly going in as a brand new owner. Until Levinson's suit was dropped, Thomas was under federal subpoena, along with Levinson and others, to answer questions concerning the multi-million-dollar wiretap suit brought by Levinson against the FBI and Central Telephone Company.

The link between the Teamsters, Levinson, and Parvin has always been clear. And Max Rubin, a director in Parvin-Dohrman, held two points in the Sands Hotel along with Parvin.

While on the subject of Parvin, it is interesting to note that, as the *Los Angeles Times* revealed on October 16, 1966, Supreme Court Justice William O. Douglas has received $12,000 a year since 1962 from the tax-exempt Albert Parvin Foundation, which in turn gets its proceeds largely from a share in a mortgage on the Flamingo Hotel.

Stated purpose of the foundation is the support of fellowship programs for students from underdeveloped nations to study at Princeton University and the University of California at Los Angeles as a means of promoting international understanding.

According to the *Los Angeles Times*, the foundation's board of directors includes two of the nation's best-known educators, Robert F. Goheen and Robert M. Hutchins. Goheen is president of Princeton, and Hutchins, former president of the University of Chicago, now heads the Center for the Study of Democratic Institutions in Santa Barbara. Douglas, as president and adviser to the Parvin Foundation, is the only official to receive regular compensation, which, in his own words, is given him "largely as an expense account" for trips in this country and abroad in connection with foundation interests.

Parvin, who laid most of the rugs in the gaming casinos of Vegas and did a good job—by Las Vegas standards—of decorating the interiors of many of the plush hotels in that community, put his foundation together in 1960 when he sold the Flamingo to the Lansburgh group. Although Parvin held the first mortgage on the hotel to cover payments owed his interior-decorating company for furnishings, Justice Douglas told the *Los Angeles Times* he thought the foundation's interest in the Flamingo had been disposed of. In any event, it appears that everyone decided to bail out of the S.S. "Flamingo," torpedoed while on a goodwill mission to Princeton and other ports.

Another recent development in Las Vegas is the reentry, on the wings of a billion dollars or two, of mystery man-industrialist Howard Hughes. Always the recluse, but perhaps feeling that being in Las Vegas puts him in show business, Hughes now employs a makeup man to give him various disguises so that he can prowl the Strip incognito. A Lon Chaney he is not, but few people have recognized him thus far.

The local officials who once tried to discourage Hughes's making the local scene by boosting land taxes on thousands of acres of his desert real estate northwest of Vegas are now sweating out his return to the gambling mecca via the acquisition of several Strip hotels and casinos as well as numerous other properties.

Among announced Hughes's purchases thus far are the following: Desert Inn (hotel and casino), with a leasehold on the hotel land, and Desert Inn golf course where the celebrated Tournament of Champions was held every year until he took over in 1967; Sands Hotel (with casino) and golf course; Castaways Casino (directly across the Strip from the Sands); Frontier Hotel property (across the Strip from the Desert Inn), making him landlord for the Frontier Hotel and Casino, which have long-term leases; Alamo Airways (adjacent to McCarran Field, in which Hughes is extremely interested); North Las Vegas air terminal; 518-acre Krupp ranch; KLAS-TV, the C.B.S. affiliate formerly owned by Hank Greenspun, publisher of the *Las Vegas Sun*; and Silver Slipper Casino.

A sixth casino purchase, the Stardust, was arranged in June, 1968, for $30.5 million, but Hughes granted a private government request that he delay announcement of his acquisition for ninety days. Attorney General Ramsey Clark wanted "an opportunity to consider the implications of the purchase," according to a Hughes spokesman, with the implied possibility of an antitrust suit being filed by the Justice Department. Had Hughes succeeded in acquiring the Stardust, he would have become Nevada's top gaming operator; the taxes collected from his casinos would have made up about 14 per cent of the state's total take from legal gambling. But apparently wanting to leave well enough alone and not stir up a hornets' nest, Hughes announced on August 15, 1968, that "the Stardust Hotel and Hughes Tool Company have terminated any existing plans for purchase of the hotel."

Finally, an October, 1968, announcement that Hughes had purchased the twenty-eight story Landmark Tower Hotel and Casino for $17.3 million and an announced agreement two months later to purchase 67 acres of Strip property, including the fire-scarred El Rancho site, for about $11 million in cash, indicate that he has run out of neither steam nor money.

These purchases, along with offers being made on countless other properties and the unimproved desert real estate he already owns, are giving pause to all of those with a vested interest in Vegas. Two schools of thought exist. According to a chamber of commerce official, who was quoted in the *Los Angeles Times*:

> There's an underlying fear that Hughes will build a fence around the town, call it Hughesville, and paint it green. Then there's the other school, people who think Hughes will eventually bring some much needed industrial diversification to Las Vegas.

One positive clue to Hughes's intentions is seen in his hiring in September, 1968, of Los Angeles airports manager Francis T. Fox, ostensibly to help build up a jet airport complex in Las Vegas. Fox, who leaves a $45,000-a-year job to take what is said, unofficially, to be a $150,000-a-year position, built the regional airports of the Los Angeles area into the world's largest. Through Fox, Hughes, who owns thousands of prime acres to the northwest of Vegas, could develop a built-in tourist communications link with the gambling empire he has acquired.

Hughes himself talks—through press releases, no one sees the man himself—of industrial diversification, which is the best thing that could happen to Las Vegas. And Nevada, which has no state income tax, no inheritance tax, and no inventory tax on items manufactured there to be shipped out of state, could look good and green to many a businessman with an eye on his pocketbook.

The big question is whether or not such industrial diversification can coexist with gambling, and this is what worries the powers that be. Can *they* get to Hughes and those who surround him? Or have *they* already done so?

One thing is certain: his buying spree has increased property values in Las Vegas—some say to the tune of about 10 per cent—after a couple of years of real doldrums. But there is also concern, voiced by one businessman thus: "Where else could you get control of a state so cheaply as Nevada? If you have economic power you have political power, and in this state you could elect both senators for about $500,000."

And so, as always, there are the questions of how much power a man will have and of how it is to be used. In Nevada, where money talks with a loud voice, this is the question of the day with regard to Howard Hughes.

The ring-around-the-rosy goes on and on in Las Vegas, but as Swifty Morgan once said: "Ashes, ashes, all fall down." We think he made it up at that.

The literary model for Damon Runyon's unforgettable "Lemon Drop Kid," Swifty is court jester to the sporting crowd, lifelong crony of comedian Joe E. Lewis and a host of entertainers who walk on the fringe of the set made up of the people who have it made, put on a few airs, and like to be amused. He is a pleasant, irascible, charming, and vulgar character—all at the same time.

Swifty, who carries a cane and sports a dapper old-time golfers' cap and a goatee, both gray, once tried to sell a stolen watch to J. Edgar Hoover. He is on the long side of sixty but looks and acts the part of a frisky young colt. And that's how he wants it to be, for Swifty Morgan has spent his life and his money betting on frisky young colts. He has followed the horses across the country, giving a lot of questionable betting advice to Joe E., who has always said that he "follows horses that follow horses."

Swifty has rubbed elbows with every top mobster in the country, as well as a few of those somewhat lower down, and can talk for hours about them—but only for laughs, not for lawmen. He knew Bugsy Siegel well and was always a welcome guest at the Flamingo. He was never allowed to pay for a meal, or even a cup of coffee, at whatever odd hour he chose to visit the dining room. So when Bugsy was murdered, Swifty mourned—and why not?

A few years ago, Swifty made a small killing at the races and decided to visit his old haunts in Las Vegas. Warm with memories of the old days, he paid a visit to the Flamingo, which at that time had just been purchased by the Miami hotelmen. The men who *really* ran the casino—Sam Cohen, with 42.75 per cent, Chester Sims, casino manager with 3.75 per cent, and Danny Lifter with 22.5 per cent—welcomed Swifty, and Sims walked with his pink-cheeked guest to the restaurant. The conversation soon drifted to Bugsy, and Swifty regaled one and all with stories that will never be printed.

Swifty soon noticed a man—Morris Lansburgh—walking around the room, saying hello and bowing to the guests. The new secretary-treasurer, 14.6 per cent owner, and major domo at the hotel was a pleasant, smiling fellow—in the latest Las Vegas image of "respectable" ownership—who had made many bucks in surplus government property after World War II, especially in instruments and jewelry, and somehow got in with the hotel crowd that saw Miami fading and Las Vegas coming to the forefront of the tourist trade.

Swifty looked and looked at Lansburgh making the rounds, and he squinted as he did so. In a little while Lansburgh made his way to Swifty's table, and Sims introduced the two men, mentioning that Swifty had been one of the first guests at the Flamingo. At that moment a waitress brought the check for Swifty's lunch to the table. Swifty cocked his head and checked the prices, though he knew Sims would sign for the check. He noticed that a ham sandwich and a cup of coffee—his lunch order—was over two dollars, and his squint deepened into a frown. Lansburgh made no move to take the check. Instead, he looked Swifty full in the face and, in his best hotel voice, asked one of the greatest con men in the world what he thought of the great changes he—Lansburgh—had made in the "Fabulous Flamingo."

For a minute Swifty looked Morris straight in the eye. Then, without a glimmer of expression he picked up his cane and rapped three times on the floor of the dining room. Looking down, away from Lansburgh's beaming face, he said, in a hushed and sepulchral voice: "Come back, Bugsy, come back!"

The rest was confusion.

So you see, Vegas has changed little except externally. The once-vivid personality evoked by the sometimes less than blue-blooded but often colorful characters who peopled its shallowed halls has been watered down. All that's left is a bigger-than-life, gaudy-and-bawdy image of a cow-town that made the big time—with the help of a few thousand flocks of sheep in men's clothing.

TWELVE

CHICAGO:

The Loch Michigan Monster

The face of Chicago is the face of a clock with a million numbers around its rim, and each of its people is a fraction of a second ruled by a mob that says: "You live, you die; you prosper, you fail. We sift the sands of the hours through our fingers."

The story of Chicago, in fact must necessarily be the story of its people, who curtsy to the mobsters—probably fearing them, sometimes profiting from their depredations, appalled by the idea, yet displaying an indifference that permits the monster to feed at will.

Yes Chicago. First in violence, deepest in dirt; loud, lawless, unlovely, ill-smelling, irreverent, new; an overgrown gawk of a village, the "tough" among cities, a spectacle for the nation;—I give Chicago no quarter and Chicago asks for none. "Good," they cheer, when you find fault; "give us the gaff. We deserve it and it does us good." They do deserve it. Lying low beside a great lake of pure, cold water, the city has neither enough nor good enough water. With the ingenuity and will to turn their sewer, the Chicago River, and make it run backwards and upwards out of the lake, the city cannot solve the smoke nuisance. With resources for a magnificent system of public parking, it is too poor to pave and clean the streets. They can balance high buildings on rafts floating in mud, but they can't quench the stench of the stockyards. The enterprise which carried through a World's Fair to a world's triumph is satisfied with two thousand five hundred policemen for two million inhabitants and one hundred and ninety-six square miles of territory, a force so insufficient (and inefficient) that it cannot protect itself, to say nothing of handling mobs, riotous strikers, and the rest of that lawlessness which disgraces Chicago.

Thus did Lincoln Steffens in October, 1903, excoriate Chicago, though he put St. Louis at the top of his list and said that "grafting" in Chicago was petty by comparison and, after Philadelphia, "most unprofessional."

Steffens was profoundly affected by a reform movement in Chicago led by John Maynard Harlan, George E. Cole, and Martin B. Madden, among others. They organized the Municipal Voters' League and tried to fight crime. "The very name was chosen," Steffens said, "because it meant nothing and might mean anything." The group went out after the board of aldermen, sixty-eight in all—fifty-seven of them "thieves," the league stated, promptly and plainly—and proceeded to defeat most of them.

Harlan, who was on the board of aldermen and fought for reform, used to tell "ghost stories" to his fellow aldermen, who together formed what was also known as the city council. Said he: "You may wake up some morning to find street lamps are useful for other purposes than lighting the streets." Or: "Some night the citizens, who are watching you, may come down here from the galleries with pieces of hemp in their hands."

The city lawmakers would fidget. "I don't like dis business all about street lamps and hemp—vot dot is?" said a German boodler—"boodler" is a word coined by Steffens to denote a "grafter" who accepts money for political favors— one night. "We don't come here for no such a business."

Carl Sandburg came up with an idealized concept of Chicago, which was, in his eyes, "Laughing the stormy, husky, brawling laughter of Youth, half-naked, sweating, proud to be Hog Butcher, Tool Maker, Stacker of Wheat, Player with Railroads and Freight Handler to the Nation." He called Chicago the "City of the Big Shoulders," but no big shoulders got there, really, until the mob and the Mafia moved in with Al Capone in 1919. Steffens had come too soon.

Capone, who is supposed to have belonged to the murderous "Five Points Gang" in New York City, was really a product of Brooklyn and the docks in the South Brooklyn and Red Hook section where Albert Anastasia came up through the ranks. Control of the piers in the harbor means control of numerous rackets. Even the big sea crabs that tear the calcium covers off the barnacles of the pilings that are laved by the sea have a racket of their own. They waltz sideways no faster for a man dumped into the river than for a dead fish. The barnacles are merely a constant buffet, always there for the taking. The only competition for the sea crabs are the shiny eels. They swim really fast.

Al Capone sealed the power of the Italian mob in New York when he killed an Irish gangster known as "Peg Leg" Lonergan, a disciple of the notorious Owney Madden. Capone was then scarred by a hoodlum named Gallucio in a street fight. What eventually happened to Gallucio is not known, but shortly thereafter, in 1919, Capone was brought to Chicago by Johnny Torrio, who took the purple mantle of crime overlordship from James (Big Jim) Colosimo. Little is known of Torrio, or of the man he deposed, except that Colosimo had married a woman who was the best known madam in Chicago and kept records of customers known to have both influence and affluence.

The Colosimo pattern has been followed since that mythical temptress, Circe, turned Ulysses' seamen into a herd of swine, but Circe never profited to the extent Mrs. Colosimo did. In fact, part of the initial financial structure of the Sahara Hotel in Las Vegas rests on the Colosimo concept, inasmuch as one of its backers from Oregon married the top madam in Portland and thereby derived much financial wherewithal. There is no record, however, that any of the Sahara's customers, like Ulysses, ever put wax in their ears to drown out the sweet voices of siren temptresses.

It is possible that Capone murdered Colosimo as a favor to Torrio. But in any case, Big Al lined up gambling and prostitution for Torrio, who had become top man on the totem pole of vice in Chicago and its northern and western suburbs by 1924.

Torrio owned three breweries and had an interest in many others, and Capone was quick to see that Torrio was not able to hold the organization together. Capone therefore moved to take the insulation away from the man who had promoted

him into the big money. There is no evidence that Torrio
went down the drain because of anything Capone leaked to
the federal government, but when Chicago police raided a
brewery in May, 1924, Torrio's immunity suddenly ended.
He was prosecuted by the government and sentenced to
nine months in jail. An attempt was made on his life before
he began serving sentence, but he was merely wounded and
fled Chicago for New York. He wound up in Florida and
retired from active mob duty—one of the few lucky ones.

Officials and judges still serving today attended the
Colosimo funeral. Some are so old they must eventually die
on the bench, for the mob won't let them quit. Once "in"
with the boys, you can't get "out," and you pay back dearly
every nickel and dime of mobster largesse.

Since 1919, when Capone came to Chicago, there have
been over one thousand mob slayings in the city, and only
two have been solved. On the other hand, about 62 per cent
of all run-of-the-mill killings—murders committed by "average"
people—are solved. The free-lance murderers are the ones who
are caught, and their nervous paranoia is very different from
the cold-blooded type of mental aberration that exemplifies
the syndicate executioner. And the mob executioners, usually
called in from far-flung parts of the country, are very clever.

Occasionally Albert Anastasia used a garrote to strangle
personal victims, but more often someone else was brought
in, someone such as "Big Greenie" Greenberg of Murder, Inc.,
Anastasia's private firm. For example, Greenberg killed
maverick longshoreman Peter Panto, one of the few water-
front workers in Brooklyn who cried out in 1942 against
various dockside evils.

When contractor Anastasia was going strong and Capone
called on the firm for "hits," an unusual method was worked
out by Phil Straus, a member of the killer team from
Brooklyn, who has since died. Phil's forte was a switchblade
knife and a moving picture theater. Phil would follow his
victim until the future corpse settled himself comfortably at
a local picture house. Then Phil would take the seat behind
him and at the proper time thrust the steel blade of his
knife through the back of the chair into his unfortunate
human target.

Capone's henchmen had a variety of ways of disposing
of victims, but the cruelest of all his practices—which had
nothing to do with death but was worse because of the

humiliation involved—concerned his dealings with the prostitutes who worked in his brothels. Capone, who ultimately died of paresis (motor paralysis of the body caused by syphilis), delivered punch cards to his brothel managers. They were much like the round cardboards given to patrons of the old fun place, Steeplechase Park in Coney Island, Brooklyn. About fifty numbers edged the cardboard disks, and these were punched as soon as a girl had finished with a customer. Often two lacily fringed disks a day were turned in by some of the more skilled whores.

Capone's inherited empire had a valuation that cannot be figured accurately since no books were ever kept, and nobody, not even the public officials, would quarrel with that. However, one raid on the gang's headquarters in April, 1925, indicated that Capone and his henchmen, Tony Arasso, John Patton, Joe Fusco, and Frank Nitti, were receiving millions of dollars from illegal activities involving beer, gambling, and prostitution. Also uncovered were customers' names and the names of federal and local officials who were being paid off.

Patton, who later became the mayor of Burnham, Illinois, was known at the time as the "Boy Wonder of Burnham," but soon after his appointment as mayor he slowly began to fade into the murky depths of time, along with Tony Arasso. Frank Nitti committed suicide, but Joe Fusco is still going strong, listed 'way down in the mob echelon as Joseph Charles Fusco. Fusco, in fact, helped build the Sands Hotel in Las Vegas along with Mack Kufferman, Mal Clarke, Ed Levinson, Meyer Lansky, and Jerry Catena.

The raid on Capone's headquarters in Cicero, where he had moved in 1923 when Bill Dever became mayor, was unusual merely because it happened and because some honest lawmen were behind it. There followed the killing, on April 27, 1926, of William McSwiggin, an assistant state's attorney, and two companions. The murders indicated Capone's utter contempt for established government, although he claimed later his gunmen meant to murder people bucking him in the beer trade.

McSwiggin was the son of Sergeant Anthony McSwiggin, for thirty years a policeman. On September 9, 1926, the father named Capone and his gang aides, Frank Rio, Frank Diamond, and Bob McCullough, as the men responsible for the machine-gunning of his son. Willie Heeney, a Capone roustabout, was named as the "fingerman" who flashed word to Capone at the Hawthorne Hotel in Chicago that McSwiggin, or whomever Heeney mistook him for, was wide open for the strike.

William McSwiggin, known as one of the ablest prosecutors of his time, was digging into the affairs of Capone and the mob and had informers who were close to the syndicate. The tumult and the shouting died in a few months with nobody in the lockup. Capone's claim of mistaken identity was considered to be quite valid by many Chicagoans.

Capone reached the peak of his power in 1927 when William (Big Bill) Thompson became mayor of Chicago. Thompson had run on a "wide open town" pledge—to the horror of reformers and the quiet apprehension of the good people of the city who generally accepted the corruption because they imagined it could not touch them. Capone's prestige soared to wild heights. He was included among those in the greeting party to welcome Commander Francesco De Pinedo's "round the world" fliers representing Italy's boss, Benito Mussolini. Official explanations for Capone's presence have a familiar echo today in the rioting in various cities in America, especially Brooklyn, where, in the summer of 1966, quasi-official authority in the form of the New York City youth board admitted to hiring gangsters to maintain order in riot-ripped areas of the city. Chicago officials said they believed Capone's presence would prevent possible anti-fascist demonstrations, implying that Capone could maintain order where the responsible authorities could not.

How close a city could come to complete criminal dictatorship cannot now be computed, but the fact is that lawmen admit it could easily flourish in what U.S. Supreme Court Chief Justice Warren has called a "Sea of Ethics," as long as a counter-sea, the "Sea of Hypocrisy," thins it out and nullifies its potency.

So Capone's star rose. The whores paid. And the cops were paid. And the numbers gangsters raked in the dough, and they paid. And the politicians were paid by the "alky cookers" in a general roundelay of corruption that made the old Tweed Ring in New York look like a polite game of musical chairs. Ultimately, however, Capone's power was built on the flesh-and-blood fact of murder, the ultimate power if an organization is willing to go that route. In 1926 twenty-nine gang killings occurred in Chicago. In less than six months in 1928 there were sixty-two bombings in the Windy City. Millions of dollars were milked from poor people by numbers racketeers, and when newsmen asked Mayor Thompson's police captain to explain the existence of such wide-scale gambling, he answered: "I am not going to interfere with policy unless I get orders from downtown. I am not going to be sent to the sticks." A few months later he became commissioner of police.

A contemporary of Capone was the storied Dion O'Banion, who ran a flower shop in Chicago and was a purveyor of roses, not a few of which had thorns that scratched Al's hide. It is not a matter of serious history that O'Banion was ultimately wiped out by Capone, but it is interesting to note the quality of loyalty inspired by the boss. For example, O'Banion, like Brooklyn's Joe Adonis, liked to ride horses and indulged his fancy whenever time could be spared from the more strenuous business of crime. It happened that one spring morning O'Banion went a-cantering, and his horse threw him, resplendent in his customary garb of a stylish horseman, into the bridle path, with all of its secondhand oats and hay. Several hours after the unfortunate accident, a group of O'Banion's cohorts went down to the stable that housed the luckless horse and shot the animal dead.

Incidents surrounding O'Banion illustrate not only a peculiar kind of honor among thieves but also how mobsters use odd businesses as legitimate fronts, as though perhaps each is pacing a troubled conscience as well as providing cover for his more nefarious activities. Flower shops and undertaking parlors were once the rage, the latter providing a convenient means of stashing an unreported dead body beneath the false bottom of a coffin housing the "legitimate" corpse.

Mortuary work was, in fact a favorite pastime of the practical mobsters in bygone days. Now there is a newer way of burying a dead man. Used car lots mash together the steel cubicles of what once were automobiles. The compressed steel is taken by railroad to rendering plants and melted down into ingots. And some ingots contain the remains of missing bad boys of the mob.

Al Capone's reign was punctuated by many things that were disquieting to the men at the top of the Mafia, which was just beginning to be put into a nationwide operation by Frank Costello. The formula worked out at the Apalachin-type meeting in Atlantic City in 1929 contained no place for

Capone; somehow he was tipped the black spot and permitted to go by the board. The Depression in 1931 saw Capone tried and convicted in federal court for evasion of income taxes, and the men who directed the syndicate—the real bosses behind Capone, no matter what he thought—let him go down the drain. History records that the federal attorneys did their work well in the jobbing of Capone, but unwritten history may yet show that Capone's day was over, anyway. The money men in the Chicago-New York axis had so decreed. In fact, he had been driving nails into his own coffin in his mistaken idea that he could not be beaten: the murder of a newspaper reporter, Jake Lingle, by gangsters; the death of the motorman on a passing streetcar, killed by a bullet intended for a hoodlum leaving police headquarters in the protective custody of a police lieutenant; the bombing of homes of State Senator Deneen and John Swanton, a candidate for state's attorney; the invasion of polling places, to kidnap election officials and steal ballot boxes, by armed thugs; the machine-gun murder of seven men, who were lined up against the wall of a garage during the bootleg liquor war—the Saint Valentine's Day massacre; and the murder of William McSwiggin.

After his 1931 conviction Capone went to jail and never again returned to Chicago. The syphilis bug was beginning to get in its effective work, and Al was put out to pasture in Florida upon his release from prison. But the organization he welded together remained intact.

Meanwhile, the criminal syndicate, which had sent Capone into exile, found itself without a steady source of revenue when the Eighteenth Amendment was repealed and the citizens of the country could purchase intoxicants without reciting the time-worn phrase, "Joe sent me." So the boys went legitimate and bought into breweries, beginning with 3.2 per cent beer and branching out into control of legal distilleries and distributorships such as Seagrams, Gold Seal, Galsworthy, Canadian Ace Brewery.

The new strategy for the organization backed by the Mafia, in Chicago and elsewhere, was simple: You lose the "alky" money, so you make it up somewhere else. There was gambling, including a host of variations. There were labor unions under duress for the wherewithal to enable them to put up a fight; it was easy to work both ends against the middle.

In Chicago, moreover, it was "more of the same." The

top men after Capone's departure were Paul (The Waiter) Ricca, Frank Nitti, and Louis Campagna. But one new area of operation was the movie industry.

The first step that led to the infamous movie shakedowns in California started when the mob took over the International Alliance of Theatrical Stage Employees and Motion Picture Operators. The head of the local motion picture operations, Tom Maloy, who opposed the hoodlums, was murdered, and a few days later a Capone henchmen took over the union and extorted thousands of dollars from Chicago theater owners. Operators from coast to coast were victimized.

George E. Browne, business agent of the union, and Willie Bioff, a panderer, labor racketeer, and Capone mob bully-boy, built up the drive for extortion funds and decided to take over all of Hollywood. A few movie men resisted, and in 1941, with the help of testimony from Browne and Bioff, who made a deal with the law, and, the mob suspected, from a strong-arm man named Nick Circella, nine racketeers were indicted, convicted, and sent to jail.

It is an old story, but, like a snowball rolling downhill, it picks up facts, half facts, and pure rumor as the years go by. Louis Campagna, Paul Ricca, Phil D'Andrea, Charles (Cherry Nose) Gioe, Ralph Pierce, John Roselli—reputed top Mafioso in the Las Vegas-Los Angeles axis at the moment—and Louis Kaufman were among those sent away in 1943.

Paroles were forthcoming as soon as the boys had served one-third of their time and after some had had their delinquent taxes paid by the mob and generally made their fiscal peace with Uncle Sam. But there remained the matter of vendettas against those who had put them in their iron cocoons.

Frank Nitti had committed suicide after being indicted, and the mob was shocked. But an even stranger aftermath was the continued payment of money to Nitti's widow, Annette, by Johnny Patton. Amounts totaled over $30,000. Such dedication to relatives of Mafiosi who die in "the line of duty" points to part of the strength of the syndicate. When a mobster or his wife can get a guaranteed pension from the mob after the boys have been served long and well, it is easy to understand that something besides terror holds the organization together.

What shocked law-enforcement agencies more, however, was the killing of Estelle Carey, cocktail waitress, in Chicago during the incarceration of her boyfriend, Nick Circella, member of the movie extortion ring. The boys felt Nick might talk too much in jail and sent a killer with a penchant for arson over to Estelle's apartment. The killer—authorities believe that Marshall Caifano, top Capone mob lieutenant and "muscle man" may have had something to do with it—tied Estelle to a chair in her apartment, poured gasoline over her, and set her afire. Her pet poodle, cowering in the corner of the room, was the only witness to the crime. Nick never talked much after that. Caifano is currently serving time for attempting to extort $60,000 from oil millionaire Ray Ryan.

Ryan himself was indicted by a federal grand jury in December, 1968, and accused of conspiracy to defraud the government and obstruct justice. The indictment alleged that in 1967 Ryan destroyed records showing that New York bookmaker Frank Erickson, now deceased, had given gift memberships in Ryan's Mount Kenya Safari Club to Mafia leaders Jerry Catena, Tommy Eboli, and Pasquale Eboli. Unindicted co-owners of the club with Ryan are actor William Holden and Swiss banker Carl Hirschmann. To date there has been no disposition of the case.

So the widow of Frank Nitti, who dealt death to himself, was paid off with cash, and the sweetheart of Circella was paid off in another grisly way as death moved in two directions for two different reasons.

Cruelty, however, is not new to the mob, as has been demonstrated in this book and elsewhere. And cruelty is just as effective a bond as kindness. Typical of the simple, amoral cruelty practiced in a conscienceless way by the hoods is the story of Chicago's Sam (Big Juice) DeStefano and his late chief enforcer, William (Action) Jackson.

DeStefano, currently serving a three-to-five-year sentence on a 1966 conviction, holds the reins of the loan-sharking business and has a habit of always being "sick" when the police come looking for him. On past occasions, while being carried off by police on a stretcher from his very nice suburban home, he has shouted to curious bystanders, through a battery-powered bullhorn, of his travails and mortifications of the flesh, all supposedly brought on by the oppression of the law. He is then usually taken to the barred ward that

Cook County jailers reserve for pestiferous people who keep each other awake with their ravings as long as they think someone is listening.

Jackson, an incredibly untidy hood, would visit the home of a recalcitrant borrower from his boss's high-interest money hoard, break in when the man's wife was at home, strip her, and inflict on her grave indignities, most of which cannot be recounted here: unusual forms of punishment even in the hardened areas of Mafia enforcement where only the men are generally worked over. Once, for example, Jackson bit the nipples off the breasts of the wife of a nonpaying borrower and spat them out on the floor.

Action, who eventually got to weigh 340 pounds, must have astounded DeStefano by his porcine proportions and sadistic proclivities. And DeStefano realized he was too dangerous to keep around; Jackson was therefore eliminated by mob killers.

Like a pig in a slaughterhouse, Jackson endured a short and swift demise, but the engineers who deal out death to Mafiosi fallen out of favor are not as good as the butchers staffing the packing plants in Chicago. Police records show that in August, 1961, Jackson was taken to a cellar and stripped naked. A barbed steel hook was then jammed into his rectum, and he was lifted, howling, to the cellar roof and left to hang there until he died. When he was later taken down, his bowels came out with the barbs as the hook was pulled free. He was later found in the trunk of a Cadillac on Lower Wacker Drive in Chicago. He still had his nipples.

Lincoln Steffens said that "Chicago is a city that wants to be led," and he lashed out against the politicians who gave away city franchises to the highest bidders, politicians who had the authorized city contracts and were paid off to steer the compass readings with a little personal magnetism. But while the syndicate makes use of such corrupt officials, the level of sophistication it is able to reach can be more closely gauged by its ability to put its victims on the spot and ripen them for extortion and payoffs, a far more effective method than that of going to the trouble of stalking them and catching them in some unlawful activity. The syndicate as a whole is not often caught doing the former, preferring to "muscle" a victim out of his bankroll. However, one case in Chicago certainly shows a certain finesse, and it is probable that the Mafia gave a grudging acquiescence to the action.

On June 24, 1966, a former Chicago police officer, John J.

Pyne, was arrested and charged by the FBI with being the mastermind of a multi-million-dollar sex extortion ring operating across the nation. It was claimed that Pyne issued phony police badges to members of his gang to extort money from men accused of being homosexuals. Pyne's racket had been extremely profitable for two years until the FBI nipped it in full bloom. In May, 1967, for example, a jury in the courtroom of Judge Hubert L. Will in the U.S. District Court in Chicago heard evidence regarding the extortion of $10,000 by Pyne and two of his men from a Provo, Utah, contractor.

In the spring of 1964 the contractor was at a convention in Chicago. While walking on a Loop street, he was approached by Robert Schwartz, aged twenty-seven, of Bellmawr, New Jersey, who identified himself as a salesman for a heavy-equipment firm. He asked the contractor to return to his hotel room to discuss business. There, Schwartz made an indecent proposal, and the contractor said he would call the authorities. Schwartz then exhibited a police badge and left. Ten days later, on March 9, 1964, Pyne and a third man, Edmund Pacewicz, went to Provo with papers that purported to include a Chicago warrant charging homosexual conduct by the contractor and documents supposedly asking for his extradition to Illinois to stand trial. The contractor handed over $10,000 to Pyne and Pacewicz and then advised the FBI of his experience.

On May 5, 1967, Pacewicz, aged forty-five, entered a plea of guilty before Federal Judge Hubert L. Will in Chicago, and Schwartz and Pyne, the other two defendants in the case, were found guilty by a jury on May 18, 1967. All three received sentences of five years in jail.

The contractor's unwillingness to be a patsy for the ring paid off in the above case, and the resulting investigation saw seventeen other persons indicted for cross-country extortion activity. It was revealed that victims included a congressman from an eastern state, who was shaken down for $40,000, a U.S. general, who paid off $2,000, and an admiral, who gave the blackmailers $5,000. One man, who held an important post in the U.S. armed services, was approached in his office in the Pentagon by ring "detectives." He subsequently committed suicide. The sex ring also operated across international lines, another victim being a British producer who paid up $3,000 in England.

What happened to the Utah contractor obviously demonstrates more finesse than the mob usually applies to its basic rackets. Perhaps a change is in sight. Certainly, Cicero mob boss Joseph Aiuppa, powerful Chicago hoodlum who dates from the Capone regime, is trying to achieve at least what he considers to be a modicum of respectability. He and his hoodlum cronies established the Yorkshire Quail Club in Kankakee County with a special permit that allowed shooting for five months a year instead of the usual forty-five days. The Illinois conservation department had approved the Yorkshire Quail Club as a state game-breeding area, but it was used as a site for hoodlum hunting parties, membership of which included well-known fixers and gamblers. However, in October, 1968, Aiuppa, whose gangland nickname is "The Doves," had his wings clipped by the then governor of Illinois, Sam Shapiro. Shapiro revoked the permit "in the public interest" after local newspapers reminded their readers that Aiuppa was convicted in Fort Scott, Kansas, in June, 1962, for killing between nine hundred and fourteen hundred migratory birds, mostly doves, when the legal limit was twenty-four. A federal judge termed Aiuppa's bag of birds "unconscionable slaughter."

Evidence shows that the Aiuppa gang likes sitting ducks as well as quail. In August, 1968, the Chicago crime commission spotlighted an incident that indicates to what extent the mob is capable of impressing its will on the public, whether it be a Utah contractor or a visiting fireman.

The report stated that vile conditions "have long prevailed in Cicero night spots dominated by Joseph Aiuppa." It gave as a case in point a visit to Chicago made in August, 1967, by a medical doctor from Sandwich, Illinois. The doctor, on a business trip, completed his work and drove to Cicero. There he entered a night spot called the Show of Shows on South Cicero Avenue shortly after midnight. He downed a drink and then walked to the Town Revue, a nearby club. He ordered one drink and remembered nothing else until about 9:00 A.M. the next morning, when he regained consciousness and found himself in a room at the Karavan Motel, two blocks away. He was nauseated and had a splitting headache.

Sitting beside him in the room, the crime commission report states, was George Hyland, aged thirty-six, who had been a worker at the Shoo-Shoo-A-Go-Go club in Cicero, described by the commission as a mob establishment.

Later the doctor told police that Hyland said: "You owe me $500 for the room and the woman; come up with the $500." At that point Joseph Aiuppa's nephew, Simone (Mike De Rose) Fulco, entered the room armed with a revolver. According to the doctor, Fulco raved like a madman and "demanded that I produce $1,600 or I'd be put into a trunk. He said I had signed blank checks for girls in a number of Cicero lounges."

Fulco displayed five blank checks allegedly bearing the doctor's signature and demanded, "I want this money in an hour." Fulco threatened him with death as an alternative.

The doctor went to the police and filed charges, following up with testimony before a Cook County grand jury, in spite of telephone threats. One caller said: "Drop the charges and you won't owe us anything."

On December 19, 1967, the grand jury handed down an indictment charging Fulco and Hyland with attempted robbery. On September 12, 1967, the Illinois liquor control commission revoked the Shoo-Shoo-A-Go-Go license. The Show of Shows and the Town Revue, managed by mob-connected flunkies, also were forced to yield their licenses, although the liquor control commission indicated that the latter club voluntarily surrendered its permit.

Jumping up the ladder of syndicate power from Aiuppa to the Capone gang leader Paul Ricca is jumping quite a distance. If ever the entire treasury of the Chicago mob is earmarked for defensive action, it will be expended toward keeping Ricca in this country. To this end a seemingly endless battle is being waged, going to every extreme. Thus in the fall of 1966 Jack Wasserman, Ricca's attorney, filed a petition in Rome asking that the Italian government declare Ricca not a citizen of Italy, and the Italian government has given indications that it might oblige. Yet it is interesting to note that in June, 1967, the Italian government nullified a murder conviction outstanding against Ricca for forty-five years, which means that Ricca would at least not have to be imprisoned if, in the event of some legal catastrophe in the United States, he is ordered deported to Italy.

Although he is over seventy, Ricca, whose real name is Paul DeLucia, give or take a few aliases, is still, with Accardo, at the top of mob hierarchy in Chicago. Ricca was born in Naples. In 1917, when nineteen years old, he murdered Emilia Parillo, one of his sister's suiters. He was convicted and sentenced to prison for two and one-half years. Upon his release, Ricca murdered a witness who testified against him in the Parillo trial, Vincenzo Capasso. He then fled Italy, was convicted in absentia, and sentenced to prison for eighteen years for the second murder. This was the conviction that was recently nullified by the Italian government, but despite this act of legal clearance, the Italians do not want him. In fact, Ricca has been so far turned down by forty-seven countries, largely because he has made a habit of mailing abroad newspaper clippings that outline his vicious career as an American gang leader.

Ricca is definitely not a dumb hood. One notable courtroom appearance by the mobster came about when he was placed on trial for perjury in Chicago's U.S. District Court in November, 1967. It was charged that Ricca had lied while testifying at deportation proceedings in 1965 about the source of $80,159 reported as "miscellaneous income" on his 1963 tax returns. Ricca said he made the money by betting at pari-mutuel windows at various Chicago racetracks. FBI agents found evidence enough to warrant an indictment for perjury, and Ricca set about explaining how his winnings were achieved.

He presented a chart showing that he placed eighty-six wagers on thirty-seven races in 1963. In each case his horse came in first. Assistant U.S. Attorney John J. McDonnell sniffed a successful prosecution at this point. How was such complete accuracy possible? "Utterly ridiculous," said McDonnell. "His horses never came in second or third. They always came in first. Isn't that the silliest thing you have ever heard of?"

The jury heard testimony for five days then acquitted Ricca. It seems that he had accomplished not one but two miracles, one at the races and the other in a Chicago courtroom.

Once in a while the underworld stops to count noses, as if to see who is still around, and these tabulations usually take place at "social" gatherings held at swank clubs or hotels. Newspapers in Chicago faithfully report the names of those present, if this determination can be made. License plates on parked autos are also checked out for the identities of party-goers.

One such gathering took place on the night of March

25, 1967, at the Edgewater Beach Hotel on North Sheridan Road in Chicago. Over one thousand persons, including two hundred important crime syndicate members attended the $25-a-plate dinner dance sponsored by the Santa Fe Saddle and Gun Club, located near Hinsdale, Illinois. The club has served as a favorite haunt for gang leader Fiore (Fifi) Buccieri and his lieutenant, James (Turk) Torello, a Cicero loan shark. The Chicago crime commission told the rest of the story in its 1967 report on Chicago crime compiled by its executive director Virgil Peterson, a former member of the FBI, as follows:

> Preceding the dinner dance at the Edgewater Beach Hotel was a cocktail party which started at 6:30 P.M. on March 25, 1967. Arriving about five minutes early was the guest of honor, Fiore Buccieri, and following him in rapid succession were Joseph Aiuppa, the crime syndicate boss of Cicero, Illinois, and Chicago near north side mob leaders Ross Prio, Joseph (Joey Caesar) DiVarco, Dominic DiBello, and William Goldstein alias Bill Gold. Other early arrivals included syndicate loan sharks William (Wee Willie) Messino and Chris Cardi as well as such underworld characters as Mike Glitta, Lawrence (Larry the Hood) Buonaguidi, Joseph Grieco, Donald Grieco, Irwin S. Weiner, Sam (Sambo) Cesario, a First Ward gambling boss, and Lawrence Rassano, a former operator of a strip tease establishment in Cicero and once a suspect in a west suburban bombing.

The crime commission report went on to name literally dozens of figures and also stated that "Chicago police officers described the dinner dance at the Edgewater Beach Hotel on March 25, 1967, as the largest assemblage of mobsters ever staged in Chicago."

A covering blanket must have been woven around the operations of the mob, and for years that blanket would seem to have had the warp and woof of its pattern outlined at least in part within the confines of a modest office building located at 134 North LaSalle Street in the heart of downtown Chicago, a building that has earned not a little scrutiny from law officers.

In 1962 the building directory in the lobby of Number 134 showed offices for the firm of Korshak, Rothman, and Marshall. Next to the Korshak outfit were the offices of California Life Insurance Company president Bernard Nemerov. The concrete, lime, and pecky cypress structure also sheltered one Mr. Sam Tucker. And the mystery of the building was that many of the occupants seemed to have more than a passing acquaintance with one another.

Sleep must have been a difficult thing to come by, though, for some of the great hearts that worked out of Number 134. What could they possibly have in common that would have brought them to the attention of lawmen? Very few people know, for nothing much has happened outwardly, but one spoor of legal manuscript led to evidence of the occupants' great proclivity for doing business with Jimmy Hoffa and the Teamsters he commands. Another pugmark trails across a dry desert to Las Vegas, where every press agent tries not to, but has to, explain why Hoffa and the Teamsters' pension fund generally provide the big guns and the ammunition necessary to justify not only his existence but also the continued existence of Las Vegas.

How does all this fit in with Chicago? A lot. Forget a microscope; take just an ordinary reading glass and focus it on the firm of Korshak, Rothman, and Marshall. Top legal figure is Sidney Korshak, a tall, black-maned, poker-faced man with an ace up his sleeve where mob connections are concerned. Korshak, whose brother, Marshall Korshak, a former Illinois state senator, is now city treasurer of Chicago, limited his practice to Chicago in the early days of his career and maintained a residence at the Seneca Hotel, then a notorious gangster hangout. But how does he fit in with the syndicate? It is often difficult to trace connections, but consider Korshak's career.

Sidney Korshak, termed by the *Los Angeles Herald-Examiner*'s labor editor in 1966 as a man who "seldom stops long enough in one place to get a wrinkle in his suit," began to call for reservations quite regularly in 1959 at the Desert Inn Hotel in Las Vegas. His neighbor at Number 134 perhaps saw to it that Korshak was never turned away, for Sam Tucker—who gave his address to the Nevada gaming control board as 1437 Eighty-Eighth Street, Surfside, Florida—owned 13.2 points in the sweaty jackpot that is the Desert Inn's gaming casino.

Korshak's "guest" tenure at the Desert Inn coincided with a move by Cleveland's racketeering Mayfield Road Gang, which during Prohibition spawned most of the Desert Inn partners, to buy their next-door neighbor, the Riviera Hotel.

The gaming commission denied the application on the basis of dual ownership; nevertheless, important gaming personnel from the Desert Inn began to show up periodically in the pit of the Riviera to keep a brotherly eye on the currency.

Korshak's reputation shaded not one bit as a result of this symbiotic merger, and within a short time he had trudged a trail through the sticky clay of Hollywood show business as an effective negotiator for really large talent—not that Dinah Shore is large, but she made her Las Vegas debut at the Riviera, as did Debbie Reynolds and Tony Martin, the perennially youthful singer for whom it was actually a "second" debut, as he had previously been a Desert Inn regular. These Korshak clients became stars in the Riviera stable, and interestingly enough, it was at about this time that the Justice Department began looking into the West Coast jukebox-talent-agency tie-ups and their controls over the entertainment industry.

A later Korshak foray into the labor-management field came to light in June, 1967, in the midst of a campaign by three unions to control the twenty-eight hundred dealers, box men, stick men, change girls, and others who police the one-way tables that siphon money from gamblers' pockets into the counting rooms of Las Vegas casinos.

Flaunting membership blanks were the American Federation of Casino and Gaming Employees, the Seafarers International Union, and the Hotel and Restaurant Workers—the latter two being AF of L-CIO affiliates. Most of the workers in Las Vegas gaming houses and hotels are already union members, but those who actually handle the green stuff have been excluded thus far.

Seafarers Union chief Paul Hall is head of a mere eighty thousand members, but he is regarded as a possible successor to AF of L-CIO President George Meany. He minces no words in describing the bosses in Las Vegas as men who do not hesitate to "use Chicago and Cleveland mob tactics."

Speaking for management, Sidney Korshak, who said he was "certainly not anti-union," claimed management sees the dealers as part of management. Korshak was speaking of the so-called elite of the gaming pits, the men who play for the house and are counted on to give their bosses an honest count. Actually, of course, "eye-in-the-sky" one-way mirrors hid the watchers who check the dealers, and the watchers have watchers who watch them.

Korshak believes that management would not fight so hard against unionization of dealers "if something could be worked out to make certain that the management people were fully in charge of employment." Las Vegas ownership obviously wants to maintain its own little Utopia, and Korshak has apparently been chosen to see that the job gets done.

Sidney Korshak's record of accomplishment for his clients once prompted Chicago newspaperman Irv Kupcinet to state that he was undoubtedly the highest paid attorney in the United States. Today Korshak resides in style in West Los Angeles and has become a party pet of movieland's social set, but there is no record of his ever having taken the California bar exams, nor is he listed in any of the California law directories. However, there is no fracture of the law, apparently, where simple bargaining and agenting are the prime concern. He also shows up on the West Coast as labor-relations man for Max Factor, the Hollywood cosmetics tycoon, and a whole string of racetracks, in addition to his other role as talent and Teamster negotiator. His numerous capabilities have so impressed Dan Swinton of the *Los Angeles Herald-Examiner* that he called Korshak "the man to move the mountains." And Swinton could be right.

Take, for example, one of the many pieces of available information about Sidney. *Life* magazine, September 1, 1967, charged that a Giancana lieutenant, Gus Alex, has "an especially warm relationship with Chicago city treasurer, Marshall Korshak, and his brother Sidney." On Alex's 1957 application for an apartment on exclusive Lake Shore Drive, he described himself as a $15,000-a-year employee of Marshall, then a state senator, and the magazine quoted a prominent mobster's testimony from a witness stand: "A message from him [Sidney] is a message from us."

At the 1963 McClellan hearings Captain William J. Duffy identified Gus Alex as a "nonmember associate" of the Chicago Mafia, and in 1967 Alex was labeled publicly by the Chicago crime commission as a "member of the Chicago crime syndicate" whose major area of influence was the Chicago Loop. After the Swiss government slapped a ten-year ban on him in 1965, following numerous visits in previous years, a letter of intercession signed by Illinois Senator Everett Dirksen was sent on Alex's behalf to Swiss officials. Dirksen, however, according to the *Chicago Sun-Times* on July 31, 1967, denied knowing Gus Alex or intervening for him.

"Such a thing might have been handled by my Chicago office as a routine matter," said Dirksen, "but I have no knowledge of it."

The umbrella of legality provided by Sidney Korshak concerns even such oddly located individuals as the workers in the vineyards of California, who, in the spring of 1966, struck against their little old winemaker bosses. Speaking through the mellifluous tones of Korshak, Schenley Distilleries announced on television that an agreement had been reached with the grape workers. A week later the Teamsters tried to "muscle" in on the AF of L-CIO, which represented the winery employees. Despite Teamster threats, name-calling, and pure muscle, the sun-drenched workers in the vineyards voted, the following September, to stay with the AF of L-CIO.

There must have been a lot of action at 134 North La-Salle, or maybe there was none if a fellow has to take time out to worry about West-Coast vineyard workers. But close to what action there was, was a man named Bernard Nemerov, president of the California Life Insurance Company. Nemerov, who owned four points in the Riviera Hotel in Vegas in 1963, came up through the ranks from Minneapolis, Minnesota, after getting to know Paul Dorfman, Hoffa's favorite insurance agent, and wound up with his own insurance company based in Oakland, California. It's strange how so many of the Number 134 roads lead in similar direction.

The association typified by some of the names of the office index at 134 North LaSalle Street goes on of course, even though some of the figures have moved away to other buildings in the city. And many of the details remain unclear—except perhaps to law-enforcement officials in Chicago and elsewhere who for one reason or another are unable to act. The convenient and unobserved meetings, in hall corridors and coffee shops—not to mention men's rooms—still take place. Locations change, but it's still business as usual.

An interesting meeting of minds, for instance, must have taken place in July, 1968, at the Teamster-pension-fund-financed La Costa Country Club—currently *the* V.I.P. spa in southern California—when a gathering was observed by law-enforcement officials. Among the cloistered participants were Moe Dalitz and Allard Roen, former executives of the Desert Inn, Allan Dorfman, of the California Life Insurance Company, Sidney Korshak, and Mrs. Jimmy Hoffa. Another attendant at the meeting, from seemingly far afield, was the

Bahamas' Big Daddy himself, Wallace Groves, who could also have an interest in Teamster moneys.

There will never be a beginning of the end for Chicago, but there will perhaps be an end to the beginning, and lawyers will be the pallbearers. Meanwhile, it is difficult to leave the continuing caprices of a modernized version of the old Capone gang in Chicago and travel across the country without stumbling upon part of the overall chain of command that seems to point to that city as being a kind of command post where anything can happen.

It should be noted that the mob boys pay strict attention to what is known—especially in Chicago—as "business." Broads and booze are more or less taboo, except in the wide-open town of Las Vegas and some of the more shadowy places in New York, New Orleans, Dallas, and Palm Springs. And even the latter city is off-Limits to the lesser hoods who go in for stick-ups, assaults, and the more juvenile proclivities of mob button men who are still wet behind the ears.

A case in point in Chicago occurred on May 2, 1962, when the police received a report that a suspicious automobile was parked in front of 1750 Superior Street. They checked and found a 1962 Ford sedan at the specified location. Crouched on the floor of the car, curled up like twin fetuses and caught literally with their switches down, were two notorious Capone syndicate hoodlums: Philip (Milwaukee Phil) Alderisio of Riverside and Charles Nicoletti of Melrose Park. The two hoods informed the investigating officers that the car did not belong to them and that they had no idea who owned it. It was 1:00 A.M., and the boys were promptly taken into custody and just as promptly released on $2,000 bail.

The car was registered in the name of a man who later proved to be nonexistent at an address that just wasn't there. The interesting thing, however, was that the car's dashboard hid three switches, two enabling the operator to disconnect the taillights, making it difficult to be followed at night, and the third turning on a small electric motor that opened a hidden compartment in the backrest of the front seat. This compartment was fitted with brackets to hold shotguns and rifles. It was also big enough for a machine gun, and the cops labeled the automobile a "hit" car—a "vehicle," as lawmen say, used to drive killers to their rendezvous with death, generally somebody else's.

Nothing ever came of the incident, and the failure to make something of the arrests proves that if you work at a thing long enough, as the mob does, you can wear down your opposition to such an extent that soon there are no disputed barricades. The Mafia has been doing just this for several hundred years, and for the past generation it has been building up insulation in this country in the form of judges, courts, and cops who are "bought" and then owe the mob something. And there lies one of the chief faults of a system whereby political selection dictates who chases what hoodlum down the street. Alderisio and Nicoletti had it made, and they knew it. They were going to stay on the job, and they knew the law-enforcement official—or whoever was in charge—wouldn't. If they were caught, they would pay bail and leave. Name the crime, and both of these men have had it tatooed on them where it won't wear off, so much so, in fact, that Alderisio's 1966 extortion conviction, now under appeal, represents merely one more step up the crime syndicate ladder.

Only one of the Chicago mobsters has ever angled tuna, a huge mackerel-like fish that courses both coasts of the United States: a silk-suited—especially for courtroom appearances—alligator-shoed, genial man who generally wears a Windsor knot in his smoothly draped tie. His name is Tony Accardo, but he is also known as "Joe Batters." "Big Tuna," which he is also called, is perhaps a better name, for the waters off Nova Scotia have been traversed many times by one of the country's leading gangsters and his trolling rigs, which have lured many a giant blue-fin tuna into close proximity.

Record catch for this species was a monster of 977 pounds, landed off St. Ann Bay, Nova Scotia, on September 4, 1950, by a lucky Izaak Walton named Hodgson. Tony, who once served as bodyguard for Al Capone and recently came out of "retirement" to reassert his control after Sam Giancana left for the Argentine, would like to beat this record, but he may have to get out that old machine gun and convert his fishing launch into a gunboat to do it.

There is really no point in trying to assess the position of Accardo, or even of Giancana, in the national crime syndicate, since these men and those who follow them and kiss their hands in the traditional greeting of the Mafia are but the rootlets of a growth so much bigger than themselves that it is difficult to understand. Certainly no public official who devotes but a few years of his life to an attempt to figure the mob can ever hope to cope with the solid core of criminality that is beyond all the common and duly regarded concepts of law and order. There is no law for the Mafia except its own.

Something must be said, however, about the princelings of the Chicago mob, the worst criminal conspiracy on the face of the earth, powered and financed by—and financing—men whose names are editorial way-stops in the columns of every newspaper across the country and abroad, but only for their social and business activities, not for their profitable dealings with Mafia underlings. The gang is hundreds of years old, but somehow its whiskers never get gray.

One of the top men for years in Chicago, pal of singer Sinatra, patron of the arts as represented by thrush Phyllis Maguire, who has long been a companion—except during a recent year's dry stretch in a Chicago jail because he wouldn't talk to the grand jury—is Salvatore Giancana, alias "Giancani," "Albert Mancuso," "Sam Mooney," "Sam Flood." Giancana is a sharp man who misses no tricks. Thus Anthony Tisci, his son-in-law, was in 1963 both a $900-a-month secretary to U.S. Representative Roland Libonati (D., Ill.) and an adviser to Mafia chieftain Giancana in a legal battle to halt FBI surveillance of the mobster.

Giancana's "at home" address in Oak Park, Illinois, is too unimportant to mention inasmuch as Tony Accardo's pad probably represents the real Fort Knox of the Chicago gang. Accardo once lived at 915 Franklin Street in River Forest, Illinois, where he was reputed to have had a vault sunk into the solid concrete of his basement and loaded with all the money he didn't know what else to do with. But by the time of the McClellan hearings in 1963, Accardo had apparently moved out, undoubtedly taking his underground valuables with him as well as his black onyx bathtub with its solid gold fixtures.

In Brooklyn, in 1950, when police officers were arrested in an investigation that sank a flock of bookmakers and sent Mayor Bill O'Dwyer's personal frigate, "Bill-O," to the bottom of the East River and Bill himself south of the border, the men sought by the grand jury used to shovel the greenbacks into cellar furnaces. If Tony Accardo didn't have his rumored basement vault, then the excess money went somewhere else—possibly pressed into a lot of campaign buttons.

After Giancana, Accardo, and Ricca, you come mostly to unimportant figures, and there is no guarantee that any of them will be alive for any length of time. But outstanding among them seems to be Marshall Caifano, alias "Johnny Marshall," also "Shoes" and "Heels," quaint appellations stuck on him by lawmen who have called him many other things, many other times.

Caifano is the hoodlum suspected of being connected with the torch death of cocktail waitress Estelle Carey, and he could be the mobster who eventually takes over in Chicago, not only to reap a harvest for himself, but also to serve as insulation for mobsters such as Ross Prio of 1721 Sunset Ridge Road, Glenview, Illinois, who has an arrest record dating back to 1929. But at present Caifano is in jail, having been convicted of fraud in 1967 and given a twelve-year prison sentence to run concurrently with the ten-year sentence he was already serving as a result of the Ryan extortion case.

The only man on record who ever really stood up to Caifano was Beldon Katleman, the owner of the El Rancho Vegas who, in 1960, had Caifano put out of the hotel because he was blacklisted by the Nevada gaming control board. Katleman's questionable reward for kicking Caifano out may have come two weeks later when the El Rancho casino was burned to the ground.

The issue of who will take over in Chicago is probably more important than the workings of civic and social groups out to improve the city, and it is no secret that the man currently being groomed for the role of gangster-guru—whatever Caifano's hopes—is Anthony J. Spilotro, protégé of Felix (The Weasel) Alderisio.

Something of a world traveler, Spilotro, a tough with a penny-polish gleaned from no school that can be found in his record of lawbreaking—which goes back to 1955—flaunts the colors of the U.S. Mafia throughout Europe with the aid of a red Mercedes. Points of call have been Amsterdam and Antwerp, where diamonds and breakfast salami are sliced, and solid gambling places and casinos in Monaco, Nice, and outlying places.

On August 2, 1964, Spilotro and a companion were picked up at the Hotel de Paris, Monaco, and questioned about the theft of $137,500 worth of jewelry from the visiting wife of a New York City oil company executive. Later, on a visit to Antwerp, Spilotro was relieved of two large cut diamonds and a switchblade knife. Although he was extensively questioned, no charges could be pressed against him, but Spilotro was—and is now—under a surveillance thumb that might keep the kettle boiling in Chicago while he goes to grade school and works his way up the long ladder to mob dominance. Others have done it before him, without the red Mercedes.

Chicago is full of hoodlums, and many of them tie in with the "licit" businessmen already mentioned. However, it also seems that wherever you turn in Chicago, you come across Jimmy Hoffa and his fountain of Teamster gold. Take the case of Guiseppe Glielmi: "Joey Glimco," as he is called.

Glimco, who lives at 629 Selbourne Drive, Riverside, Illinois, and has a total of thirty-six arrests—for larceny, robbery, assault with intent to commit murder, and auto theft—has served only twenty days in jail. But then Glimco is a Teamster man. For example, Glimco arranged an astounding deal in the operation of Teamster Local 777 having to do with the rebate of Teamster Union dues to the Yellow Cab Company and the Checker Taxi Company in the amount of $327,491.46. The companies said the rebates over a period of twenty years ending in 1959 were made in order for them to pay the additional help necessary to operate the union checkoff system for collection of employees' union dues. Glimco, beloved of Hoffa, who attributes Joey's troubles to "bad headlines," didn't object when the union paid for his house: $26,000 in Teamster dues money. But Hoffa wasn't around in February, 1969, when Joey was fined $40,000 for violations of the Taft-Hartley Act.

Glimco is only one example of Hoffa's Chicago connections. One can, however, be sure that there will be continuous syndicate and Teamster action as long as their cooperation is profitable.

A fuse was lit for a spell—a brief candle in the darkness that usually shrouds investigative processes where hoodlums are concerned—when Henry Peterson, chief of the Justice Department's organized crime and racketeering section, spoke out during an informal panel discussion at the National Conference on Crime Control in Washington late in March, 1967.

Peterson claimed he knew for a "moral certainty" that "in the upper echelons there is an amalgamation" between the Cosa Nostra and the Teamsters Union and the International Longshoremen's Association. He also said the Justice Department had "identified about 5,000 persons in the nation as members of Cosa Nostra."

Peterson's unexpected bombshell of testimony was cut off by the moderator of the panel, deputy director of the President's Crime Commission Henry S. Ruth, who said: "We're going to move on to another subject." And top officials of the I.L.A. and the Teamsters challenged Peterson to prove his allegation, perhaps secure in the knowledge that the man would have to go through many channels to be able to do this.

Actually, testimony taken by Senator John McClellan's rackets committee and the hearings into organized crime underscore Peterson's contentions, and public statements made by Jimmy Hoffa on behalf, for instance, of Joey Glimco bear Peterson out. The expressed friendship, evidenced by appearances at social functions and, more important, gangster funerals, of Hoffa and I.L.A. lieutenants indicates ties that fun deep and wide. The FBI, which questioned Joe Valachi for a year before he testified to the McClellan committee on organized crime, has all the evidence necessary. All Peterson needs is a chance to talk.

There have been other indications of government suppression of damning evidence. For instance, while praising the work of the Chicago crime commission at a civic gathering in October, 1967, during Chicago Crime Prevention Week, George P. Hunt, *Life* magazine managing editor, deplored what he called censorship of an official document linking Chicago politicians to the mob. Hunt, who also declared that "the present organized crime program of the federal government is a colossal failure," charged that a sixty-three-page report, ordered by the government and prepared by J. Robert Blakey, Notre Dame law professor, was "reduced to four footnotes" by the White House in the final report of the President's Commission on Law Enforcement.

One thing is certain: while Hoffa doesn't wear long hair, he *is* "bigger than Jesus" to certain people in many parts of this country and the world. His crucifixion may start another religion, or end a really bad kind of faith, for the almost two million truck drivers who are helplessly hooked one way or the other by the syndicate—though they must admit there will never be a Cloud Nine or a harp for any of them if they follow the Hoffa-Glimco-Ricca-Accardo-Giancana Chicago recipe.

Meanwhile, in spite of murders ordered over the years for the benefit of the Mafia, not enough has been done to secure successful and lasting convictions; yet as recently as September, 1966, after an almost four-year moratorium on capital punishment in California, there sat in San Quentin over fifty men awaiting execution. These men waiting to die may be slobs, but their pictures and records indicate that few if any of them ever wore a silk suit in his life or had his nails manicured or had enough money in the bank to hire a lawyer. Certainly not one of them is allied in any way with the Mafia killer-types who have spilled more blood in Chicago since Capone's time than that shed by the average Latin-American revolution or the charge Teddy Roosevelt led up San Juan Hill.

In this connection, moreover, not a little of the blame must be placed on the shoulders of the congressional chefs in Washington who have for years placed the mob's culinary monstrosities before the noses of their hungry, but unknowing, constituents. Lift the top of the Capitol dome and sniff for yourself the aroma created by the questionable recipes of a host of questionable minds.

EPILOGUE

The men joined together today in what is known as the syndicate live quite differently from, and play a game that is incomprehensible to, the average citizen. Their claim is already staked out on the moon, you can be sure, and its future waxing and waning will be measured against what the mob can get out of it: whether the profit can be derived from earth or from the Mafia's presence—in absentia, as usual—behind the forces that create the machinery necessary to put flesh and blood in just another position to make a profit for them.

These apes no longer toss coconuts out of trees; they have now pledged themselves to a complete abortion of the law that has given them unlimited power.

The mob boys have exchanged their kinky coats for the very sharp splendor and protection of legal garments designed by men far removed from them intellectually but, for the most part, bound to them by the fear of death. And while the apes themselves seem not to worry about death, in their ultimate winding sheets there are always legal threads—at God knows what cost.

There are silk suits for the boys at $400 apiece, silken girls at a trifle more, and suckers galore, but most of all, there is the pervading, remembered atmosphere of what once was their own poverty—in Palermo, Sicily; in Boyle Heights, Chicago; in South Brooklyn; in the back streets and unwashed, hot alleys of Everytown that spawned the Bugsy Siegels, the Lepke Buchalters, and the people who served them out of fear and fond hope.

These people have put their pennies into hot hands and nickel-plated slot machines over the years, and the machines, like the silken girls, have acquired a patina of social respectability. The fingerprints on their shiny surfaces are those of a host of captive gamblers. The whole state of Nevada lies in chains, and the people who live there *and can change things* seem happy to be forging the links of their own perpetual imprisonment.

The joy of compulsive gambling springs, perhaps, from its very lack of joy, but the proprietors who rake in the money have no need for laughter. Joe E. Lewis once said, "Las Vegas—the only place you can have a good time without enjoying yourself!" and that goes for any gambling joint. But the big question is: "Where does the dough go?" "Who gets it and stashes it away?"

Most people work eight hours a day for their security, but the mob works twenty-four, and there is no man in the world too big for the boys to take on. Take the savings and loan saga, for example.

It appears that a funnel for funds to be siphoned out of the country by racketeers was fashioned in 1960, when it was discovered that Maryland was a honey pot for investors. It took only three incorporators with a total risk of $30 to form a savings and loan association and send out a milk train to investors with a promise that pure cream would be delivered in return. We have named a few of the mob men, and their apologists, who moved in fast. And it is therefore interesting to note that on January 8, 1966, Mayor Sam Yorty of Los Angeles demanded an investigation of "lame duck wholesale handing out of savings and loan charters" by the outgoing administration of Governor Pat Brown, and that in a letter to Attorney General Thomas C. Lynch, the only leading elected officer in Brown's official family to be reelected, Yorty minced no words. He charged that "a sudden speedup of pending applications" came about following pressure on Brown's savings and loan commissioner by top politicians.

On December 31, 1961, Laurence M. Stern of the *Washington Post* asked: "How was it possible for men with major criminal records and dubious financial backgrounds to go into Maryland and traffic in millions of dollars worth of savings drawn from an unsuspecting public?"

Stern stated that part of the answer lay in the fact that Maryland, until late 1961, had no controls over the "phenomenally burgeoning savings and loan business." Savings accounts in Maryland associations were, he said, in institutions that were federally regulated and insured and that state officials were "not worried" about the solvency of these firms or their ability to make good on losses. Cited also were some four hundred additional associations with a combined $250 million in savings that are either uninsured or privately insured. And Stern concluded: "Official suspicions are that some of these associations have served as funnels for hot or dirty money."

Stern didn't say where the money came from or went to—which perhaps indicates a lack of liaison with the FBI—but he did ask how a stolen $100,000 treasury note made its way from a New York broker's office to the safe of the First Continental Savings and Loan Association of Chevy Chase.

It would seem that the high interest rates granted by many savings and loan groups—"Give us your savings and we will loan them"—represent earnings made possible by the mob's usage of "your savings" in "front" enterprises and by the accumulated gratuities acquired through the use of mob money, bastard currency that has to be legitimatized.

In fact, several of the savings and loan groups sanctioned by Maryland failed, and investors were left holding empty money bags. Consequently, a Department of Building, Savings and Loan Association was set up in Maryland to police operations of the non-federal segment of the industry, and to keep in check such excesses as practiced by at least one private savings and loan insurance company, Security Financial Insurance Corporation, which at the time was headed by Maryland House Majority Leader A. Gordon Boone. Boone had been provided with $450,000 to establish the company by a Chicago attorney, Henry McGurren, and a cast of prominent fellow Democratic politicians backed the venture too. Then it was discovered that with less than $1 million in surplus the firm was insuring on one policy a $12-million Utah association!

Before the lid was clamped down, however, people from all points of the compass got in on the honey pot. For example, there was the Las Vegas-inspired account in Anjon Savings and Loan whose history has already been referred to. Anjon Account 804 was apparently established, at least partly, for the purpose of gathering funds to purchase stock of the Merritt Savings and Loan Association. But it is curious to note the names and pedigrees of the Las Vegans and others who banded together where there was money to be made:

Charles D. Baker, former mayor of Las Vegas	$ 5,000
Edward J. Barrick, point owner in three Las Vegas casinos	10,000
George R. Bieber, Chicago attorney	5,000
Irving Blatt	10,000
C. R. Bramlet	2,000
Irving Devine, Las Vegas gambler whose wife was named by *Life* as a mob courier	25,000
M. J. DiBiase, Las Vegas contractor	5,000
James Genlert	5,000
J. E. Hazard	5,000
Herbert H. Jones, Las Vegas attorney	5,000
Clifford Jones, former lieutenant-governor of Nevada	10,000
Harry B. Lahr	5,000
Floyd Lamb, state senator of Nevada	5,000
Edward Levinson, hotel operator and Doc Stacher's man	12,500
Wayne G. Osborn	5,000
John Pullman, onetime president Bank of World Commerce	5,000
Preston A. Parkinson	10,000
M. A. Riddle, head of the Dunes Hotel	5,000
Emanuel Schwartz	5,000
B. E. Seigelbaum, friend of Levinson	12,500
Michael Silvagni	5,000
Sav-Way Investment Company	5,000
Charles Turner	5,000
L. Schofer	1,000
Joe Wells, Las Vegas contractor and onetime owner (in name) of the Thunderbird Hotel	10,000
Paul Weinert	5,000
Sam Ziegman	5,000
Bank of World Commerce	23,000

So there you have the lineup of depositors in a savings and loan association that is, in a very large way, a class above that of the three-member, $30 type that plagued investors with Maryland charters.

The names are indicative of the current trend in America's financial morality, and a lot can be gleaned by studying them. On the list are politicians who make the laws, attorneys who oversee them, labor leaders on both sides of the fence who use them, and gambling men—gambling men with underworld connections who like to take advantage of them if they can. Put them all together and they don't exactly spell mother; it's something more like smother, and the innocent public is the victim who is fast running out of air.

The influence of gangland in the field of money lending, and that business' rise from the obviously insufficient nomenclature and violence associated with the "juice racket" has been outlined by crime reporter Ray Brennan, who pointed out that the syndicate operation utilizes Illinois state laws that authorize acceptance agencies to deal in stocks, bonds, warehouse receipts, bills of lading, and other commercial paper. Such agencies could also be used for disposing of merchandise hijacked from interstate trucks. Three financial agencies under recent investigation in Chicago were incorporated under Illinois charters, Brennan said. A gangster known as Charles (Chuck) English is president of two of the companies, the Lormar Acceptance Company and the B. & D. Acceptance Company. "A third is bossed by Frank Padula, 55, known as the king of the jukeboxes in Chicago and downstate Illinois," according to the *Chicago Sun-Times*. Probers, the paper said, have uncovered evidence that such companies are apparently used to transmit huge sums of money between criminal mobs located in cities from coast to coast.

The disclosures came as a result of investigations by the Illinois crime commission, then headed by Charles Siragusa, who formerly spearheaded U.S. Treasury Department probes into narcotics smuggling from illicit, Mafia-controlled drug centers in Europe.

Said David E. Bradshaw, Chicago lawyer and member of the state crime commission: "Racketeers can feed tainted money, stocks, bonds and warehouse receipts for stolen goods into one end of such an apparatus and the paper would come out the other end, scrubbed and cleaned and ready to be put into legitimate banking channels."

Both English and Padula, who have long arrest records but have never spent a night in jail, are prominent in operations of a jukebox monopoly with estimated gross profits of $18 million a year, all of which is ladled out to the crime syndicate, the newspaper charged. And such activities are not confined to the United States. In October, 1967, *Life* editor Hunt told Chicagoans of the mob's apparent move into Brazil, where the boys were supposedly trying to persuade the government to authorize the minting of $9 million worth of new coins to be used in syndicate slot and vending machines thoughtfully flooded into the country by Charles English and Jackie (The Lackey) Cerone. English and Cerone, who was indicted in February, 1969, on gambling charges, were said to be running the operation, but it is interesting to note that the report arose when Sam Giancana was working his way down to the Argentine.

Such, and other, foreign adventures mean that syndicate profits eventually have to be taken out of the country, not only to be away from the prying eyes of the IRS and, in some cases, to be washed clean for legitimate reentry, but also to be worthwhile to the foreign branch of the Mafia. Lucky Luciano used an order of Catholic nuns to transport money to him from Brooklyn. When the nuns, who had been conned into the act by a man named Balsalmo, traveled to Italy every so often, the cash was left in Rome.

And so it goes. The information has been available to the FBI for decades, but it is stymied at the eighteenth hole every time—whenever the government is called upon to make a choice.

The answers to the mystery of the crime syndicate in America—and around the world, for the boys all know each other—lie, most probably, in the vast sums deposited in Swiss and other foreign banks. Many of the top gamblers in the United States own interests in such banks, and it is not always a question of transferring hard cash. Sometimes merely letters of credit change hands, which indicates that U.S. bankers are lending full cooperation.

So the Mafia law of *omerta* is observed by the respectable banker families, some of whom in Switzerland are so rich that it is not unusual for them to discourage the placement of a deposit of less than $100,000.

Take the Mafia money out of these banks, and you would see a financial panic that could displace quite a few governments. The American dollar supports the economy of Europe in many ways, the least known of which is perhaps through the billions tossed into numbered bank accounts by the mob. And yet it all boils down to the beginning: a two-dollar bet made on a street corner in Anytown, U.S.A.

And everywhere the prospects for the mob widen.

Dollar-poor governments around the world desperately need an international shot in the arm. And instead of the usual loan from the United States, they sometimes look to an influx of U.S. gambling men to help get the tourists to visit. The new countries of Africa and the private American bankrolls that finance hotels in the strangest places all have their eyes on the potential gaming take. And the Mafiosi are willing to accommodate them—on their own terms.

Freetown, Sierra Leone, built a casino overlooking the Atlantic Ocean, and clicking roulette wheels and the whap of playing cards sound a counterpoint to trumpeting elephants and talking drums. A European-style casino is run in the government-owned Federal Palace Hotel in Lagos, Nigeria, by an outfit that also operates two casinos in Egypt. The Club Africana in Accra, Ghana, has assorted games of chance, and another casino is opening near Victoria Falls in Rhodesia, and may finance a large part of the cost of that country's abdication from the British Commonwealth.

All this may have been adding to the perturbation of Croesus, Aristotle Onassis, who in 1966 challenged Monaco's Prince Rainier on ownership of the legendary gambling house at Monte Carlo, a casino that long ago "busted out" many of Europe's aristocrats. The story is that Onassis threw all his shares in the outfit on the open market and that, under the law, the state was compelled to buy them. Possibly Onassis "cashed out" on what looked like a bad deal. The casino was very much out-of-date and quite without customers. At any rate, in March, 1967, the government of Monaco announced payment of close to $8 million for Onassis' 500,849 shares. Perhaps Rainier, who reportedly wants to modernize Monte Carlo, may know of a couple of Las Vegas-type fellows who can come in, throw a new rug on the floor, and really make a fast buck for the place. Anything can happen, but the handwriting seems to be on the wall for Monte Carlo as more and more tourists are heading for Las Vegas, Freeport, and Paradise Island.

Ultimately, of course, the trouble lies at home: the two-dollar bets at one end of the scale and the attitude of the Supreme Court at the other.

The wiretapping conflict is not as complicated as it sounds, but the mob lawyers realize that in the computerized electronic world of today their clients would not stand a chance if the full power of the law could also use the full power of science to aid it. Hence the clamp-down on "bugging" devices and the mob-directed publicity campaign to frighten the American public into believing that it is being spied on at every turn. And since everyone seems to be trying to get the better of the government where income taxes are concerned, there exists a *sub rosa* pricking of the conscience. Has everyone, all of a sudden, identified with the likes of the Accardos, the Giancanas, the Costellos, and the assorted dope-smugglers, counterfeiters, and other criminals the lawmen are *really* after?

The really hard fact of the case for and against wiretapping—which could be called "delousing"—is laid out clearly and voluminously in a report made by G. Robert Blakey, Notre Dame professor of law and contributor to a treatise called "Task Force Report: Organized Crime," a 1967 publication of the President's Commission on Law Enforcement and Administration of Justice. Among other things, Professor Blakey said:

> The most sophisticated use of these techniques—where the goal has been a criminal trial—has been made by the Office of the District Attorney of New York County. It has been testified that without electronic surveillance techniques, specifically wiretapping, this office could not have achieved the convictions of James "Jimmy Hines" [Tammany power for many years], John Paul "Frankie" Carbo, Charles "Lucky" Luciano and Anthony "Little Augie Pisano" Carfano.

Yet in spite of his well-publicized "all out war on crime," even former President Johnson came out against eavesdropping of any kind except in the extreme case of tracking down a plot to assassinate the president. He thereby eliminated one of the most lethal weapons lawmen have against the criminal syndicate and, in effect, cast the protective cloak of the presidency over the machinations of the mob. One cannot help wondering if Johnson's motivations might not have included the fear of similarly garnered evidence exposing other Bobby Bakers.

It is not beyond imagination that if the decline in law enforcement goes too far, vigilantes will take over again—it's an old American custom. The Constitution, where the enforcement of anti-criminal laws is concerned, contains the seeds of its own destruction. The alternatives are clear: either we get the mob, or it gets us. If the latter process is allowed to continue unhampered, the Constitution will be valueless.

APPENDICES

APPENDIX I

Phi Beta Mafia

Anthony Accardo: FBI #1410106, also known as "Big Tuna" because of his proclivity for tuna fishing. Born April 28, 1906, in Chicago. A bodyguard for Al Capone. Developed the technique of carrying machine guns in violin cases in the early days of the Prohibition era. Reported to have become boss of the Chicago criminal syndicate in 1943, coming up through the ranks with an assist from Sam Giancana. From 1957 to 1966 relinquished control to Giancana. Probably reasserted control after Giancana's disgrace in 1966—an event still to be nailed down by police intelligence. Wears silk suits and likes fancy bathtubs with gold fixtures. Defied, with the help of syndicate-oriented lawyers and judges, every attempt to wipe out his underworld prestige.

Vito Agueci: FBI #889944D. Emigrated from Sicily to Canada during the early 1950's. Became, with his brother Albert, part of an underworld operation that set up outlets for heroin smuggled into Canada from Italy. In Toronto the brothers used a bakery as a front for their illegal activities, thus bringing themselves into contact with Stefano Magaddino, top Buffalo racketeer and friend of Mafia kingpin Vito Genovese. The vendetta killing of Al Agueci in 1961 indirectly led to the revelations of Joseph Valachi and details concerning the Cosa Nostra conspiracy in the U.S.

Ismael Barragan: FBI #455305. Born Jan. 15, 1914. Lives in Tijuana, Baja California, and Los Angeles, Calif. Associate of Juan and Roberto Hernandez in the narcotics smuggling racket and, according to the U.S. Bureau of Customs, is responsible for bringing tons of marijuana across the border into the U.S. Criminal record includes arrests for murder, narcotics violations, and, in Feb., 1968, possessing 1754.498 grams of heroin. Source of marijuana probably is the Guadalajara area; of heroin, the Sinaloa area on the Mexican mainland. Owns the Rancho Los Palmos, 20 miles south of Tecate. Is known to accept merchandise, guns, and jewelry in exchange for narcotics.

Anthony Joseph Biase: FBI #36521. Born Sept. 6, 1908, in Omaha, Neb. Lives at 2207 Mason St., and probably is leading Mafioso in Omaha. Frequents the Owl Smoke shop at 610 South 16th St. Arrested for burglary, theft, and, numerous times, bookmaking. Criminal associates, according to authorities, include his brothers, Sam, Louis, and Benny and Samuel Carollo of Kansas City, Mo. Also tied in with Louis Ventola, listed by the police as a onetime resident of Las Vegas, Nev. Associated with Anthony Marcella, now serving a 40-year term for narcotics trafficking in Los Angeles and San Francisco, and Louis Fiano, and through him with top Mafioso Vito Genovese.

Frank Bompensiero: FBI #337240, also known as "The Bump." Born 1905. Lives at Pacific Beach in San Diego, Calif. Has a formidable roster of friends among the hoodlum element, among them James Fratianno and Louis Tom Dragna, but his importance in the California syndicate is a matter of debate by authorities. Yet to live down being called a "dumb hoodlum" by Anthony Pinelli after being sentenced to state prison in 1955 for 5 years on a conviction of 3 counts of bribery. Put in the spotlight, probably by informant, in 1955, when, police records indicate, declared to be head of the Mafia in the San Diego area, a perhaps erroneous assumption.

Joe Bonanno: FBI #2534540, also known as "Joe Bananas." Born 1905 in Sicily. Identified by Joseph Valachi as head of a family of Cosa Nostra members that included narcotics smuggler Carmine Galante. Business interests throughout the U.S. Criminal record includes arrests for grand larceny, possession of a gun, and obstruction of justice. Highly independent operator within Mafia ruling council.

Russell A. Bufalino: FBI #691589. Born Oct. 29, 1903, in Montedoro, Sicily. Lives at 304 E. Dorrance St., Kingston, Pa. Criminal record goes back to 1927 and includes arrests for vagrancy, petty larceny, receiving stolen goods, and, as a result of attending the Apalachin meeting—which he, according to McClellan committee records, arranged—conspiracy to obstruct justice charges. On the latter count sentenced in 1960 to 5 years in jail and fined $10,000 though his appeal was successful, as were those of all who attended the Apalachin meeting. According to McClellan committee records, "one of the most ruthless and powerful leaders of the Mafia in the United States." Also engaged in narcotics trafficking, labor racketeering, and dealing in stolen jewels and furs. Frequents the Medico Electric Motor Co. in Pittston, Pa. Owns the Penn Drape and Curtain Co. of Pittston, and has an interest in other Pittston and New York City dress manufacturing companies. According to McClellan committee records, associates with Santo Volpe, Sam Mannarino, Frankie Carbo, James Plumeri, etc., many of whom are labor racketeers. Fond of prizefights, rarely missing a heavyweight championship contest. Left thumb and index finger amputated.

Leonard Calamia: FBI #366116, also known as "Culanis." Born Jan. 2, 1911, in Kansas City, Mo. Many arrests on record. Served one year in jail on a narcotics-law conviction in 1936. Questioned in 1945 regarding the murder of a government witness, Carl Caramussa, in June, 1945, in Chicago. In 1966 named by government as one of 15 most important narcotics violators. In 1967 lived in San Francisco, Calif. On Dec. 23, 1948, arrested in Albuquerque, New Mexico, and charged with the murder in California of Nick De John, a Chicago hoodlum who had migrated west. Three other men were also indicted, but all defendants were subsequently released when then San Francisco District Attorney Pat Brown called off the prosecution.

Gerardo Vito Catena: FBI #144036. Born Jan. 2, 1902, in Newark, New Jersey. Has lived at 21 Overhill Rd., South Orange, N.J. Owns or controls many business firms in New Jersey, where he has concentrated his criminal activities with such men as the late Lucky Luciano, Joe Adonis, Frank Costello, Anthony Strollo, and Charles Tourine. Since 1923 arrested on charges of robbery, hijacking, bribing a federal juror, and suspicion of murder. Used strong-arm methods to gain control of vending machines in northern New Jersey, aided by Abner Zwillman, late underworld political fixer in that state.

Nick Civella: Listed by the McClellan committee with brother Carl as criminal associate of important, though lesser, men in the Mafia setup in Kansas City. Despite denials, was at the Apalachin crime conclave, according to federal authorities. With Carl and an associate, Max Jaben (Motel Grzebienacz), a top enforcer in the Kansas City underworld, was among 11 men forbidden by the Nevada gaming control board to enter casinos in that state. Others from Kansas City reputed to be close to Civella are Michael and Joseph Lascoula, who have long criminal records.

Anthony Corallo: FBI #269969, also known as "Tony Ducks" because of his skill in dodging process servers. Good friend of labor leader Jimmy Hoffa. Involved in rackets that include gambling, labor racketeering, extortion, strong-arm, and other gangster activities. In June, 1968, convicted in New York City of conspiracy to commit bribery after 10 days of testimony that linked the Mafia with City Hall and sent several individuals to jail including James L. Marcus, a city commissioner and close friend of Mayor John V. Lindsay. Principal territory has been Queens County in New York City, where he has used an automobile agency as a front.

Frank Costello (Francesco Seriglia): FBI #936217, also known as "The Prime Minister" of the national crime syndicate. Born Jan. 26, 1893, in Calabria, in the Italian "boot." After coming to the U.S., for years resided at 115 Central Park West, New York City. Naturalized in 1925. Criminal associates include every known racketeer in the U.S., if not the world. Criminal history goes back to 1908 and includes arrests for assault and robbery, concealed weapons, conspiracy, contempt, and income-tax evasion. Has valuable real estate holdings in New York City and interests in at least one Las Vegas casino. For years was an influential factor in the selection of many candidates for public office who were associated with Tammany Hall in New York City. Derived much of his early income via gem smuggling from abroad: one of his carriers, killed in an airliner crash while on a mission, was carrying $600,000 worth of gems, which were scattered far and wide over a southwestern area in the U.S.

Louis Coticchia: FBI #1427493, also known as "Lou Brady." Born Feb. 25, 1920, in Cincinnati, Ohio. First arrested in 1936 in Ohio for robbery. Other charges filed in Miami and in Hot Springs, Ark. In 1938 sent to jail in Cleveland for 4 years on charges of assault with intent to commit rape. Later received 5 years in jail in Baltimore for receiving stolen goods. Wide range of activity and friendship with top Mafiosi such as Santo Trafficante, Jr., perhaps fitted him for the job of Mafia courier. Confidence vested in him by the gambling element was reflected by jobs he held as pit boss in casinos in Las Vegas, Nev., and Havana, Cuba. Arrested in Tampa in 1963 on suspicion of grand theft and found to have previously visited a motel in Miami under the name "Luiz Paulino Bailey" from Rio de Janeiro, Brazil. Missing for several years.

Frank Cucchiara: FBI #4477, also known as "Frank Caruso," "Frank Russo," "Frank the Spoon." Born March 29, 1895, at Salemi, Sicily. Lives in Watertown, Mass. Naturalized in 1931 at Boston, despite arrests in 1925 in Boston for possession of morphine and dynamite. Rapidly came up the ladder of crime to a position of rackets importance in that city, working hand in glove with Ray Patriarca, New England boss, and important members of the Mafia throughout the East. In 1932 picked up on suspicion of murder. Attended the Apalachin meeting in 1957. Named by the McClellan committee as an operator of gambling joints in the North End of Boston and a financier of narcotic transactions. Interests in Watertown in restaurants and a cheese company.

Joseph J. Di Carlo: FBI #286967, also known as "Jerry the Wolf," "Joe the Gyp," and "Joe DeCarlo." Born Nov. 8, 1899, in Vallellunga, Sicily. Acquired a derivative citizenship in the United

States. Associated for many years with the Magaddino brothers of Buffalo, N.Y. Confidant of Mafia chieftain Joseph Massei of Detroit; believed to be currently engaged in illegal gambling in the greater Miami area, where Massei has long been a power. Criminal record dates from 1920 and includes arrest for assault, coercion, intimidating witnesses, and violation of federal narcotics laws. Has been utilized as a killer by the Magaddinos, according to McClellan committee records, and is now in Florida after having been forced to leave the Buffalo area by police.

Louis Tom Dragna: FBI #4677209. Born July 18, 1920. Nephew of the late Mafioso Jack Dragna, once boss of bosses in California. Seems to be reaching for the syndicate crown in that state. Lives in Covina, Calif. Second-in-command now under Nick Licata, venerable clan elder. Has surrounded himself over the years with men known to police from coast to coast as hard-line criminals, both Mafia and non-Mafia types, including his lieutenant, Harold Meltzer, Joe Sica, and boxing racketeers Frankie Carbo and Frank Palermo—the latter three of whom are all now serving time in Leavenworth for extortion in the shakedown of a well-known fighter. Has influence in Las Vegas, according to police records, where he has placed friends in position of influence in several casinos and is friendly with men involved in skimming operations.

Carmine Galante: FBI #119495. Born Feb. 21, 1910, in New York. Known as one of the most ruthless criminals in the U.S. Many aliases and an arrest record that lists crimes since 1921. Many associates in Montreal, Canada. Considered to be a prime candidate for the world Mafia throne, ranking with the late Charles Luciano and Lucky's superiors in Sicily. Is a confidant of Vito Genovese, Joseph Bonanno, and others and was a major factor in the successful plot to murder Carlo Tresca, the anti-fascist editor, in New York in 1943, according to testimony before the McClellan committee. Has traveled to Palermo, Sicily, for consultations with world Mafia leaders. In July, 1962, was sentenced to 20 years for conspiracy to violate the narcotics laws.

Joseph Gallo: FBI #120842A, also known as "Joe the Blond." Born April 6, 1929, in Brooklyn. A member of the so-called Young Turk group in the Mafia. With brothers Larry (now dead) and Albert ("Kid Blast" Gallo), once challenged—unsuccessfully— the might of the late Joseph Profaci, the Brooklyn don. Power has waned, although he is considered to be a "comer" in the Brooklyn Mafia barony. A good friend of Carmine Lombardozzi, a *capo* in the Carlo Gambino family of New York City. Criminal record dates from 1947 and includes arrests for burglary, kidnapping, attempted sodomy, and felonious assault.

Carlo Gambino: FBI #334450, also known as "Don Carlo," "Carlo Gambrino," and "Carlo Gambrieno." Born Aug. 24, 1902, in Palermo, Sicily. Attended the Apalachin meeting as representative of a powerful Mafia faction in New York City. Involved with his brother Paolo in large-scale narcotics and alien smuggling, according to McClellan committee records. Served 22 months in prison on income-tax evasion charges. Criminal associates have included Lucky Luciano and Thomas Lucchese (both now dead) and gambling chieftain Meyer Lansky. In the paper-products business in Brooklyn, N.Y., and owns a "labor consultant" firm in Manhattan. Married to his first cousin, Vincenza Castellana. A son, Tom, married Frances Lucchese, daughter of Thomas Lucchese.

Vito Genovese: FBI #861267, also known as "Don Vitone." Born Nov. 21, 1897, in Naples, Italy. For years maintained a home in Atlantic Highlands, N.J. Reputed head of the Mafia organization in the United States. Now serving time in a federal prison for narcotics violations. Criminal record dates back to 1917 and includes arrests for burglary, concealed weapons, auto homicide, and murder. Attended the Apalachin meeting in 1957. An intimate of former New York Mafia boss Frank Costello and the late Lucky Luciano as well as top-ranking officers in the U.S. armed forces during the occupation of Italy in World War II.

Sam Giancana (Salvatore Momo): FBI #58437, also known as "Sam Mooney Giancana," "Sam Flood," "Albert Mancuso." 60. Currently in the Argentine after a flood of publicity knocked him off the syndicate throne in Chicago. An ex-convict: arrested and rearrested in three murder investigations before he was 20 years old; served time for auto theft, burglary, moonshining, and refusing to tell a federal grand jury of syndicate operation. Arrested over 60 times on various charges. Boss of Chicago crime syndicate from 1957–1963, when he paid a forbidden visit to a gambling lodge known as Cal-Neva, on Lake Tahoe's Crystal Bay and was entertained by Phyllis McGuire of the McGuire sisters. Adverse publicity about the visit to the lodge, which was partly in California and partly in Nevada, sent his fortunes tumbling. Later, in Mexico City in Dec., 1966, before moving onto the Argentine, renewed his romance with Miss McGuire, who was driven from the airport by Richard Cain, real name Richard Scalzetti, onetime chief investigator for former Cook County Sheriff and now Governor of Illinois Richard B. Ogilvie.

Vincent Gigante: FBI #5020214, also known as "The Chin." Strong-arm man and suspected killer for the Vito Genovese family. A former professional boxer. Better known as the prime suspect in the attempt to kill declining underworld chief Frank Costello in May, 1957. Two years later found guilty, with Genovese and 13 others, of violating the federal narcotics laws and sentenced to 7 years in jail.

Anthony Giordano: FBI #1624141. Born June 24, 1914, in St. Louis, Mo. Rise in the syndicate underscored by arrests dating back to 1938, including charges of carrying concealed weapons, robbery, holdups, income-tax evasion, and counterfeiting tax stamps. On the latter charge sentenced to 4 years in prison in Sept., 1956. Inherited a sinister mantle dating back to the initial influx of Mafiosi into St. Louis in 1916. Criminal associates include Ralph Quasarano of Detroit and Frank Coppola, supposedly now in Sicily but known to be a frequent visitor to Mexico, where he meets with syndicate buddies from the U.S. Has ties to New Orleans through Sam Vitale and others.

Joey Glimco (Giuseppe Glielmi): FBI #238623. Born 1909 in Salerno, Italy. After making three applications, naturalized in 1943—despite a police record that showed 34 arrests—when he was assistant business agent of the Taxicab Drivers Union of Chicago, Local 777. Has served no time in jail or prison, but has been charged, at one time or another, with larceny, disorderly conduct, vagrancy, murder, attempted murder, and robbery with a gun. Recently fined on a federal indictment with having accepted gifts from two Chicago businessmen—who were indicted with him—in violation of the Taft-Hartley Act. Hoodlums named as his associates during a Senate hearing in 1959 were Tony Accardo, Paul Ricca, the late Jack Guzik, Gus Alex, and the late Louis Campagna, whose last will and testament was witnessed by Mrs. Glimco.

Leroy Jefferson: FBI #2028068. Born Feb. 1, 1919, in Warran, Ark. Long considered to be "the largest individual narcotic trafficker" and a "source of supply" for other top-echelon Negro traffickers in California, Oregon, and Washington. Made his first rackets money as a pimp. Handled heroin deliveries throughout the U.S. and Mexico and was able to get his hands on such vast quantities that, according to McClellan committee records, "several New York Italian groups were actually 'fighting' to get him as a customer." When arrested by the Los Angeles police on June 2, 1958, was carrying $32,430; common law wife, Delores Mitchell, had $5,765. Police claim to have broken up the Jefferson organization with convictions in three conspiracy cases involving Jefferson and his crew.

Meyer Lansky: Nearly 70. With his brother Jake rules the gambling roost of the crime syndicate and may be the direct link between unknown moneyed nabobs who stash away mob dollars in foreign banks and the cash vaults of the U.S. criminal cartel. Ran gaming houses for the syndicate in Havana, Cuba, under the Batista regime, then moved operations to British-owned Bahamas and thence to other islands in the Caribbean. Served with mobster Benjamin Siegel as enforcer for Louis Buchalter, industrial racketeer in New York's garment section. Lives and flourishes by respect for the Sicilian element in the mob, as exemplified by a remark he made when notorious Las Vegas gambler "Russian Louie" Strauss disappeared after a card game while in the company of hoodlums Jack Dragna and Marshall Caifano: "That's the last time a Jew will cheat a Sicilian in this town."

James V. Lasala: FBI #690454. Born June 4, 1904, in Brooklyn. Operates as a wholesale distributor of narcotics on the West Coast, maintaining ties in New York City for "business" purposes. Considered one of the most important dope traffickers in northern California, obtaining huge supplies of heroin from the Mafia's eastern branch. Uses extreme caution while making contact with other traffickers or customers, but fell afoul of the law in Feb., 1954, when he was sentenced to 4 years in prison for selling narcotics obtained from Christoforo Rubino of New York City.

Nick Licata: FBI #2585380. Born Feb. 20, 1897, in Camporeale, Tampani, Italy. Probably the most influential syndicate member in the Southwest. Came to the U.S. in 1913, and worked his way up into Mafia ranks with an amazing ability to dodge interference, if not surveillance, from the law, despite association in one form or another with syndicate subchiefs Louis Tom Dragna, Frank Bompensiero, James Fratianno, and others. Lives in the Royal Arms Apartments in Torrance, Calif., and has been associated over the years with every important gangster in the West. Record includes a small fine and a 30-day suspended sentence for refilling liquor bottles in 1945. During a probe of California rackets by a state assembly subcommittee, said he knew nothing of the Mafia and was cited for contempt for refusal to answer other questions. Charges were dismissed in November, 1959. Became boss in southern California after the death on Jan. 10, 1968, of Frank DeSimone, of Downey, Calif., who represented the southern California branch of the Mafia at the Apalachin meeting and was considered a top enforcer. Interests reach Dallas, Tex., and Detroit, Mich., where he is related by marriage to William Tocco.

Peter Licavoli: FBI #237021. Born in St. Louis; therefore immune from deportation. Rules Detroit's Mafia hierarchy with Joseph Zerilli, John Priziola, Angelo Meli, and William Tocco—though all are answerable to Joseph Massei, retired elder of the Detroit complex now in Florida. Owns the Grace Ranch in Tucson, Ariz., and was associated with narcotics trafficker Nicola Gentile and, through Gentile, with Luciano. Legitimate business interests are legion, and a fair chunk of the Las Vegas Strip is reputed to be in his hip pocket.

Peter Joseph LoCascio: FBI #986365, also known as "Mr. Bread." Born June 10, 1916, in New York City. Lives in Copiague, Long Island, N.Y., frequenting the Lower East Side (Little Italy) section of Manhattan. A vicious and feared hoodlum. Criminal associates include Joseph and Pete DiPalermo, John Ormento, who attended the Apalachin meeting, Rocco Mazzie, James Picarelli, and Sammy Kass. Since 1935 arrested for federal liquor-law violations, conspiracy, and New York State narcotics-law violations. Business interests in the Ennis Construction of Lindenhurst, Long Island, N.Y., and Peppi's Restaurant in Forest Hills, N.Y., according to McClellan committee records.

Carmine Lombardozzi: FBI #290869, also known as "The Doctor." Over 50. Has been involved in gambling, shylocking, labor racketeering, vending-machine and jukebox rackets, extortion, strong-arm action, and murder, according to records provided by New York City police. Member of Gambino family in New York. Frequents cafés in the Flatbush and Coney Island sections of Brooklyn, where he orders cheese and prune Danish pastry and coffee in the wee hours of the morning. Was given a "suspended" underworld sentence for mismanagement of a jukebox concession in Brooklyn after the late Joseph Profaci interceded for him with Mafia chieftains. Has served less than 5 months in jail since his first arrest in 1929 and has the kind of record his bosses like—1 incarceration out of 22 pinches.

Joseph Paul LoPiccolo: FBI #790022C, also known as "Joe." Born April 28, 1918, in Chicago, Ill. Considered by authorities to be an important member of the Mafia. Arrested during an investigation in Miami. Convicted on a federal narcotics charge in Aug., 1958; sentenced to 20 years. Lives, when not in jail, on East 69th St., New York City, and at 621 44th St., Miami. Frequents both the Vesuvio Restaurant and the Paddock Bar, 50th and Broadway, in New York City, according to McClellan committee records, and is a partner in the Rock Creek Fluorspar Mining Co., in Hardin County, Ill. Often travels to Philadelphia and Chicago and friendly with hoodlums Santo Trafficante, Jr., and Joseph DiPalermo.

Stefano Magaddino: FBI #7787220. Born Oct. 10, 1891, in Castellammare, Sicily. With his brother Antonino controls syndicate operations in the Buffalo-Niagara Falls area of New York. Lives on Dana Drive, Buffalo, and for years operated a funeral parlor and other "legitimate" fronts, including a linen service and the Power City Distributing Co., of Niagara Falls. Arrested in 1921 in New York as a fugitive from justice (homicide) for the Avon, N.J., police department. Provides a link in the chain of Mafia influence that stretches from Boston across the Great Lakes area to Minneapolis. Is believed to have been at the Apalachin meeting, escaping the police raid there across nearby fields and woodland.

Carlos Marcello (Calogero Minacori): FBI #292542. Born Feb. 6, 1910, in either Tunisia or Guatemala, depending on whose word you take. Mafia chief of New Orleans. Barony extends across the borders of states adjourning Louisiana, and owns vast tracts of land and myriad "legitimate" businesses. Also has a stranglehold on every racket and racketeer in Louisiana—even the shrimp, through his many boats. Has spent time in the penitentiary for selling marijuana, but has not been incarcerated as long and as many times as the authorities would like. Received special political favors over the years, including a full pardon by Governor O. K. Allen, then a political ally of Huey Long, for an assault conviction. Efforts to deport him reached a climax in 1961 when he was "dropped off" in Guatemala—where he had claimed he had been born—by U.S. immigration officials. Promptly returned to the U.S. and has been here ever since. No other country wants to take him. Helping govern Louisiana fief are six younger brothers. Adheres to Mafia principles perhaps more fervently than any other boss of bosses in the country.

Harold Meltzer: FBI #113017, also known as "Happy." Operates large bookmaking and prostitution syndicates in California and is associated with the more important labor organizers on the West Coast. Confidant of California gangland figure Louis Tom Dragna. Appears to be a world traveler for the organization, having visited Canada, Cuba, Hong Kong, Japan, Hawaii, and the Phillipines in recent years. In 1951 pleaded guilty in a conspiracy case following a probe by the Federal Bureau of Narcotics and was sentenced to 5 years in prison. Has associates in Oklahoma, Texas, Baltimore, Miami, Las Vegas, and Boston, and ranks with gaming chieftain Meyer Lansky in the syndicate hierarchy.

Michele Miranda: FBI #91524, also known as "Mr. Big," "Mike," and "Frank Russi." Born July 26, 1896, in San Giuseppe Vesuviano, Naples, Italy. Attended the Apalachin meeting as a leader from the New York area. Is one of the most feared and ruthless Mafiosi in the country, concentrating his attention on New York City's garment industry—inherited in part from the notorious industrial racketeer, Louis Buchalter—and on rackets once shared with Thomas Lucchese. Last known address: 167 Greenway North, Forest Hills, N.Y. Travels to Florida, Canada, and Italy and has an interest in Cuban enterprises. Has spent much time in jail with a record dating from 1915.

Salvatore Mussachio: FBI #191344, known also as "Sally the Shiek." Related by marriage to the family of the late Giuseppe

Magliocco, who headed one of New York City's larger families before he died of natural causes in Dec., 1963. Now nominal head of the family, may be superseded by a *caporegime* in the Magliocco empire named Joseph Colombo. Has 22 arrests and 1 conviction on his record sheet. A suspect in the slaying of two people in 1938. Friend of Frank Livorsi and Livorsi's associates such as Vito Genovese, John Stopelli, and members of the Tocco and Meli families of Detroit. Claims to be in the fish business and to be a barber and a baker. Also probably a social lion: had two tables at the Tocco-Profaci wedding in Brooklyn in June, 1955.

Raymond Patriarca: FBI #191775. Born March 17, 1908, in Providence, R.I. Began his criminal career as a bodyguard for bootleggers and led a charmed life, for was known to have planned the hijacking of many shipments of alcohol he was hired to guard. Long enjoyed the favor of top mobster Frank Costello. Controls the lotteries, bookmaking, dice games, and wire services in the New England area, particularly in Boston and Worcester, Mass., and also in Broward County, Fla. As one of the many gangsters involved in the makeup of the gambling complex in Las Vegas was very influential in the affairs of the Dunes Hotel. Inherited his criminal empire from Mafia chieftain Phillip Bruccola, former boss in New England now residing in Italy. Convicted on March 8, 1968, for conspiracy to commit murder, is now free on bond, appealing a 5-year prison sentence and $10,000 fine. Latest sentence raised his conviction record to 6, for a variety of offenses including violation of the Mann Act.

Anthony Pinelli: Also known as "Tony." Born 1899 in Calascibetta, Sicily. Came to New York City in 1913 as an immigrant. Has never become a citizen. Has entertained top Mafia figures at his home in Sierra Madre. Revered by his syndicate friends. Presently is the object of deportation proceedings as a result of his 1966 guilty plea to charge of evading federal income taxes for the year 1959. In 1960, despite the fact he did not live in his "district," monopolized gambling and other rackets around Gary, Ind. According to the late Robert Kennedy, former chief counsel of the Senate rackets committee, used profits from the rackets to acquire valuable real estate in southern California and was put in charge of Gary-East Chicago gambling in 1954 by Tony Accardo and Sam Giancana. Has been reported linked with two known mobsters who attended the Apalachin meeting: John Sebastian LaRocca and Gabriel Mannarino.

Al Polizzi: FBI #118357, also known as "The Owl." Arrived in the U.S. from Siculiana, Sicily, on March 15, 1900. One of the "most influential members of the underworld in the United States," according to U.S. Senate investigators who also point out, in a review of underworld statistics compiled by the McClellan committee, that he somehow managed to retire and get away from the action in Cleveland, Ohio, before it became the bailiwick of the Mayfield Road Gang headed by Moe Dalitz. Shaped the course of syndicate events for years in Cleveland and has a police record that starts in 1920. Lives in Coral Gables, Fla., and is a buddy of Frank Milano of California, *caporegime* of an area that embraces southern California and includes operations in Mexico.

Raffaele Quasarano: FBI #736238, also known as "Ralph," "Gino," "James Quasamoni," and "Jimmy Q." Born Dec. 20, 1910, in Mauch Chunk, Pa. Lives in Grosse Point Woods, Mich. Is considered a top-level Detroit underworld member and narcotics trafficker. Criminal record dates from 1931 and includes arrests for disorderly conduct, armed robbery, shooting, wiretapping, gambling, and violation of federal narcotics laws. Owns a barber-supply business, a furniture company, a housing development, and a gymnasium in Detroit. Father-in-law Vito Vitale is an underworld leader in Italy. Listed as criminal associates by authorities are most of the principal members of the Detroit underworld including Angelo Meli and John Priziola, and a fair smattering of New York City characters including Frank Costello, Frank Livorsi, and Frank Coppola, narcotics dealer deported to Italy.

Vincent John Rao: FBI #792086C. Born 1898. Considered a *consiglieri* in the Mafia structure of the family of the late Thomas Lucchese. Appeared at one time to be in line as successor to the throne. Has real estate holdings in East Harlem and currently lives in Yonkers. "Legitimate" interests include paint companies, housing projects, and parking lots. Is the owner of, or has an interest in, the Parkway Motel at Elmsford, N.Y., according to McClellan committee records. Has five arrests, one for homicide, but has never been convicted. Named by John F. Shanley of the New York City police department as an associate of mobsters Mike Coppola, Joe Rao—no relation—and Willie Moretti, a New Jersey gambling kingpin until his slaying in a tavern in Palisades, N.J., in 1951. Also according to Shanley, is interested in gambling, using Nunzio Arra, also known as "Frank Arra," a business agent for a lathing union, as a lieutenant.

Paul Ricca (Paul DeLucia): FBI #832514, also known as "Felice DeLucia," "Paul Viela," "Paul Villa," "Paul Salue," "Paul Maglio," "Paul Barstow," "Paul (The Waiter) Ricca," and "The Porter." Born 1898 in Naples. Apparently has resumed his leadership of the Chicago mob, sharing the throne with Anthony Accardo. A favorite of certain factions in the Teamsters Union. Arrest record dates back to 1927. Served time for conspiracy and income-tax evasion. Arrested twice in his native Italy for murder;

convicted once. Is up for deportation, but is undeportable because no foreign country will grant him residency. With Accardo took the Fifth Amendment almost 200 times during questioning before the McClellan committee, dodging questions concerned with an illegal attempt to seize control of the Chicago liquor industry. Once bodyguard to Al Capone. Became boss of bosses in Chicago after Capone died, until income-tax troubles—solved at one point when the Teamsters Union "bought" Ricca's home for $150,000, far above the appraised value—created so much publicity that Accardo, then Sam Giancana, took over.

John Roselli (Filippo Sacco): FBI #333986. Born 1905 in Esteria, Italy. Claims Chicago birth, but was recently found guilty of falsifying his birth record in the U.S. In 1968 faced deportation and a fine of $2,000. Also, along with several other men, charged in 1968 with conspiracy to cheat members of the Friar's Club in Los Angeles through the use of electronic devices during gin-rummy games. Arrived in the U.S. on September 16, 1911. In 1921 arrested by federal narcotics agents in Boston and released on bail. Jumped bail, somehow wangled his way out of the charge, and changed his name to Roselli. Early associates included Abner Zwillman of New Jersey and Al Capone in Chicago. Convicted in 1944 as one of the principals in the Bioff-Browne movie extortion case, sentenced to 10 years in prison, and released on parole on Aug. 13, 1947, after serving 3 years and 7 months. Close associate of hoodlum chieftain Louis Tom Dragna in California. Seems to be in charge of the Los Angeles-Las Vegas gambling axis. Dresses in the latest fashion. His steel-gray hair, thin face, and bright piercing eyes are well known in almost every Las Vegas gambling casino, but prefers the Desert Inn.

Joseph Sica: FBI #343378. Born Aug. 20, 1911, in Newark, N.J. Considered an extremely rough and hardened criminal. Lengthy criminal record includes arrests since 1928 for robbery, murder, extortion, narcotics, and other serious crimes. Now serving time in Leavenworth for extortion. Connections extend coast to coast and criminal associates include his brothers Alfred, Frank, and Angelo. Well known to all racketeers in southern California. Listed in McClellan committee records as an important Mafia leader who is known as a killer, travels with a body-guard, and has dipped his fingers in the narcotics trade. In early 1950 with 15 other gangsters was indicted in California for conspiracy to sell narcotics, but the case was thrown out when the principal government witness, Abraham Davidian, was shot to death while sleeping in his mother's home at Fresno, Calif.

Anthony C. Strollo: FBI #4282858, also known as "Tony Benda" and "Tony Bender." Born June 18, 1899, in New York City. Is mystery man of syndicate. Disappeared on April 18, 1962, from his home in Fort Lee, N.J., during a family ruckus with the reigning Brooklyn don Joseph Profaci. For years was one of the most powerful racketeers in the U.S., concentrating his attention on the northern New Jersey dock area. An intimate of most of the top racketeers. Arrest record dates back to 1926. A hoodlum known as Joseph Lanza was his enforcer for many years.

William Tocco: FBI #534742, also known as "Black Bill." Born in Terrasina, Italy. A member of the board of reigning Mafia dons in the Detroit area. Related by marriage to Mafiosi throughout the country. Said to share the rule in Detroit with Joseph Zerilli. Illegal activities, listed by the McClellan committee, include gambling, bootlegging, burglary, robbery, larceny, and tax evasion. Rise to power in Detroit had beginning in the 1930's, when the Italian mobsters took over from the non-Mafia members of the famous Purple Gang. Son, Anthony, is married to Carmela, daughter of the late Joseph Profaci of Brooklyn.

Santo Trafficante, Jr.: FBI #482531B. Maintains residence in Tampa and Miami, where he operates lucrative rackets operation. Lived at one time in Havana, Cuba, operating gaming casinos under the Batista regime. With advent of Castro, returned to the U.S. where he inherited rackets controlled by his father, Santo Trafficante, Sr., who died in 1954. According to government files, attended Apalachin meeting and is an associate of such criminals as Meyer Lansky, Joseph Bonanno, Sam Giancana, Sam Mannarino, and Joseph Riccobono. Was among guests at the marriage of Carmela Profaci to Anthony Tocco in June, 1955. Later appeared at a reception in the Hotel Commodore with others, including 13 men who attended the Apalachin gathering. Early in 1968 visited, for reasons unknown, Singapore, Hong Kong, and South Vietnam. Is an intimate of Louisiana Mafia chieftain Carlos Marcello.

Joseph Valachi: FBI #554, also known as "Joe Cago," "Joe Cargo," "Joe Kato," "Joseph Siano." Born Sept. 22, 1903, in New York City. Criminal associates included, before his arrest and appearance before the McClellan committee, Joe Adonis, Anthony Strollo, John Stopelli, etc. Criminal record includes arrests for burglary, robbery, and carrying concealed weapons. In 1960 pleaded guilty to federal narcotics-law violations and was thereafter instrumental in exposing the inner workings of the Mafia. Bailiwick was the upper East Side of New York City, where he was, among other things, a wholesaler of heroin.

Joseph Zerilli: FBI #795171C. Born in Terrasina, Sicily. One of the five ruling dons of the Detroit Mafia family. Supposed to have exercised the greatest continuing influence through the years on the Detroit syndicate structure, though some police officials claim that Pete Licavoli, whose brother Dominic is married to Zerilli's daughter Rosalie, really is the Detroit boss. Listed by McClellan committee as having been involved in almost every form of illegal activity: extortion, mayhem, and murder; burglary, robbery, and larceny; bootlegging and illegal possession of weapons. En route to the Apalachin meeting but turned back when he found out there was trouble, according to Detroit police.

APPENDIX II

Las Vegas Casino Licensees

The following is a listing of licensees in some of the larger downtown and Strip casinos in Las Vegas. Gambling licenses are issued by the Nevada State Gaming Control Board, and those listed here were in effect as of May 1, 1968.

(C.O. stands for Corporate Officer.)

Desert Palace, Inc., dba CAESAR'S PALACE
Las Vegas, Nevada

	Shares
ADLER, Abraham: 6304 Fairlane Dr., Baltimore, Md.	100
AGRETTO, Ralph: 3322 Berwyck, Las Vegas, Nev.	50
ALPERSTEIN, Jerome: 1701 Woodholme Ave. Pikesville, Md.	50
AXELROD, Max: 15610 Van Aken Blvd., Cleveland, O.	150
BEALLO, Herman: 3570 Las Vegas Blvd., Las Vegas, Nev.	110
COHEN, John (deceased): 115 Peterborough St., Boston, Mass.	100
DEVERELL, George: 1639 Parkchester Dr., Las Vegas, Nev.	100
FACCINTO, Albert: 1337 St. Jude Circle, Las Vegas, Nev.	100
FRANK, Walter B.: 7107 Grand Ave., Cleveland, O.	110
GLICKMAN, Howard: 1422 N. Sweetzer, Dept. 300, Los Angeles, Calif.	100
GOLDBERG, Nathaniel: 1444 E. Baltimore St., Baltimore, Md.	400
GRASMICK, Louis J.: 303 Valdene Ct., Timonium, Md.	50
GROBER, Bert M.: 356 Desert Inn Rd., Las Vegas, Nev.	200
GUNION, Fred A., M.D.: 1148 N.E. 99th St., Miami, Fla.	50
JACOBS, Nathaniel: 7505 Long Meadow Rd., Baltimore, Md.	366
JACOBSON, Edward: 1 Charles Center, Baltimore, Md.	110
JACOBSON, Morris: 4201 Cathedral Ave, N.W., Apt. 810, West Washington, D.C.	100

JACOBSON, Nathan S.: 1 Charles Center, Baltimore, Md.   650
JANIEN, Cedric: 416 E. 50th St., New York, N.Y.   400
KADAN, Leonard: 13937 Cedar Rd., Cleveland, O.   75
KLIM, William: 3051 Kishner Dr., Apt. 201,
    Las Vegas, Nev.   100
KLINE, Sam: 8201 16th St., #18, Silver Springs, Md.   100
KOREN, Eugene B.: 445 Desert Inn Rd., Las Vegas, Nev.   100
KOVENS, Irvin S.: 6203 Verdene, Baltimore, Md.   100
KRAUSE, Marvin: 350 Desert Inn Rd., Las Vegas, Nev.   100
KURLAND, Sanford: 13937 Cedar Rd., Cleveland, O.   75
LEVIN, Leonard: 3512 Autumn Dr., Baltimore, Md.   100
MALLIN, Stanley: 2367 Mohigan, Las Vegas, Nev.   555
McINTOSH, Jud: 7 Lake Shore Dr., Avondale Estates, Ga.   325
NEWMAN, Jake: 2220 Juana Vista, Las Vegas, Nev.   100
PERENCHIO, Robin: 13240 Stone Ridge Pl.,
    Sherman Oaks, Calif.   100
RACKIN, Martin L.: 628 N. Foot Hill Rd.,
    Beverly Hills, Calif.   110
RAINESS, Julius: 3407 Midfield Rd., Baltimore, Md.   110
ROGERS, Ben J.: 2030 Thomas Rd., Beaumont, Tex.   150
ROGERS, Nathan: 2190 Thomas Rd., Beaumont, Tex.   150
ROGERS, Sol J.: 2195 Thomas Rd., Beaumont, Tex.   150
ROGERS, Victor J.: 2025 Thomas Rd., Beaumont, Tex.   150
ROSENBERG, Harry: 8211 Anita Rd., Baltimore, Md.   50
SARNO, Jay: 3541 Maricapa Way, Las Vegas, Nev.   1400
SCHUMAN, Ruth: 1701 Woodholme, Pikesville, Md.   50
STEIN, Daniel: 4849 Koval Lane, Las Vegas, Nev.   200
WALD, Harry: 4793 Koval Lane, Las Vegas, Nev.   100
WATNER, Lloyd: 1112 Race St., Baltimore, Md.   55
WEINBERGER, William S.: 4777 Koval Lane, #3,
    Las Vegas, Nev.   200
SHENDAL, Dean: 548 Ellen Way, Las Vegas, Nev.   200
CLAIBORNE, Robert C.   50
HORTON, Starr W.   100
JOHNS, Charles B.   100
KAMINSKY, Moe   50
PEARLMAN, Samuel   100
PLATT, Leonard   40

Casino Operations, Inc., dba LAS VEGAS HACIENDA
Las Vegas, Nevada

Casino Operations, Inc. Proprietary Interests   *Percentage*
WARREN BAYLEY INVESTMENT COMPANY   81.88
    BAYLEY, Warren (Estate) (Judith Bayley,
        Executrix): c/o Hacienda Hotel, Las Vegas Blvd.,
        Las Vegas, Nev.   100.00

MAGLEBY, C.: 109 S. 3rd St., Las Vegas, Nev.   C.O.
INMAN, B.: 93 E. Reno Ave., Las Vegas, Nev.   C.O.
CURFEW, L. S.   10.62
SEIDEMAN, Ben: 1532 S. 7th St., Las Vegas, Nev.   3.75
SEIDEMAN, R.: 117 N. Hamilton Dr.,
     Beverly Hills, Calif.   3.75

Casino Operations, Inc., Beneficial Interests
SOUTHERN NEVADA INVESTORS LTD.   60 N.P.
JARRATT, Charlotte: 9069 Chaney Ave., Downey, Calif.   6.63
BAYLEY, Warren (Estate) (Judith Bayley, Executrix):
     c/o Hacienda Hotel, Las Vegas Blvd.,
     Las Vegas, Nev.   31.38
MATTHEWS, V.: Litchfield Rd., Norfolk, Conn.   4.42
OVERHOLSER, J. H.: 4961 Palomar, Tarzana, Calif.   5.44
SEIDEMAN, Ben: 1532 S. 7th St., Las Vegas, Nev.   3.32
SEIDEMAN, R. M.: 117 N. Hamilton Dr.,
     Beverly Hills, Calif.   3.32
SEXTON, Sophia: 10017 Wiley Burke, Downey, Calif.   2.20
MULCONNERY, Florence: Belair Apts. Apt. 118,
     2001 Beverly Plaza, Long Beach, Calif.   2.20
MULCONNERY, William J. (Estate) (Florence
     Mulconnery, Executrix): Belair Apts, Apt 118,
     2001 Beverly Plaza, Long Beach, Calif.   6.18
TERRAZZI, E.: 1218 S. St. Andrews, Santa Ana, Calif.   2.20
CURFEW, Harold: 7913 Melva St., Downey, Calif.   5.52
HOFUES, F. (Estate): 6803 Lakewood Blvd., Dallas, Tex.   2.20
DESSEL, Louis: 4502 Highland Pl., Riverside, Calif.   4.42
CRAFT, Shields B.: 2451 Brickell Ave., Apt. PH-T,
     Miami, Fla.   5.52
MARTELL, LeRoy and Emma: 114 S. Locust,
     Visalia, Calif.   3.72
BORIS, James E.: 6333 S. 3rd, Los Angeles, Calif.   2.20
RANKAITIS, John: 7401 Naylor, Los Angeles, Calif.   1.33
MILLER, Hubert: 7953 Mt. Vernon, Lemon Grove, Calif.   1.13
HESSE, R. E.: 933 E. Gross, Tulare, Calif.   3.05
JAME, Mabel E.: 1130 Fiske St., Pacific Palisades, Calif.   2.20
BAYLEY, Patrick K.: 179 'S' St., Salt Lake City, Utah   1.33

Consolidated Casino Corporation, MINT HOTEL Division
Las Vegas, Nevada

Percentage
HUGHES, John P.: 750 Rancho Circle, Las Vegas, Nev.   30
JAMES, Howard P.: Las Vegas, Nev.   70
THOMPSON, Earle: 3501 Maryland Pkwy., Villa 74,
     Las Vegas, Nev.   C.O.

FITZGERALD, Maurice E.: 1701 Ivanhoe Way,
    Las Vegas, Nev.   Casino Mgr.
HINKLE, Jess W.: 1808 Ivanhoe Way, Las Vegas, Nev.   C.O.
BENNETT, William G.: 4113 Fortun Ave.,
    Las Vegas, Nev.   Adm. Ofc.

Consolidated Casino Corporation, SAHARA HOTEL Division
Las Vegas, Nevada

	Percentage
HUGHES, John P.: 750 Rancho Circle, Las Vegas, Nev.	30
JAMES, Howard P.: 2020 Bannies, Las Vegas, Nev.	70
HINKLE, Jess W.: 1808 Ivanhoe Way, Las Vegas, Nev.	C.O.
THOMPSON, Earle F.: 3501 Maryland Pkwy., Villa 74, Las Vegas, Nev.	C.O.

Consolidated Casino Corporation, THUNDERBIRD HOTEL
Division
Las Vegas, Nevada

	Percentage
HUGHES, John P.: 750 Rancho Circle, Las Vegas, Nev.	30
JAMES, Howard P.: Skyland, Zephyr Cove, Nev.	70
THOMPSON, Earle F.	C.O.
HINKLE, Jess W.	C.O.
BENNETT, William G.	C.O.

Flamingo Resort, Inc., dba FLAMINGO HOTEL
Las Vegas, Nevada

Owner	*Percentage*
TRACY INVESTMENT COMPANY	100
KERKORIAN, Kirk: 37 Country Club Lane, Las Vegas, Nev.	Pres.
BENNINGER, Fred	V.P.
ALJIAN, James D.	Sec./Treas.
PECHULS, Rose	Dir.

Licensees, Operating Company	
KERKORIAN, Kirk	Chmn.
BENNINGER, Fred	Pres./Dir.
ALJIAN, James D.	Sec./Treas.

PECHULS, Rose	V.P./Dir.
GOODWIN, Ernest	V.P./C.O.
NEWMAN, James W.	V.P./C.O.
SCHOOFEY, Alex J.	C.O.

Four Queens, Inc., dba FOUR QUEENS CASINO-HOTEL
Las Vegas, Nevada

	Percentage
ABRAMSON, Einar: 1816 S. 17th St., Las Vegas, Nev	1.5
ADELSON, Mervyn: La Costa Country Club, Costa Del Mar Rd., Rancho La Costa, Calif. 92008	2.0
BARNES, F. E., Jr.: 2917 Mason Ave., Las Vegas, Nev.	1.5
BELLANGER, H. L.: 2913 Colanthe Ave., Las Vegas, Nev.	4.0
CALLAHAN, T. J.: 367 Desert Inn Rd., Las Vegas, Nev.	7.5
COULTHARD, G. W.: 601 Rancho Circle, Las Vegas, Nev.	1.0
GABRIELE, Julius: 1201 Buehler Dr., Las Vegas, Nev.	1.0
GAMBARANA, Edgar: 501 Park Way E., Las Vegas, Nev.	2.0
GARTH, Max: 3115 Dona Marta Dr., Studio City, Calif.	1.0
GINSBURG, M. E.: 1100 N. Alta Loma Rd., Los Angeles, Calif.	2.0
GOFFSTEIN, Ben, Estate: 353 Desert Inn Rd., Las Vegas, Nev.	15.0
GOLDMAN, H. A.: 1001 N. Crescent Dr., Beverly Hills, Calif.	4.0
GOLDMAN, Norris J.: 1634 Tower Grove Dr., Beverly Hills, Calif.	1.0
HAM, A. W., Jr.: 1337 Cashman Dr., Las Vegas, Nev.	4.0
HAM, A. W., Jr. (Trustee for Pattea Reid Tueller): 1337 Cashman Dr., Las Vegas, Nev.	1.0
HAZAN, M. A.: 1822 Doheny Dr., Los Angeles, Calif.	2.5
KRAFT, B. F.: 531 Park Way E., Las Vegas, Nev.	2.0
LAXER, G. B.: 7813 Chesterfield, Knoxville, Tenn.	1.0
MACK, J. D.: 1501 S. 6th St., Las Vegas, Nev.	6.0
MACK, J. D. (Trustee and Melvin MOSS, Trustor, for Ellen Joy Moss and Rosemary Beth Moss): 1501 S. 6th St., Las Vegas, Nev.	4.0
MACK, J. D. (Trustee for the Center Trust): 1501 S. 6th St., Las Vegas, Nev.	2.0
MACK, J. D. (Trustee for the Peter Trust): 1501 S. 6th St., Las Vegas, Nev.	2.0
MOLASKY, Irwin A.: 43 Country Cub Lane, Las Vegas, Nev.	2.0
MORSE, H. S.: 712 N. Sierra Dr., Beverly Hills, Calif.	3.0
NABAT, A. S.: Fremont Hotel, Las Vegas, Nev.	1.0
PAPAGNA, William T.: 1932 E. Oakey Blvd., Las Vegas, Nev.	1.0

PARVIN, Albert B.: 2220 Avenue of the Stars,
   Los Angeles, Calif.   3.0
ROTHBERG, G. Harry: 321 S. Beverly Dr.,
   Beverly Hills, Calif.   4.0
WELLS, H. A.: 750 Brown St., Reno, Nev.   4.0
WELLS, Joe (Estate): 725 Rancho Circle, Las Vegas, Nev.   4.0
WELLS, Robert: 1580 Circle Dr., Reno, Nev.   2.0
WHITE, N. L.: 55 Country Club Lane, Las Vegas, Nev.   1.0
LANDWIRTH, Michael   3.0
MISSLER, Earl B.   1.0
STEWART, John D.   2.0

FREMONT CASINO CORPORATION
Las Vegas, Nevada

Percentage

PARVIN, Albert B.: 2220 Avenue of the Stars,
   Los Angeles, Calif.   45
GOLDMAN, Harry A.: 9105 Carmelita, Beverly Hills, Calif.   45
GOLDMAN, Norris: 1634 Tower Grove Dr.,
   Beverly Hills, Calif.   10
FALBA, Frank: 4777 Koval Lane, Apt. 4, Las Vegas, Nev.   C.O.
HILL, James: 27 Country Club Lane, Las Vegas, Nev.   C.O.
NABAT, Abe: c/o Fremont Hotel, Las Vegas, Nev.   C.O.

GOLDEN NUGGET
Las Vegas, Nevada

Shares

BLAINE, G. C.: 1623 Hastings Ave., Las Vegas, Nev.   8,827
KING, C. C.: 880 Rancho Circle, Las Vegas, Nev.   4,100
GREENE, W. E.: 1224 Park Circle Dr., Las Vegas, Nev.   12,000
HIRSCH, C. J.: 2104 Santa Rita Dr., Las Vegas, Nev.   C.O.
BRICK, Arthur: P.O. Box 610, Las Vegas, Nev.   68,856
CAFFERTY, Jack D.: 2411 Mason, Las Vegas, Nev.   100
GRIFFITH, R. B.: 400 Rancho Circle,
   Las Vegas, Nev.   % Rentals
MARTIN, W. M.: 2824 Ashby, Las Vegas, Nev.   % Rentals
MARK, M. H.: 611 First Federal Bldg.,
   Indianapolis, Ind.   % Rentals
DAHLIN, Ray: 298 S. Anza, El Cajon, Calif.   % Rentals
BOYD, William: 1110 Douglas Rd.,
   Las Vegas, Nev.   % Card Room
PIEPER, Jack K.: 3609 Fortune, Las Vegas, Nev.   % Casino

ROSE, Gordon: 2339 Sandy Lane, Las Vegas, Nev.	% Casino
WILLIAMS, John: 2209 Mesquite Ave., Las Vegas, Nev.	% Casino
WORTHEN, Robert: 1315 Norman, Las Vegas, Nev.	% Casino
ABRAMS, Lucille: 1599 Williams St., Denver, Colo.	20,000
BERNSTEIN, Dr. Peter M.: 2531 W. McNichols Rd., Detroit, Mich.	26,000
CAHLAN, A. E.: 3211 Ashby, Las Vegas, Nev.	41,600
CASTELLUCCI, Bernard and Jennie: 919 W. 84th St., Los Angeles, Calif.	22,000
COOPER, Chester C.: 3000 Ashby Ave., Las Vegas, Nev.	30,490
HAUGEN, Marian Virginia: 5229 Morgan Ave. S., Minneapolis, Minn.	40,200
HOUSSELS, Mrs. J. Kell: 1012 S. 6th St., Las Vegas, Nev.	20,000
IDE, Mrs. Rozan: c/o Crown Jewelry Store, Great Falls, Mont.	20,000
KELLER, Mitzi H. (Executrix for Norman Keller): 905 Ironwood Dr., Las Vegas, Nev.	32,000
KROLOFF, Robert: 2650 California St., Apt. 1, Mountain View, Calif.	26,000
McAFEE, Guy (Estate): Box 610, Las Vegas, Nev.	45,200
McMICHAEL, J. W.: 1615 Maryland Pkwy., Las Vegas, Nev.	26,000
MASEK, Irma D.: 13421 Fairfield Lane, Apt. 55–1, Seal Beach, Calif.	20,000
PURCELL, Kermit	20,000
RYAN, Martin S.: 1231 Bartlett Bldg., Los Angeles, Calif.	24,000
STEIN, Freida: Box 610, Las Vegas, Nev.	20,000
WITTUS, Max and Lucille (Trust): 2121 Santa Ynez Dr., Las Vegas, Nev.	10,000
LAZARD-VANIER, Marie Louise	25,800

Hotel Conquistador, Inc., dba HOTEL TROPICANA
Las Vegas, Nevada

	Shares
DENVER, Edward J.: 860 DeWitt Pl., Apt 1407, Chicago, Ill.	200.0
FEINBERG, Preston: 401 Parkway W., Las Vegas, Nev.	2,284.3
FIELDS, Jackie: 1313 S. 16th St., Las Vegas, Nev.	516.0
HOUSSELS, J. K., Jr.: 380 Rancho Circle, Las Vegas, Nev.	3,066.6
HOUSSELS, J. K., Sr.: 1012 S. 6th St., Las Vegas, Nev.	3,066.6
KALLIS, Jack A.: 1130 S. Canal, Chicago, Ill.	918.8

KALLIS, Morton: 1130 S. Canal, Chicago, Ill.	281.6
MIRSKY, Solomon B.: 3180 Lake Shore Dr., Chicago, Ill.	2,189.3
SALTZ, Sidney: 412 S. Wells St., Chicago, Ill.	1,976.0
URBAN, Louis: Route 1, Dundee, Ill.	525.0
VALENTINE, Grace A.: 1040 Bayview Dr., Suite 520, Fort Lauderdale, Fla.	400.0

Hughes Tool Company, dba THE CASTAWAYS CASINO
Las Vegas, Nevada

	Percentage
HUGHES, Howard R.: 3145 Las Vegas Blvd. S., Las Vegas, Nev.	100
HOLLIDAY, Raymond M.	Pres.
GAY, Frank W.	Sr. V.P.
MONTROSE, Maynard E.	Sr. V.P.
COLLIER, Calvin H., Jr.	V.P./Treas.
CONNER, Earl M.	V.P.
KISTLER, William A., Jr.	V.P.
LESCH, James R.	V.P.
MARTIN, Daniel J.	V.P.
MYERS, Park L.	V.P.
PAYNE, Lyle L.	V.P.

Hughes Tool Company, dba DESERT INN
Las Vegas, Nevada

	Percentage
HUGHES, Howard R.: 3145 Las Vegas Blvd. S., Las Vegas, Nev.	100
BRADY, Rodney H.	C.O.
COLLIER, Calvin H., Jr.	C.O.
CONNER, Earl M.	C.O.
GAY, Frank W.	C.O.
HARNED, Malcom S.	C.O.
HOLLIDAY, Raymond M.	C.O.
HOOPER, Rea E.	C.O.
KISTLER, William A., Jr.	C.O.
LESCH, James R.	C.O.
MONTROSE, Maynard E.	C.O.
MYERS, Park L.	C.O.
PAYNE, Lyle L.	C.O.
PEDERSON, Don E.	C.O.
RANKIN, William E.	C.O.

SCHAAF, Charles E. C.O.
STINSON, Leon B. C.O.

Hughes Tool Company, dba FRONTIER HOTEL
Las Vegas, Nevada

	Percentage
HUGHES, Howard R.: 3145 Las Vegas Blvd. S., Las Vegas, Nev.	100
HOLLIDAY, Raymond M.	Pres.
GAY, Frank W.	Sr. V.P.
MONTROSE, Maynard E.	Sr. V.P.
COLLIER, Calvin H., Jr.	V.P./Treas.
CONNER, Earl M.	V.P.
KISTLER, William A., Jr.	V.P.
LESCH, James R.	V.P.
MARTIN, Daniel J.	V.P.
MYERS, Park L.	V.P.
PAYNE, Lyle L.	V.P.

Hughes Tool Company, dba SANDS HOTEL
Las Vegas, Nevada

	Percentage
HUGHES, Howard R.: 3145 Las Vegas Blvd. S., Las Vegas, Nev.	100
HOLLIDAY, Raymond M.	Pres.
GAY, Frank W.	Sr. V.P.
MONTROSE, Maynard E.	Sr. V.P.
COLLIER, Calvin H., Jr.	V.P./Treas.
CONNER, Earl M.	V.P.
KISTLER, William A., Jr.	V.P.
LESCH, James R.	V.P.
MARTIN, Daniel J.	V.P.
MYERS, Park L.	V.P.
PAYNE, Lyle L.	V.P.

Hughes Tool Company, dba SILVER SLIPPER
Las Vegas, Nevada

	Percentage
HUGHES, Howard R.	100

HOLLIDAY, Raymond M.	Pres.
GAY, Frank W.	Sr. V.P.
MONTROSE, Maynard E.	Sr. V.P.
COLLIER, Calvin H., Jr.	V.P./Treas.
CONNER, Earl M.	V.P.
KISTLER, William A., Jr.	V.P.
LESCH, James R.	V.P.
MARTIN, Daniel J.	V.P.
MYERS, Park L.	V.P.
PAYNE, Lyle L.	V.P.

M. & R. Investment Company, dba DUNES HOTEL
Las Vegas, Nevada

	Percentage
RIDDLE, M.A.: 2808 Brown Circle, Las Vegas, Nev.	35.28
RICH, Charles: 2622 W. Charleston Blvd., Las Vegas, Nev.	12.00
WYMAN, Sidney: c/o Dunes Hotel, 3650 Las Vegas Blvd. S., Las Vegas, Nev.	21.00
RICE, Robert: 1311 S. 5th Pl., Las Vegas, Nev.	7.72
DUCKWORTH, George: 1400 Westwood, Las Vegas, Nev.	6.00
ENGEL, Howard I.: 1621 Westwood, Las Vegas, Nev.	5.00
BASSINGER, Wilbert: Route 1, Industry, Pa.	1.00
GENGERELLA, Louis: 1109 Beaver, Midland, Pa.	1.00
HERSCH, Joseph: 1805 N. Whitley, Hollywood, Calif.	1.00
STEINBAUM, Jerome: 1109 Tower Rd., Beverly Hills, Calif.	2.00
GOLDSTEIN, David: 3478 Paradise Rd., Las Vegas, Nev.	2.00
SCHAFER, Leonard: 1716 Chapman Dr., Las Vegas, Nev.	1.00
APCAR, Frederick: 1499 Cayuga Pk., Las Vegas, Nev.	5.00
RIDDLE, Norma: 2808 Brown Circle, Las Vegas, Nev.	C.O.
CAMPBELL, Leonard J.: 400 Parkway, East Las Vegas, Nev.	C.O.

N.L.V. Casino Corporation, dba SILVER NUGGET
North Las Vegas, Nevada

	Percentage
RIDDLE, Major A.: 2122 Edgewood, Las Vegas, Nev.	51
RIDDLE, Norma F.: 2122 Edgewood, Las Vegas, Nev.	C.O.
WIENER, Louis, Jr.: 1700 Chapman Dr., Las Vegas, Nev.	C.O.
THOM, Arthur	C.O.
ROVINSKY, Meyer	5

KAUFMAN, David M.   5
RUBIN, Gabriel   5
COHEN, Herbert S.   5
APCAR, Frederic   10

Prell Hotel Corporation, dba ALADDIN HOTEL
Las Vegas, Nevada

Shares

ATOL, Elias J.: 908 Benedict Canyon, Beverly Hills, Calif.   12
AGRON, Oscar: 1812 E. St. Louis, Las Vegas, Nev.   8
BERMAN, Adolph (deceased: Estate of): 907 S.
    Gramercy Pl., Los Angeles, Calif.   4
BRILL, John H.: 2100 Jefferson St., San Francisco, Calif.   2
CLARK, Paula C.: 3784 Central Park Dr., Las Vegas, Nev.   2
COBLENTZ, Alexander: 1609 S. 6th St., Las Vegas, Nev.   4
FEINBERG, Harry: 3187 Silver Saddle St., Las Vegas, Nev.   4
GARBIAN, Albert: 449 Desert Inn Rd., Apt. 47,
    Las Vegas, Nev.   8
GARFIELD, Pearl: 1001 N. Odgen Dr., Los Angeles, Calif.   2
GILBERT, Gil: 1700 Rexford Dr., Las Vegas, Nev.   20
GILBERT, Sanford L.: 3177 Brazos St., Las Vegas, Nev.   2
GOLDMAN, Harry A.: 9105 Carmelita, Beverly Hills, Calif.   20
HASTIE, Carl J., Jr.: 241 Sands Ave., Apt. 105D,
    Las Vegas, Nev.   4
HILTON, Harriet Z.: 6904 Munsee Lane, Indianapolis, Ind.   8
HOFFMAN, Jack: 3944 Lemon Ave., Long Beach, Calif.   4
KEAYS, John E.: 809 Chabot Dr., Las Vegas, Nev.   2
KONYS, James J.: 561 Bonita Ave., Las Vegas, Nev.   10
KRANTZ, James J.: 2224 Juana Vista, Las Vegas, Nev.   2
KRYSTAL, Sydney D.: 9255 Doheny Rd., Los Angeles, Calif.   14
McLEOD, Norval B.: 804A S. 3rd St., Las Vegas, Nev.   2
MELVIN, Jack: 1924 S. 6th St., Las Vegas, Nev.   4
MESSER, Saul: 6332 Shawnee, Las Vegas, Nev.   10
MORSE, Harvey S.: 110 E. 9th St., Los Angeles, Calif.   8
PARVIN, Albert B.: 2220 Avenue of the Stars,
    Los Angeles, Calif.   8
PORTNOY, Sylvia: 1010 Pamela Dr., Beverly Hills, Calif.   12
POSNER, Stanley M.: 252 N. Kenter Ave.,
    Los Angeles, Calif.   2
PRELL, Melvin S.: 2280 Mahigan Way, Las Vegas, Nev.   8
PRELL, Milton: 3667 Las Vegas Blvd., S., Las Vegas, Nev.   80
PRELL, Sheila L.: 3667 Las Vegas Blvd., S., Las Vegas, Nev. 20
RIVERA, James: 908 Hassett St., Las Vegas, Nev.   4
ROTHBERG, G. Harry: 400 N. Oakhurst Dr.,
    Beverly Hills, Calif.   20
ROWAN, Hyman L.: 107 W. Broadway, Long Beach, Calif.   4

ROWAN, Sam: 3649 Country Club Dr., Lakewood, Calif.   4
SCHAYER, Charles M.: 100 Locust St., Denver, Colo.   3
SIMS, Ernest A.: 4673 Happy Valley Ave., Las Vegas, Nev.   4
SPECKS, Granville I.: 1421 Dobson St., Evanston, Ill.   10
STERN, Martin, Jr.: 8221 Sunset Blvd., Los Angeles, Calif.   4
STERN, Stuart: 8506 Spring View Dr., Indianapolis, Ind.   10
TOPPER, Ronald: 2630 Sherwood, Apt. 6, Las Vegas, Nev.   4
ZICKLER, Joyce F.: 7150 N. Pennsylvania St.,
   Indianapolis, Ind.   12
MAJOR, Bernard A.   10

HOTEL RIVIERA, Inc.
Las Vegas, Nevada

	Shares
GOLDMAN, Harry A.: 120 N. Robertson Blvd., Los Angeles, Calif.	1,600
SILBERT, Harvey L.: 9601 Wilshire Blvd., Beverly Hills, Calif.	4,000
MAGNA CORPORATION: 246 W. 44th St., New York, N.Y.	4,000
HARRISON, Charles J.	1,600
ABRAMS, Samuel	800
ATOL, Frank	1,200
MARTIN, Tony	1,600
KREMS, Nathan S.	1,600
CARTER, Charles T.	800
MILLER, Herschel M.	1,600
MILLER, Louis	1,600
MILLER, Ross	3,200
ROSENBERG, Joe	800
STOKES, E. Yale	800
GOODMAN, J. Dee	800

New Hotel Showboat, Inc., dba SHOWBOAT CASINO
Las Vegas, Nevada

	Percentage
CONWAY, Nelson: 319 S. 3rd St., Las Vegas, Nev.	9.0
HOUSSELS, J. K., Jr.: 380 Rancho Circle, Las Vegas, Nev.	18.0
HOUSSELS, J. K., Sr.: 1012 S. 6th St., Las Vegas, Nev.	31.5
KELLEY, Joseph: 830 Kenny Way, Las Vegas, Nev.	8.0
MOORE, R. Julian: 273 Sands Ave., Apt. 3, Las Vegas, Nev.	5.0
MORLEDGE, Fred: 2040 Edgewood Dr., Las Vegas, Nev.	5.0

PARKER, Judd: 605 Lacy Lane, Las Vegas, Nev.   4.0
ZETTLER, George: 2043 Canosa, Las Vegas, Nev.   2.5
VALENTINE, Harold L.: 1040 Bayview Dr.,
    Fort Lauderdale, Fla.   10.0
SHUGART, James W. (Executor of the Estate of James C.
    Shugart): 1656 Christy Lane, Las Vegas, Nev.   7.0

STARDUST HOTEL
Las Vegas, Nevada

DALITZ, Moe B.: Stardust Hotel, Las Vegas, Nev.
JONES, C. J.: Desert Inn Hotel, Las Vegas, Nev.
DREW, John F.: 333 Desert Inn Rd., Las Vegas, Nev.
JAFFE, Milton: Stardust Hotel, Las Vegas, Nev.
DONNELLEY, John A.: Stardust Hotel, Las Vegas, Nev.
BENEDICT, Alvin: Stardust Hotel, Las Vegas, Nev.
STILLINGS, George L.: 5101 Evergreen Ave., Las Vegas, Nev.

APPENDIX III

Charts

The following fourteen charts are provided in the hope that they will help the reader define his ideas concerning the nature and scope of organized crime in the country.

Charts 1–11 are adapted from the charts published in the printed "Hearings (Organized Crime and Illicit Traffic in Narcotics) before the Permanent Subcommittee on Investigations of the Committee on Government Operations, United States Senate, Eighty-Eighth Congress, September 1963–August 1964."

Chart 12 is taken from the "Task Force Report: Organized Crime, 1967" (prepared for the President's Commission on Law Enforcement and Administration of Justice).

Chart 13 is adapted from a document drawn up by the Los Angeles police department.

Chart I

THE VITO GENOVESE FAMILY

VITO GENOVESE *Boss*

THOMAS EBOLI *Acting Boss* GERARDO CATENA *Underboss* MICHAEL GENOVESE *Messenger* MICHELE MIRANDA *Consigliere*

Capiregime

Michael Coppola
Pasquale Eboli

Thomas Greco
Richard Boiardi

VINCENT ALO REGIME	JAMES ANGELINA REGIME	MICHAEL COPPOLA REGIME	PASQUALE EBOLI REGIME	RICHARD BOIARDI REGIME	MICHELE MIRANDA REGIME

Vincent Alo
James Angelina

Soldiers — Buttons	*Soldiers — Buttons*	*Soldiers — Buttons*	*Soldiers — Buttons*	*Soldiers — Buttons*	*Soldiers — Buttons*
Nicholas Bolangi	Louis Barbella	Charles Albero	Dominic Alongi	Joseph Agone	Settimo Accardi	John Gregory Ardito
Lawrence Centore	Joseph Barra	Alfred Cupola	Edward Capobianco	Philip Albanese	Albert Barrasso	Lorenzo Brescia
Francesco Cucola	Morris Barra	Anthony DeMartino	Joseph DeNegris	Ottilio Caruso	Anthony Boiardi	Anthony Carillo
Aniello Ercole	Earl Coralluzzo	Benjamin DeMartino	Cosmo DiPietro	Mike Clemente	Paul Bonadio	Frank Celano
Frank Galluccio	Tobias DeMiccio	Theodore DeMartino	Alfred Falcco	George Filippone	Thomas Campisi	Salvatore Celembrino
August Laietta	Mattew Fortunato	Pasquale Erra	Anthony Florio	Joseph Lapi	Antonio Caponigro	Alfred Criscuolo
Gaetano Martino	Paul Marchione	Anthony Ferro	Mario Gigante	George Nobile	Charles Tourine, Sr.	Pete DeFeo
Aldo Mazzarati	John Savino	Joseph Lanza	Vincent Gigante	Michael Spinella	Peter LaPlaca	Joseph Lanza
Sabato Milo		Frank Livorsi	Michael Maione		Ernest Lazzara	Alfonso Marzano
Rocco Perrotta		Philip Lombardo	Vincent Mauro		Andrew Lombardino	Barney Miranda
James Plenrelli		Felix Monaco	Gerardo Mosciello		Paul Lombardino	Carmine Persico, Jr.
Louis Prado		Louis Pacella	Sebastian Ofrica		Anthony Marchitto	David Petillo
Rudolph Prisco		Joseph Paterra	Joseph Pagano		Anthony Peter Riela	Mathew Principe
Nicholas Ratemi		Al Rosato	Pasquale Pagano		Salvatore Chiri	Frank Tieri
Batisto Salvo		Anthony Salerno	Armando Perillo			Eli Zaccardi
George Smurra		Ferdinand Salerno	Girolamo Santuccio			
Gaetano Somma		Angelo Salerno	Fiore Siano			
		Dan Scarglatta'	John Stopelli			
		Giovanni Schillaci	Joseph Valachi			
		Frank Serpico				
		Joseph Stracci				
		Joseph Tortorici				

Chart 2

THE CARLO GAMBINO FAMILY

CARLO GAMBINO *Boss*

JOSEPH BIONDO *Underboss*   **JOSEPH RUCCOBONO**' *Consigliere*

Capiregime

Anthony Sedotto   Charles Dongarro
Anthony Zangarra   Peter Ferrara
Joseph Colazzo   Carmine Lombardozzi
Aniello Dellacroce   Ettore Zappi

Soldiers—Buttons

Paul Castellano
Paolo Gambino
Arthur Leo
Rocco Mazzie

Alex D'Allesio	Giuseppe LoPiccolo	Giacomo Scalici
John D'Allesio	Frank Luciano	Joseph Scalici
Mike D'Allesio	Aniello Mancuso	Salvatore Scalici
Charles DeLutro	Genaro Mancuso	Giacomo Scarpulla
Nicholas DiBene	Joseph Manfredi	Mike Scandifia
Alex DeBrizzi	James Massi	Al Seru
Charles Gagliodotto	Frank Moccardi	James Stassi
Frank Gagliardi	Sabato Muro	Joseph Stassi
Michael Galgano	Frank Pasqua	Felice Teti
Pasquale Genese	Michael Pecoraro	Arthur Tortorella
Anthony Granza	Dominick Petito	Peter Tortorella
Frank Guglieimini	Larry Pistone	Paul Zaccaria
Sally Guglieimini	Anthony Plate	
Joseph Indelicato	Hugo Rossi	

Andrew Alberti
Germaio Anaclerio
Joseph Armone
Eduardo Aronica
Peter Baratta
Charles Barcellona
Frank Barranca
Ernesto Barese
Sebastiano Bellanca
Salvatore Bonfrisco
Michael Bove
Anthony Carminati
James Casablanca
Matthew Cuomo

Chart 3

THE GAETANO LUCCHESE FAMILY

GAETANO LUCCHESE *Boss*

STEFANO LASALLE. *Underboss*   VINCENT JOHN RAO *Consiglieri*

Capiregime

Joseph Lucchese	Salvatore Santoro
John Ormento	Carmine Tramunti
James Plumeri	Natale Evola
Joseph Rosato	

Ettore Coco
Anthony Corallo
Joseph Laratro

Soldiers—Buttons

John Dioguardi	Neil Migliore	Joseph Silesi
Charles DiPalermo	Vic Panica	Nicholas Tolentino
Vincent Corrao	Andinno Pappadia	Angelo Tuminaro
Joseph DiPalermo	Anthony LoPinto	Joseph Vento
Salvatore Granello	Vincent Potenza	Anthony Vadala
Anthony Lisi	Calogero Rao	Sam Valente
Salvatore LoProto.	Charles Scoperto	Tom Valente
Salvatore Maneri	Salvatore Shillitani	James Vintaloro

Frank Arra
Nicholas Bonina
Frank Campanello
Paul John Carbo
Sam Cavalieri
Donato Laietta
Edward D'Argenio
John Di Carlo
Thomas Dioguardi

318

Chart 4

THE GIUSEPPE MAGLIOCCO FAMILY

GIUSEPPE MAGLIOCCO *Boss*

SALVATORE MUSSACHIO *Underboss*

Capiregime

Sebastiano Aloi	Harry Fontana
Simone Andolino	John Franzese
Salvatore Badalamenti	Ambrose Magliocco
Leo Carlino	Nicholas Forlano
Joseph Colombo	John Oddo

Soldiers—Buttons

Anthony Abbattemarco	Albert Gallo, Jr.	Frank Profaci
Cassandros Bonasera	Joseph Gallo	James Sabella
Alphonse D'Ambrosio	Lawrence Gallo	Modesto Santora
Salvatore D'Ambrosio	Philip Gambino	Joseph Schipani
Bartolo Ferrigno	Gaetano Marino	Giuseppe Tipa
Cosmo Frasca	Sebastiano Nani	Joseph Yacovelli

Chart 5

THE JOSEPH BONANNO FAMILY

JOSEPH BONANNO   *Boss*
CARMINE GALANTE   *Underboss*
FRANK GARAFOLO   *Consigliere*
JOSEPH NOTARO   *Caporegime*

Soldiers—Buttons

James Colletti
Michael Consolo
Rosario Dionosio
Nicholas Marangello
Frank Mari
John Petrone
Angelo Presinzano
Frank Presinzano
Philip Rastelli
George Rizzo
Michael Sabella
Joseph Spadaro
Costenze Valente
Frank Valente
Nicholas Zapprana

other capiregime unidentified

Chart 6

BUFFALO, NEW YORK, ORGANIZATION

STEFANO MAGADDINO *Boss*

FREDRICO RANDACCIO *Underboss*

Lieutenants

John Cammillieri
Pascal Natarelli
Roy Carlisi
Steven Cannarozzo

Section Leaders

Salvatore Brocato
Joseph Fino
Salvatore Bonito
Daniel Sansanese
Paul Briandi
Anthony Perna
Salvatore Rizzo
Pascal Politano
Sam Lagattuta
Salvatore Miano
Michael Tascarella

Relatives of Boss

Antonio Magaddino
James LaDuca

Chart 7

RHODE ISLAND AND BOSTON, MASSACHUSETTS, ORGANIZATION

PHILIP BRUCCOLA *Former Boss*   RAYMOND PATRIARCA *Boss*   GENARO J. ANGULO

RHODE ISLAND

Henry Tamello
Antonio Lopreato
Americo Bucci
Louis J. Taglinetti
Frank Morrelli
John Candelmo
Dominic J. Biafore
Francis Joseph Patriarca
Alphonse Capalbo
Albert Le Pore
Santino Ruggerio
Giuseppe Simonelli
Frank Forti
Richard Ruggerio
Frank Ferrara
Albert Joseph Vitali
Alfredo Rossi

BOSTON, MASS.

Frank Cucchiara
Anthony Sandrelli
Larry A. Zannino
Joseph Lombardi
Francesco P. Intiso
Leo Santaniello
Peter J. Limone
Michael Rocke
Joseph Anselmo
Santo Rizzo
John Gugliemo
Ralph Lamattina
Theodore Fuccillo
Henry Selvitelli
Nicholas A. Giso
Samuel Granito

Chart 8

THE MAFIA ORGANIZATION IN THE TAMPA, FLORIDA, AREA

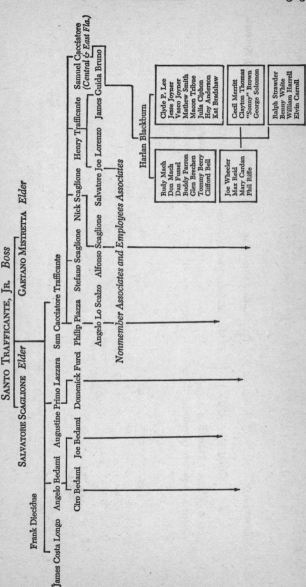

SANTO TRAFFICANTE, JR. *Boss*

SALVATORE SCAGLIONE *Elder* GAETANO MISTRETTA *Elder*

Frank Diecidue

James Costa Longo Angelo Bedami Augustine Primo Lazzara Domenick Furci Philip Piazza Stefano Scaglione Nick Scaglione Henry Trafficante Samuel Cacciatore *(Central & East Fla.)*

Ciro Bedami Joe Bedami Sam Cacciatore Trafficante Angelo Lo Scalzo Alfonso Scaglione Salvatore Joe Lorenzo James Guida Bruno

Nonmember Associates and Employees Associates

Harlan Blackburn

Rudy Mach
Don Mach
Dan Fussel
Buddy Parron
Glen Breechen
Tommy Berry
Clifford Bell

Clyde P. Lee
Jesse Joyner
Vasco Joyner
Mathew Smith
Macon Trabue
Julia Cliphon
Hoy Anderson
Kat Bradshaw

Joe Wheeler
Max Reid
Mary Cardan
Phil Riffe

Cecil Merritt
Clayton Thomas
"Sonny" Brown
George Solomon

Ralph Strawder
Benny White
William Harrell
Elvin Carroll

Chart 9

THE MAFIA ORGANIZATION IN THE DETROIT AREA

Ruling Council

Joseph Zerilli	John Priziola	Angelo Meli	William Tocco	Peter Licavoli

Administrators and Heirs Apparent

Joseph Zerilli	John Priziola	Angelo Meli	William Tocco	Peter Licavoli
Michael Rubino Salvatore Lucido	Joseph Massei Dominic P. Corrado	Joseph Bommarito Santo Perrone	Raffaele Quasarano Michael Polizzi	Anthony Giacalone Vincent A. Meli

Chiefs *(Zerilli, Priziola)* — Lieutenants *(Meli, Tocco, Licavoli)*

Joseph Zerilli	John Priziola	Angelo Meli	William Tocco	Peter Licavoli
Dominic Corrado Joseph Triglia Tony Teramine Anthony Cimini Vito Giacalone	Peter Vitale Paul Vitale Joseph Barbara, Jr. Joseph Bommarito Joseph Moceri	Eddie Guarella	Frank Meli Benedict Bommarito Sam Finazzo Dominic Cavataio	Julian Cavataio Peter Cavataio Salvatore Serra Sam Caruso

Section Leaders

Joseph Zerilli	John Priziola	Angelo Meli	William Tocco	Peter Licavoli
Angelo Lombardi Anthony Imburnone Danny Bruno Pete Trupiano Peter Maniaci Dominic Bommarito Joe Coppola Pete Lombardo	Nick Ditta Vincent Finazzo Michael Bartalotta Sam Lobaido	James Macagnone James Galici Joseph Lobaido Leonardo Monteleone	Mario Agosta Sam Giordano Arthur Gallo Frank Mudaro	Frank Randazzo Joe Brooklier Ricco Priziola Tony Randazzo Dominic Allevato Paul Cimino

Windsor, Canada, Segment

Joe Catalanotte *(Lieutenant)*   Nicolas Cicchini *(Section Leader)*

Onofrio Minaudo *(Lieutenant)*

Chart 10

CHICAGO-ITALIAN ORGANIZATION

Overall Chicago Area, Bosses and Lieutenants

SALVATORE GIANCANA	DOMINIC BRANCATO	JOHN CERONE
SAM BATTAGLIA	FELIX ANTHONY ALDERISIO	GIUSEPPE GLIELMI
ANTHONY ACCARDO	ROCCO FISCHETTI	ROCCO DESTEFANO
PAUL RICCA	ROSS PRIO	FRANK CARUSO
DOMINIC NUCCIO	FRANK FERRERA	FIORE BUCCIERI
DOMINIC DIBELLA	MARSHALL CAIFANO	WILLIAM ALOISIO
	FRANCESCO CIRONATO	

West Side

William Daddano	Leonard Gianola	Mario A. DeStefano	Ned Bakes	Joseph A. Ferriola	Rocco Potenza	Frank Fratto
Charles English	James Mirro	Sam DeStefano	Dominic Blasi	Ernest Infelice	Louis Rosanova	Frank Eulo
Frank Buccieri	Charles Nicoletti	Vito DeStefano	Samuel Cesario	Vincent J. Inserro	Rocco Salvatore	James Torello
Joseph Aiuppa	Anthony Pitello	John DeBiase	Eco James Coli	John Lardino	Joseph Siciliano	Phillip Mesi
Albert Capone	Louis Briatta	Rocco DeGrazia	Dominic Cortina	John L. Manzella	Tarquin Simonelli	Frank Manno
John Capone	Albert Frabotta	Charles Tourino, Jr.	Joseph Colucci	Sam Mesi	Frank Teutonico	Nick Manno, Jr.
Matthew Capone	Joseph Gagliano	Dominic Volpe	Americo DePietro	William Messino	Nick Visco	Sam Manno
Ralph Capone	Joseph Fusco	Sam Ariola	Anthony Eldorado	Rocco Paternoster	Joseph A. Accardo	Thomas Manno

North Side

Placido Divarco	Frank Orlando	James Polichert	Anthony DeMonte	Michael Glitta	L. Buonaguidi	Joseph LaBarbara
Joseph Liscandrella	Joseph Liscandrella	Samuel Liscandrella	Frank Liscandrella	Cosmo Orlando	Ben J. Policheri	

South Side

George Tuffanelli	James Rott	James Catura	James R. Cordovano	Anthony DeLordo	Charles B. DiCaro	Joseph N. DiCaro
	Anthony Passdea	Louis Tornabene	Frank C. Tornabene	Joseph Caruso	Anthony DeRosa	

Chart 11

NONMEMBER ASSOCIATES OF
CHICAGO-ITALIAN ORGANIZATION

Overall Chicago Area

MURRAY HUMPHREYS
RALPH PIERCE
GUS ALEX
LESTER KRUSE
FRED THOMAS SMITH
LEONARD PATRICK
DAVID YARAS

West Side

Joseph Corngold
Elias Argyropoulos
August Dierolf Liebe
Edward Vogel
Leo Rugendorf
John Wolek
William Block
Nick Bravos
George J. Bravos
Maish Baer
Frank Zimmerman
Gus Spiro Zapas
Jack Patrick

North Side

William Goldstein
Joseph Arnold
Robert Furey
Phillip Katz
Irving Dworetzky

South Side

Bernard Posner
Arthur Markovitz
Michael Markovitz
Hyman Gottfried

Chart 12

AN ORGANIZED CRIME FAMILY

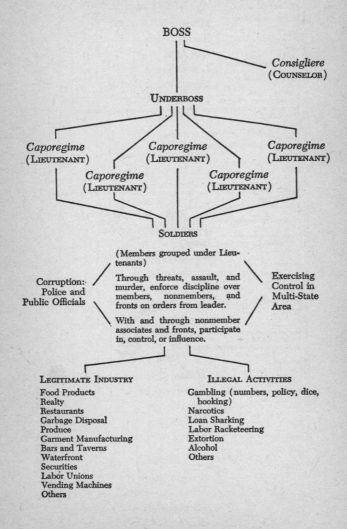

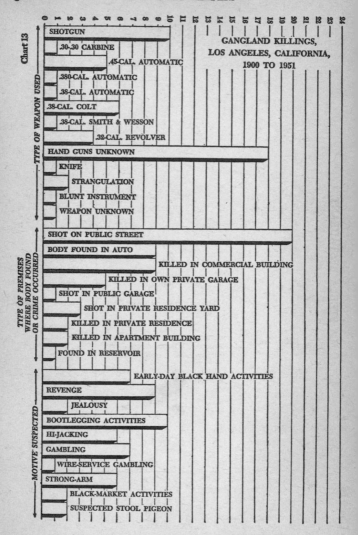

Chart 13

GANGLAND KILLINGS,
LOS ANGELES, CALIFORNIA,
1900 TO 1951

TYPE OF WEAPON USED

SHOTGUN
.30-30 CARBINE
.45-CAL. AUTOMATIC
.380-CAL. AUTOMATIC
.38-CAL. AUTOMATIC
.38-CAL. COLT
.38-CAL. SMITH & WESSON
.32-CAL. REVOLVER
HAND GUNS UNKNOWN
KNIFE
STRANGULATION
BLUNT INSTRUMENT
WEAPON UNKNOWN

TYPE OF PREMISES WHERE BODY FOUND OR CRIME OCCURRED

SHOT ON PUBLIC STREET
BODY FOUND IN AUTO
KILLED IN COMMERCIAL BUILDING
KILLED IN OWN PRIVATE GARAGE
SHOT IN PUBLIC GARAGE
SHOT IN PRIVATE RESIDENCE YARD
KILLED IN PRIVATE RESIDENCE
KILLED IN APARTMENT BUILDING
FOUND IN RESERVOIR

MOTIVE SUSPECTED

EARLY-DAY BLACK HAND ACTIVITIES
REVENGE
JEALOUSY
BOOTLEGGING ACTIVITIES
HI-JACKING
GAMBLING
WIRE-SERVICE GAMBLING
STRONG-ARM
BLACK-MARKET ACTIVITIES
SUSPECTED STOOL PIGEON

Chart 14

LA STELLA RESTAURANT

CARLO GAMBINO
Boss of Gambino family

CARLOS MARCELLO
Boss of New Orleans

SANTO TRAFFICANTE, JR.
Boss of Tampa, Fla.

ANTHONY COROLLO
Member of Marcello family

FRANK GAGLIANO
Member/associate of Marcello family

JOSEPH N. GALLO
Caporegima in Gambino family

ANTHONY CARILLO
Soldier in Genovese family

MICHELE MIRANDA
Consigliere in Genovese family

POSITION SEATED AT TABLE

JOSEPH COLOMBO
Boss of Colombo (Profaci) family

THOMAS EBOLI
Acting boss of Genovese family

DOMINICK ALONGI
Soldier in Genovese family

JOSEPH MARCELLO, JR.
Member of Marcello family

ANIELLO DELLACROCE
Caporegima in Gambino family

INDEX

A

Abati, Michael, 203
Accardo, Anthony, 17, 98, 186, 187, 188, 192, 233, 263, 271–273, 276, 287, 293, 297, 299
Accardo, Martin, 98
Adamo, Girolamo, 181–182, 183, 185, 188
Adams, Sherman, 198
Adonis, Joe, 11, 17–18, 90–95, 100, 115, 171, 173, 177, 188, 222, 256, 289, 300
Advance Vending Company (Newark, N.J.), 37
Ageuci, Al, 20, 48–52, 68, 287
Ageuci, Vito, 48–52, 287
Ahern, Frank, 202–204
Aiuppa, Joseph, 262–263, 265
Aladdin Hotel (Las Vegas), 230, 311
Alamo Airways, 246
Alcohol Beverage Control Act, 176, 206
Alderisio, Felix, 273
Alderisio, Philip, 270, 271
Alderman, Jerome, testimony before McClellan Committee, 87–88
Alex, Gus, 268, 293
Alioto, Joseph L., 213
Allen, O. K., 151, 296
Allied Military Government, 31
Alo, Vincent, 41, 43, 92, 232, 233
Aloha Motel (Miami), 97
Aloi, Sebastian, 19–20
Alouette Restaurant (San Francisco), 202
Altamura, Thomas, 97–98

Amico, Michael, 51–58; testimony before McClellan Committee, 51–52, 53–55, 57
Anastasia, Albert, 29, 93, 94–95, 132, 252, 253
Anderson, Robert, 109
Angersola, George, 123
Angersola, John, 43, 99, 123
Angiulo, Gennaro, 64, 70, 233
Anselmo, Joseph, 233
Anslinger, Harry J., 215–216
Antinori, Ignazio, 91, 95
Apalachin meeting, 17, 75, 94, 95, 181, 182, 288, 289, 292, 293, 295, 296, 297, 300, 301; Little Apalachins, 159, 232, 240
Arasso, Tony, 254
Ardizzone, Joe, 169–170
Arra, Nunzio, 298
Astor, Lady, 120
Atol, Frank, 236

B

Bacon, Sir Ranulph, 112, 114
Baioni, Larry, 64, 70
Baker, Bobby, 125, 131, 133–145, 195, 199, 241, 284
Baker, James, 113
Balke, John, 74
Balletto, George, 66
Baltimore Colts, 109–110
Bank of World Commerce, Ltd. (Nassau), 129–130
Barbara, Joseph, Jr., 80–81, 200
Barboza, Joe, 68–70
Barragan, Ismael, 287
Basile, Jimmy, 169